I0639610

LOST IN
THE DARK
AND OTHER EXCURSIONS

Other Books by John Langan

Novels
The Cleaving Stone (forthcoming)
The Fisherman
House of Windows

Collections
Corpsemouth and Other Autobiographies
Children of the Fang and Other Genealogies
Sefira and Other Betrayals
The Wide, Carnivorous Sky and Other Monstrous Geographies
Mr. Gaunt and Other Uneasy Encounters

CRITICAL ACCLAIM FOR
JOHN LANGAN'S CORPSEMOUTH

"John Langan's enviable range encompasses the whole panorama of horror, from the psychological to the cosmic, the monstrous to the deeply and movingly human, the insidiously disturbing to the thoroughly nightmarish. His imagination never falters or flinches, and his flavoursome prose is a literate pleasure to read."

—WHC Grand Master Ramsey Campbell

"In his masterful new collection, John Langan puts cosmic horror back where it belongs: in our basements, on our crumbling streets, in the crevasses that open in our relationships with our loved ones. These stories don't just pay homage to the Old Gods: they give them fresh lives. Meaning ours."

—Glen Hirshberg, author of *Infinity Dreams*
& the Motherless Children trilogy

"There are certain writers who go straight to the top of my reading list, and John Langan is in that company. One of the finest and most surprising writers working in the tradition of the uncanny."

—Kelly Link, author of *The Book of Love*

CRITICAL ACCLAIM FOR
JOHN LANGAN'S CHILDREN OF THE FANG

"Langan (*The Fisherman*) draws inspiration from Stephen King, H. P. Lovecraft, David Lynch and other masters of the strange and horrific to create an impressive collection of 21 tales as terrifying as they are mysterious. […] This well-crafted collection will delight fans of dark, literary horror."

—*Publishers Weekly*

"Langan is my standard by which all other short stories are measured. There is something in this collection that will stand out as your favorite, relish your time in these Genealogies to find it."

—*Cemetery Dance*

CRITICAL ACCLAIM FOR
JOHN LANGAN'S *THE FISHERMAN*

"*The Fisherman* is an epic, yet intimate, horror novel. Langan channels M. R. James, Robert E. Howard, and Norman Maclean. What you get is *A River Runs Through It*...Straight to hell."

—Laird Barron, author of *Not a Speck of Light*

"...at turns epic and personal, dense yet compulsively readable, frightening but endearing. Already among the year's very best dark fiction releases."

—Adam Cesare, author of *Clown in a Cornfield*

"Reading this, your mouth fills with worms. Just let them wriggle and crawl as they will, though—don't swallow. John Langan is fishing for your sleep, for your soul. I fear he's already got mine."

—Stephen Graham Jones, author of *I Was a Teenage Slasher*

"John Langan's *The Fisherman* isn't about fishing at all. Yes, there's fishing in it, but it's really about friendship, loss, and bone-deep horror. What starts as a slow, melancholy tale gains momentum and drops you head first into a churning nightmare from which you might escape, but you'll never forget, and the memory of what you saw will change you forever."

—Richard Kadrey, author of *The Everything Box*

"John Langan's *The Fisherman* is literary horror at its sharpest and most imaginative. It's at turns a quiet and powerfully melancholy story about loss and grief; the impossibility of going on in the same manner as you had before. It's also a rollicking, kick-ass, white-knuckle charge into the winding, wild, raging river of redemption. Illusory, frightening, and deeply moving, *The Fisherman* is a modern horror epic. And it's simply a must read."

—Paul Tremblay, author of *Horror Movie*

LOST IN THE DARK
AND OTHER EXCURSIONS

JOHN LANGAN

WORD HORDE

PETALUMA, CA

Lost in the Dark and Other Excursions © 2025 by John Langan
This edition of *Lost in the Dark and Other Excursions*
© 2025 by Word Horde

Cover art by Matthew Jaffe
Cover design by Scott R Jones

Illustration on page 236 by Kayla Heikkinen

All rights reserved

Edited by Ross E. Lockhart

An extension of this copyright page can be found on page 291.

First Edition

ISBN: 978-1-956252-10-1

A Word Horde Book
http://www.WordHorde.com

TABLE OF CONTENTS

For Fiona

INTRODUCTION

VICTOR LAVALLE

The danger of writing *about* John Langan, is that you risk trying to write *like* John Langan. That is a fool's errand. Because nobody writes like John Langan. There are many writers who I might classify as related to him, but they strike me as ancestors, forebears not contemporaries. Algernon Blackwood; M. R. James; T.E.D. Klein; Henry James's keen interest in human consciousness; and that master of the expansive short story, Alice Munro. So maybe it's more precise to say no one writes like John Langan *these days*.

Lots of people are saying that we're in the middle of another horror boom—one that might actually rival the heyday of the '80s, that incandescent era that gave us King, Straub, Rice and Barker—I would like to think so. If I went through the list of writers knocking it out of the park these days, national and international, I could fill a page or two. And I'd still, inevitably, forget a few. John is on that list of course, mapping out a particular kind of interiority, where even the digressions feel emotionally fraught, intellectually invigorating, and dramatically weighty. A territory all his own.

The Fisherman announced him as a tremendous writer on the world stage ʾat I had the good fortune of encountering his first novel, *House* s, in 2009, and falling headfirst into the knotty, discursive, emo-

1

tionally thorny elements that I would only realize, with time, signaled the essence of a John Langan tale.

In that novel, a woman named Veronica Croyden tells the story of her husband's disappearance. Her husband is Roger Croydon, a Dickens scholar, who was once her professor. Roger's son was killed in Afghanistan and this has sent Roger down a pathway of grief. These characters all live inside the Belvedere House, a location that has its own ties to things ephemeral, magical. The grief that has animated Roger, the animus we learn about between father and son, the complicated history of Veronica's life, all this is related to us over the course of the novel and the Belvedere House, in some way, seems fueled, even animated, by the force of those powerful feelings.

So far, so good. You could offer these basic narrative elements to a dozen writers and I bet they'd turn in fairly enjoyable versions of the Gothic's traditional haunted house tale. That is not what I experienced as I read *House of Windows*. I can't say what I expected as I turned each page, but the expected was rarely what I received. Rather than trying to describe what happened from one scene to the next, one conversation or another, it feels more honest to relate the sensation. Above all else, as the novel spun on, I found myself relaxing into a *tale*.

The American Heritage Dictionary of the English Language offers a definition that seems most useful here. And already I find myself imagining a reader—perhaps even John Langan himself—rolling his eyes as I fall into the "here's dictionary definition" portion of this presentation. *Oh, how clever, are you in seventh grade?* The urge to appear smart enough to talk about John's work is real, at least for me. Let's just treat this particular aside as a flash of insecurity and leave it at that.

The American Heritage Dictionary of the English Language defines a tale as "a recital of events or happenings; a report or revelation." *House of Windows* is, in essence, one long recital. Veronica relates the story and that element matters as much as the story itself. This might serve as an essential fact about so much of the Langan's fiction: the teller matters as much as the tale. A feature, not a bug, as the cliché goes.

Lost in the Dark and Other Excursions collects stories published between 2017-2020. Thirteen stories, a few of them, particularly "Natalya, Queen of the Hungry Dogs," are quite substantial. And yet while the pieces here all bear the stamp and style of John Langan, the breadth of mood and tone

INTRODUCTION

truly impresses.

Because John can be such a heady writer, I don't often see his sense of humor credited as it should be. If you've ever met him in person, spent time over a meal, or even just listened or watched him interviewed, you can quickly appreciate his playfulness and wit. While some of the pieces here can be grim and troubling—we are talking about a collection of horror stories after all—what a pleasure to be caught off guard when Langan tells a story that just makes you laugh. Dare I say *chortle.*

"Madame Painte: For Sale," the story of a man and his garden gnome, is even funnier than that brief summary suggests; "Errata," a playful romp about a misprint in *The Fisherman;* and the cautionary morsel that is "Clapping Teeth and Driving Beats;" each of these, all of these, are just so much damn fun to read. And they play so nicely with/against the stories that get under the skin and rattle your bones.

"Natalya, Queen of the Hungry Dogs" offers the most sustained experience in the collection. Settle into a story that asks, at its heart, how much someone would do for a friend. How far would one go to help that friend, let's say, put his affairs in order. The story builds to a place of true mayhem, even terror, and it also moved me emotionally which, in the end, the most effective horror must do.

Last, I would highlight "Haak" as a story I have already read three times because it is, to put it mildly, a damn masterpiece. This story manages to be, in a way, *everything* that makes John Langan such an absolute wonder as a writer: a tale within a tale; the mythic blending with the mundane; erudition not merely for the sake of showing one's knowledge but in service to the story; surprising twists and connections; moments of playfulness and wit; a surprising and satisfying conclusion, and it all ends with a quote from Mallarmé! Who else is pulling off half of that, let alone all of that? Fucking no one, that's who. Only John Langan.

Long may he reign.

Victor LaValle
May 31, 2025
Bronx, NY

MADAME PAINTE: FOR SALE

"This?" the man behind the counter says. "Why, this is Madame Painte."

The figure is short, a foot and a half tall, and squat, about the same dimensions across, composed of what might be porcelain. The face is round, the eyes squeezed shut by the wide smile lifting the cheeks. A pointed hat fails to conceal the pointed tips of the figure's ears. It wears a long apron dress over a peasant blouse. A somewhat typical garden gnome, you think, except for the colors, from which it obviously derives its name. It's been painted without regard for the margins of clothing and skin. Black, green, and orange slash down the figure from right to left. The face is mostly dark green, the hat orange mixed with black. A splash of white paint traverses the closed eyes; the effect is less a mask and more a piece of webbing. You saw the figure sitting to the left of the door to the antique shop as you walked up the path to it and were so struck by its remarkable grotesquerie that you lifted and carried it inside, setting it on the front counter. On the way, you read the notecard strung to the top of the hat: MUST BE KEPT OUTSIDE.

"I didn't mean its name," you start.

"Of course not," the man says. He's on the small side, more wiry than slender. Based on the ratio of salt to pepper in his mustache and hair, he's somewhere in the deep middle of middle age. He says, "You meant the warning."

"Must be kept outside," you read. "Why must?"

"The official reason is, she's covered in lead paint."

You step back from the counter, wipe your hands on your jeans. "There's an unofficial reason?"

"There's a story," the man says. "Would you like to hear it? It's brief."

"Um. Sure," you say, but do not move any closer.

"Madame Painte," the man says, "hails from Holland by way of Guam by way of Australia. She was part of a line of garden ornaments manufactured by a factory outside of Amsterdam in the 1980s. I'm not sure how she traveled to the western Pacific, possibly via cargo ship. I know she was decorating the front lawn of a house in Yigo by 1995. This was the residence of a colonel stationed at the U.S. Air Force base there. She was already sporting her distinctive paint job; though I'm unclear who gave it to her. It may have been the colonel's wife, whose name was Priscilla. As I understand it, she was an artist—bit of an amateur anthropologist, too. She's the first person I'm aware of who insisted the figure be kept outside. This was when she sold it to a young Australian couple, Trudi and Lenard Niles, visiting the island. The colonel had been transferred back stateside, and he and his wife had decided to take the opportunity to thin their possessions. The Nileses—well, mostly Trudi—were quite infatuated with the Madame. Priscilla was reluctant to part with her, said she couldn't let her go with just anyone. The Nileses thought she was trying to up the price, but that wasn't it. She'd give the figure away for free to the exactly right person. I guess the young couple wasn't quite perfect, because she took their money, but they were good enough for her to part with Madame Painte. Only after they'd sworn to keep her outside their home, though.

"This was how the figure made her way from Guam to Canberra."

"Let me guess," you say, "the couple brought her inside their house."

"Not at first, no," the man says, "but eventually, yes. Initially, they placed her in their back garden, next to a tall claret ash. The Nileses had a small metal table and pair of chairs near that spot. When the weather was warm, they would bring their morning coffee there. Trudi was a writer, a travel writer; Lenard was high up in an electronics company. After he went off to the office, she would carry her notebook, and later her laptop, to the table and work on whatever article was due that month. Actually, she wrote an article about the trip to Guam, which is how I know as much as I do about

Priscilla and the promise she extracted."

"What changed?" you say. "I mean, what made the couple break their promise?"

The man shrugs. "I don't know. I'm not certain anything did change, which is to say, I'm not sure there was a moment when one of them looked at the other and said, 'The time has come for us to forsake our vow.' I suspect their promise wasn't that much to begin with, just words said to get what they wanted. Then one day, years later, they decided to redecorate, and thought their garden ornament would look better in a corner of the living room. If they recalled their conversation with the colonel's wife, their pledge to her, it was in a bemused, hey-do-you-remember way. They cleaned the dirt and insects off Madame Painte, and brought her inside."

"And?"

"At first, nothing. As I said, they were redecorating, painting walls, replacing furniture, putting in a new kitchen. For a time, the interior of their house was fairly chaotic. Madame Painte sat in her corner and waited."

"Waited for what?"

"The right moment. Months had passed. Everything had calmed; the house was in its new configuration. One night, Lenard woke up to use the toilet. On his way back to bed, he saw something on the wall outside the room. It was a splash of white, as if someone had swiped a paintbrush across that spot, or as if moonlight were reflecting off a mirrored surface in the living room. He waved his hand in front of it, which had no effect. He placed his palm against it, but could feel no difference in texture. To the best of my knowledge, he did not notice a resemblance between the white streak on the wall and the white mask Madame Painte wore.

"Next morning, after her coffee and writing, Trudi saw that a patch of the wall beside the bedroom door was discolored, faded the way paint gets after years of direct sunlight. She touched the spot, and it crumbled under her fingertips. She found it strange, especially since the surface had been painted so recently, but she decided it must be some form of dry rot. When she discussed it with Lenard over dinner, he mentioned his late-night vision, but neither drew any conclusions from it. They made plans to call a contractor.

"A couple of days later, Trudi saw the white streak. Once again, it was late at night, the house dark. She had stayed up finishing an article whose deadline she had let draw too near. Walking into the bedroom, she glimpsed something white draped over the hindquarters of Toro, the Nileses' cat, who was asleep at the foot of the bed. So tired was she that she took the white streak for moonlight shining through the venetian blinds; only later would she realize it had been a new moon that night.

"In the morning, Toro was gone from the bed, which was not unusual, and he didn't come for his breakfast, which was. Trudi found him in the garden, when she brought her coffee out there. (Lenard had left for an early meeting.) The minute she sat, she heard a low moan from somewhere nearby. She recognized it as the cat, but it was a sound he'd never made before, halfway between a complaint and a warning. It raised the hairs on the back of her neck. She stood, called the cat's name. He uttered that weird groan again. She looked around the garden. He wasn't hard to find: what remained of him lay under a bush—some variety of hakea, I think it was."

"What do you mean, 'what remained'?"

"From a little below his midsection, the cat had shriveled, the fur gone, the skin blackened and shrunken against the bone. It was what you might have expected to find had the cat been dead for years. He was panting, obviously in pain, unable to understand what had happened to him. Trudi's first impulse was to take him to the veterinarian, but Toro wouldn't let her near him, hissing and clawing at her as she reached for him. She had to settle for calling the vet, who promised to stop by after her office was closed. By then, it was too late. Toro had bared his fangs at some unseen foe, and breathed his last. The vet was puzzled, to say the least. This degree of atrophy suggested some type of venom, but the speed with which it had acted was, in her experience, unprecedented. She asked to take Toro's remains to her office for an autopsy, which Trudi consented to. As the vet lifted him, though, the cat…came apart. His lower portion crumbled and his insides slid out onto the ground. The vet removed what she could, but it was a messy business."

"Did she find anything?" you say.

"Not exactly," the man says. "She phoned Trudi a day or two later. From what she'd been able to see under the microscope, the cat's cells had collapsed, lost their integrity and dissolved into one another. It's the kind of effect certain kinds of spider venom have on their victim's tissues. There was more. The worst affected portions of Toro were completely dry, every last drop of moisture drained from them. Of course, Trudi wanted to know what spider or other creature had done this to her cat. The vet didn't know. It was a familiar joke that Australia was full to the brim with deadly wildlife, but nothing she was acquainted with operated in this fashion on mammals of any size. Possibly, they were dealing with an invasive species. She was going to make some calls, ask if anything new had snuck into people's back gardens. In the meantime, Trudi should be careful, and should tell her husband to be careful, as well.

"During the following day, there was a moment Trudi looked at Madame Painte, at the white swath across the figure's smiling face, and was struck by the resemblance between the decoration and the white stripe she had seen on Toro. Hadn't Lenard mentioned a white mark on the wall outside their bedroom? She remembered the promise she'd made to Priscilla. For an instant, the details threatened to cohere into a bizarre and awful whole. As quickly as the thought occurred to her, however, she rejected it. It was ridiculous, absurd, like something from an old horror story. Over dinner that night, she shared the idea with Lenard. He nodded at the coincidence, but dismissed it, as well.

"Do I have to tell you what happened, next? Sometime late in the night, Trudi dreamed she sat up in bed, looked at Lenard asleep beside her, and saw the splash of white traversing his face, from just above his right eyebrow down to the left corner of his mouth. In her dream, she wasn't afraid as much as curious. With the index and middle fingers of her right hand, she touched the white streak where it crossed Lenard's nose. It was like brushing her fingers against a spider web. She lowered her head onto her pillow, and was instantly asleep."

"It wasn't a dream, was it?"

The man shakes his head. "It was not. You can imagine the sight that greeted Trudi when she woke that morning. She ran screaming into the street, and who can blame her? Eventually, the police were called, and the emergency services, but it was all over. The best anyone could do for poor Lenard was opine that at least he hadn't suffered, and how could they be sure? Initially, there was some suspicion of foul play. The idea was that Trudi had murdered Lenard by pouring acid on him while he slept. There were too many problems with the theory for it to hold up very long, not least of which was the coroner's report. This showed that Lenard had died from something that had liquefied a portion of his face, skull, and brain, then drained the liquid, all without spilling a drop on the pillow. The closest analogue the M.E. could suggest was a spider melting its victim's insides with its venom and slurping them out. But like Trudi's veterinarian before him, he couldn't name an arachnid capable of dissolving and consuming this amount of tissue. Eventually, the cause of death was settled on as a previously unknown strain of MRSA.

"Which was bullshit, but more acceptable than the explanation Trudi was giving."

"Madame Painte."

"To anyone who would listen, she repeated the story that had become overwhelmingly, hideously obvious to her. She refused to reenter the house, and it wasn't long until she was taken to the hospital, where she was given a bed in the psychiatric ward. No doubt, she was prescribed a sedative, at minimum. When all was said and done, she agreed to return home, but she insisted that the figure be removed from the living room, first. Her doctor decided it was easier to comply with this request than continue to go back and forth with her. Someone—it might have been the psychiatrist, herself—entered the house, located Madame Painte, and brought her to a local charity shop. She went so far as to follow Trudi's instructions and stipulated that the figure must be sold with a warning to keep her outside.

"This was how I found her. The charity shop listed some of its merchandise online. I subscribe to a couple of groups that keep an eye out for unusual pieces. The instant Madame Painte popped up on my screen, I clicked the purchase button."

"Weren't you, I don't know, nervous?"

"No—although that was because I didn't know the full story behind her. Not that I do, now: let's say I didn't know Trudi and Lenard's portion of it. I assumed the instruction to keep the figure outside had to do with the paint that had been used on her. I went so far as to e-mail the charity shop, but they weren't much help. What I've told you I learned from Trudi, who sent me a long e-mail a few months after I set Madame Painte outside my front door. For weeks, Trudi had been plagued by a combination of guilt and anxiety at passing on the Madame without disclosing her history, until she decided the only thing for her to do was contact whoever had purchased the figure. The charity shop supplied my e-mail, and she wrote me the whole strange, sad story."

"And you believed her?"

"I didn't not believe her. Before I opened this place, I was a cop in Albany for twenty years, and as the saying goes, I've seen some things. Business was slow, which let me do a little digging online. Lenard's death had made national news, briefly, and had sparked a series of articles about the dangers of drug-resistant super-bacteria. Based on the information included in the initial report, I was able to track down the veterinarian, who confirmed the details of Toro's death. In the end, I decided there was nothing wrong with leaving Madame Painte where she was. She seems happy enough watching the front door, and I've noticed a decrease in the local rodent population." The man smiles thinly.

"What do you think, I mean, what is she?"

"Aside from the focal point for a woman who suffered an excruciating loss? I don't know. My father was a big fan of Kipling, Stevenson, and this sounds like the kind of story one of them would have written. White people encounter a cursed object in the mysterious east—which, my older daughter would say, is pretty racist. (She's working on her Ph.D. over at Amherst.) I suppose it is. I wonder if there mightn't have been something wrong with the figure early on, right after she emerged from the factory. Maybe something attached to her, or was attached to her, whatever the white mask is. Maybe a version of what happened to the Nileses took place in a pretty house beside a canal, and the decision was made to send her far away, to the other side of the earth, where she wouldn't harm any more Dutch folks. Like dumping your supernatural toxic waste in a place whose inhabitants you don't give a rat's ass about."

"Why not just smash her, then, solve the problem that way?"

"What if I let loose whatever's in or on her?"

"Sounds like that's happening already."

"Only if she's kept inside," the man says. "Apparently, Priscilla, the colonel's wife, had her in their garden for years without any problems. There are fewer mice, chipmunks, around, but I can tolerate that."

"You sound like her caretaker."

"I suppose. That's one way of looking at it."

"Then why have her for sale?"

"Because it's a big responsibility. One I'm not certain I completely believe in, but I feel better erring on the side of caution. I would be happy to pass the care of Madame Painte onto someone I could be satisfied would maintain it with due diligence.

"Now that you've heard the story, the question is, Is that someone you?"

There is a moment, which is not that long but which will lengthen in your memory, when you think it might be. Not for any good or noble reason, but due to the cause that chased you out of your house this morning, sent you driving east on the Thruway until you took the first exit for Albany and wound up here: your grandfather, ninety-two, who lives in the basement apartment under you and your spouse's home. His brain clotted by dementia, but his body strong from a lifetime of construction work, he has been expelled from the last three nursing homes to which you've brought him. He can live on his own, he insists. Surrendering to necessity, you and your spouse have refurbished the basement to a reasonably safe space for him, from which he nonetheless flees once a week, usually to the next-door neighbors', to whom he appeals for protection from the strangers he says have kidnapped and imprisoned him. This is not to mention the daily trials, the small acts of meanness, vindictiveness, the piss and shit left on the bathroom floor, the stale and rotten food hidden under the bed and in the cushions of his easy chair, the sudden insults and rages. He could live another ten years, his doctor has said, he could give up the ghost tomorrow. You didn't sign up for this, you've said to yourself with increasing frequency, neither of you signed up for this.

Madame Painte might be the solution to your dilemma. Yes, the story is likely so much fantasy, but suppose it isn't? Just suppose. Your grandfather wouldn't have to know she was there. You could wait till he's asleep, hide her in his bedroom closet. Didn't the man say Lenard hadn't felt any pain? Plus, how would—how could—such a thing be traced back to you?

The wave of horror that sweeps through you carries the, "No, it isn't," from your mouth before you realize you've said it.

"That's all right," the man says. "Feel free to keep browsing. I'm sure you'll appreciate, I'd like to return the Madame to her proper place."

"Sure," you say, your face burning with shame.

For politeness's sake, you spend a few minutes wandering the shop's narrow aisles while its proprietor carries the figure out to the front step. Once he's behind the counter again, you depart the antique shop at something close to a run. The man nods to you as you pass him; in reply, you lift your left hand in a half-wave.

You can't help yourself: as you hurry up the front walk, you cast a glance over your shoulder at Madame Painte. She smiles her closed-eye smile at you, as if she knows you'll be back.

LOST IN THE DARK

TEN YEARS AGO, SARAH FIORE'S *LOST IN THE DARK* TER-RIFIED AUDIENCES. NOW, ON THE ANNIVERSARY OF THE MOVIE'S RELEASE, ITS DIRECTOR HAS REVEALED NEW INFORMATION ABOUT THE CIRCUMSTANCES BEHIND ITS FILMING. JOHN LANGAN REPORTS.

I

Pete's Corner Pub, in the Hudson Valley town of Huguenot, is a familiar college-town location: the student bar, at whose door aspiring underage patrons test their fake IDs against the bouncers' scrutiny, and inside which every square inch is occupied by men and women shouting to be heard over the sound system's blare. Its floor is scuffed, its wooden tables and benches scored with generations of initials and symbols. More students than you could easily count have passed their Friday and Saturday nights here, their weekend dramas fueled by surging hormones and pitchers of cheap beer.

During the day, Pete's is a different place, its patrons older, mostly there for its hamburgers, which are regarded by those in the know as the best in town. A few regulars station the bar, solitary figures there to consume their daily ration of alcohol and possibly pass a few words with the bartender.

Between lunch and dinner, the place is relatively quiet. You can bring your legal pad and pen and sit and write for a couple of hours, and as long as you're a good tipper, the waitress will keep warming your cup of decaf. The bartender has the music low, so you can have a conversation if you need to.

This particular afternoon, I'm at Pete's to talk to Sarah Fiore. To be honest, it's not my first choice for an interview, but it was the one location on which we could agree, so here I am, seated in a booth at the back of the restaurant. The upper half of the rear wall is an unbroken line of windows that curves inward at the top, for a greenhouse effect. I'm guessing it was intended to give a view out over the town, but the buildings that went up behind the bar frustrated that design. Still, they provide plenty of natural light, which must save on the electric bill.

It's Halloween, which seems almost too on the nose for the interview I'm here to conduct. Already, small children dressed as characters from comic books, movies, and video games wander the sidewalks, accompanied by parents whose costumes are the same ones they wear every day. I see Gothams of Batmen, companies of Storm Troopers, palaces of Disney princesses, and MITs worth of video game characters. There are few monsters, which saddens me, but I'm a traditionalist. In a couple of hours, the town will host its annual Halloween parade, for which they'll close the lower part of Main Street. It's quite a sight. Hundreds of costumed participants will assemble in front of the library—just up the street from Pete's—and process down towards the Svartkill River, which forms the town's western boundary. Once there, they'll turn into the parking lot of the police station, where they'll be served cider and donuts by members of the police and fire departments, accompanied by the mayor and other local officials. I find it quite sweet.

In the interest of full disclosure, I should add here, while we're still waiting for Sarah Fiore to arrive, that she and I know one another. Specifically, she was my student twenty-one years ago, in the first section of Freshman Composition I I taught at SUNY Huguenot. She was in her mid-twenties, settling down to pursue a degree after several years of working odd jobs and traveling. She was a big fan of horror movies, wrote several essays about films like *Nosferatu* (the original), the Badham *Dracula*, and *Near Dark*. We spent fifteen minutes of one class arguing the merits of *The Lost Boys*, much to the amusement of her fellow students. After the semester was over, I occasionally bumped into Sarah in the hallways of one building or another, which was how I learned that she was transferring to NYU for their film program. I told her she would have to make a horror movie.

Eleven years later, when *Lost in the Dark* was released, I remembered our exchange. I hadn't seen Sarah since that afternoon in the Humanities building, had no idea how to get in touch with her, to offer my congratulations for her good reviews. "A smarter *Blair Witch Project*": that's the one that sticks in my mind; although the only thing Sarah's film shares with Eduardo Sànchez and Daniel Myrick's is its reliance on hand-held cameras for the faux-documentary effect. Otherwise, *Lost in the Dark* has a much more developed narrative, both in terms of the Bad Agatha backstory and the Isabelle Price main story. The sequels did a lot to perpetuate the brand, and helped to add Bad Agatha to the pantheon of contemporary horror villains. Sarah's involvement with these films was limited, but she pushed for J.T. Petty to direct the second, and she reached out to Sean Mickles to bring him in for the third. As a result, you have a trilogy of horror movies by three different directors that work unusually well together. Sarah's sets up the story, Petty's explores the history, and Mickles's does its weird meta-thing about the films. While her name is on the fourth and fifth movies as producer, that had more to do with the details of the contract her agent worked out for her. Recently, there's been talk of a *Lost in the Dark* television series. AMC is interested, as is Showtime. There have been a couple of tie-in novels, and a four–issue comic book published by IDW.

Truth to tell, I think a good part of the continuing success of the *Lost in the Dark* franchise has to do with its Halloween connections. It didn't hurt the original film to be released Halloween weekend, and whoever thought up giving away Bad Agatha masks to the first dozen ticket buyers was a promotional genius. Plastic shells with a rubber band strap, they were hardly sophisticated, but there was a crude energy to their design, all flat planes and sharp angles. An approximation of the movie's makeup, the masks captured the menace of the character. It's the eyes that do it, especially that missing left one. The bit of black fabric glued behind the opening gives the appearance of depth, as if you're seeing right into the center of Bad Agatha's skull and the darkness therein. The last I checked, one of the original masks was going for four hundred dollars on eBay. The versions that have been released with each subsequent *Lost in the Dark* installment have varied in execution (though a colleague said that the mask she received was the best thing about the fourth movie), but they've become part of the phenomenon.

Throughout this time, Sarah Fiore has kept herself busy with other projects. She wrote and directed two films, *Hideous Road* (2009) and *Bubblegum Confession* (2011), and was director for *Apple Core* (2012). She wrote and directed the 2014 Shirley Jackson documentary for PBS's *American Masters*, which was nominated for an Emmy. With Phil Gelatt, she co-wrote an adaptation of Laird Barron's "Hallucigenia" that John Carpenter was rumored to be considering. Yet none of these movies or scripts has attached to her name the way the *Lost in the Dark* series has. For the most part, she's borne this with good grace, expressing in numerous interviews her gratitude for the films' success.

While not inevitable, it's hardly surprising that, in today's short-term-memory culture, any work of art with staying power is going to be milked for all it's worth. In the case of the original *Lost in the Dark*, this means a celebration of the movie's ten-year anniversary. There's a special-edition Blu-Ray with an added disk full of bonus features, screenings of the film in select theaters, and a new batch of Bad Agatha masks. Plus, the announcement that Takashi Shimizu has signed on to direct the sixth *Lost in the Dark* movie, which is supposed to herald a bold new direction for the franchise. None of this is especially remarkable; much lesser films receive much grander treatment.

What is of note lies buried within the fifteen hours of new footage on the Blu-Ray's bonus disk. There's a forty-minute group interview during which Sarah, and Kristi Nightingale, who was her director of photography, and Ben Formosa, who played Ben Rios, sit around a table with Edie Amos of *Rue Morgue* discussing the origins and shooting of the movie. It's the kind of thing film geeks love, behind the scenes of their favorite film. There's a pitcher of water on the table, a glass in front of each participant. Sarah sits with her elbows on the table, her hands clasped. She's wearing a black linen blouse, her long black hair pulled back in a ponytail. Kristi leans back in her chair, the mass of her curly brown hair springing from underneath an unmarked blue baseball cap. A black and white Billy Idol, circa *Rebel Yell*, sneers from the front of her white sweatshirt. Ben has shaved his head, which, combined with noticeable weight loss, gives him the appearance of having aged more than his former companions. The red dress shirt he's wearing practically glows with money, an emblem of the success he's enjoyed in his recent roles. Edie sits with a tablet in front of her. Her oversized round glasses magnify her eyes ever-so-slightly.

The conversation flows easily, and the first fifteen minutes are full of all sorts of minutiae. Then, in response to a question about how she arrived at the idea for the movie, Sarah looks down, exhales, and says, "Well, it was supposed to be a documentary."

At what she assumes is a joke, Edie laughs, but the glance passed between Kristi and Ben gives the lie to that. She says, "Wait—"

Sarah takes a sip from her water. "I'd known Isabelle since NYU," she says, referring to Isabelle Router, who plays the ill-fated Isabelle Price. "She was from Huguenot, which was where I'd done my first two years of undergrad. We kind of bonded over that. She knew all about the area, these crazy stories. I was never sure if she was making them up, but any time I went to the trouble of fact-checking them, they turned out to be true. Or true enough. That's why she was at school, for a degree in Cultural Anthropology. She wanted to study the folklore of the Hudson Valley.

"Anyway, we kept in touch after we graduated. I landed a position working for Larry Fessenden, Glass Eye Pix. Isabelle went to Albany for her doctorate. There was this piece of local history Isabelle wanted to include in her dissertation. She'd heard it from her uncle, who'd been a state trooper stationed in Highland when she was growing up. Sometime around 1969 or '70, a train had made an unscheduled stop just north of Huguenot. This was when there was a rail line running up the Svartkil Valley. Even then, the trains were on their way out, but one still pulled into the station in downtown Huguenot a couple of times a day. This was the night train, on its way north to Wiltwyck. It wasn't very long, half a dozen cars. About five minutes after it left town, the train slowed, and came to a halt next to an old cement mine. A pair of men was waiting there, dressed in heavy coats and hats because of the chill. (It was only mid-October, but there'd been a cold snap that week. Funny, the details you remember.) No less than five passengers said they witnessed a woman being led off the very last car on the train by one of the conductors and another woman wearing a Catholic nun's veil. None of the passengers got a good look at the woman between the conductor and the nun. All of them agreed that she had long black hair and that a man's overcoat was draped across her shoulders. Other than that, their stories varied: one said that she had been bound in a straitjacket under the coat; another that she'd been wearing a white dress; a third that she'd been in a nightgown and barefoot. The woman didn't struggle, didn't appear to notice the men there for her at all. They took her from the conductor and the nun and, guiding her by the elbows, steered her toward the mine opening. Before anyone could see anything more, the train lurched forward.

"I suppose that might've been all, except one of the passengers was so bothered by what she'd seen that she called the police the minute she walked in her front door. The cops in Huguenot didn't take her seriously, told her it was probably nothing, the engineer doing someone a favor. This was not good enough for our concerned citizen, who went on to dial the state police, next. Their dispatcher said they'd send someone out to have a look. Isabelle's uncle—what was his name? John? Edward?"

"Richard," Kristi Nightingale says. She is not looking at Sarah.

"Right, Richard, Uncle Rich," Sarah says. "He was the one they sent. It was pretty late by the time he reached the old access road that led to the mine. He told Isabelle he didn't know what to expect, but it wasn't a pair of fresh corpses. He stumbled onto the men ten feet inside the mine entrance. One had been driven forward into the wall with such force his face was unrecognizable. The other had been torn open."

"Wait," Edie says, "wait a minute. This is real? I mean, this actually took place?"

Sarah nods. "You can check the papers. It was front page news for the *Wiltwyck Daily Freeman* and the *Poughkeepsie Journal* for days. Even the *Times* wrote a piece on it: 'Sleepy College Town Rocked by Savage Killings.'"

"Well, what happened?"

"Nobody knew," Sarah says. "The whole thing was very strange. Apparently, the dead men were the same pair who had met the woman off the train. It turned out they were brothers from somewhere down in Brooklyn, Greenpoint, maybe. I can't remember their name, something Polish. Neither of their families could say what they were doing upstate, much less why they'd been waiting at the mine. Nor was there any trace of the conductor or the nun. All of the convents within a three-hour radius could account for their residents' whereabouts. The conductor who had been working that section of the train was a new guy who didn't return the next day, and whose hiring information turned out to be fake. Of the mysterious woman, there was no trace. The police searched the mine, the surrounding woods, knocked on the doors of the nearest houses, but came up empty-handed.

"There were all kinds of theories floating around. The most popular one involved organized crime. There used to be a lot of Mafia activity in the Hudson Valley. They had their fingers in the local sanitation businesses. Great way to dispose of your rivals, right? The story was, they also used some of the old mines and caves for the same purpose. In this version of events, the woman had been brought to the mine to disappear into it. Whoever she was, she or someone close to her was guilty of a particularly grievous trespass, and this was the punishment.

"But then what? How had she turned the tables on her captors and killed them? Not to mention, in such an… extravagantly violent manner. You could imagine adrenaline allowing her to overpower one of the men, seize his gun and shoot him and his partner before they had the chance to react. Crushing a man's skull against a rock wall, cracking his friend's chest open, were harder to believe. Plus, neither one showed evidence of having been armed.

"Maybe the woman hadn't been there to be murdered; maybe she was there to be traded. She'd been kidnapped, and the mine was the place her abductors had selected to return her to whoever was going to pay her ransom. Or she was a high-class prostitute, being transferred from one brothel to another. Either way, the scheduled meeting went pear-shaped and the men died. It didn't explain why they had done so in such a fashion, but the cops liked it better, it felt more probable to them.

"There were other, wilder explanations offered, too. The dead guys were Polish. This was the end of the sixties, the Cold War was in full swing, and Poland was slotted into the Eastern Bloc. Were the brothers foreign agents? Was the woman a fellow spy who had failed in her duties? Had she been sent here to be liquidated? Then rescued by other spies? Or were the brothers working for the US government, and the woman a captured spy who had to vanish? These weren't the craziest scenarios, either. *Rosemary's Baby* was pretty big at this time, which may explain why some people picked up on the detail of the nun who stepped off the train. Could it be that the woman had been carrying the spawn of the Satan, or otherwise involved in diabolical activities? It would account for the savagery of the brothers' deaths—the Devil and his followers are pretty ferocious—if not for what the men had been doing at the mine in the first place. It's been a while since the Catholic Church sanctioned anyone's murder.

"In the end, the investigation dead-ended. Officially, it was left open, but in the absence of any credible leads, the cops turned their attention elsewhere."

Sarah drinks more water. "Within a year or two, the local kids were telling stories about the woman in the mine. Some of them portrayed her as criminally insane, delivered to the place to be kept in a secret cell constructed for the sole purpose of confining her. Other accounts made her a witch, dropped at the mine for essentially the same purpose, imprisonment. Whether she was natural or supernatural, the woman escaped her bonds, slaughtered her jailors, and was now on the loose, ready to abduct any child careless enough to allow her too close. A few years later, when *The Exorcist* was released, the narrative adapted itself to the film, and the woman became demonically possessed, transported upstate for an exorcism, which obviously had failed. It was one of the peculiarities of the story, the way it shaped itself to the current cultural landscape. The woman morphed into a teen with dangerous psychic abilities, an alien masquerading as a human, even a vampire. For older kids, venturing into the mine, especially at night, and especially at Halloween, became a rite of passage. After the railroad stopped running in the seventies, high school and college kids would drive to the access road and hike to the entrance to build bonfires and drink.

"A similar process happens all over the country—all over the world. Something bad happens, and it hardens into the seed for stories about a monstrous character. This was what Isabelle's dissertation director said. There was nothing unusual about the woman in the mine, as the local kids called her. Isabelle disagreed, said she had additional information that distinguished this narrative from the rest. Once again, it involved her uncle, Rich, the cop.

"Ten years to the date after he answered his first call about the mine, he received a second. A group of high school seniors had been partying outside the entrance, and one of them had gone into it on a dare. That was three hours ago, and there had been no sign of him since. A couple of the other kids started in after their missing friend, but could find no trace of him as far as they dared to go. Everybody panicked, and eventually someone who was sober enough drove home and phoned the police. The Huguenot cops were busy with a costume party at one of the university's dorms that had gotten out of hand when someone spiked the punch with acid, so the call was booted to the state troopers. Rich suspected a Halloween prank, probably by the missing kid on his friends, possibly by all the kids on the cops. Despite that, he drove to the access road and made his way on foot to the spot.

"There, he encountered a dozen teenagers convincing enough in their panic that he decided they must be telling the truth. Flashlight in hand, he set off into the mine to search for their friend. He wasn't nervous, he told Isabelle. Sure, he remembered the bodies of the men he'd discovered a decade before, but he'd seen a lot of dead bodies in the meantime, and if none was quite as bad as those two, a few had come close. The dark had never bothered him, nor did the thought of being underground. He was more concerned about the debris littering the floor, rocks of varying sizes, dusty boxes, rusted bits of old machines, the occasional tool. His feet crushed fast food containers, kicked the bones of small animals, clanged on an empty metal lunchbox. There was one good thing about the clutter: it allowed him to track the missing student without much difficulty.

"He came across graffiti farther inside the mine than he would have expected. Most of it was of the familiar variety, names of people, sports teams, bands. There were hearts encasing the names of lovers, peace symbols, even the anarchist A. He stumbled through a heap of beer cans, whose musical clatter wasn't as comforting as he would have liked. Finally, he came upon the portrait."

"Portrait?" Edie says.

"A woman's face," Sarah says, "done in charcoal on a patch of rock about head level. Whoever she was, Rich said, she was striking. Long black hair, high, strong cheekbones, full lips. Her left eye had been smeared, which made it look like a hole into her skull. The artist had given the picture a force, a vitality, Rich struggled to define. He said it was as if she were two seconds away from stepping right out of the rock.

"By this point, he was pretty far in. Any sounds of the high school students had long since ceased. He was grudgingly impressed that the kid had traveled this distance. On the right, the tunnel he'd been walking opened

on a shallow chamber. He swept his light across it, and stopped. There was
a bed in there, its metal frame spotted orange with rust from the damp,
its mattress black with mold. Lying half on the bed was a long piece of
clothing—a straitjacket. He entered the room, lifted the restraint to check
it. Mold blotched the material. What wasn't mold was covered in writing,
in symbols. He saw rows of crosses, stars of David, crescent moons, other
figures he didn't recognize, but assumed were religious, too. He held up the
straitjacket, passed the light over it. The right front side and sleeve were
stained with what he was certain was blood. He replaced the garment on
the bed, and heard a footstep behind him.

"It was some kind of miracle, Rich said, he didn't spin around gun in
hand and shoot whoever was there, or at least brain them with his flashlight.
Of course it was the missing student, who'd gotten himself good and lost
in the mine's recesses and only come upon Rich through dumb luck. 'Why
didn't you call for help?' he asked the kid. Because there was someone else
down there, the kid said. A woman. He'd seen her at the other end of one
of the tunnels, right before the torch he was carrying guttered out. There
was something wrong with her face, and when she saw him, her expression
made him turn and run as fast as he could. For he wasn't sure how long,
the student had been hiding, listening for the sound of her footfall. He'd
thought Rich was *her*, and had debated fleeing further into the mine before
she saw him. Now that he'd found Rich, it was imperative the two of them
exit this place without delay.

"Had he been listening to the kid outside, Rich told Isabelle, beside the
fire he and his friends had built, he would have taken his story with a block
of salt. This far into the mine, the only source of light his flashlight, facing
the stone cell with the weird straitjacket, the tale sounded less incredible.
The student was all for bolting for the entrance, which Rich nixed. They
needed to pay attention to their surroundings, he said, or the two of them
would get lost, and the kid didn't want that, did he? 'No way,' the kid said.

"The walk back to the surface took a long time. Rich did his best to
remain calm, not let the student's hysteria affect him, but there was a stretch
of tunnel, about halfway to the exit, in which he was suddenly certain he
and the kid were not alone. The hair on the back of his neck lifted, and his
mouth went dry. For fear of spooking the student, he didn't want to stop,
but the echo of their feet on the walls made it difficult to decide if the sound

he thought he was hearing, a whispering noise, like fabric swishing over rock, was more than his imagination. He didn't want to put his hand on his gun, either, though the spot between his shoulders itched, as if something was stalking him and the kid, just a handful of footsteps behind them in the dark. The kid picked up on it, too, and asked him if there was someone else there with them, if *she* had found them. Rich heard the panic rising in the student's voice and said no, it was only the two of them. If the kid suspected him of lying, he didn't say anything.

"At last—at long last, Rich walked the student out of the mine and into the waiting arms of his friends, who were overjoyed at their reappearance. It was all he could do, Rich said, not to look back into the mine. He was afraid he'd see a woman standing inside it, something terribly wrong with her face."

There's a moment of silence, during which both Kristi and Ben fidget. Finally, Edie says, "That's…incredible."

"Isabelle thought so," Sarah says. "A couple of years after that, the stories about the woman in the mine gained a new detail: the left side of her face was scarred. Whether the student Rich had retrieved told his story, or other kids ventured into the mine and discovered the drawing he'd seen, that became part of the description. It didn't hurt that the first *Nightmare on Elm Street* was released around that time, with its disfigured villain. The point is, there was something interesting going on, and Isabelle already had enough information to justify further research and analysis. She told me she was planning to make the woman in the mine the center of her dissertation, an instance of the way traditional folk story was affected by the presence and pressure of newer narrative forms. The professor overseeing the project disagreed. She more than disagreed, she told Isabelle her idea was a non-starter. Instead, she wanted Isabelle to go south, to Kentucky, where there were reports of a lizard monster that had been spotted during a local disturbance at the end of the sixties. It wasn't that Isabelle wasn't interested in the lizard monster, but she had done a lot of work on the other topic, and she didn't want to drop it. Her professor's attitude left her unsure what to do, scrap what she had and start over, or look for another director who would be more agreeable to her plans. Either way, she was watching the completion of her dissertation recede into the future. Which happens, but is still a bummer.

"Enter me. Through five years of busting my ass, I had convinced Larry that I could and should be trusted with a camera and a small crew. We were searching for the right project for me. I read a lot of scripts; nothing clicked. I tried writing a couple of screenplays, myself, but they weren't any better. Then one night, I'm talking to Isabelle on the phone. We spoke every couple of weeks, caught up on what each of us was doing. She'd been telling me about the woman in the mine forever, since undergrad. I must have heard the story a thousand times. This particular night, the thousand and first time, things fell into place, and I realized I had my movie right in front of me. I would take Isabelle's research project, and I would put it onscreen. I would make a documentary about the woman from the mine, about the whole weird thing. Isabelle had assembled a huge archive. There were audio interviews with twenty people. There were hundreds of photographs. There were maps. There were police reports, train schedules, articles about mining. Before I even started, I figured I had a good portion of what I needed for my movie. Production costs would be relatively low, which is never a bad thing for a beginning filmmaker. Sure, a documentary wasn't exactly the most exciting debut, but I planned to jazz it up by filming an excursion to the mine. We'd take a look around inside, see if we couldn't find the drawing Isabelle's uncle had described. If we did—or better, if we located the straitjacket—it would give the film an added *oomph*.

"Isabelle didn't need much convincing. She saw the documentary as a middle finger to her professor, a way of demonstrating exactly how wrong the woman was. I doubted it would matter to her; her head sounded as if it was pretty tightly wedged up her own ass. But the idea led Isabelle to sign on with me, so I didn't argue."

"Hold on," Edie says, "hold on. Did you make this? Are you telling me *Lost in the Dark* is a documentary?"

"No," Sarah says, "no, it's—it's more complicated than that." For the first time in the interview, she is flustered. Both Kristi and Ben appear to be barely containing the impulse to bolt. "We went to the mine—this was after Isabelle and I had put together a rough introduction, twenty minutes laying out the story of the mysterious woman. Her uncle Rich was retired in Tampa, but we interviewed him via phone and he repeated everything he'd told Isabelle. I had arranged for a professor from SUNY Huguenot who specialized in folklore to sit down for a conversation with Isabelle about the woman.

"First, though, I wanted to shoot our trip. I planned it for Halloween, because how could I not? That was when everything had started, when kids built their bonfires outside the entrance, when Rich had ventured into its tunnels. I had my crew: Kristi on camera, George Maltmore on sound, a couple of film students who'd agreed to do whatever we needed them to. The barest of bones. And Isabelle, who was our guide. I gave George and Isabelle handheld cameras and Priya and Chad a camera to split between them. I wasn't expecting anyone to catch anything remarkable; I liked the idea of having shots from other perspectives.

"At dusk on Halloween, we entered the mine. I was certain we'd run into kids partying there. In fact, I was counting on it. I wanted it as an illustration of an annual event, a local ritual. But there was no one there. As far as setbacks go, it wasn't bad. After filming the mine's exterior, we walked into it."

Edie waits a beat, then says, "And…?"

"And we came out again," Sarah says. "Eventually."

II

A synopsis of *Lost in the Dark* is simple enough: an academic leads a film crew into an abandoned mine in search of a mysterious woman who disappeared there decades ago. While in the mine, the crew is plagued by strange and frightening incidents, culminating in a confrontation with the missing woman, who is revealed to be a supernatural creature. After she brutally murders most of the crew, the others flee deeper into the mine. The movie ends with the survivors proceeding into the dark, pursued by the woman.

The devil lives in the details, though, doesn't he? After all, you could make a terrible film from such a plot. There are three scenes, I think, on which the movie's success depends. It seems to me a good idea to pause here a moment and consider them. The IMDB listing for *Lost in the Dark* features what has to be one of the most thorough descriptions of any film listed on the site. At twenty-three thousand words, it's clearly a labor of love. In the interest of not re-inventing the wheel, I'd like to quote its summaries of the scenes I'm interested in. This is how the movie begins:

JOHN LANGAN

SYNOPSIS OF LOST IN THE DARK (2006)

The content of this page was created directly by users and has not been screened or verified by IMDB staff.

Warning! This synopsis may contain spoilers.

See plot summary for non-spoiler summarized description.

Professor Isabelle Price (Isabelle Router) is being interviewed in her office. Thirty-five years ago, she says, on Halloween night, a woman was brought by train from Hoboken, New Jersey, to a spot north of the upstate New York town of Huguenot. As she speaks, the screen cuts to a shot of 1960's-era passenger train speeding across farmland, then back to her. The woman's name, she says, was Agatha Merryweather. The screen shows a graduation-style portrait of a young woman with dark eyes and long black hair. The image switches to a large blue and white two-storey house. In a voiceover, the professor says that for the previous four years, Agatha Merryweather had been confined to the basement of her parents' home in Weehawken, New Jersey. During that time, neighbors reported frequent shouts, screams, and crashes coming from the house. The photograph of the house is replaced by one of police reports fanned out over a desktop. The Weehawken police, the voiceover continues, responded to one hundred and eight separate noise complaints; although only at the very end did they actually enter the house. The camera zeroes in on the report on top of the pile. When the Merryweathers opened the front door to their house, Professor Price says, the police saw the living room in shambles, furniture upended, lamps smashed, a bookcase tipped over. They also saw Agatha Merryweather, age twenty-one, crouched in one corner of the living room, wearing a filthy nightdress. The screen shows a photograph of a middle-aged man and woman, him in a brown suit, her in a green dress. Agatha's parents, the voiceover says, assured the officers that things were not as they appeared. Their daughter was not well, and every now and again, she had fits. The police thought the couple was acting strangely, so they entered the house. One of them approached the girl. The screen shows an open door, its interior dark. The other officer, Professor Price says, was drawn to the door to the basement. As the camera focuses on the darkness within the doorway, she says, He noticed that the door had been bolted and padlocked, but that the bolt and the lock had been torn loose when the door was thrown open, apparently with great force. There were no working lights in the basement, but the officer had his flashlight. He went downstairs, and discovered a bare, empty space, with a pile of blankets for a bed and a pair of buckets for a toilet. The walls were covered in writing, row after row of crosses, six-pointed stars, crescent moons, other symbols the cop didn't recognize. The smell was terrible.

The screen returns to Professor Price, sitting at her desk. From behind the camera, the interviewer (Gillian Bernheimer) asks what happened next. The answer to that question, the professor says, is very interesting. While the police were going about their business, Mrs. Merryweather was on the phone. As you can imagine, the officers were certain they had stumbled onto a case of child abuse. Before they had finished questioning Mr. Merryweather, a black car pulled up in front of the house. Out steps Harrison Law, the Archbishop of Newark, with a couple of assistants. The film shifts to a clip of a heavyset man wearing a bishop's mitre and robes and holding a bishop's crozier, greeting a crowd outside a church. The officers were surprised, the professor says, and even more surprised by what the archbishop said to them: This woman is under the care of the Church. She is suffering from a terrible spiritual affliction, and her parents are working with me to see that she returns to health.

The screen returns to the professor. The interviewer asks how the police reacted. Professor Price says, They were very impressed. This was when the Church still commanded considerable respect. For an archbishop to intervene personally in a situation was unusual. The cops were willing to give him a lot more leeway than they would in a similar situation today. Although, she adds, to his credit, one of the officers still wrote a fairly extensive report on the incident, which is how we know about it.

The interviewer asks if there was any follow-up. The professor shakes her head. She says, The report was filed and forgotten. However, she was able to track down one of the Merryweathers' former neighbors. This person, who did not want to be identified, said that the morning after the police made their incursion, they watched Agatha Merryweather be led down the front steps of her house by a priest and a nun. She appeared to be wearing a straitjacket. The priest and nun helped her into the backseat of a black car. The black car drove off, and that was the last the neighbor saw of Agatha. Professor Price says she asked the neighbor if they remembered the date of

Agatha's departure. As a matter of fact, the neighbor said, they did. It was Halloween.

What were the priest and nun doing there? the interviewer asks. The professor says she can only guess. She's been in touch with the Archdiocese of Newark, not to mention, Harrison Law, who currently holds a position at the Vatican. Neither was any help. The Archdiocese claims to have no record of contact between the former archbishop and the Merryweathers. Harrison Law says that the assistance he offers those under his pastoral care comes with a guarantee of utter discretion.

The interviewer says, It sounds like the Church was a dead-end. Which leads me to ask, How did you learn about Agatha Merryweather in the first place? And what led you to connect her to the woman who left the train outside Huguenot?

Professor Price says, Bear with me. She holds up a photocopy of a drawing. It shows the face of a young woman with dark eyes and long black hair, and bears a strong resemblance to the photograph of Agatha Merryweather. She says, This was made by a police sketch artist in Wiltwyck, New York, after several of the passengers who were on that train called the police to express their concern. All of their reports agreed that the woman was wearing a straitjacket, and was accompanied by a priest and a nun. The professor lowers the piece of paper. She says, The passengers also agreed that Agatha and her companions were met another pair of men, also priests, outside the entrance to the mine formerly run by the Joppenburgh Cement Company. The police might have passed off the reports as not worth more than a call to St. John's in Joppenburgh to ask if their priests had met someone off the Wiltwyck train. However, one of the reports came from a local judge, who insisted on a more thorough investigation. This, Professor Price says, is how they found the bodies.

Bodies? the interviewer asks. The professor is replaced by a series of black and white crime-scene photographs. They show a pair of naked men lying side by side next to the wall of a cave. Their legs are together, their arms are at their sides, and their eyes are shut. Their throats have been torn open, down to the bone. There are long scratches on their faces and their arms. The wall beside them is splashed with blood, as is the floor near them. In voiceover, Professor Price says, These two were found by the officers who were sent to check the site. As you can see, their clothes, any jewelry they might have been wearing, whatever might have identified them, has been removed. The evidence was that they were killed after a brief, fierce struggle. Obviously, the cause of death was the wound to each man's throat. The medical examiner said their throats had been ripped apart by a set of teeth, most likely human, though he noted irregularities in the bite marks that he failed to elaborate. After their deaths, the men were stripped and positioned together. Whoever had tended to the corpses had been careful to leave no traces of themselves. As for the assailant: a scattering of bloody hand- and footprints were found near the top of the tunnel wall, nearly twelve feet up. They retreated into the mine for twenty-five feet, and stopped.

The professor returns to the screen. The interviewer asks her what exactly she's saying. Professor Price says she doesn't know. For eight days, the police conducted a substantial investigation. The murders were front page news in papers up and down the Hudson Valley. They were the lead story on all the local TV news broadcasts. There was a lot of concern that a homicidal maniac or maniacs was on the loose. One of the local papers speculated that the killings might be the work of a Manson-style cult. Huguenot was quite the counterculture mecca at this time. After a few days, the story moved from the front page to page two or three, but it was still very much news. A couple of the passengers on the train thought the dead men were the priests who had helped Agatha Merryweather off the train, but none of the local clergy admitted to knowing them. The sketch I showed you was published in the paper, shown on TV. This was how Agatha Merryweather was identified as the woman on the train. A couple of her former neighbors saw the sketch and called the local police to say they recognized her. The police went to the Merryweathers' house but it was empty, the couple nowhere to be found. None of the neighbors had seen them leave. Apparently, the police did some kind of follow up with the Church, but they don't appear to have had any more success than I did.

The professor says, In Huguenot, the police searched for Agatha in surrounding homes and buildings, and turned up nothing. They brought in dogs in hopes they might discover something. Two of the dogs pissed themselves, then started fighting with such ferocity their handlers needed help separating them. A third dog went into the mine a hundred yards, sat, and started to howl. The police had dismissed the bloody hand- and footprints on the wall as some kind of red herring; although they hadn't been able to explain why the false lead had been placed in such an outlandish place. Now, they decided to search the mine. They broke out the flashlights and set off into its tunnels in pairs.

The interviewer asks if they found anything. Professor Price says, They did. In one of the mine's side passages, the police came across what was left of a straitjacket. It was stiff with dried blood, and had been ripped open by its wearer. More officers were brought in to assist in the effort. Several reported hearing sounds ahead of or behind them, footsteps, mostly, though one pair of officers described something growling close to them. The police said they were concentrating their efforts on the mine, which was where they were reasonably certain their suspect was hiding. And then…nothing. The search was called off.

Called off? the interviewer asks. The professor nods. Why? the interviewer asks. The professor says, No one knows. The mine remained the best lead. There was no trace of Agatha Merryweather anywhere else. When they heard about it, the local papers tried to get to the bottom of what had happened, but the police stonewalled them. It didn't take the papers long to move onto other stories. Since that time, no more has been done to determine Agatha Merryweather's fate.

Really? the interviewer asks. The professor says, I've made a pretty through search. There are stories the local kids tell, legends, but nothing in the way of formal investigation. Oh, Professor Price says, but I did learn one more odd fact in the course of my research. The bodies of the murdered men that were left at the mine's entrance? Three days after they arrived at the county morgue, they were claimed, by a John Smith, of Manhattan. The interviewer says, An alias? Professor Price nods. She says, I haven't talked to every John Smith who was living in the city at that time, but I'm pretty confident whoever came for those corpses did so under a fairly blatant pseudonym. Why? the interviewer asks. The professor says, That question comes up a great deal, doesn't it? If we're going to answer it, then I think we need to start with the place where Agatha Merryweather was last seen. We have to go to the mine.

The second scene occurs two-thirds of the way through the movie. By this point, we're well into the mine. In addition to Isabelle Price, we've met Carmen Meloy, the director; Kristi Fairbairn, the cameraperson; George

Slatsky, the sound person; and Ben Rios and Megan Hwang, the interns. We've passed the entrance, with its remnants of parties past, its scattered garbage, beer cans, and bottles, random articles of clothing, and graffiti, including the warning about "Bad Agatha," a name everyone in the film crew, with the exception of Isabelle, picks up. Following the old map of the mine Isabelle has folded into her knapsack, we've descended the main tunnels, running across strange, rusted pieces of machinery, shovels and other tools, a dusty copy of *Playboy* that's been a source of temporary amusement. Along the way, we've had snippets of Isabelle recounting the story of Agatha Merryweather, as well as moments of the crew reacting to the tale. We've encountered the portrait of Agatha's face, split between a normal right and a cadaverous left half; we've flinched when Ben touches it and jumped in our seats when he starts screaming, only to laugh with nervous relief as his outburst dissolves into laughter, and Megan calls him an asshat.

We've worked out some of the relationships among the crew, as well. Ben and Megan are involved; she's worried about how her parents will react to her dating someone who isn't Korean. We catch the tail end of a couple of heated, whispered exchanges between them. George is short-tempered, preoccupied with his ten-year-old daughter, for full custody of whom he's locked in legal combat with his ex-wife. Kristi is unhappy from the start with this project, a sentiment exacerbated by a mild case of claustrophobia. Carmen spends much of her time checking in with the others, consulting on technical matters, touching base on personal ones. Isabelle is focused on searching the mine with an intensity that's unnerving; she gives the strong impression of being in possession of additional information she has not shared with her companions.

(A pause here to say that Isabelle Router deserves credit for a remarkable job of acting. Granted, her part is based to a large extent on her actual background, she nonetheless delivers an exceptional portrait of a woman struggling to maintain her composure in the face of pressures external and internal.)

On the soundtrack, sounds that started as background noise, barely distinguishable from the clamor of the crew proceeding, have increased in volume substantially. Some are identifiable: a low, weak sobbing, the kind that comes at the end of hours of crying; the rattle and click of a small rock being knocked across the floor into another rock. Some are harder to place:

a metallic ping, and a sudden, deafening roar that sends the film crew into wide-eyed panic, racing headlong through the tunnels as the sound goes on and on.

This is what brings them to a low opening on their left, into a small cave where they spend a solid minute shouting, cursing, and screaming, until the noise drains away and we're left with their mingled panting. Only now do they notice the chamber they've entered. Overhead, the ceiling slopes down into darkness. To either side, walls that are marked with rows of unfamiliar symbols stretch to join it. Directly in front of the crew, a narrow trench bisects the floor, running away into blackness. The bottom of the trench is streaked with blackish-red liquid. Despite the warnings of the others, Ben Rios kneels and extends a hand to the substance. When he raises his fingertips to his nostrils, he pulls his head back, lips wrinkling in disgust. "Blood," he says, as we knew he would.

While the others digest this news, Isabelle Price is on the move, sweeping her flashlight over the weird figures on the walls. Geometric shapes—mostly circles within circles—punctuate long lines of characters that appear almost hieroglyphic. She directs her light to the floor, and picks out something scratched on the rock, a rectangle the size of a dinner tray. YES is incised in its upper left hand corner, NO in its upper right hand corner. The letters of the alphabet line the inside of the rectangle, beginning with A below the YES and Z under the NO. A series of lines, some more recent than others, loop from letter to letter to the flat stone positioned at the rectangle's center. The lines seem to have been drawn in blood. Isabelle lifts the flat stone and turns it over, revealing its underside smeared with shades of red. Rock in hand, she crosses to the trench, where she kneels to dip the rock in the blood there. As the crew members exclaim and ask her what she's doing, Isabelle returns to the primitive Ouija board and replaces the stone within it. She beckons Ben and Megan to join her, but Ben refuses. After a brief debate, George says he'll take part in the professor's little séance. Passing his equipment to Ben, he lowers to his knees to Isabelle's right; Megan is on the left. There's a whispered exchange off camera, Kristi asking Carmen what the fuck is going on, Carmen telling her to keep shooting.

Here's how the IMDB entry describes what happens next:

Professor Price says, Rest your fingers on the stone lightly, like this. She places the tips of her fingers on the stone. Megan and George do the same. The professor says, Good. Now, clear your minds.

Megan asks, How are we supposed to do that? Have you seen where we are?

Just do the best you can, Professor Price says. You can close your eyes, if it helps.

Megan shakes her head no, but George shuts his eyes. He says, All right, what next?

The professor closes her eyes. She asks, Is anyone there?

Nothing happens.

Professor Price says, Is anyone there?

Slowly, the stone scrapes across the floor. Megan screams, but keeps her fingers on it. George says, What the hell? The professor says, Easy. Stay calm. Keep your hands on the planchette.

Megan says, The what?

George says, The stone.

Right, Professor Price says, the stone. Her eyes are open. The stone settles on YES. The professor nods. She asks, Who is there?

The stone slides from YES to the letter A beneath it. Then to G, back to A, to T, to H, and back to A. Professor Price says, Agatha.

Kristi's voice says, Holy shit. Ben Rios crosses himself.

The professor asks, What happened to you, Agatha?

The stone spells out T-R-A-P-P-E-D.

Professor Price says, Trapped? You were trapped here, in the mine?

The stone moves to YES.

The professor asks, Why?

The stone spells B-A-D.

Professor Price says, You were bad.

The stone spells B-A-D.

The professor frowns. She asks, How were you bad?

The stone does not move.

Professor Price says, How were you bad, Agatha?

The stone spells out B-L-O-O-D.

The professor says, I don't understand. How were you bad, Agatha?

George says, Seems pretty obvious to me. She was doing something with blood. Ben says, Maybe she was drinking it.

The stone slides to YES.

Professor Price says, Please, let me do the talking. What were you doing with blood, Agatha?

The stone moves to NO.

The professor says, All right. Who trapped you here, in the mine?

The stone spells K-L-E-R-O-S.

Megan asks, Who is Kleros? George shakes his head. Professor Price says nothing. Ben says, I think it's Greek. Carmen asks, Greek? Ben says, yeah. It's like the root of clergy.

The professor asks, Where are you from, Agatha?

The stone moves to NO.

Professor Price repeats the question.

The stone does not move.

The professor exhales. She asks, Can we help you, Agatha?

The stone does not move.

Professor Price waits for an answer. None comes. She asks, Are you still there, Agatha?

The stone does not move.

Megan asks, What happened? George says, We lost her. He sits back, lifting his hands from the stone. Megan does the same. The professor maintains contact for a few seconds more, then she sits back, too.

Kristi says, What the fuck was that? Carmen says, Yeah, Isabelle, what's going on?

Isabelle Price starts to speak, but her answer is interrupted by George shouting, Shit! and scrambling backward. Megan screams and stumbles to her feet. The professor raises her hands, startled.

The planchette stone is bleeding. All over its surface, drops of blood appear, swell, and collapse into streams that trickle to the edges of the stone and spill onto the floor. Kristi shouts, Fuck! Megan turns and collides with Ben. Blood pools around the planchette stone. Professor Price stares at it. Carmen says, Isabelle, what the fuck is happening? Blood spreads over the words and letters of the Ouija board. Ben mumbles something. George is praying, Our Father, Who art in Heaven. Blood flows to the edges of the trench in the center of the cave and slides into it. Kristi says, What is this? What is this? What are we seeing? What? Carmen tells everyone to move away from the blood, to come over beside her. The crew does, except for the professor. Carmen says, Isabelle. Come here, Isabelle.

Professor Price turns around. Her face is blank. Her left eye is red, blood pouring from it down her cheek.

The third and final scene is, of course, the movie's climax. By now, the movie's title has been realized, as the film crew has emerged from the cave to discover that their panicked flight has carried them off Isabelle's map. Despite following several seemingly familiar paths, they have remained lost. Their complaints have grown more hysterical.

In the meantime, Carmen has succeeded in coaxing Isabelle out of the trance-like state into which she fell. The sclera of her left eye is still stained red with hemorrhages, but it's no longer actively bleeding. Prompted by Carmen and Kristi, she has revealed some of the secrets we've suspected her of harboring. Her research on Agatha Merryweather, she says, led her to a website that's kind of a clearinghouse of weird information. There was an entry for the Bound Woman of the Mine that sounded as if it might connect to the information she'd already gathered. The site kept crashing her computer, so she wasn't able to read all of the listing, but the portion she finished was intriguing. It concerned a fourteen-year-old girl who had been responsible for a series of terrible murders in northwestern New Jersey during the early nineteen sixties. This was farm country, near the Pennsylvania line. For some reason, after her apprehension by the sheriff, the local Catholic priest was brought in to consult on the case. This led to another pair of priests being summoned, an older man and a younger one, whose accents no one recognized. They said they were members of a small order, the Perilaimio. Eventually, the girl was released into their custody on the condition she remain confined to her house. At some point thereafter, she, her parents, and the priests were discovered to have fled for an unknown destination. There was talk of a search for her, but it came to nothing.

When Kristi asks what any of this has to do with anything, Isabelle reveals that the website gave a name for the girl: Agatha Merryweather. Obviously, with the assistance of the Church, she and her family fled east, where they were resettled in Weehawken. The question was, why?

"She was possessed," George says. "That's where this is heading, isn't it?"

That is what she thought, Isabelle says, until she looked into the order to which the priests belonged, the Perilaimio. It's an old, old group, maybe

37

older than the Church itself.

What is she talking about? Megan wants to know. How can there be a part of the Church that came before it?

Like Christmas trees, Ben says, or Yule logs. Pagan things the Church folded into it.

That's it exactly. The Perilaimio, Isabelle says, were charged with managing the Keres.

Which means what? Kristi asks.

Death-spirits, Ben says.

Death-spirits? Megan says. How does he know this stuff?

He took Greek in high school, Ben says.

Does he mean ghosts? Megan says.

Sounds like devils to him, George says.

No, Isabelle says. These are beings of the primordial dark, beyond the Church's sway. They depend on blood to maintain their presence in this world. They can't be cast out, or destroyed, only contained.

Which is what happened here, George says. Agatha Merryweather was brought to this place to imprison her.

That's her theory, Isabelle says. At first, she read this entire story as a case of a mentally ill girl subjected to a prolonged victimization by religious maniacs. The mine, she assumed, was intended as a jail, primitive but low profile. Most likely, the men who transported her to upstate New York planned for her to die in these tunnels, of malnutrition or disease.

Why would they have thought this? Kristi says. Didn't Isabelle just say the death-spirits couldn't be killed?

It's complicated, Isabelle says. The Keres are fundamentally violent; they can't be killed by violent means. However, if their host dies of natural causes, they lose their hold on it.

This makes no sense, Kristi says. How does any of this make sense?

The point is, Carmen says, Isabelle thought they were dealing with a crazy person.

Honestly, Isabelle says, she was sure Agatha had been dead for years. The most she expected was to find her remains.

Instead, Kristi says, they have…this. What they have.

"Us," George says, "lost. In the Dark. With a monster."

Their wandering has brought the crew to another unfamiliar location, a small chamber whose rough walls recede at regular intervals to what appear to be doorways. This is the IMDB summary of what ensues:

Ben shines his flashlight on the recess furthest to the right. It shows solid rock. He swings the light to the left. The next recess opens on a passageway. He swings the light to the left, to the recess directly across from him. It is solid, too, but there is something on the rock at approximately head level. It is the same portrait the film crew saw at the beginning of the expedition, a woman's face, the left half a skull. Megan shrieks. Kristi says, What the fuck? Ben says, It's only another drawing, and crosses to it. He reaches out his free hand to touch it. He says, See?

His flashlight goes out. Megan shrieks again. Carmen says, Ben? George says, Now is not the time for screwing around, kid. He aims his flashlight at the recess.

There is a flurry of motion. Ben screams. George's flashlight beam swings from side to side, trying to keep up with the action. Kristi shouts. Carmen points her flashlight in Ben's direction. She says, There! There! Ben continues screaming. There is someone grabbing him from behind. White arms wrap around his neck and chest. White legs encircle his waist. A head with long black hair presses against his neck. Ben grabs at the arms. He slaps at the head. He stumbles back into the wall. Megan screams, Someone do something! Professor Price shouts, Agatha! Agatha, stop!

Agatha growls and tugs her head back. There is the sound of flesh tearing, followed by a hiss as blood sprays from Ben's open throat. He drops to his knees, slaps at Agatha's hands, and falls forward, Agatha still clinging to him. She drops her head to his neck. There is the sound of her slurping his blood. Kristi says, Holy shit. Megan screams, You fucking bitch! and runs at Agatha, raising her flashlight as a club. Agatha ducks her swing and leaps onto her. She knocks Megan onto her back, and rips her throat out. Kristi says, Jesus Christ.

George says, We have to get out of here. He runs from the chamber. Agatha jumps off Megan onto the wall. She hangs on it like a spider. Professor Price shouts, Agatha! Please! Agatha! Agatha scrambles up the wall and out of the light. Carmen sweeps her flashlight around the ceiling. Kristi shouts, Where did she go? Where is she? The professor shouts, Agatha! Please!

Agatha drops onto Carmen. Her flashlight spins away. She screams. Agatha growls. Kristi and Professor Price scramble out of the way. There is the sound of Carmen struggling. Kristi shouts, Come on! Let's go! Now! Carmen shouts, wait! Help me! Kristi says, I'm sorry, and runs through the passageway Ben discovered. Carmen shouts, Kristi! Agatha snarls. The professor says, Agatha, please, then follows Kristi. Carmen screams.

The screen goes black.

After five seconds, there is a clatter and the screen fills with Kristi's face, illuminated by the camera light. She says, I don't know why I'm doing this. There's no way either of us is getting out of here. I can hear her—Agatha. She's coming closer. Kristi begins to cry. She says, I just wanted to say, I'm sorry about Carmen. I couldn't do anything about Ben and Megan. Maybe I couldn't have helped Carmen, either, but I'm sorry. She wipes her eyes with the back of her hand. She says, And George, if you make it out of this place, and somehow see this, fuck you, you chickenshit piece of shit.

The camera turns to show Isabelle Price's face. Kristi says, You never told us everything, did you? Professor Price shakes her head. Kristi asks, Anything you want to say now? Isabelle shakes her head. Kristi says, You know this is all your fault. The professor nods. Kristi says, We're going to leave this camera here, in hopes that someone will find it. Which is about as stupid as all the rest of this, but hey, why stop now? She sets the camera down, turned to light the tunnel she and Professor Price are headed down. She says, We still have a flashlight. We'll hold off using it as long as we can, to save the batteries. Professor Price starts along the tunnel. Kristi follows. When she is almost out of view Kristi stops and turns. She says, I can hear her. Hurry.

The women disappear into the darkness. For the next three minutes, the credits roll over the scene. Once the credits are finished, the camera light dims. There is the sound of bare feet slapping stone. Agatha's face fills the screen. Her features are those of a young woman, covered in blood. Her eyes are wide. Blood plasters her hair to her forehead and cheeks. The screen flickers. Agatha's left eye is an empty socket, her left cheek sunken, her lips on this side drawn back from jagged teeth. The screen flickers again, goes to static, then goes dark.

LOST IN THE DARK
III

It's the teacher in me: I can't help wanting to discuss all the things *Lost in the Dark* does right. The opening, for example, which imparts a substantial amount of background information to the viewer without sacrificing interest, as well as the Agatha Merryweather narrative, itself, which taps into the enduring fascination with the Catholic Church and its secrets (which, if I felt like being truly pedantic, I would point out is one of the ribs of the larger umbrella of the Gothic under which the movie shelters). Or the way the film suggests there's even more to the Agatha narrative than we've been told, than anyone's been told. Only Isabelle Price knows the full story, and to the end, she keeps back some portion of it. By making her the model for the portraits of Agatha the crew encounter, a similarity no one mentions, the movie visually suggests a connection between the women, which contributes to the audience's growing sense that the characters are in a situation that's much worse than they understand. (It's one of the enduring conceits of the film that the identity of the actress who portrays Bad Agatha has never been revealed. The credits assign the part to Agatha Merryweather. I'm of the camp that would wager money Isabelle Router played the monster; it fits too well with the portrait ploy not to be the case.)

Were it not for Sarah Fiore's interview in the Blu-Ray extras, this article might address itself to exactly such a critical analysis. That interview, though, changed everything. According to Sarah, the trip into the mine to shoot footage for Isabelle Router's documentary lasted much longer than they had planned, almost twenty hours. During that time, the crew became lost, wandering out of the mine into a series of natural tunnels and caves. While underground, they had a number of strange experiences, about half of which at least one member of the crew caught on film. They returned to the surface with a couple of hours of decent footage that was not what they had been planning on. After a rough edit, Sarah sat down with Larry Fessenden to watch the film. He loved it. He also thought she had abandoned her plan for a documentary in favor of an outright horror movie. Thinking quickly, Sarah responded to his enthusiasm by saying that yes, she had decided to go a different route. Fessenden offered to produce a feature-length version of what he'd seen, on the condition that Sarah revise the script to give it a more substantial narrative. Since there was no actual script at that moment, his request was both easier and harder to fulfill; nonetheless, she agreed to it. She also agreed that she should keep as much of what she'd shown him as they could in the longer film. This turned out to be about forty minutes of an hour and forty minute movie. Isabelle Router was willing essentially to play herself, as were Kristi Nightingale and George Maltmore. The interns, Priya and Chad, had no interest in taking part in another expedition to the mine, so they were replaced by a pair of actors, Ben Formosa and Megan Park. Rather than juggle the roles of director, scriptwriter, and actor, Sarah hired Carmen Fuentes to play her. The rest is cinema history.

If we're to believe Sarah, *Lost in the Dark* was built from another film, a piece of fiction constructed using a significant portion of non-fiction. I use the "if" because, as soon as word of her interview got out, the question of its authenticity was raised. After all, this was a filmmaker who had started her career with a faux-documentary. What better way to mark the ten-year anniversary of that production than with another instance of the form, one designed to send audiences back to pore over the original movie? By those who took this view of Sarah's revelations, she was variously praised for her cleverness and decried for her cynicism. I've swung back and forth on the matter. I did my due diligence. The narrative Sarah relates, of the mysterious woman who stepped down from the train to Wiltwyck, the murdered men at the entrance to the mine, is true. You can read about it online, in the archives of the *Wiltwyck Daily Freeman* and the *Poughkeepsie Journal*. Confirming Isabelle Router's uncle's story proved more difficult. Richard Higgins died in Tampa three years ago. I located one of his former colleagues, Henry Ellison, who confirmed that Rich had gone into the mine to retrieve that dumbass high school kid. Of any more than that, Rich never spoke to him.

Still, there's sufficient evidence that Sarah Fiore was telling at least some of the truth. This doesn't mean there was a documentary shot between her discovery of this information and *Lost in the Dark*. Once again, I did some digging and came up with contact information for all but one of the members of the (supposed) original crew. Wherever Chad Singer currently resides, it's beyond my rudimentary sleuthing abilities to locate. Of the remainder of those involved, Priya Subramani listened to my introduction, then hung up and blocked my number. Kristi Nightingale told me to go fuck myself; I'm not sure if she also blocked me, since there didn't seem much point in calling back. George Maltmore instantly was angry, demanding to know who the hell I thought I was and what the hell I thought I was playing at. Despite my best efforts to reassure him, he became increasingly incensed, threatening to find out where I lived and show up at my front door with his shotgun. Finally, I hung up on him. Somewhat to my surprise, Larry Fessenden spoke to me for almost half an hour; although he did so without answering my question in a definitive way. Sure, he said, he remembered the film that Sarah had brought to him. It was a terrific piece of work. Was what he saw a documentary? I asked. Ah, he said, yeah, that was the story making the rounds, wasn't it? He couldn't remember Sarah saying that to him at the time, but it would be something if it turned out to be true, wouldn't it?

Yes, I said, it would.

Even more unexpectedly, Isabelle Router agreed to talk. Once *Lost in the Dark* was done shooting, she and Sarah had an argument which resulted in a falling out that has lasted to this day. Isabelle returned to Albany, to work on her Ph.D. at the state university, only to leave after a single semester. For the next few years, she said, she was kind of messed up. She moved around a lot, did…things. Eventually, she pulled herself together, settled in Boulder, where she became a yoga instructor. She asked me if I had spoken with anyone else, and what they had said. Isabelle was particularly interested to know if I'd talked to Sarah. That I had been her teacher was of great interest; she wanted to know what Sarah had been like as a student. When it came to the question of the documentary, her answers grew vague. Yes, they had done some preliminary filming in the mine. In fact, they'd gotten kind of lost down there. Did I know that the idea for the movie, for all of the supernatural stuff, was hers? It came out of the research she'd been doing for her dissertation. You did shoot a documentary first, I said.

"I don't know that I'd go that far," Isabelle said. "We were just lost in the dark. Sarah got that much right."

Nor could I coax any more definitive statement from her. There was enough in Isabelle's words for me to take them as supporting Sarah's claims, but not enough to settle the matter. Not to mention, the more I paged through the notes I'd taken from all of the interviews, the less certain I was that I wasn't being played for a sucker. The extremity of Priya, Kristi, and George's reactions—their theatricality—added to Fessenden's bland non-answers and Isabelle's ambiguous replies, seemed intended, scripted, to give the impression that not only had the documentary been filmed, it had recorded an experience singularly unpleasant. On the other hand, quite often, the truth looks glaringly untrue; as Tolstoy said, God is a lousy novelist.

In the end, I would need to speak with my former student. Rather than a phone conversation or e-mail exchange, Sarah suggested we meet in person. Halloween, she was scheduled to attend a special late-night screening of *Lost in the Dark* at the Joppenburgh Community Theater. Why didn't we get together before that? She'd bring her laptop; there were clips she could show me that would prove interesting. I agreed, which has brought me here, seated at the back of Pete's Corner Pub, while trick-or-treaters make their annual pilgrimage.

IV

Sarah Fiore enters the bar as she used to enter my classroom, walking briskly, head down, oversized bag clutched to her side. The heels of her boots knock on the wood floor. She's wearing a hip-length black leather coat over a white blouse and black jeans. With her head tilted forward, her long black hair curtains her face. Before the hostess on duty can approach her, she's crossed to where I'm sitting and slid into the bench across from me. Since I didn't meet her until she was in her mid-twenties, I don't see as dramatic a change in her as I often do with my former students. That said, time has passed, which I've no doubt she notices in the tide of white hairs that has swept both sides of my beard, and is washing through what brown remains on my chin. We exchange greetings, Sarah orders a martini from the waitress who's hurried to the booth, and she slides a gray laptop from her bag. She places it on the table in front of her, unopened. Hands flat on either side of it, she asks me if I've talked to the other members of the original crew.

With the exception of Chad Singer, I say, I have, and relay to her abbreviated versions of our conversations. She smirks at Kristi Nightingale's cursing, drops her head in an attempt to conceal a laugh at George Maltmore's furious show. Larry Fessenden's non-committal response receives a nod, as does Isabelle Router's remark about them being lost in the dark. "She was intrigued to learn that I had been your teacher," I add, but it draws no further response from Sarah.

The server returns with Sarah's drink, asks me if I'd like more coffee. I decline. If you need anything, she says, and leaves.

"All right," Sarah says after tasting her drink. "How should we do this?"

"Why don't we start with a question: why now? Why wait ten years to reveal this new information? Wouldn't it have been simpler to do so back when the movie was first released?"

"Possibly," Sarah says. "I don't know. At the time, Isabelle and I weren't on speaking terms. We still aren't, but then, it was new. We'd had this massive fight—things didn't just turn ugly, they turned hideous. Everything felt pretty raw. Part of me did want to go public with the documentary stuff, but it was mostly because I thought it would hurt Isabelle. She was back at graduate school, working on her dissertation. If word got out that she'd been part of this crazy documentary project, I figured it would make her study less pleasant.

"For once in my life, though, I listened to my inner Jiminy Cricket and did the right thing. For a long time after that, I was so busy, I didn't have time to think about the footage. Really, when I sat down for the interview with *Rue Morgue*, I had no intention of mentioning any of that stuff. It just…came out. I don't see the harm in it, now. I mean, Isabelle left her doctoral program, didn't she? Isn't she a massage therapist or something?"

"Yoga instructor," I say. "But you have to admit—"

"The timing is highly suspicious, yes. I can't blame anyone who thinks that. It's what I would say."

"You, however, have the original documentary."

Sarah nods. "I do." She raises the laptop's screen. "The problem is, we're living in an age where it's easy to fake stuff like this. If you have the re-sources, you can put together something that would fool everyone up to and maybe including the experts. Although, why would you want to?" She lifts a hand to forestall my answer. "Yeah, publicity, I know. It's a case of diminishing returns. If all I was after was to generate interest in the movie, I would have ended my story saying that the original footage was lost, wiped when my computer crashed. It wouldn't be worth whatever meager spike in sales you might project for me to go to the trouble of creating a new fake film."

"Which is exactly the sort of thing I'd expect you to say, if you were trying to pass off a fake movie as authentic."

"Yeah," she says, sweeping her fingers over the computer's touch pad to bring it to life. "The thing is, if you want to believe something's a conspiracy, you will. No matter what I say, one way or the other, it'll be evidence of what you're looking for."

"Fair enough."

"Okay." She taps keys, and turns the computer ninety degrees, allowing me a view of the screen. The window open shows a woman's head and shoulders foreground right, the entrance to the mine background left. It's Isabelle Router, her face burnished by the same late afternoon sunlight that paints the rock face behind her bronze. "This is how we began," Sarah says. "Isabelle standing in front of the mine, reciting the history of the mystery woman. We could watch it, but you already know the story, right?"

"Right."

"Let's…" She fast forwards ten minutes. We're inside the mine, rough rock walls and ceiling, scattered trash on the floor. To anyone who's seen *Lost in the Dark*, it's a familiar shot, although the voices are different. Somewhere off screen to the right, Chad Singer is saying, "Am I going to have to carry this for very long? Because it is heavy." From what sounds as if it might be behind the camera, George Maltmore is muttering about the acoustics of this damn place. Much closer, Kristi Nightingale says, "Eww," at the desiccated carcass of a small animal, likely a mouse. "We had to swap out the soundtrack for something more atmospheric," Sarah says to me. "Plus, Chad had left, so we couldn't use his voice." She pauses the video. "There's plenty more of this kind of thing I can show you, if that's what you want." She advances five minutes, to the crew encountering a piece of Jack-Kirby-esque machinery the approximate dimensions of a refrigerator, its yellow paint faded and flaked away in patches, the large round openings in its sides strung with cobwebs. A leap of another six minutes brings us to the comic relief of the ancient *Playboy*, its cover and interior pages crumpled. The crew's jokes approximate those in the later film. Ten minutes more down the dark tunnel brings the first surprise of the interview, the portrait of a woman's face on the rock wall. It's exactly as it appears in *Lost in the Dark*. Despite myself, I flinch, say, "Jesus. This is for real?"

"It's what we found," Sarah says.

I stare at the waves of the woman's hair, the lines of her cheekbones and nose, the weird smearing on the right hand side of the drawing, which gives the left half of the face a roughly skeletal appearance. I fight the urge to reach my fingers to the screen. "I assumed—I mean, I know Isabelle's uncle mentioned it in his story, but I figured he invented it."

"Me, too," Sarah says. "It seemed hard to believe, didn't it? Like something out of a horror movie."

"Who did it?" I can't stop looking at the portrait, which is in some ways no different from what I've seen previously, and in other ways has been fundamentally changed. Stranger still, the portrait's resemblance to Isabelle remains as strong as ever. "I mean, did Isabelle have any friends who were artists?"

"She swore it wasn't her," Sarah says. She lets the movie play. The camera pans from the tunnel wall to Isabelle, who is not pleased. "Very funny," she says.

"What do you mean?" Kristi says.

"You think I don't know who this is?"

"Isabelle," Sarah says, "we didn't do this."

"Yeah, right," Isabelle says.

"Seriously," Kristi says.

"You think we had something to do with this?" Priya Subramani says.

"Obviously," Isabelle says. "How else do you explain it?"

"Um, someone drew it," Chad says. "Someone who isn't one of us."

"Are you sure?" Isabelle says.

"Yeah," Chad says. "When my friends say they didn't do something, I believe them."

"What would be the point?" Sarah says. "Why would we do this, and then lie to you about it?"

Doubt softens Isabelle's features, but already, she's invested too much in the argument to yield the point. Plus, she doesn't want to contemplate the implications of the crew telling the truth. She says, "Whatever," and turns away.

The camera swings to Sarah, who blows out through pursed lips while rolling her eyes.

"Probably should have omitted that last bit," she says, tapping the touch pad and freezing the screen. "After we returned from the mine and were going through the footage, Kristi suggested that maybe Isabelle was responsible for the drawing. I told her there was no way, she was being ridiculous. Had she not seen Isabelle's reaction to the thing? When the group of us met to screen what Kristi and I had put together, she asked Isabelle about the portrait point blank. I didn't stop her. I'll admit: I was curious. Isabelle acted genuinely surprised at the accusation, enough for me to believe her. Although, when I think about her performance in *Lost in the Dark*, how well she acted, I wonder."

"Why would she have done that?"

"To back up the story that had brought us there in the first place," Sarah says.

"I don't know," I say. "That seems like a little far to go."

"Well." Sarah brings the movie ahead another ten minutes, hurrying the crew through a pair of large spaces whose flat ceilings rest on rock columns the girth of large trees. In the second chamber, their flashlights pick out a shape to the right, a dark mound like a heap of rugs. Flashlights trained on the thing, they cross the space toward it. As they approach, the mound gains definition, resolving into the carcass of a large animal. When they reach it, Sarah returns the film to normal speed.

"—is it?" Chad is saying.

"I think it's a bear," Sarah says.

"No way," Kristi says.

"There are bears here?" Priya says.

"Yes," George says, "black bears." He steps away from the group to circle the remains.

"Be careful," Priya says.

"Yeah, George," Chad says, "watch yourself."

"Relax," George says, "this fellow's been dead a long time." He crouches next to the bear's blunt head, playing his light back and forth over it. His eyes narrow. "What the hell?"

"What?" Sarah says.

"What is it?" Priya says.

"From the looks of things," George says, "something tore out Gentle Ben here's throat."

"Is that strange?" Chad says.

"What could do that?" Kristi says.

"I have no idea," George says. "Another bear, maybe. A mountain lion, I guess."

"Hang on—I want to see this," Kristi says. The camera moves around the animal's prostrate form to where George sits on his heels, his flashlight directed at the bear's head. Its eyes are sunken, shriveled, its teeth bared in a final snarl. The right canine is missing, the socket ragged, black with blood long-crusted. What should be the animal's thick neck is a mess of skin torn into leathery ribbon and flaps, laying bare dried muscle and dull bone. "Jesus," Kristi says.

"Should be more blood," George says. He sweeps his flashlight over the floor around them, whose dust and rock are unstained. "Huh."

"What does that mean?" Priya says.

"Could it be, I don't know, poachers?" Chad says.

"Black bear isn't protected like that," George says. "You're supposed to have a license, but if you shot one by mistake, you wouldn't need to go to this amount of trouble to hide it. Not to mention, I don't know what gun would inflict this type of wound."

"Maybe it was shot," Chad says, "and came in here to escape, and another bear got it."

George shrugs. "Anything's possible. Doesn't explain the lack of blood, though."

"I do not like this," Kristi says.

"Hey," Priya says, "where's Isabelle?"

Sarah pauses the movie.

"What happened to Isabelle?" I say.

"She…wandered off," Sarah says.

"In a mine?"

"Yeah," Sarah says, "that was what the rest of us thought."

"Where did she go?"

"All the way to the end of the mine, and then further. There's a network of caves the mine connects to. We spent most of the shoot searching for her—about fifteen hours." The next twenty minutes of the film advance in a succession of scenes, each of which leaps ahead another half hour to hour and a half. The expressions on the crew's faces oscillate between irritation and worry, with intermittent stops at fatigue and unease. Sarah says, "We hadn't brought much in the way of food or drink; we hadn't expected to be down there for more than a couple of hours. We ran out of both pretty quickly. Not long after, Chad floated the idea of turning around, heading for the surface, where we could call for help, bring in some professionals to locate Isabelle. Kristi was aghast at the thought of abandoning her here. The others agreed. We kept on moving further underground. Isabelle had left enough of a trail for us to follow; although there were a couple of times we really had to search for it. Finally, we arrived at this spot."

She taps the touchpad. The screen shows the tunnel dead-ending in a shallow chamber filled with junk: rows of rusted barrels, any identifying marks long flaked off; cardboard boxes in various stages of mildewed collapse; shovels and pickaxes, mummified in dusty cobwebs; a stack of eight or nine safety helmets leaning to one side.

"Shit," Sarah says.

"What do we do now?" Chad says.

"Go back," George says, "see if we can pick up the trail again at that last fork."

"Hang on," Kristi says. The view moves behind the row of barrels closest to the wall. As the camera's light shifts, so do the barrels' shadows, swinging away from the rock to reveal a short opening in it. "Guys," Kristi says, bringing the camera level with her discovery. Manhole-sized and -shaped, the aperture admits to a brief passage, which ends in darkness.

"What is it?" Sarah says.

"Some kind of tunnel," Kristi says. The opening swims closer.

"What are you doing?" Sarah says.

"Wait," Kristi says. The screen rocks wildly as she crawls the passage.

"Hey!" George calls.

Kristi emerges into a larger space. Curved walls expand to a wider exit. The camera scans the floor, which is strewn with an assortment of stones. A rough path pushes through them. "Guys!" Kristi shouts.

The film jumps to Priya scrambling out of the tunnel. Chad helps her to her feet. To the left, George says, "Is everyone sure about this?"

"No," Chad says.

"I don't know," Priya says.

"Do you want to abandon Isabelle down here," Kristi says, "in the dark?"

"It's worth checking out," Sarah says. "We'll go a little way. If we don't see any sign of her, we'll turn around."

"What the fuck is she doing here?" Priya says.

"When we find Isabelle," Sarah says, "we'll ask her."

Another cut, and the crew is standing in blackness that extends beyond the limits of their flashlights. Ceiling, walls are out of view; only the rock on which they're standing is visible. Chad and Kristi shout, "Hello!" and, "Isabelle!" but any echo is at best faint. "Where are we?" Priya says. No one answers.

In the following scene, an object shines in the distance, on the very right edge of the screen. "Hey," Kristi says, turning the camera to center the thing, "look." The rest of the crew's lights converge on it.

"What…?" Priya says.

"It looks like a tooth," Sarah says.

"It's a stalagmite," George says. "Or stalactite. I get the two confused. Either way, it isn't a tooth."

"It's not a stalagmite," Chad says. "The surface texture's wrong. Besides, you usually find stalagmites and stalactites in pairs, groups, even. Where are the others?"

"So what is it, Mr. Geologist?" George says.

"It's a rock," Kristi says.

It is; though both Sarah and George's identifications are understandable. Composed of some type of white, pearlescent mineral, it stands upright, tapering from a narrow base to a flattened top the width of a tea saucer. Halfway down it, there's a decoration, which, when the camera zooms in on it, resolves into a picture. Executed in what might be charcoal, it's a face, the features rendered simply, crudely. In the scribble of black hair, the black hole of the left eye, it isn't hard to recognize the repetition of the portrait near the mine's entrance. "What the fuck?" Kristi says.

"What is this?" Priya says. "What is happening here?"

"Um," Chad says. The view draws back from the face to show Chad standing beside the stone, in the process of picking up something from its flattened top. Frowning, he raises a thin, shriveled item to view. "I think this is a finger."

"Jesus Christ," Kristi says. "Are you sure?"

"No," he says, replacing the digit gingerly, as if it might shatter.

"What the hell is this?" George says.

"We need to leave," Priya says. "Right now, we need to leave."

"I think she might be right," Kristi says.

"Just a little further," Sarah says. "Please. I know this is—this is scary, I know. But please…We can't leave Isabelle here. Please."

"What makes you think she's even in this place?" George says.

"I do not want to be here anymore," Priya says. "We have to leave."

"Sarah," Kristi says.

Without another word, Sarah walks past the strange rock in the direction the crew was heading, her flashlight spreading its beam across the floor in front of her.

"Hey!" Kristi says.

"What is she doing?" Chad says.

"Making a command decision," George says.

"Are we going to follow her?" Chad says.

"What choice do we have?" Kristi says. "We already lost Isabelle." The camera moves after Sarah.

From behind, Priya says, "This is so unfair."

After the next cut, the screen shows Sarah a half-dozen steps in front of the crew, trailing her light through blackness. "Sarah," Kristi says. "Wait up." The others join her in calling Sarah's name, urging her to slow down. "Come on!" Priya says.

When Sarah stops, it isn't because of the requests directed at her. Her light slides over the cave floor to her left, illuminating a low line of dark rocks. As she changes direction toward it, so do the others, aiming their lights at her destination. "What now?" George says.

Less than a foot tall, the line is composed of stones fist-sized and smaller. They're black, porous, distinct from the rock on which they're arranged. At either end, the row connects to a shorter line of the same rock, each of which joins another longer row of rocks, forming a rectangle the dimensions of a large door. The space within it sparkles and flashes in the lights. Chad kneels and reaches into the rectangle, towards the nearest piece of dazzle, only to snatch his hand back with a "Shit!"

"What is it?" Priya says.

"Glass," Chad says, holding his fingers to display the blood welling from their tips. "It's filled with broken glass." He sticks his fingers into his mouth.

"Fuck," Kristi says.

"What does this mean?" Priya says.

"Yeah, Sarah," Kristi says, "what the fuck is this?"

"I—" Sarah starts, but George interrupts her: "Shh! Hear that?"

"What?" Kristi says.

"I do," Priya says.

"What?" Chad says.

"Over here," George says, waving his light at the blackness on the far side of the stone rectangle. "Listen."

Everyone falls silent. From what seems a long way away, a faint groan is audible.

"Is that Isabelle?" Chad says.

"Who else would it be?" Kristi says. "Come on." Now she takes the lead, skirting the edges of the stone design as she heads in the direction of the moaning. "Isabelle!" Kristi shouts. "We're here!"

In the middle distance, the cave floor shimmers white. This is not the crystalline fracture of broken glass; rather, it's the flat glow of light on liquid. "What the hell?" Kristi says. She is approaching the shore of a body of water, a lake, judging by the stillness of its surface. Given the limited range of the camera's light, the lake's margins are difficult to discern, which gives it the impression of size. This close to the water, the groaning has a curiously hollow quality. The camera swings right, left, and right again. "Isabelle!" Kristi shouts.

The rest of the crew catches up to her. Exclamations of surprise at the lake combine with calls to Isabelle. Flashlight beams chase one another across the water, roam the shore to either side. "Where…?" Kristi says.

"There," Sarah says, pointing her flashlight to the right. At the very limit of the light's reach, a pale figure stands in the water, a few feet out. Camera bouncing, the crew runs toward it.

Arms wrapped around herself, Isabelle Router stands in water ankle deep. Her eyes are closed, her mouth open to emit a wavering moan. Priya splashes into the lake, at Isabelle's side in half a dozen high steps. When Priya touches her, Isabelle convulses, her groans breaking off. Her eyes remain closed. "It's all right," Priya says. "Isabelle, it's all right. It's me. It's Priya. We're here."

"Priya?" Isabelle's voice is a hoarse whisper.

"Yeah," Priya says, "it's me. Everyone's here. We found you. It's all right."

Isabelle opens her eyes, lifts her hands against the lights.

"Isabelle," Sarah says, "are you okay?"

"You're here," Isabelle says.

"We are," Sarah says.

"What happened to you?" Kristi says.

"You're all right," Priya says.

Isabelle drops her eyes, mumbles something.

"What?" Priya says.

Her gait stiff-legged, Isabelle sloshes toward the shore. She does not stop once she's on dry land; rather, she continues barefoot past the crew, the camera tracking her. "Wait a minute," Kristi says, "where are you going?"

Without looking back, Isabelle says, "Out."

"That's it?" Kristi says. "We go to all this trouble and…that's it? 'Out?' Really?"

"Kristi," Sarah says.

"No, she's right," Chad says.

Priya steps out of the water. "She's obviously freaked out," she says.

"She's obviously a pain in my ass," Kristi says.

"Guys," Sarah says, "could we have this discussion while we're keeping up with Isabelle?"

"Yeah," Chad says, "it'd suck to lose her a second time."

"Shut up, Chad," Kristi says.

Three quick scenes show the crew traversing the darkness that lies between the subterranean lake and the tunnel to the mine. Even after she cuts her right foot on a rock, leaving a bloody footprint until the others catch up to her and insist on bandaging it, which George does, Isabelle maintains a brisk pace. She does not let up after they have reentered the mine; though the comments from the others shift from complaint to relief. Throughout, Kristi continues to return to the question of what happened to Isabelle, asking it at sufficient volume for her to hear; Isabelle, however, does not answer.

Not until they have reached the portrait of the woman nearer the mine's entrance does Isabelle stop. Immobile, she stares at the artwork as the rest of the crew gathers around her.

"What now?" Kristi says.

In reply, Isabelle screams, a loud, high-pitched shriek that startles everyone into stepping back. The scream goes on, and on, and on, doubling Isabelle over, breaking into static as it exceeds the limits of the recording equipment. While Isabelle staggers from foot to foot, bent in half, her mouth stretched too wide, the soundtrack cuts in and out, alternating her screaming with an electronic hum. The members of the crew stand stunned, their expressions shocked. Tears stream from Isabelle's eyes, snot pours from her nostrils, flakes of blood spray onto her lips and chin. The audio gives up the fight, yielding to the empty hum. Finally, Priya runs to Isabelle, puts her arms around her, and steers her away from the drawing, toward the exit. While she remains doubled over, Isabelle goes with her. Chad and George follow. For a moment, Sarah studies the portrait, then she, too, turns to leave.

The camera remains focused on the wall, at the weird image that so strikingly resembles Isabelle Router. It zooms in, until the half-skeletal portion of the face fills the screen. As it does, the soundtrack recovers. Isabelle is still screaming, the sound echoing down the mine's tunnels. The picture goes black. "Directed by Sarah Fiore" flashes onto the screen in white letters.

"And that's it," Sarah says, freezing the film.

"Huh," I say. I'm suddenly aware that in the time I've spent viewing Sarah's video, the sun has dropped behind Frenchman's Mountain, hauling night down after it. The autumn light has slid from the windows at the back of the bar, leaving a tide of blackness pressed against them. I can hear the shouts and shrieks of the trick-or-treaters, somewhere in that darkness. It's absurd, but after spending the last hour immersed in the film's subterranean setting, I have the impression that the blackness of the mine has escaped into the night. I swallow, say, "That's something."

"Larry was worried it was too oblique," Sarah says. "He liked it, but he thought the film needed developing. I was—it was surreal, you know? I had this documentary I'd put together that showed…I don't know what, and here was this filmmaker I respected treating it as if it was fiction, and I realized, *Yeah, you could watch it that way,* and then I thought, *Wait, was that what it was?*" She shakes her head.

"Did you ever think of telling him the truth?"

"For about half a second, until he started throwing around budget numbers, talking about possible distributors. All of it was extremely modest, but compared to what I was used to—that, and the chance it represented for me as a director—well, it wasn't much of a decision.

"My biggest concern was Isabelle. She was in pretty rough shape after we exited the mine. Priya drove her to the ER in Wiltwyck right away. She had stopped screaming not long after she left the picture, but her throat was a mess. She was exhausted, dehydrated, and there was something wrong with her blood: the white blood cell count was too high, or too low; I can't remember. Anyway, she was in the hospital for a couple of days. I assumed she'd have no interest in a return trip to the mine, to put it mildly, but I felt I owed it to her to fill her in on the new plan."

"And?"

"And she was completely into it, which was a surprise. She offered to help me with the screenplay, and she had some great ideas. A lot of the Bad Agatha stuff came from her." Seeing me opening my mouth, Sarah holds up a hand to forestall the inevitable question. "Yes, I asked her what had happened while she was on her own down there. She shrugged off the question, said she'd gotten lost and freaked out. Okay, I said, but what made her leave us in the first place?

"She heard something, what sounded like someone calling her name. She already thought the rest of us were pranking her with the woman's portrait; she assumed this was more of the same. Her intent was to find whoever was saying her name and kick them in the ass. Instead, she lost track of where she was, and then she had a little bit of a breakdown, and that was all she could remember clearly until she was in the hospital."

"Did you believe her?"

"Yes," Sarah says, drawing out the word, "but I was pretty sure there was more she wasn't telling me. I couldn't figure out how to persuade her to let me in on it. She told me she was fine with returning to the mine, but I was pretty nervous about it. Honestly, I would have been happier if she'd refused. The problem was, Priya and Chad had already bowed out, which meant we couldn't use as much of the documentary footage as I wanted. If Isabelle hadn't agreed, then we would have had to shoot an entirely new film, which might have exceeded our meager budget. So I went with her, and I have to admit, she did a terrific job. For all the years I'd known her, I had no idea she was such a convincing actress."

"What caused the two of you to fall out?"

Sarah frowns. "Creative differences."

"Over?"

"A lot of things." As if she's just noticed the night outside, Sarah says,

LOST IN THE DARK

"Holy shit. What time is it?" She closes the window on the laptop and squints at the corner clock. "I better go," she says, folding the computer shut. While she slides it off the table into her bag, I say, "Anything else you'd like to add?"

"It's funny," she says, easing out of the booth, "there have been moments when I've thought about posting the video online, putting it up on You-Tube with no fanfare, letting whoever discovers it make of it what they will. Except, I knew people would view it as a publicity stunt, some old footage I'd stitched together to generate new interest in my movie. I had no plans to mention it during the interview for the anniversary edition, until there I was, talking about it. Once I started, I figured, why not?"

"And people still thought it was a hoax."

"Yeah. What are you gonna do?"

The walk from the booth to the bar to pay the bill is no more than twelve or fifteen feet, yet it seems to take us an hour to make it. My thoughts are racing, trying to fit what I've heard and seen this afternoon with everything else I know about Sarah and the film. After all, I'm the horror writer; it's why the editors of this publication have asked me to conduct this interview. I'm supposed to judge the veracity of Sarah's footage and, assuming I accept it as true, trace its connections to *Lost in the Dark*, explain the ways in which the fiction refracts the facts. It's a favorite critical activity, isn't it? especially when it comes to the fantastic, demonstrating how it's only the stuff of daily life, after all. The vampire is our repressed eroticism, the werewolf our unreasoning rage. The film Sarah has shown me, though, isn't the material of daily life. I don't know what it is, because to tell you the truth, I'm more of a skeptic than a believer these days. Strange as it sounds, it's one of the reasons I love to write about the supernatural. The stories I tell offer me the opportunity to indulge a sense of the numinous I find all too lacking in the world around me. But this movie…I can't help inventing a story to explain it, something to do with an ancient power captured, brought to a remote location, and imprisoned there. Those dead men at the entrance, maybe they were there as a sacrifice, a way to bind whatever was in that nameless woman to the mine. The stuff inside the tunnels, the caves beyond, was that evidence of someone or someones tending to the woman, worshipping her? And Isabelle Router, her experience underground, was the movie that she co-wrote an act of devotion to something that found her in the dark?

57

I half-remember the line from Yeats about entertaining a drowsy emperor.

None of it makes any sense; it's all constructed with playing cards, waiting for a sneeze to collapse it. I pay the bill, and we walk out of Pete's. The sidewalks have filled with a mass of children and parents making their slow way up Main Street to the library to assemble for the Halloween parade. Zombies stagger along next to Clone Troopers, while Batman brings up the rear. Clown parents carry ladybug children. Frankenstein's bride towers over the Hobbits surrounding her. Witches whose pointed green chins are visible beneath the broad brims of their black hats talk to fairies sporting flower crowns and wings dusted with sparkles. There's a kid costumed as a hairy dog, an adult dressed as a boxy robot. The Grim Reaper swings a mean-looking scythe; Hermione Granger flourishes her wand. Vampires in evening dress walk beside superheroes in gaudier colors. A few old-fashioned ghosts flutter like sheets escaped from the clothes line.

A number of Bad Agathas are part of the procession, one of them quite small. This diminutive form darts through the crowd to where Sarah and I are standing. The mask the girl tilts at us is too big for her. It's an older design, the features angular, the left eye socket a black cavern. Sarah's eyebrows lift at the sight. The girl raises her right hand. She's holding a Bad Agatha mask, which she offers to Sarah.

Sarah hesitates, then accepts the mask. Apparently released by her act, the girl sprints away into the costumed ranks. Sarah considers Bad Agatha's stylized face, as if studying a photograph of an old acquaintance. She turns the mask over, tilts her head forward, and slides Bad Agatha's face over hers. She straightens, turns to me. Whatever witty remark I was preparing dies on my tongue. Without another word, Sarah turns and joins the parade.

MY FATHER,
DR. FRANKENSTEIN

Hi Dena,

Here are the endnotes for my review of Dan Franklin's *My Father, Dr. Frankenstein*. I'm afraid I may have gone a bit overboard in providing historical context for Franklin's book, but I think it's useful for understanding the circumstances under which Josiah Franklin undertook his research. Dan Franklin's account of his struggles with addiction—not to mention, what sounds like some form of schizophrenia—is compelling, but it assumes a great deal of background knowledge about his father and the man's work that I'm not sure the average reader has. Despite Josiah Franklin's reputation within the scientific community, and the books that have been written about him already, his life and career are more specialized subjects.

Anyway, feel free to include these as you see fit. Hope all's well.

Best,

John

ENDNOTES

1. Daniel Franklin's description of his father as Dr. Frankenstein is more indicative of his sentiments toward the man from whom he had been estranged so long and so bitterly than it is an accurate comparison. As presented in Mary Shelley's famous novel (1818, rev. 1831), Victor Frankenstein discovers the means for reanimating dead tissue and then cannot resist following his discovery to its logical end. By and large, the various cinematic incarnations of the scientist, from Colin Clive (1931) to Kenneth Branagh (1994), have been faithful to this initial conception of him. If such literary allusion truly is necessary, then it might be better to focus on Dr. Moreau, the titular figure in H.G. Wells's *Island of Dr. Moreau* (1896). Moreau's focus on manipulating animal life places him in relative proximity to the projects with which Josiah Franklin occupied himself. Of course, Franklin and Frankenstein sound similar enough to justify Daniel Franklin making a kind of half-pun; that, and the monstrous outcomes of his father's first experiments.

2. The exact quotation is found in James Whale's *Bride of Frankenstein* (1935), where it is uttered by the sinister Dr. Pretorius: "To a new world of gods and monsters!" One may hear in the toast an echo of Shakespeare's, "O brave new world, / That has such people in't" (*Tempest* V.1.205-206).

3. Josiah Franklin's concern—even obsession—with the end of the world has been traced to a variety of sources. Although Daniel Franklin insists that his father had left his religious upbringing long behind, in favor of what he calls a "quasi-pagan agnosticism" (45), this may be underestimating the matter. Gunterson has pointed out that the faith of Josiah's childhood, Seventh-Day Adventism, places a good deal of emphasis on the Apocalypse, which it envisions within a particularly American context (32). Similarly, Daniel Franklin spends only a few pages on his paternal grandfather, Samson, noting that the man partook of the mania for bomb shelters that swept the nation during the 1950s. Yet, as Molloy emphasizes, Samson Franklin's experiences in the Second World War lent the construction of his backyard shelter a real urgency (11). A private in the United States Army, Samson was part of the forces that occupied Japan after its surrender. Stationed

near Hiroshima, he had a first-hand view of the devastating effect of what would now be called a weapon-of-mass-destruction, and he shared some of what he saw with his oldest son—who in turn passed the stories on to his son. While Daniel Franklin discounts the significance of the Cuban Missile Crisis (1962) to Josiah's development, it is hard to believe that the threat of nuclear annihilation it promised would not have had a profound effect on someone of his particular upbringing.

4. See William Butler Yeats "The Second Coming" (1920).

5. Far-fetched as the idea may appear now, the global cooling scenario origi-nally was presented in a more restrained, even understated manner (e.g. Kukla and Matthews's "When Will the Present Interglacial End?" [1972]). It took a figure such as Nigel Calder to transform speculation about long-term climate change into anxiety over a "snowblitz," a sudden, catastrophic shift in the weather that would usher in a new ice age in a matter of decades, as opposed to centuries or millennia. Calder's work at the beginning of the 1970s was complemented at the other end of the decade by a group desig-nating itself "The Impact Team," which further popularized the idea of an incipient ice age in 1977's *The Weather Conspiracy: The Coming of the New Ice Age*. (A dramatization of such a drastic change forms one of the crucial scenes in the film, *The Day After Tomorrow* [2004], in which the young protagonist must literally outrace a sudden freeze. This suggests that the idea of the snowblitz retains something of its potency.) There is no reason to doubt Daniel Franklin's assertion that his father, pursuing post-doctoral work at M.I.T., did not take the prospect of a snowblitz seriously. That said, the prospect of a global catastrophe, even a fictional one, clearly struck a chord with Josiah. If nothing else, it prompted him to his first, sustained speculation as to how the human form might be altered to meet the chal-lenges of an environment grown hostile—how, as Josiah put it, "evolution might be hurried up."

6. A copy of the paper may be read online through the Franklin archive at the University of Boulder (c.f. http://ucblibraries.colorado.edu/archives/franklin/surmounting-the-snowblitz/)

JOHN LANGAN

7. The word "bionic" was originated by American physician and retired U.S. Air Force colonel Jack E. Steele. Originally, Steele intended the term to describe the study of biological mechanisms as a means of solving challenges in mechanical engineering. However, the word's meaning expanded to include the use of artificial enhancements of and replacements for human organs and limbs. In no small part, this was due to the success of Martin Caidan's novel, *Cyborg* (1972), and the TV series it subsequently inspired, *The Six Million Dollar Man* (1973-1978). Inspired by Steele's ideas, Caidan created an astronaut gravely injured when his vehicle crashes, whose right arm, legs, and left eye are replaced by mechanical equivalents, which provide him with a number of augmented abilities. Despite the term's more colorful associations, bionics has remained an active field of study, both in its general and specific senses, since its inception.

8. As the apex predator of the Arctic region, the polar bear (*Ursus maritimus*) was not an unreasonable model for Josiah Franklin's "modified human form." Skilled hunters, the bears are also equipped with extensive fat reserves, which allow them to survive periods when no prey is to be found. Their fat combines with tough skin and layers of fur to insulate the bears from punishingly cold temperatures. Franklin's paper suggested using bionics essentially to graft what he viewed as the bear's most significant features onto a human being. A course of steroid injections would increase muscle mass. Hands and feet would be surgically enlarged, to improve load distribution on frozen surfaces and to improve swimming. Nails would be replaced with claws fashioned from a neutral metal (probably a titanium alloy). What Franklin called a "pseudopelt" would be attached to the skin through an extensive network of sutures. Composed of a breathable under layer covered with two layers of synthetic fur, the pseudopelt was intended for the frigid climate of the new frozen globe. Plastic surgery to the head would reduce the ears—and their potential for frostbite—and shape the brow to provide better protection from the glare of sunlit snow and ice. Franklin weighed enlarging the jaw to insert additional teeth (polar bears have forty-two), but decided the extra teeth were unnecessary. The principal challenge to his design, Franklin wrote, lay in replicating the bear's considerable fat supplies. In order for the typical human to have sufficient fat stores to survive a significant time without food, other elements of the organism

62

must be compromised, to a dangerous degree. In the absence of equivalent reserves of fat, his modified human would require near-constant access to substantial amounts of food. While Josiah's paper went largely unnoticed by his peers, it did attract the attention of the Department of Defense, which contributed increasing amounts of funding to his next several projects.

9. "Sasquatch," of course, is an Anglicization of the Halkomelem name for the cryptid popularly known as Bigfoot. Daniel Franklin's use of the word to describe the end result of his father's proposal is another indication of his sentiments toward the man and his work. His speculation concerning the connection between his father's trips to Colorado and the reported sightings of Sasquatch in the area should not be taken seriously.

10. Although the prospect of nuclear war had been present since the Soviet Union successfully detonated an atomic bomb on August 29, 1949, there had been instances when such a conflict appeared likely, even imminent. As early as the Korean War (1950-1953), the U.S. Strategic Air Command sent ten B-29s carrying unarmed atomic bombs to the U.S. territory of Guam for possible use against the Soviet-backed North Korean forces. U.S. President Harry Truman admitted in a November 1950 press conference that he had contemplated using these weapons, and while he never did, such an admission did little to ease global anxieties about the possibility of nuclear conflict. Within the United States, fears of a nuclear exchange with the Soviet Union led to widespread construction of public and private bomb shelters, such as the one Josiah Franklin's father, Samson, built in the backyard of the family home in Boulder, Colorado (see Molloy for a fuller discussion of this). From October 16-28, 1962, the Cuban Missile Crisis brought the U.S. and the U.S.S.R. to the brink of nuclear war, and while the immediate aftermath of the crisis saw both sides implement measures to lessen the chances of such a situation repeating itself (i.e. the establishment of a hotline between Washington, DC and Moscow), it was by no means the end of nuclear tensions between the nations. In addition, the People's Republic of China successfully tested a nuclear weapon on October 16, 1964, and although their nuclear arsenal was not as extensive as the Soviet Union's, it further complicated the international nuclear situation. During the 1980s, as U.S. President Ronald Reagan and British Prime Minister

Margaret Thatcher embraced a more confrontational stance toward the U.S.S.R., tensions again increased. The shootdown of Korean Air Lines flight 007 by Soviet jets on September 1, 1983 dramatically heightened tensions between the United States and the Soviet Union, as did NATO exercise Able Archer 83 two months later (indeed, a number of historians of the Cold War have argued that the NATO war game brought the world as close to nuclear war as it had been since the Cuban Missile Crisis, as certain Soviet leadership elements viewed the exercise as a cover for the preparation of an actual nuclear attack). Although the second half of 1983 would mark the last significant flare up in Cold War hostilities, for Josiah Franklin, now affiliated with the U.S. Army Natick Soldier Research, Development & Engineering Center (NSRDEC) in Natick, MA, these events appeared to presage imminent nuclear war. As a result, he suspended his work on the enhanced combatant program (see Gunterson) to devote his efforts toward modifying the human form to maximize its chances of surviving a post-nuclear-conflict world.

11. First broadcast in November of 1983 to an estimated audience of 100 million viewers, the ABC television movie, *The Day After*, dramatized the effects of a nuclear exchange between the U.S. and the U.S.S.R. on two communities in the American Midwest. In his memoirs, President Ronald Reagan credited the film with influencing his decision to engage in the negotiations with the Soviets that would lead to the 1987 Intermediate-Range Nuclear Forces Treaty. For Josiah Franklin, the movie was "a hellishly evocative depiction of the nightmare I work day and night to find a pathway through" (quoted in Molloy).

12. The lyric is from Barry McGuire's 1965 song, "Eve of Destruction."

13. A redacted copy of the paper may be read online through the Franklin archive at the University of Boulder (c.f. http://ucblibraries.acolorado.edu/archives/franklin/a-nuclear-metamorphosis/). A version of the essay was rejected by the editors of *Would the Insects Inherit the Earth and Other Subjects of Concern to Those Who Worry About Nuclear War*, who described it as "too fanciful" for their book.

14. Since Wilhelm Röntgen's discovery of x-rays in 1895, the diagnostic applications of radioactive elements have been part of medical research and practice. As early as 1896, Leopold Freund employed x-rays in a therapeutic fashion to remove a mole from a patient. In the first decades of the twentieth century, a host of over-the-counter health supplements containing radioactive substances were advertised as treating conditions including arthritis, rheumatism, and constipation. Several leading scientists, most notably Marie Curie, cautioned against such drugs, arguing that the effects of prolonged exposure to radioactive elements were poorly understood. By 1927, Hermann Joseph Muller had established the relationship between irradiation and heightened risks of cancer and genetic mutation. (He would be awarded the Nobel Prize in Medicine for his research in 1946.) From the 1950s, radiation therapy became one of the principal avenues of treatment for cancer, though with increasing concern for the consequences of the therapy on the patient's potential offspring.

15. Muller's experiments irradiating fruit flies with x-rays to explore the effects on their genes were cited by Franklin as one of the inspirations for his proposal.

16. While Josiah Franklin had no formal plans to engage in mapping the human genome, the enterprise became necessary once he decided to focus his research on modifying human embryos. (A series of early experiments using radioactive materials to selectively mutate mature individuals had ended in a catastrophe, which resulted in closed-door Congressional hearings that put Josiah's career in serious jeopardy, and which have spawned a host of urban legends concerning his "monster men" [see Gunterson]). Franklin's research coincided with the first years of the Human Genome Project, which developed from a series of workshops and essays by leading scientists on the topic during the mid-1980s. The official enterprise began in 1990, its co-founders the U.S. Department of Energy and the National Institutes of Health. An international consortium of scientists from nations including the U.K., France, and China contributed to the process, whose target date for completion was set for fifteen years. However, a preliminary map was completed in 2000, five years ahead of schedule, while the final map appeared two years early, in 2003. Because of the nature of his work,

Josiah Franklin's contributions to the project had to be made through a series of intermediaries. As a result, it is difficult to evaluate his claim that his research helped bring the mapping to its early conclusion; though it seems an exaggeration.

17. Anecdotal reports of the atomic blast sites at Hiroshima and Nagasaki listed cockroaches among the first organisms to return to the areas. This gave rise to the popular notion that, in the aftermath of a nuclear war, those insects would inherit what was left of the earth, an assertion that was repeated in an interview given by H. Bentley Glass to the *New York Times* in 1962 and that subsequently achieved the status of quasi-fact. The insects are quite hardy, able to survive up to 62,500 REM, as compared to just 800 REM for humans. Other insects can withstand higher levels still—the parasitic wasp *Habrobracon hebetor* can endure 180,250 REM—but Josiah Franklin found a number of other advantages to cockroach physiology that caused him to select the insect (specifically, the American cockroach [*Periplaneta americana*]) as the model for his second modified human form. Through targeting of specific genes with infinitesimal amounts of what he called his radiation cocktail, Franklin intended to cause a human embryo to mutate in certain pre-determined directions. For example, the skin would develop as a harder surface, strengthened by elevated amounts of calcium carbonate and made water-resistant by wax secreted from its pores. The jaw and teeth would be reinforced, the interior of the mouth and upper digestive tract toughened, to allow the consumption of a wider range of sustenance, while the mid- and lower digestive tract would be adjusted to allow nutrition to be drawn from less promising fodder. Augmentation of the bone marrow would enable it to produce a glycerol-based "antifreeze" in the event of the severely cold temperatures accompanying the inevitable nuclear winter. The most significant change Franklin proposed, however, was to the rate of cell division throughout the body. Humans are vulnerable to radiation because it interferes dramatically with ongoing cell replication, disrupting it to lethal effect. The cockroach, in comparison, undergoes cell division at a profoundly slower pace, approximately once a week, which limits the damage radiation can cause. Thus, after an initial period of rapid growth, the cells in Franklin's modified human form would replicate at a substantially reduced rate. This would result in a smaller organism; Franklin

estimated its average height as just over one meter.

18. Although Josiah Franklin's proposed modification chamber was microscopic in scale, his son has a point: it is hard not to be struck by the resemblance to the famous laboratory set in James Whale's *Frankenstein* (1931).

19. Perhaps the principal challenge to Josiah Franklin's plan for his post-nuclear-conflict humans was one of timing. Even in the case of a "snow-blitz," there would be adequate time to alter human beings to meet the changed environment; in the case of a nuclear war, however, civilization would be in smoking ruins before the necessary procedures could be performed. Franklin's proposed solution was the creation of a small population of his modified humans well in advance of any conflict. This would allow ample time to raise and educate a sufficient number of them to counter any sudden catastrophe. While Daniel Franklin enjoyed frightening his middle- and high-school friends with stories about the monsters his father kept in their house's extensive basement—and while he hints at actually having witnessed something under their residence in Natick—there remains no credible evidence to support any of these claims.

20. The Cold War came to an end over a two-year period that began on November 9, 1989 with the fall of the Berlin Wall and concluded on December 26, 1991 with the dissolution of the Soviet Union. While both the United States and the members of the Russian Federation maintained their nuclear arsenals, the symbolic "Doomsday Clock" of the *Bulletin of the Atomic Scientists* was set back to seventeen minutes to midnight, the furthest from that time and the catastrophe it represents the clock's hands ever have been. Despite this, Josiah Franklin continued work on his post-nuclear-war modified human until 1998, when U.S. President Bill Clinton ordered a review of biological threats to the country. Franklin's participation in this review was minimal, yet it spurred him to put aside the research that had consumed him for the last decade and half in favor of a new project designed to address this threat. The extent to which Daniel Franklin's increasingly erratic behavior had distracted his father, with the result that he failed to appreciate the full implications of the end of the Cold War, is difficult to gauge; though certainly Daniel's struggles with heroin addiction

throughout the early and mid-1990s—resulting in a series of stays in rehab facilities—occupied a significant portion of his father's attention.

21. Ironically, the end of the Cold War revealed the extent of the former U.S.S.R.'s biological weapons programs. Although the U.S.S.R. was a signatory to the 1972 Biological Weapons Convention, whose express purpose was to prohibit the production of bioweapons, this had little effect on their actual activities. These were overseen by the Biopreparat, a nominally civilian bureaucracy that managed a series of secret laboratories, each dedicated to developing a different biological pathogen for military use. Documents whose release was approved by Russian President Boris Yeltsin in 1992 disclosed efforts at weaponizing the anthrax bacterium (*Bacillis anthracis*), the accidental release of which in Sverdlovsk (now Yekaterinburg) in 1979 led to at least one hundred fatalities from "Anthrax 836." A 1995 report indicated that the Soviets, building on research captured from the Imperial Japanese army at the end of the Second World War, had spent decades working toward a weaponized smallpox virus (*Variola major*), finally succeeding by using a strain of the disease retrieved from the 1967 Indian outbreak (and christened "India-1967"). Also in 1992, Yeltsin ordered all biological weapons within Russia destroyed, but numerous analysts agree that his directive was almost certainly disregarded, in part if not in whole.

22. The United States's biological weapons program was approved by President Franklin Roosevelt in 1942; the following year, the U.S. Army Biological Warfare Laboratories were established at then-Camp Detrick in Maryland. For the next quarter-century, the U.S. military worked on enhancing the effectiveness of many of the same pathogens as their Soviet counterparts. Although the United States did not suffer the same weapons-related accidents as the U.S.S.R., there was substantial testing of biological agents on unwitting subjects, many of them in the U.S. military. In addition, there were accusations of U.S. use of biological weapons during the Korean War, and against livestock targets in Cuba in the 1960s; though these charges remain subject to debate. (The extent of Josiah Franklin's knowledge of these events is unclear. The position he took at Defense Advanced Research Projects Agency [DARPA] in Arlington, Virginia, in 1995 would have permitted him access to a significant amount of classified

information.) The U.S. bioweapons program came to its end in 1969, when President Richard Nixon officially ended it and ordered all stockpiles of biological agents destroyed. This was accomplished by 1973. Since then, the official position of the United States government has been that any research it conducts in this area is purely defensive in nature; though concerns continue to be raised about the exact parameters of that study.

23. In 1984, members of the Rajneeshee group deliberately contaminated salad bars in the Oregon city of The Dalles with home-grown *Salmonella Typhimurium*. This was done in order to influence the outcome of a local election in which the group had a stake. Seven hundred and fifty-one people were affected, forty-five of them hospitalized. No one died as a result of the attack, but Josiah Franklin saw the group's actions as demonstrating the frightening ease with which a non-state actor could obtain and employ a biological pathogen, to potentially devastating ends.

24. Published in 1994, *The Hot Zone: A Terrifying True Story* grew out of an article *New Yorker* writer Richard Preston had contributed to the magazine in 1992, "Crisis in the Hot Zone." The article focused on the 1989 Reston Incident, during which a number of long-tailed macaques (*Macaca fascicularis*) at the Hazleton Research Products' Primate Quarantine Unit in Reston, Virginia, were found to be infected with a hitherto-unseen strain of Ebolavirus. While what would become known as Reston Ebolavirus was eventually found to be non-threatening to humans, its relationship to the more lethal species of the virus, combined with the research facility's proximity to Washington, DC, led to a significant portion of the macaques being euthanized. Building on the magazine piece, the book describes a number of viral hemorrhagic infections, details their past outbreaks in sub-Saharan Africa, and speculates on their potential to spread to Europe and the United States. A massive success, the book reached the number one spot on the *New York Times* non-fiction bestseller list. With the benefit of two decades' hindsight, it seems clear that Preston's book owed a measure of its popularity to anxieties about the ongoing HIV-AIDS epidemic, which had foregrounded the threat posed by hitherto-unfamiliar viral infections.

25. A heavily-redacted copy of the paper may be read online through the

Franklin archive at the University of Boulder (c.f. http://ucblibraries.colorado.edu/archives/franklin/a-symbiotic solution-to-the-coming-plagues/).

26. The origins of nanotechnology can be traced to a 1959 talk by Richard Feynman, "There's Plenty of Room at the Bottom," which raised the possibilities for technological advances created by the increasing ability to control individual atoms. Feynman's ideas were picked up by K. Eric Drexler in his 1986 book, *Engines of Creation: The Coming Era of Nanotechnology*, in which Drexler forecasts a wide range of applications for nanotechnology, from information storage to human medicine. Drexler's predictions had been spurred by the development of the scanning tunneling microscope in 1981; while the use of the device to manipulate individual atoms in 1989 appeared to show his ideas in action. As Josiah Franklin already was working at a microscopic level with his embryo modification chamber, the notion of moving to an even smaller scale did not require a significant adjustment in his perspective.

27. With the exception of the scanning tunneling microscope, the necessary technology remains classified by the U.S. government.

28. For Josiah Franklin, the challenges posed by biological pathogens were considerably more complex than those presented by nuclear weapons (or, for the matter, a sudden ice age). Depending on the disease, the effects could vary widely, necessitating modifications to the human form that would allow an ongoing adaptive response. As was the case with his previous proposals for altering the human form to meet an apocalyptic threat, Franklin looked to the animal kingdom for inspiration. His focus this time was on the Egyptian plover (*Pluvianus aegyptius*), more popularly known as the "crocodile bird," for its supposed symbiotic relationship with the Nile crocodile (*Crocodylus niloticus*). According to the Greek historian Herodotus, while the crocodiles were resting on the banks of the Nile, they would open their mouths to allow the birds to hop into them. Rather than consuming the plovers, the crocodiles would allow the birds to pick through their teeth for any traces of food left in them. In this way, the birds would feed, and the crocodiles have their teeth cleaned. Although the story of the crocodile bird has not been documented by modern science,

it provided Josiah with a conceptual model for his third modified human form. Instead of radically altering human physiology to adapt it to a hostile landscape, he would supplement it with a population of symbiotic organisms designed to assist it in overcoming the most virulent diseases. Research into animal resistance to disease led Franklin to another crocodilian, the American alligator (*Alligator mississippiensis*), whose robust immune system allows it to survive open wounds submerged in swamp water teeming with a host of microorganisms. Through extensive modification using specialized nanomachines, Josiah proposed adapting macrophages isolated from the alligator's blood to enable them to function within human beings. Much of what he envisioned remains subject to DARPA secrecy protocols, but it appears to have involved splicing the animal's white blood cells with the individual human's, in order to avoid rejection by the host. The human appendix would be employed as a kind of reservoir for these augmented white blood cells, a portion of which would be released when the immune system registered a severe enough response to an infection. Outside the customized environment of the appendix, the modified cells would die in a matter of hours, but this would be ample time for them to destroy whatever disease was present. According to Josiah's calculations, the appendix of a typical adult human could contain sufficient reserves of his adapted macrophages to see that person through half a dozen significant epidemics.

29. Despite Daniel Franklin's accusations, there is no evidence that the 2009 car crash that claimed his father's life in Colorado was anything other than an accident caused by wet leaves and a sharp turn in the road. The quotation is from William S. Burroughs.

30. Approximately six weeks after Daniel Franklin turned in the final copy-edits for *My Father, Dr. Frankenstein*, he was found dead in his apartment in Ellicott City, Maryland, by his landlord. Since completing the manuscript of his memoir in late 2014, Daniel's behavior had grown increasingly erratic, as he struggled against and eventually relapsed into heroin addiction. Whether or not the end of what had been six years drug-free was caused by revisiting the material covered in his book is impossible to say with certainty, but the coincidence is difficult to ignore. Daniel's drug use apparently fostered a growing conviction that he had been experimented upon

by his father during his last stay in rehab, leaving him "infested," as he put it, with Josiah Franklin's creations, which Daniel insisted were concentrated in his appendix. (The echo of his father's final project is striking, particularly as the Franklin archive had yet to post the edited version of Josiah's final paper; though it is possible that he had shared some of the details of his work with his son.) Because of the alterations his father had made to him, Daniel said, heroin no longer offered the profound escape it once had. In addition, he felt his consciousness changing in ways he struggled to articulate, but that appeared to involve heightened impulses to aggression and violence. Consultations with a number of physicians failed to reveal any abnormalities in his health, and he could not convince the doctors to conduct exploratory surgery to examine his appendix. Nor did sessions with several therapists yield a resolution to his sense that he had been fundamentally altered. Finally, Daniel Franklin took matters into his own hands, and attempted to remove his appendix himself. After disinfecting his bathroom with bleach and covering it in sterilized sheets, he lay on the floor on his back. Positioning a pair of mirrors to allow him a better view of the surgical site, he swabbed his lower abdomen with iodine, then injected the area with a mixture of lidocaine and epinephrine. Using a folding lockback knife with a 3 ¾-inch blade, he made a four-inch incision in his abdominal wall. Remarkably, he succeeded in reaching his appendix; once there, however, he sliced the appendicular artery lengthwise, creating a wound that he was unable to suture successfully. The resulting bleeding both complicated his task and gave it added urgency. This likely led to the slip that drove the knife into his external iliac artery. While Daniel Franklin attempted to address this even more serious injury, he had neither the training nor the tools to do so. He lost consciousness in short order, and bled to death on his bathroom floor not long thereafter. When his body was discovered, EMTs were summoned to the scene, but it was too late. The official report mentions that his appendix was found on the floor next to him; apparently, he had succeeded in his final task. What became of the organ afterward is unclear.

A SONG ONLY
PARTIALLY HEARD

This is the story he doesn't tell.

Not because no one will believe him (although no one would), and not because of the stares he knows his account would provoke, the poorly concealed laughs and muttered remarks ("Crazy," "What the fuck is he talking about?" "Goddamn boss's cousin"). No, the reason Horacio Martinez keeps his story to himself is that it won't make a difference, won't return Hector to life, won't alter the judgment of the sheriff's deputies, who have ruled the death an accident, which Horacio supposes it was, only one with slightly less randomness than the declaration implies.

There's something else, too, a reason under the reason. What he saw, what he heard, not only when his friend died, but in the moments before and after it, was like nothing his ears and eyes have experienced, not during his decade here, in Wiltwyck, upstate New York, and not during his decade growing up in San Juan. He isn't sure how to describe it; although *holy* occurs to him. It's a term from his childhood, redolent of incense and candlewax, from when he was devout, when he spent each week anticipating the candle he would light at the foot of the Virgin, when his daily dress included his Maltese cross and his scapula, when every morning he checked his children's missal to see which saint's feast day it was. Uttering it now puckers his lips with embarrassment, unless it's as half of a curse. But it

73

attaches itself to Hector's death with a force which will not be denied, and he supposes this means it's correct.

Following the departure of the police, everyone has been sent home with pay for the remainder of the day, a nod to compassion on the part of cousin Fernando qualified by the fact that the work day had less than an hour left. Shocked as even the older men were by the violence of Hector's end, the employees were happy to take advantage of the boss's generosity, most of them walking down and across the street to the bar which occupies the ground floor of a large, three-story house on the corner there. No one paid much attention to Horacio, who found it easy to stay behind after the chain-link gate was rolled closed. To be certain his failure to depart wouldn't be noticed, he kept to the other side of the white trailer that serves as Fernando's office, remaining there as the echoes of his coworkers' voices faded into the distance. Once the only sound is the whoosh of a car passing by, Horacio peeks his head around the trailer, confirms the yard is empty, and crosses to where the *Helen Leucocia* sits in her ship cradle.

She's the tug half of an ATB, an articulated tug and barge combination, brought to the shipyard Fernando manages on the northern bank of the Redout Creek for an assortment of repairs and renovations. Her almost comically high bridge has been removed entire and set to one side, where a designated team works on it. A second team labors inside the ship's rounded hull, while a third, to which Hector and Horacio were assigned, has tended to the tug's exterior, inspecting and mending small injuries to the surface, in a couple of places replacing what can't be fixed. Horacio hasn't been at the shipyard long enough to be trusted with any truly significant job, nor does he find the work particularly easy to learn, but once he masters a task, he does so with a thoroughness which has attracted grudging nods from his coworkers, whose respect for him has grown as he has demonstrated himself more competent than his first week on the job indicated (about which, the less said, the better). Though he doesn't care for the work, he finds it oddly satisfying, and as his father is fond of saying, you don't have to like a job if the money is good, which it is. Give Fernando this much credit: he pays his workers well.

Overhead, one of the massive collars that encircle the tug's propellers hangs, like something from a jet. To the right, on the other side of the keel, the space the second collar occupied is empty, the hull torn and hanging down in strips. Directly beneath it, jagged pieces of metal, some the size of windows, doors, begin a path which stretches the twenty or so feet to the edge of the yard, where it drops to the surface of the creek seven or eight feet below. On a sunny summer day like this one, you can stand at this ledge and look through the clear water at schools of fish maintaining their positions in the current. This is the spot Hector was when, with an ear-splitting shriek, the collar tore loose from the tug and crashed to the ground, rolling toward the creek, leaving shards of itself behind as it went, revealing the propeller it contained. Tangled with half a dozen lengths of metal, each a razored whip, the propeller struck Hector.

Although he witnessed his friend's death, Horacio isn't certain exactly what he saw happen to him. He isn't sure he wants to know. One instant, Hector was turning to the Juggernaut rumbling toward him; the next, he appeared to move in several different directions at once. The propeller and its metal necklace rolled off the edge of the yard into the creek, taking the better part of Hector with it, leaving behind his right arm below the elbow and a slice of his skull, the flesh stubbled from his recent buzz cut. His blood rained from the air in fat droplets. Already knowing it was too late, Horacio ran to the place his friend had been in time to watch the propeller rock to a halt, half-submerged in the water splashing around it. He saw Hector's leg bobbing in the current, caught on a strand of metal wound around one of the propeller's blades. Horacio scanned the water, could distinguish no more of Hector amidst the turbulence the propeller had stirred. But there was something else, between the shore and the propeller, a movement at the creek's churning surface, a shape that glowed crimson and gold with the sunlight, that resolved into a form more shocking than the sight of Hector's leg floating in the Redout. Horacio's glimpse of it lasted for what seemed to be minutes, yet couldn't have been more than a couple of seconds, before he was joined by a handful of the other workers, all searching for Hector and crying out as they saw what remained of him, when the thing beneath the water darted out of view.

It was a woman: why not say that? Because she was like no woman he's ever seen. She was drifting on her back, her long gold hair spreading around her head in a cloud. He guesses she was naked, if that's the right way to describe skin crosshatched with dark red and gold scales. What appeared to be trains of red silk, each the length of her long body, attached to her forearms, her hips, her calves, and rippled in the surrounding water. They reminded him of Ocho, the beta fish Fernando keeps in the office, and he understood that they were fins. From eyes a uniform blue (azure), she regarded him, an unreadable expression on her face. Tiny silver fish darted around her. In her gaze, he felt the weight of an intelligence ancient and strange.

There was one more detail, a sound, distant and musical, what might have been a song. The memory of it lingers, hours after he (thinks he) heard it. Almost, he can pick out lyrics, though the language is foreign to him. They have a plaintive quality that evokes images of clusters of rocks washed by foaming seas, of the sun high and unforgiving in a blue, blue sky. *Come*, the lyrics seem to be pleading, *come here, join me below the waves, where everything is calm, peaceful. Come to the peace of the kelp forests, of the eel dens, of the lobster roads. Come down to where ships lie in quiet rust and rot. Come let the small crabs and fish feast on you, give yourself to the sea, to the sea, to peace.*

This, the woman with her trailing red fins, her blue (azure) eyes on him, the song he (thinks he) heard, comprise the secret story, the experience he cannot help thinking of as holy. There is no doubt in his mind Hector was gripped by a similar but more intense version of it in the moments preceding the accident. Horacio noticed him at the edge of the yard, his head tilted toward the creek. Nothing remarkable about that, but in the final second of his life, as Hector turned to the swirl of metal screeching toward him, Horacio saw reflected in his friend's face an experience of profound beauty. It was as if a beam of light were shining directly on his features, illuminating them, casting them into sharper relief. Horacio was reminded of endless paintings of ecstatic saints, bathed in the light of God. When the propeller and its looping shards struck him, Hector must have thought the beauty that illuminated him was killing him.

Or so Horacio imagines. He walks out from under the *Helen Leucosia*. Police tape flutters around the trail of metal fragments leading to the edge of the yard. There, patches of Hector's blood still stain the ground. In the creek, the propeller rises like a bizarre idol. Hector's leg has been retrieved from it, along with what other pieces of him the police divers could locate. Horacio gives the men their due: they worked for a good couple of hours, searching for and retrieving his friend's remains with care and deliberation. With the exception of his left hand and a scoop of his lower back, the divers succeeded in recovering all of Hector, for which Horacio is grateful to a degree that surprises him. He is unclear whether the search for those last fragments of Hector will continue tomorrow, or if as much of him has been found as is going to be; he suspects the latter. In which case, assuming the police give the okay, the early part of the morning will be spent lifting the propeller from the Redout, inspecting it, and deciding if whatever damage it suffered can be repaired, or if a replacement will have to be ordered.

Horacio would like Fernando to choose the second option, for the propeller to be melted down, destroyed, but he assumes this is unlikely. Though battered and dented by its murderous transit, the propeller appears basically sound, able to be fixed, and a new one would be expensive, much more costly than the life of a man from Santo Domingo who enjoyed spending his Sunday afternoons with his girlfriend and her daughter, picnicking one place or another. At the end of Horacio's first, disastrous week at the shipyard, Hector invited him to join them on the weekend, which he did, and while Horacio had little to say to either Megan or Ella, he appreciated their smiling friendliness enough to join the three of them again a couple of weeks later, and intermittently thereafter, as recently as this past Sunday, when the four of them took an order of Chinese takeout to the picnic benches at Wiltwyck Point, an arm of land reaching into the Hudson. As Ella tip-toed across the rocky beach to splash in the river, Megan calling after her not to go too far, Hector and Horacio studied the boats traveling the water, from the sailboats whose sails belled from their masts, to the speedboats galloping from the crest of one wave to the next, to a combined ATB making its slow way south. Unlike Horacio, Hector loved boats, loved working on them, loved being out on them. He named the different types of sailboats, the horsepower of the speedboats' engines, the top speed of an articulated tug with and without its barge. This afternoon, he was most interested by an enormous oil tanker which had dropped anchor a couple of hundred yards north of them, almost beneath the Wiltwyck-Rhinecliff Bridge. "That's an old one," he said. "Early sixties. Didn't know any of them were still in service. Can you see what flag she's flying? I swear, my eyes are no good any more." Horacio squinted, but did not recognize the colors. "It's grey," he said, "or black, with some kind of design on it in yellow. I think it's a triangle, but the sides are all wavy. That could be the wind, though. Whose flag is that?" Hector didn't know, nor could either of them read the letters in which the tanker's name and country of origin were written. Hector ventured they were Russian or Greek; Horacio guessed Thai or Sanskrit. Later, as they were packing up to leave, they saw water venting from a hatch in the tanker's flank. Frowning, Hector said, "They aren't supposed to do that." "What?" Horacio said. "The water," Hector said, pointing to the green stream foaming into the Hudson. "That's sea water. They use it for ballast, to keep the ship stable. They aren't allowed to dump it up here. This is fresh water. Who knows what's in that shit?" Horacio shrugged. "What can you do?"

What can you do? He doesn't know what he expects, standing here as the creek eddies round the propeller. Another glimpse of the strange woman? To hear her song as Hector did, in all its terrible loveliness? To what end? He shakes his head. The sensation of what he cannot stop thinking of as holiness, as the sacred in all its awful glory, is unbearable. It is as if he is being torn apart. He feels himself caught in a narrative whose parameters he cannot identify, a minor character moved by a plot he does not understand. Sudden disgust twists his lip, propels him away from the water at a brisk pace. If he hurries, maybe he can catch up to the others at the bar.

If he remained in place, staring into the water, would he make out the woman floating a half-dozen feet down, amidst a grove of green weeds, her fins wrapping around her like red robes? Would he see Hector's hand in hers? Would he watch her lift it to her perfect mouth, take one of the fingers between her lips, and strip the waterlogged flesh from the bones with her delicate, razored teeth?

THE DEEP SEA SWELL

"It may be that the gulfs will wash us down"
—Alfred, Lord Tennyson "Ulysses"

I f she hadn't argued with the man, Susan thinks, they could have
been in a first-class cabin, instead of down here, at the bottom of the
bloody ferry. The floor tilts forward. There's a great swooshing sound,
the sensation of plunging down a steep slope, the briefest of pauses, and a
tremendous BANG that rattles the ship's hull. Slowly, the floor levels, then
tilts backward. The swooshing returns, accompanied now by the feeling of
being on a roller coaster as it climbs a sheer set of tracks. Somewhere near,
somewhere inside the ferry, Susan hears the steady drone of a motor. The
sweet stink of fuel (diesel?) swirls near the floor, below the bunk on which
she's lying. On the bunk above, her husband snores intermittently. The
Dramamine they took an hour ago knocked Alan out, the lucky bastard;
whereas all it did for Susan was sand the edges off the dizziness and nausea,
freeing her mind to run through every disaster-at-sea movie she's seen, from
Titanic to *The Poseidon Adventure* to that cheesy horror film, what was it
called, *Leviathan*? Something like that.

The sail up from Aberdeen wasn't this bad, not nearly. She'd never been
on a ferry like this before. The nearest thing had been the ship they'd taken
out to Martha's Vineyard on their honeymoon, which was maybe half the
size of this one? Less than that? This was a proper ocean-going vessel, built
to cross the roughly two hundred nautical miles between the northeast of

Scotland and the Shetlands, which, as Alan delighted in saying, lay closer to Norway than they did the UK. There was something romantic about traveling by ship, she'd thought, a notion of taking your time, enjoying the journey as well as the destination. They spent much of the journey in bed, trying to work out the mechanics of sex on a surface that was rising and falling with the sea. She was Sexy Susan, the sailor's friend; he was Able Alan, always up for adventure.

That was in the first-class cabin to which they'd been upgraded after she passed one of the ship's crew a twenty-pound note. She'd been quite pleased with the luxury, which consisted primarily of a room done in seventies-era paneling and set high enough in the ship to have its own window, but less so once they'd been in Lerwick for a day and Alan's university friend, Giorgio, informed her that, as long as there were cabins available, the ferry staff were supposed to upgrade passengers free of charge. "They pocket the money, you know," Giorgio said, which had let the air out of her self-satisfaction, and left her determined not to be taken advantage of again. In turn, this led to her challenging the crew member who requested twenty quid for a boost to first-class lodgings on the return voyage. (Possibly, it was the same man: several of the staff appeared related, cousins or even brothers, short, broad fellows wearing grey sweater vests under their blue blazers and over their shirt-and-ties, their faces red, their curly hair black yielding to grey.) "You know," Susan said, "one of my friends in Lerwick told me an upgrade to first class is supposed to be no charge."

"Did they?" the man said, raising his bushy eyebrows as if to indicate his surprise at such a statement.

"Yeah," she said, nodding.

"Well…" The man smiled, shrugging and spreading his hands.

"My friend said you guys keep the money."

Whatever warmth was in the man's performance chilled. "It's twenty pounds," he said.

Which was how they descended she isn't certain how many flights of stairs to the corridor that brought them here, to a narrow room with bare white walls and a pair of economy-sized bunkbeds in it. "Think of it this way," Alan said, "we're experiencing the full range of travel options."

Those options included a mid-winter storm, whose center lay somewhere to the east, but which had stirred the North Sea to a tumult. They climbed to the dining area, but already, Alan was queasy and opted for a cup of tea and a packet of digestive biscuits, leaving Susan to order a Coke and the fish and chips, which she ate half of before a sudden squall of nausea caused her to set down her knife and fork and not pick them up again. The two of them tried sitting in the large padded chairs positioned in front of the wall of windows that looked out over the ferry's stern, but night had fallen hours ago, with the heavy blackness of early January at a northern latitude. All that was visible was an expanse of blackness with a cluster of orange lights twinkling in the far distance that Alan thought was an oil rig. Although the sea was more sound than sight, the rise and fall of those lights added a visual dimension to the ferry's see-sawing movement. "Next time Giorgio wants to see us," Alan said, "we'll fly." It was an extravagant promise: the tickets from Edinburgh weren't too far shy of what it had cost them to cross the Atlantic from Newark.

"Or he can take the ferry," Susan said.

Not long after, they descended the stairs to their cabin a second time. Gazing out the windows wasn't doing anything for him, Alan said, and Susan agreed. The more she stared at it, the more uneasy the dark outside—its sheer thoroughness—made her, until she could feel panic nipping at the edges of her mind. "It's as if we're already at the bottom of the sea," she said.

"Whoa," Alan said, "touch wood," knocking the chair's armrest. "Although," he added, "it's pretty deep, here. I imagine it's calm, down there."

"You just have to go through the whole drowning thing," Susan said.

"Will you stop?" Alan said, rapping the armrest again.

"You and your superstitions."

"The middle of the ocean is not the place to test them."

She supposed he had a point.

In the cabin, they dry-swallowed the Dramamine tablets Susan had in her bag and climbed into their bunks. Alan sang, "Yo-ho, blow the man down, / Yo ho, blow the man down."

"Now who's tempting fate?" she said.

"It's only a song," he said, his words slurring as the pill tugged him into unconsciousness.

"Remember that when we're saying hi to King Neptune."

"Hey," he began. The rest of his reply disappeared into a mumble.

Despite herself, Susan knocked on the cabin wall. It wasn't wood, but it was the best she had.

The next hour passed with stomach-churning monotony. The ferry rose and fell, rose and fell. Alan snored, snorted, went back to snoring. The distant engine churned steadily. In the corridor outside the cabin, a little girl's voice asked a question Susan couldn't decipher. The ocean rushed along the hull. A woman, likely the girl's mother, said they were just going for a wee lie down. The smell of fuel made Susan's nostrils bristle. Someone laughed as they passed the cabin. The ship slid down into a pause that lasted a second too long, as if the waves were weighing whether to let the vessel continue its descent, all the way down. A woman, the same one from before, said she was just going to the toilet. The sea smacked the ship like a giant's hand, BANG.

In an odd sort of way, Susan has thought, this trip has been all about the ocean, salt water threading its way through her and Alan's winter vacation like a recurring theme in a longer piece of music. The flight across the north Atlantic was only the second time she had traversed the ocean, and she spent the daylit hours of the voyage gazing out the scuffed and scratched window beside her seat at the corrugated grey expanse visible through the gaps in the clouds below. Alan's parents' house in North Queensferry was one of a half-dozen on a cul-de-sac set on a high bluff overlooking the stretch where the Forth River merged with the North Sea. The sea was a constant companion as they drove their tiny rental up Scotland's east coast, stopping for an early lunch at an Indian place outside St. Andrew's, a wander around the ruins at Stonehaven, and then a couple of days in Aberdeen, revisiting Alan's university haunts and a few of his friends who had settled in the city. With one of those friends and his partner, they walked a rocky beach washed by the waves they would ride to Shetland, where Alan's friend Giorgio ran a small chip shop overlooking Lerwick harbor.

Once they were ashore on Shetland, however, something about the sea changed—or, to be more accurate, something about her perception of it shifted. The afternoon of their arrival, Giorgio took them for a quick jaunt to a spot where the land on either side of them shrank toward the road, until they were between a pair of narrow beaches onto which water splashed in long foaming rolls. "On that side," Giorgio said, pointing right, "is the North Sea. On this side," pointing left, "is the Atlantic." No matter where they went, it seemed, salt water was visible. When she mentioned this to

Giorgio, trying to keep her tone light, carefree, he nodded and said, "Aye, someone told me once you're never more than three miles from open water on Shetland." No doubt the landscape of the island, low hills bare of trees, contributed to the sensation, but she began to feel horribly exposed, surrounded by the ocean, which, if you thought about it, could rise and wash over the place without much effort at all.

Nor did the stories Giorgio liked to tell help matters. An amateur historian of the Shetlands and their surrounds, he possessed a seemingly endless supply of narratives about the islands. In the majority of them, the sea figured prominently. They would begin with a bold, almost ridiculous assertion. "You know," he would say over drinks at one of the pubs, "Shetland was part of the actual Atlantis." Then, as she and Alan coughed their beers, he would raise his hands and say, "No, I'm not talking about that Disney rubbish. I mean Doggerland. You've heard of it, yeah? No? Ten, eleven thousand years ago, during the last ice age, all the seas were lower. The water was bound up in the glaciers, right? From Shetland down to Orkney and Scotland, over to Europe, was dry land. You could walk across the North Sea, the English Channel, and folk did. There was a whole civilization spread across the place. As the ice started to melt, though, the sea crept closer. Some of the archeologists think it was a process of years, decades, and that the people living there had plenty of time to pack their things and leave. I've heard others say it was more catastrophic, an ice dam broke and sent hundreds of millions of gallons of water rushing through all this low-lying land. That's where your story of Atlantis comes from."

Another afternoon, as they were sitting in Giorgio's car on a local (smaller) ferry from the main island to the neighboring island of Yell, Giorgio said, "When you were coming up, did you notice there was a point the sea went all choppy—I mean, worse than what you'd been used to?" Susan and Alan exchanged glances. Had they? "Maybe," Alan said. "Aye, that was you passing Fair Isle," Giorgio said. "The sea behaves funny there, has to do with currents or some such. You know there was a fellow drowned out there? This was during my granddad's time. It was a man from away down in Edinburgh, a professor—from Edinburgh University, must have been. He was an anthropologist, studied the prehistoric sites in the north of Scotland, the Orkneys, up Shetland way. This chap took an interest in Fair Isle—in the ocean floor off the island. Something had washed up on one of the

83

island's beaches, and it found its way into this professor's hands. I'm not sure what it was, but it got the man all worked up. He decided he needed to have a look under the water next to the island. This was none of your scuba diving; this was one of those suits with the big round helmet and the hose up to a boat on the surface. Fellow hired a couple of locals out of Aberdeen to man the boat and mind the air pump, and another pair of lads from Fair Isle to help them. The lot of them took the boat to the spot the professor had calculated was the best bet to search for more of whatever it was brought him there in the first place. Over the side he went. This was what you'd call a low-tech rig, no diver's telephone. Well. Maybe an hour into the professor's dive, a storm blew in. The sky went dark, the wind rose, and the next anyone knew, the rain was bucketing down, the waves spilling over the sides. It's no fun to be in a big ship when the weather turns against you, and this boat was far from big. At first, the lads thought they could ride out the storm. I gather they gave it their best, but it wasn't long before they realized that this was not a workable plan. The sea was heaving, and none of them had the experience to maintain their position in these conditions. They tried to contact the professor—there was no telephone, right, but they had this system of bells he'd set up for basic communication. One bell on the boat, and a tiny one in the helmet. I'm not sure exactly how it worked. Morse Code, I'm guessing—had to be. Anyway, as things went from bad to worse topside, the crew were signaling the professor, SOS, COME BACK. If he heard them, he didn't answer. Now the boat was riding waves halfway to vertical. Water was foaming onto the deck from every side. It was all the lads could do to keep from being swept overboard. And still no response from the professor. Funny, the things you'll do in a crisis. One of the crew grabbed a hatchet and, chop, cut the diving suit's air hose. That was the end for the professor. You have to hope he found whatever he was looking for." Susan said, "That's terrible. What happened to the crew?" "Oh," Giorgio said, "they made it back safely. Went straight to the police and confessed everything. Only problem was, each man said he was the one had picked up the hatchet, and nothing anyone could threaten or promise would persuade any of them to change his story. In the end, none of them was charged, and the professor's death was ruled an accident. The body was never recovered."

Still a third time, as they were treating Giorgio to dinner at a nice restaurant in a small hotel located on the shore of a slender inlet, he set down his salad fork and said, "There's a ghost in this hotel, you know, right in this very room. A woman dressed in a long dark green dress and a short jacket, with a little hat. Like the style women wore at the beginning of the last century. She sits at one of the tables over there." He pointed to an alcove at the other end of the dining area. "It's always after the last customer has left, and one of the staff is cleaning up. I used to date a lassie had seen her on two separate occasions. The first time, she ran out of the room as if the Devil himself was clutching at her heels with his pointy nails. The second time, Colleen (that was the lassie's name) stayed put. She said the woman stood, turned around, and walked to the door. Her face was in shadow, that was the way Colleen described it. She couldn't manage a good look at her. She said the woman passed through the door, the way you hear ghosts doing. Colleen ran to the door and opened it. Although it was late, this was during the summer, so there was plenty of light for her to watch the woman cross the lawn to the water and keep going, out into it until she was gone, submerged, hat and all. No one knows who she is, or was. Another drowning victim, right? Sometimes I wonder, though: what if we have it backwards? What I'm trying to say is, instead of someone who used to live on land returning to it, maybe it's someone, or something, whose home is the water coming up to have a look and see what all the fuss is about." "Really?" Susan said. "No," Giorgio said, "I'm just speaking out my arse. Still, the ocean is deep and dark and full of secrets, right? Isn't there a saying to the effect that we know more about outer space than we do the bottom of the sea?" "I don't know," Alan said, "sounds good, though." "Aye, so it does," Giorgio said.

Between Giorgio's stories, and the omnipresent water rolling to the horizon, Susan found herself revising her opinions of life beside the ocean. Since she and Alan had met at a mutual friend's house in Bourne, on the mainland side of the Cape Cod canal, Susan had declared it her fondest wish to return to the area to buy a house overlooking the ocean. It was a favorite fantasy, one she indulged by scrolling through online real-estate listings. That such houses were out of their price range by a factor of several hundred percent was of no real concern. Alan was doing well enough at his architecture firm to make the daily commute to Manhattan worthwhile, and the director of Penrose College's art museum was sufficiently pleased with her performance to hire Susan full-time. They saved what they could, and eventually, they would be in a position to afford a place in Bourne, or further out on the actual Cape, in Orleans or even Wellfleet. In the meantime, they had their friend's house to return to. Her dream was in part a declaration of loyalty to the place where she and Alan had so improbably found one another. But she also fancied the Cape an appropriate symbol for the relationship they had discovered, a place of fundamentals, land and sea and sky. Not once had it occurred to her that part of the reason she could appreciate the Bay at Scusset Beach was because the entire continent was behind her, thousands of miles of mountains and hills, cities and plains. Even way out on the end of the Cape, in Provincetown, there was the sense of being connected to something larger, a solid mass of land. Five days on Shetland, and she had learned that being on the margin between sand and water was a different thing from being surrounded by the ocean. Giorgio diagnosed what she described to him as island fever. "It's not for everyone, living up here," he said. "The sea…" He shrugged, as of the word was explanation enough.

BANG. As if making Giorgio's point, the water smacks the hull directly outside her bunk, from the sound of it. The metal groans, a loud complaint that lasts an ominous length of time. Susan stares at the wall next to her. The dread she's been managing since they sailed into the storm surges within her. Her heart breaks into a full gallop. Should she wake Alan, grab their bags, head for the upper decks, closer to the lifeboats? She doesn't know. She can't draw enough air into her lungs. The edges of her vision darken. She's burning up. The panic attack isn't the first she's had, but it's without doubt the worst. She can't keep lying down; she's suffocating. She throws off her blanket, sits up as the ferry begins another slide down down down… She grips the edge of her bunk, braces her feet against the floor. BANG. The ship protests, asking how much more of this abuse it's expected to take. Susan has to get out of here. She grabs Alan's bunk, uses it to haul herself to standing. On the other side of the hull, water swooshes as the floor tilts back. She crosses to the door in four lurching steps, opens it, and exits the cabin.

The corridor outside the room is empty, the rest of the cabin doors shut. No sign of the little girl and her mother, the laughing passer-by. Susan isn't so distracted she can't think, *Well, good for them.* One hand on the wall, she turns left, toward the stairs. The ferry levels, tips, lunges. The wool socks she's wearing slide on the floor. She flattens on the wall. BANG. The impact shudders through her. While the ship tilts to climb the next swell, she scuttles along the wall as fast as her feet and hands will move her, which isn't as fast as she'd like, but it occupies her while the ferry slides up and then down. BANG. By the time the ship has summited the following waves, Susan has reached the doorway to the stairs. *Alan*, a distant part of her mind objects, *what about Alan?* She plunges into the stairwell.

It's like trying to play some demented fun-house game, climbing the stairs as they rock this way, then that. Although each stair is covered in studs to aid traction, they benefit her socks little, and she clings to the guard rail with both hands. The acoustics of the space make it sound as if the water streaming past the ship is filling the stairwell, while each BANG shivers all the stairs at once. She manages four flights, two decks, before she has to abandon the stairwell.

As she emerges into a corridor more or less the same as the one she left, the lights dim, then brighten, then go out. "Oh, come on," she says. With a click, emergency lights pop on at either end of the corridor. "Thank you." She backs against the wall to her left and slides down it until she's sitting. Her heart is still racing, but the short excursion she's taken has left her exhausted. Maybe it's the Dramamine having more effect, too. If it weren't for her pulse jackhammering, she'd swear she would pass out right here. She places her hands on the floor to either side of her to help with the ferry's relentless rocking, which feels as if it's grown worse. *We must be close to Fair Isle*, she thinks. *Isn't that the place Giorgio said the sea was especially rough?*

Another BANG and a horrible smell floods her nostrils. She claps her hand over her mouth. For an instant, she wonders if a sewage pipe has broken under the waves' pounding, only to reject the idea. This is not the pungent stink of shit. It's the reek of a beach—of a North Atlantic beach at low tide, a medley of decaying flesh and baking plant matter. Tears blur her eyes. At the same time, the temperature in the corridor drops, heat escaping as if out a hole in the ferry's side. The cold that swirls into its place is thick, gelid. There's something else, a note in the atmosphere that reminds her of nothing so much as the worst arguments she and Alan have had, when hostility foams and froths between them. Malice washes over her. She swallows, shakes her head.

To her left, movement on the floor draws her eye. An eel, long and skinny, slides away from her. It isn't an eel: it's a length of hose, dun-colored, the end closest to her ragged, vomiting water as it moves. That's the source of the awful smell, the cracked and peeling hose that's being dragged toward and through the doorway at the far end of the corridor, making a sound halfway between a hiss and a breath. She can't see what's on the other side of the threshold; the emergency lights cast a veil of brightness her vision cannot pierce.

Even were she not schooled in hundreds of horror films, Susan would know that following the foul-smelling hose to whatever is dragging it would be a bad idea. In fact, she has no intention of hanging around this location one second longer than is necessary. She pushes to her feet, and staggers up the corridor to the exit to the stairs.

Up or down? She opts to climb. It's slow going. The stairs are like an enormous metronome. She loses her footing twice, has to clutch the railing to keep from tumbling down. Her heart is still pounding, her skin burning, but she isn't sure if it's from the panic attack continuing or her brush with what was standing beyond the lights at the other end of the corridor. *Or both*, she thinks, one of her favorite rhetorical sayings returning to haunt her: *Why does it have to be either/or? Why can't it be both/and?* When the water smacks the hull, the BANG echoes through the stairwell like thunder. The best Susan can do is two flights of stairs, and then she stumbles out the doorway to the next deck. The motion of the ship combines with her slick footing to send her into the wall opposite; she catches most of the impact with her arms, but the force drops her to one knee.

At least the lights are working properly on this level. That revelation, however, is accompanied by another: the terrible smell permeates the air here, too, and with it are the same cold and the same impression of overwhelming malevolence. A noise equal parts a breath and a hiss jerks her head up, to watch a peeling and cracked hose snaking along the floor. *How…?* The thing drawing the hose toward it halts the thought. Susan has the impression of a figure the approximate size and shape of a man, its hide studded with barnacles, strung with seaweed, a single round eye staring out of its misshapen head. Hatred rolls off it in waves. Before her mind can process what she's looking at, she's back in the stairwell, her legs propelled not so much by fear as by some deeper impulse, something that precedes and pre-empts rational thought. (*How…?*) The same response sends her down the stairs, flight after flight, until she's back where she started, at the deck where Alan lies slumbering on his bunk in their cabin. Alan: for the first time in what feels an eternity, she thinks of her husband as more than a name. What if he woke to find her missing? What if he went in search of her, and encountered whatever is stalking the hallways? Fear for him runs down her spine like ice water. She staggers across the tilting floor into the corridor.

The monster is waiting for her. It swipes at her with oversized hands, and would probably have her if her feet didn't slip and dump her on her ass. The pain registers dimly; she's already scooting backward, her attempted escape hindered by the floor tilting her toward the monster. It leans to grab her legs, spilling a rain of tiny green crabs onto them. Susan jerks her legs back, avoiding the thing's grasp, and slaps at the crabs scrambling over her pajamas. She twists onto her stomach, crawls for the stairwell. The ferry levels, and she pushes to her feet. Stiff-legged as Frankenstein's monster, the thing lurches after her. The floor slopes forward. Struggling not to lose control of her balance, she slides on the soles of her socks, as if ice-skating. The monster's feet clatter behind her. She's almost at the stairwell. The sea pounds the ferry, BANG. The monster reaches, catches her left arm, and swings her in a long arc all the way around it into the wall. She tries to get her right arm up to protect her head, but she still sees a brilliant flash of white, feels the impact rattle her teeth. The monster releases her arm, steps in close, catches her by the shoulders. She's spun to face it, pressed against the wall by heavy hands.

This close, the stench brings her to the verge of fainting. Arctic cold envelops her, extinguishing the remaining heat the panic attack kindled in her skin. She twists from side to side, trying to loosen the thing's hold on her, but its grip is unbreakable. Its eye flashes. Malice batters her, its ferocity utter, unrelenting. She turns her head from the thing, closes her eyes—

—and she is somewhere else, a place mostly dark, here and there dim, an expanse of bare mud ornamented with rocks. Shadowy forms, each the size of a large dog, float languidly in the air, and she sees that they're fish, which means she's underwater, from the look of things, somewhere deep. In front of her and to the right, maybe twenty yards away, a light spreads a yellow cone through the murk. It's a large flashlight, carried in one hand by a figure wearing a diving suit, rounded helmet and all. Its air hose rising behind it, its heavy boots *raising clouds of mud, it trudges toward a low heap of rocks. Long, rectangular, the rocks have a consistency of size and shape that gives them the appearance of having been carved into their present forms. When the flashlight's beam illuminates designs grooved into their surfaces, Susan understands that she's looking at an archeological site, that she's watching the protagonist of Giorgio's Fair Isle diver story as he sees the object of his expedition. (Which means...) His flashlight ranges over the stones, picking out symbols she doesn't recognize, concentric circles, a triangle with rounded corners, a crescent like a smile. Other characters are obscured by mud and algae. The arrangement of the stones suggests that they've fallen over onto one another. Before one of them, the diver stops, directs the flashlight to a spot immediately in front of him. Something flashes in the mud. Slowly, ponderously, the diver kneels, reaching down with his free hand. He brushes away a layer of mud, and as he does, sends a small white object tumbling up from its resting place. It's a wonder that he's able to catch it, but catch it he does, and holds it up for view. Susan is too far away to see his discovery in much detail. It's circular, the diameter of a saucer, composed of a white material that shines in the flashlight beam. The diver turns it over, examines the other side, then slides it into a bag hung down his chest. He rises and continues toward the piled stones. As he draws closer to them, his flashlight seeks out the gaps between the rectangles. What it reveals quickens his pace. At the pile, he bends forward, bringing his helmet as close as he can manage to one of the larger spaces between them, holding the flashlight beside his helmet. He slides his other hand into the gap. Whatever he's after resists his efforts. He withdraws the flashlight and turns to the side, to extend his reach. He doesn't see the slender white hand shoot out from the space and grab his arm. By the time he's aware of the contact, the hand has pressed his arm further down into the gap, where the space narrows, wedging it there. The diver pulls back, but his arm is stuck fast. The hand retreats amidst the stones. The diver releases his flashlight, which is looped to his wrist, and attempts to use that hand to pull the other free. It's no use. He pulls; he pushes. He shakes his trapped hand with such fury, Susan can imagine his screams ringing in his helmet. He stops, lets go of his hand and turns as best he can to look behind him. Undulating like a sea serpent, the air hose to his suit descends the water, bubbles venting from its torn end as it falls. Frantically, the diver flails at the back of his suit, where the hose attaches, but he can't maneuver his arm to it. Even if he could grab hold of the hose, it's hard to see what good that would do him. The same thought appears to occur to the diver, who surrenders his attempt. As the hose snakes across the mud, he turns again to the stone heap, sagging against it, his helmet coming to rest above the space that has trapped him. If he isn't dead already, he will be soon. The white hand steals from between the stones and trails its fingers across his faceplate, almost lovingly—*

Susan recoils from the sight, and confronts the monster holding her, which, she sees, is no monster, but the diving suit in which Giorgio's professor met his watery end. The barnacles, the seaweed, the tiny green crabs scuttling across it, are the yield of decades beneath the water, as are the dents that have misshapen the helmet, the cracks that spider-web the faceplate's glass. It has looped the hose around itself like a bandolier. She can't say if there's anything left of the suit's former inhabitant, though she doubts it. What has remained is his anger, his rage at having made the find of his career, of his life, and then been abandoned to death. Contained in the suit, that fury, burning with the blinding flame of an underwater welder's torch, has sustained it, has maintained its integrity long after time, salt water, and the ministrations of a thousand ocean creatures should have dissolved it.

It is terrifying; she has to escape it. She drives the heel of her right palm into the faceplate, hears a chorus of snaps. The helmet draws back, as if surprised. She strikes again, missing the faceplate, hitting the metal beside it with a hollow bong. A surge of hatred blasts her. When she tries to hit the thing a third time, it releases her left shoulder to swat her hand away. It catches her by the throat and squeezes. Never mind that she was years from birth when the professor drowned, that she hasn't the slightest connection to this tragedy. She is here now, the accident of her presence as good a reason for the thing's hostility as any. Fingers thick and cold dig into her neck. She grabs its hand, searching to pry open its grip. It is inhumanly strong. She cannot breathe. Her vision contracts. Somewhere distant, the sea strikes the ferry's hull, BANG. She lets go of the hand, opts for another round of blows, punching the suit's shoulders, chest, striking the hose wound around it, searching for a last-second vulnerability. Her knuckles tear on barnacles, slip on seaweed, rebound from the hose wrapping it. *Oh, Alan*, she thinks. Her arms feel incredibly heavy. She can't have much time left. *Goddamn it*, she thinks, *Goddamn it*, the curse summoning a last surge of strength. Muscles screaming for oxygen, she punches as hard and fast as she can, One two three four.

With a crack, her right fist connects with an object that breaks under its impact. There's a burst of something between them, a soundless explosion. The hands at her neck and shoulder fall away. Gasping for air, Susan collapses into the wall, her fists still out in a trembling attempt at a guard. The diver steps away from her, its hands pushing aside the hose, searching through the seaweed decorating its chest, to a woven bag hung from its neck. Within the bag, the shards of a white disk slide against one another. The damage to the bag's contents confirmed, the diver's hands drop to its sides. The cold is bleeding from the air, taking with it the awful smell. The figure retreats another pace. Its malevolence gutters and puffs out. Susan has the impression of something behind the suit, retreating at great speed through the wall, out of the ship, an impossible distance. On slightly unsteady legs, the diver lumbers to the exit and proceeds into the stairwell. Its heavy boots clank on the metal stairs.

Susan feels no desire to follow. With a kind of visionary certainty, she knows that the diver is going to continue its climb until it reaches a level that admits to the ferry's exterior. If enough of the force that animated it remains, it will walk to a bulwark, lean forward, and allow the weight of its helmet to carry it over into the heaving waves. If not, one or the other of the crew members will come across an astonishing discovery, the remains of an old diving suit, apparently washed onto the ferry by the storm. Perhaps they'll examine the contents of the bag around its neck, perhaps the professor will receive his recognition yet. Or perhaps not.

For the moment, all Susan wants to do is to return to the cabin where she hopes she will find her husband fast asleep. There's still a long way to go and the storm has not abated. In the morning, Alan will ask her why she's wearing gloves and a scarf. She'll say that she'll tell him once they're back at his parents', safely removed from the sea, and all its marvels and horrors.

HAAK

Today, Mr. Haringa was wearing a scarlet waistcoat with gold trim and gold buttons under his usual tweed jacket and over his usual shirt and tie. A gold watch chain looped out of the waistcoat's right pocket, through which the outline of a large pocket watch was visible. While Mr. Haringa was required to dress professionally, as were all staff and students at Quinsigamond Academy, he did so without the irony and even mockery evident in the wardrobe choices of many students and not a few of his colleagues: cartoon character ties, movie print blouses, black Doc Martens. His jackets and trousers were in dark, muted colors, his white button-down shirts equally unassuming, and his half-Windsor-knotted ties tended to blue and forest green tartans. If he added a sweater vest to the day's ensemble, which he did as fall crisped and stripped the leaves of the school's oaks, then that garment matched the day's color scheme. "It's like he likes dressing this way," the occasional student muttered, and though delivered disparagingly, the remark sounded fundamentally accurate.

For Mr. Haringa to appear in so extravagant, so ornate an article of cloth-ing was worthy of commentary from the majority of the student body, and a significant minority of his fellow teachers; although the conversation only circled, and did not veer toward, him. Aside from the scarlet and gold waistcoat, whose material had the dull shine of age, Mr. Haringa behaved in typical fashion, returning essays crowded with stringent corrections and un-sparing comments, lecturing on the connection between Coleridge's *Rime of the Ancient Mariner* and Robert Bloch's "Your Truly, Jack the Ripper" to his two morning sections, and discussing the possible impact of Maturin's *Melmoth the Wanderer* on Browning's "Childe Roland to the Dark Tower Came" with the first of his afternoon classes. By his second class, the change in his attire had receded in the students' notice.

A few in the final session wondered if the waistcoat was related to that date on the course syllabus, which had been left uncharacteristically blank. They had completed two weeks of exhaustive analysis of Conrad's *Heart of Darkness*, during which they had lingered at each stop on Marlow's journey into the interior of the African continent to meet the elusive and terrible Kurtz, examining sentences, symbols, and allusions with the care of naturalists cataloging a biosphere. Ahead lay a selection of Yeats's poetry, including "Second Coming," which several students had mentioned they knew already but which Mr. Haringa assured them they did not. This afternoon, however, was a white space, unmapped terrain. As the rest of the syllabus was a study in meticulous planning, it seemed impossible for the gap to be anything other than intentional.

When Mr. Haringa entered the room, he strode to the desk, removed his jacket and hung it on the back of his chair, loosened the knot of his tie, pulled it from his neck, draped it over the jacket, and unbuttoned the top button of his shirt. Had he appeared stark naked, the students could not have been more shocked. He extracted the pocket watch from the waistcoat and opened it. Although gold, or gold-plated, its surface was scratched and dented. With his left hand, he gave the crown a succession of quick turns. Roused to life, the timepiece emitted a loud, sharp ticking. Watch in hand, Mr. Haringa said, "Anyone who wants to leave is free to do so. For next class, please be sure to read 'Sailing to Byzantium' and be prepared to discuss it."

The students exchanged glances. Mr. Haringa offering them the opportunity to depart class before the bell—after one or two minutes past the bell—was almost as startling as the scarlet waistcoat, the removal of his jacket and tie. One of the better students raised her hand. Mr. Haringa nodded at her. She cleared her throat and said, "Are you serious? We can go?" The class tensed at the directness of the question, ready for it to provoke their teacher's notorious sarcasm.

But his razored wit remained in its scabbard; instead, he said, "Yes, Ashley, I'm serious. If you want to leave, you may."

Another student raised his hand. "What happens if we stay?"

"You'll have to wait to find out."

In the end, slightly less than half the class accepted the offer. Once the door had closed on the last student's departure, Mr. Haringa closed the watch and returned it to its pocket. "Aidan," he said, "would you get the lights?"

For an instant, the classroom was plunged into darkness. Someone laughed, nervously. There was a click, and a series of lights sprang on around the room's perimeter. Positioned at the base of the walls, each cast upward a crimson light whose long, oval shape suggested a window. A trick of their placement made the lights appear to hover ever-so-slightly in front of the painted brick. A couple of the students wondered when Mr. Haringa had been in to set up so elaborate a display. They had watched him walk to his car yesterday afternoon, and they had seen him exiting it this morning. Not to mention, the teacher had not impressed them as especially proficient in technology. Perhaps another faculty member had helped him? Mr. Baillie, maybe?

Despite the fabric enveloping it, the pocket watch was louder in the crimson space, every tick opening into a tock. Yet when Mr. Haringa spoke, his voice, though low, was clear. "You will recall," he said, "that, following his trip up what was then the Congo River, Joseph Conrad became ill. As does Marlow, yes. Unlike Marlow, Conrad went to a spa in Switzerland the year after his trip, to continue his recovery. He was suffering from a variety of complaints, including gout, which likely was unrelated to his time on the Congo, recurrent malaria, which likely was related to his months on the river, and pain in his right arm, which may or may not have been connected to his recent activities. Oh, and there was something wrong with his hands, too, a strange swelling. To put it mildly, he was not in good shape.

"The spa he went to overlooked a mountain lake. A small steamboat, not unlike the one Conrad had captained on the Congo, ferried passengers to and from the spa to a modest town on the opposite shore. From his chair on the spa's front porch, Conrad could watch it chug across the lake's smooth blue surface. He found the sight simultaneously comforting and unnerving. Eventually, once he was feeling well enough, he left his chair, ventured down to the landing, and bought a ticket for the crossing. When the boat reached the town, he did not disembark; instead, he remained onboard as the vessel took on a fresh load of passengers and set off for the spa. At the dock, he stepped off and made his way up to the spa.

"Conrad repeated this trip the next day, and the one after that, and every day thereafter for a week and a half. Finally, the steamboat's captain introduced himself to him. His name was Heuvelt. He was from Amsterdam, originally, had commanded a merchant vessel in the Dutch East Indies for twenty years before retiring to the Swiss mountains, where he had established the steamboat service and was now as busy as he had ever been. He was approximately ten, fifteen years older than Conrad, late forties to early fifties. In a letter, Conrad described him as weather-beaten to handsomeness. The two of them had a pleasant exchange. Conrad complimented Heuvelt on his vessel. Heuvelt invited him to try the wheel. Conrad declined, politely, but he and Heuvelt continued their conversation over the course of their next several visits, trading stories of their respective ocean voyages. According to everyone who knew him, Conrad was an accomplished raconteur, and apparently Heuvelt was reasonably gifted, as well. Their daily meetings, Conrad wrote, did as much to restore him to well-being as any of the spa's therapies. Eventually, he accepted Heuvelt's offer to steer the boat, to the irritation of the young local whose job it was. Heuvelt was impressed with Conrad's handling of the boat, and soon this became part of their daily routine. Conrad would board the steamboat, assume the wheel, and he and Heuvelt would converse while he guided the boat back and forth across the lake.

"After another couple of weeks, Heuvelt asked Conrad if he would be interested in joining him onboard that evening, around sunset. There was something he wished to show Conrad, a peculiarity of the lake Heuvelt thought he would find of interest. Conrad agreed, and a few hours later, was waiting alone on the landing as the steamboat pulled up to it. To his surprise, Heuvelt had the wheel, his young man nowhere to be found. 'This is not for him,' Heuvelt said, which sounds more odd, and even ominous, to us than it did to Conrad: ship captains are notorious for keeping secrets from their crew, no matter that the crew consists of a single man. Whatever their destination, Conrad understood Heuvelt was trusting him to keep it to himself.

"Heuvelt turned the boat toward the other end of the lake, which was hemmed in by steep mountains. About halfway to their destination, the sun set, leaving in its wake a crimson sky. The water caught the light, and it was as if, Conrad wrote, they were steaming across a tide of blood, beneath a bloody firmament."

For an instant, a handful of students had the impression that the light saturating the classroom was in motion, as if they were seated on the steamboat with the writer and his friend. The tick-tock of Mr. Haringa's pocket watch echoed like an enormous grandfather clock. The students shook their heads, and returned their attentions to the teacher. A couple of them noticed that, despite the red filter laid over everything, Mr. Haringa's waistcoat remained visible as its own distinct shade of the color, but did not know what, if any, significance to ascribe to this.

His words still audible through the pocket watch's see-sawing progress (perhaps he was wearing a microphone?), Mr. Haringa proceeded: "With the sun setting, the mountains ahead grew shadowed. As the boat drew closer to them, Conrad saw that what he had taken for a recess among the peaks was in fact a steep valley, through which a surprisingly wide river rushed into the lake. Heuvelt tuned the wheel to bring the prow in line with the river, and started them up it. To either side, rock walls rose, reducing the sky to a single red strip. There was a light on the boat, but Heuvelt made no move toward it. Conrad wondered if the man was attempting to impress him. If so, he was succeeding. While the river was sufficiently broad to admit the steamboat's passage, rocks and clusters of rocks pushed up through its current every few yards, requiring a skill at navigation Conrad did not think he would have been able to summon. He assumed Heuvelt was steering them toward another lake, because he could see no way for the boat to turn around in the river, but he did not want to distract Heuvelt from his task by asking him if to verify his assumption.

"They rounded a bend in the river, and there in front of them a great tree stood in the midst of the water. Easily a hundred feet high, a third that in girth, it was like no tree Conrad had seen anywhere in his travels, which, as you know, had been considerable. Deep grooves ran up its bark, clumps of moss and small plants filling the channels. Pale lichen tattooed the tops of the ridges. High overhead, thick branches formed a crown like a vast umbrella, from which a network of vines hung in loops and lines. To show him such a thing might well have been Heuvelt's intent, but the steam-boat showed no signs of stopping, so Conrad assumed there was more to come. In order to circumvent the enormous obstacle, Heuvelt had to steer perilously close to its vast trunk, an arm's length away, less, and this close, Conrad could feel the tree's age. This was an ancient of its kind; when the Romans were laying roads across their empire, the tree already stood proud. Conrad stretched out a hand to touch the hide of so venerable a being, only to be warned off completing the act by a shake of Heuvelt's head.

"On the other side of the tree, the river spread out dramatically. Dozens of trees, each the same species and dimensions as the one they had cleared, reared from the water, a flooded forest. In the twilight, the trees reminded Conrad of great beasts, a herd of prehistoric animals gathered in the water to relieve the heat of the day. It was an astonishing sight, which had not been so much as hinted at during Conrad's time at the spa. This strained belief. Surely, he thought, a location as remarkable as the one into which the steamboat continued should be the pride of its location, should it not?"

Within each of the red lights around the classroom, a darker form appeared, a thick column suggestive of the trunk of a tree, viewed from a distance. While Mr. Haringa's pocket watch counted its time, the shapes to the class's left became larger, the light on that side dimmer, as if the students were sailing this way. A handful of them felt the floor shift under the soles of their shoes, rising and falling as it would were they on the deck of a boat pushing up a river.

Although he had not changed his position in front of his desk, Mr. Haringa's voice sounded closer; eyes closed, each student might have believed their teacher was seated beside them. As he continued with his narrative, the shadowy forms bisecting the rest of the red lights expanded, until it seemed the immense trees of his story surrounded the class. He said, "Employing signposts Conrad could not identify, Heuvelt sailed a winding course through the forest. Although he considered himself possessed of a superior sense of direction, Conrad soon lost track of which way they were traveling. Thinking he would regain his bearings by checking the stars already visible overhead, he leaned out from under the boat's roof. But he recognized none of the constellations burning in the sky from which the last traces of red had yet to vanish. This was impossible, of course, and he wondered if the crowns of the trees spreading between him and the stars were in some way distorting his view, which was not much more likely, but preferable to the other explanations available. He retreated beneath the roof and saw Heuvelt watching him, the expression on the man's face an indication that he knew and had shared Conrad's observation. Such confirmation was almost too much to bear, Conrad later wrote; rather than acknowledge it, he asked Heuvelt if their destination had a name.

"In reply, Heuvelt said, 'Haak.' During his years at sea, Conrad had picked up a smattering of Dutch, but this word was unfamiliar to him. He started to ask for a translation when the steamboat chugged out of the trees into a wide pool in which sat the wreck of a great ship. It was a Spanish galleon, what you or I might imagine as an old-fashioned pirate ship, with three masts for its sails, a raised deck at its rear, and square windows perforating the sides for its cannons. Centuries had passed since such vessels had been in widespread use. The ship was tilted to the right, its wood blackened with age. Gaping holes in its left flank exposed its ribs. Its foremast had broken near the base and tipped into the water. The mainmast and mizzenmast were intact, the ragged remains of their sails and rigging draped from them like faded bunting. Amidst the tattered canvas, Conrad picked out shapes dangling from the masts, the corpses of a score of men, their flesh desiccated, their clothing rotted. They had been hanged, their hands tied behind their backs."

Now the darker columns within the red lights faded, to be replaced by a variety of shapes. At the front of the room, shadowy arcs suggested a ship's ribbing, while thick diagonal lines to either side of the students stood in for the tilted masts. Interspersed among these shapes were the silhouettes of men at one end of a heavy rope, their necks crooked. Only the lights at the back of the class were absent any form, and the glow they cast forward highlighted Mr. Haringa in a hellish luminescence through which the waistcoat was visible in its own scarlet hue. The pocket watch had increased in volume to the point its TICK-TOCK shuddered the students' desks, and not a few of them wondered how much longer it would be until a teacher in one of the neighboring rooms stuck their head in the door to request Mr. Haringa turn down the noise.

His voice in each student's ear, Mr. Haringa said, "Conrad was stunned. As if a flooded forest in the Swiss mountains was not fantastic enough, the wreck of a huge, ocean-going ship in its midst defied explanation. There was no river large enough to have borne the galleon anywhere within fifty miles of the place. In his time at sea, Conrad had heard sailors relate glimpses of islands not on any maps, of vessels from centuries gone by. He was enough of a rationalist to ascribe the majority of these accounts to old and incomplete maps, to the confusion of distance and poor eyesight, but he was also enough of a sailor, himself, to recognize that the immensity of the ocean held room for all manner of things. Although he had thought them far from the sea, it appeared the sea was not far from them. Combined with the unfamiliar constellations overhead, the remains of the ship indicated Heuvelt had taken them into one of those strange countries whose coastlines he had heard described.

"Heuvelt guided them around to the galleon's top side, keeping a wide distance between the steamboat and the masts with their tangle of sails. Throughout the trip so far, he had maintained a more or less constant speed, which he reduced as they circled the wreck. One eye on the ship, one on their course around it, he said, 'You have heard of the Armada, yes? The great fleet the Spanish king sent to invade England when Elizabeth was her queen. One hundred and thirty ships, it was said. It was defeated by the English navy's ships, which were smaller and faster, and its tactics, which were superior. There is no one as ruthless as an Englishman. The Spanish captains chose to flee up the English and Scottish coast. Their enemies pursued them all the way. North of the Orkney Islands, the Spaniards turned west, intending to sail down the western side of Scotland into the Irish Sea. As they entered the open Atlantic, however, a ferocious storm greeted them. All along northwest Scotland and northeast Ireland, Spanish sailors were shipwrecked and came ashore. Many were killed by the populace. A few were given shelter by those Britons unfriendly to their queen.

"'There was one ship whose captain sought to escape the catastrophe of the Armada by sailing directly into the storm. He trusted his ability to navigate the wind and waves, and his crew to follow his commands. The English captains saw him heading toward the gale and allowed him to go, sure the Spaniard would not outlive his disastrous choice.

"'You know what it is like on a ship during a storm. The English were not wrong to let the Spanish vessel escape; they must have assumed the captain was choosing to die in this fashion, rather than at the edges of their swords. They were not familiar with this commander, Diego de la Castille, who was new to the responsibility of a ship but was a gifted sailor and inspiring leader. Although Poseidon struggled mightily to bring the vessel and its crew to his watery halls, the captain outmaneuvered him, and exited the other side of the storm.

"'Perhaps the old god had the last laugh, though, because when the wind quieted and the waves calmed, the ship was in a location not even the most seasoned hand recognized.'

"Conrad said, 'This place.'

"'Yes,' Heuvelt said, 'this place of great trees rising from the water, of a hundred scattered islets.' The steamboat had drawn opposite the tip of the mainmast. So distracted had Conrad become by Heuvelt's story that he did not notice the boy crouched on the end of the mast until he uttered an exultant, blood-curdling whoop and leapt toward them. Heuvelt had kept a good fifteen yards between their boat and the mast, but the child crossed the distance effortlessly. He landed on the steamboat's roof with a solid bang, scurried along it to the front of the boat, and dropped onto the deck before the men. Only Heuvelt's raised hand restrained Conrad from fleeing the short sword whose tip was suddenly pointed at his throat. Already, Heuvelt was speaking, a patois of Spanish and another tongue Conrad recognized as Greek, but of an older, a much older form. From what Conrad could understand, the man was urging calm to the child aiming his blade at the base of Conrad's neck. Panos, Heuvelt called the boy, who was perhaps ten or eleven, his long hair sunbleached, his bronzed forearms and legs bare, latticed with white scars. He was wearing a scarlet coat whose sleeves had been hacked off above the elbows, and whose ragged hem hung down to his calves; despite the antique style, Conrad saw its gold brocade and knew it at once as the garment of a ship's captain. Underneath the coat, the child was dressed in a tunic stitched together from large yellowed leaves. A worn strip of leather served him as a necklace for a steel hook, of the kind a man might substitute for a hand lost to violence. Conrad recalled the name Heuvelt had given this place and said, 'This is Haak?'

"Without pausing his speech to the boy, Heuvelt nodded. He was slowing the boat to a crawl. The child's weapon was wavering, but was still far too close to Conrad's skin for him to feel free to move. Its tapered blade was notched, scratched, a record of many campaigns. The design reminded Conrad of illustrations he had seen in books on the ancient world. How strange it would be, he thought, to die on the point of such a sword now, at the end of the nineteenth century, with all its marvels and advances.

"As Heuvelt continued urging the boy to calm, he reached into his coat and withdrew from it a gold pocket watch. The child's eyes widened at the sight of it. Heuvelt wound the timepiece, then held it out. 'Go on,' he said, 'take it.' He'd brought it for the child. Quicker than Conrad could follow, the boy dropped the blade from his neck, leapt across the deck to Heuvelt, snatched the watch from his hand, and retreated with it to the prow. While the child hunched over the pocket watch, pressing it to one ear, then the other, Heuvelt said to Conrad, 'You have heard of the Roman captain who was sailing near Gibraltar when a loud voice declared, "The Great God Pan is dead." The captain sent word of this to the Emperor, who decreed three weeks of mourning for the passing of so important a deity. He was one of the old gods, Pan, foster-brother to Zeus. Now he is pictured as a dainty faun, but he was nothing of the kind. He was wild, savage, the cause of sudden panic in the forest. How could such a one die, eh? He did not. He withdrew into himself, made of his form a place in which he could retreat. Or perhaps that place was always what he had been, and the face he showed the other gods was a mask he put on for them. Either way, he left the society of gods and men. Who can say why? He remained undisturbed for a thousand years, more, long even as a god measures time.'

"Conrad was an experienced enough storyteller to recognize where Heuvelt's tale was headed. He said, 'Until the Spanish captain and his crew arrived to rouse Pan from his slumber.'

"'It is a dangerous thing,' Heuvelt said, 'to wake a god. Pan was both angry at the presumption and intrigued by the sight of these new men on a ship the like of which he had not seen before, dressed in strange clothing, and armed with shining weapons. His curiosity won out, and instead of appearing to them in his full glory, he chose the form of a child.'

"Conrad started. He had expected Heuvelt to declare the boy an orphaned descendent of the Spaniards. He said, 'Do you mean to say—'

"'Of course,' Heuvelt said, 'Pan did not reveal his identity to the strangers. They took the child who stared at them from a rocky islet in this unfamiliar place as another castaway. They brought him onboard their ship. A man of some learning, the captain knew enough classical Greek to converse with the boy. Over the next several days, he asked him how he had come to this location, if he knew its name, if he was alone. But the only information the child would offer was that he had been here many years. The captain concluded the child had been shipwrecked with his parents as an infant, and his father and mother subsequently died. Why the boy spoke antique Greek was a mystery, but already, the men were teaching him Spanish, and the child was showing them locations of fresh water, and fruit, and game, so the captain decided to allow the mystery to remain unsolved. As for Pan, whom the men had named Pedro: after a millennium of solitude, he found he enjoyed the company of men much more than he would have anticipated.'

"'Obviously,' Conrad said, nodding at the wreck, the corpses dangling from its masts, 'something changed.'

"'There lived in the waters of this place a great beast, a crocodile, such as you may have seen sunning themselves on the banks of the Nile, though bigger by far than any of those. This was an old man, a grandfather croc, veteran of a hundred battles with his kind and others. Blind in one eye, scarred the length of his thick body, he was as cunning as he was ferocious. Their first days here, one of the sailors had sighted him, surveying the ship from a distance, and his size had amazed the crew. A few of the men suggested hunting him, but the captain forbade it, cautious of the risk of such an enterprise. As the monster gave them a wide berth, his command was easily followed.

"'A few weeks after that, the crocodile capsized one of the ship's boats and devoured three of the crew. It may be that the attack was unprovoked, that the beast had been studying the sailors, stalking them. Or it may be that the sailors had disobeyed their captain's order and gone in search of grandfather croc. Well. Either way, they found him, much to their sorrow. The survivors fled to the ship, where they relayed the tale of their attack to their fellows. As you can imagine, the crew cried out for vengeance, a demand the captain gave in to. He led the hunt for the monster, and when the sailors found the crocodile, engaging him in a contest that lasted a full day, it was the captain who struck the killing blow, at the cost of his good right hand. The sailors towed the carcass to the ship, where they butchered it and made a feast of the meat, draping the hide over the bowsprit as a trophy.

"'Pan was not on the ship for any of this. He would leave the company of the Spaniards for a day or two to wander his home. He would visit the sirens who lived in a hole in the base of one of the great trees, and who sang of the days when they drew ships to break themselves on their rocky traps, so that they might dine on the flesh of drowned sailors with their needle teeth. Or he might watch the Cimmerians, who lived on a rocky island on the far side of the trees, and whose time was spent fighting the crab men who crept from the water to carry away the weak and infirm. Or he would seek out the islet in whose crevice was the living head of a demigod who had offended Pan and been torn asunder by a pair of boars as a consequence. Oh yes, this place is large and full of strange and wonderful things.

"'Wherever the god had been, when he returned to the ship and saw the crocodile's skin hanging from its front, his wrath was immediate. Grandfather croc had been sacred to Pan, and to kill him was a terrible trespass, no matter how many of the men he had eaten. Pan stood in the midst of the sailors feasting on the crocodile's meat and declared war on the vessel and its captain, pledging to kill them to the man. You can appreciate, the crew saw a child threatening them, and if a few were annoyed at his presumption, the majority were amused. The captain chided him for speaking to his friends so rudely, and offered him some of the wine he had uncorked for the celebration. Pan slapped the goblet away, and fled the ship.

"'The next time the Spaniards saw the god, he was armed with the blade you have inspected so closely. As one of the ship's boats was returning from collecting fresh fruit, it passed beneath the limb of a great tree where Pan was waiting. He dropped into the middle of the boat and ran through the men at its oars. The rest scrambled for their weapons, but even confined to such a modest form, Pan was more than their equal. He ducked their swings, avoided their thrusts. He slashed this man's throat, opened that man's belly. Once the crew was dealt with, he threw the food they had gathered overboard and left.

"'As it happened, though, one of the first men Pan stabbed was not dead, the sword having missed his heart by a hair's breadth. Still grievously wounded, this sailor nonetheless was able to bring the boat and its cargo of corpses back to the ship, where he lived for enough time to describe Pan's attack. The crew were outraged at the deaths of their mates, as was the captain, but he was as concerned at the loss of the fruit the men had been transporting.

"'The following day, he sent out two boats, one to carry what food could be found, the other to guard it. Before they had reached the islet that was their destination, the men sighted Pan curled in a hollow in one of the trees, apparently asleep. Thinking this a chance to avenge their fellows, they rowed toward him. As they drew closer, the Spaniards heard voices, women's voices, singing a song of surpassing loveliness. They searched the trees, but saw no one. One of the men looked into the water, and directed the others to do likewise. Floating below the surface were the sirens, their limbs wrapped in long trains of silk. Pan liked them to sing of his life as it had been, when he and his foster-brother, great Zeus, had spent their days roaming the beaches of Crete, peering into the pools the tide left, on their guard for Kronos's spies. The approach of the boats distracted the sirens from their duty. Long years had passed since they had tasted the flesh of any man but the Cimmerians. From the shores of Crete, their song changed to the delights awaiting the sailors under the water. Wasting no time, one of the younger men leapt to join them. He was followed by all his fellows save one, an old hand mostly deaf from decades manning the cannons. To him, the sirens' song was a distant, pleasant music. He was the one who would return to the ship to relate the fates of the others. He would describe the sirens darting around the men, keeping just out of reach. Like many sailors of the time, none of those who had pursued the sirens could swim; not that it would have made much difference in this case. Maybe they would not have drowned so quickly. That was bad, but what was worse was when the sirens began to feed. Their song ceased, and the old hand who had watched his mates die saw that their beautiful robes were in fact long fins growing from their arms and legs, and that their pretty mouths were full of sharp, sharp teeth. So frightened was the sailor that he forgot about Pan until he was fleeing. Then he saw the god awake, on his hands and knees, leaning forward to watch the water grow cloudy with blood.

"'If the captain grieved the loss of his men, and so soon after the deaths of the others, he regretted the loss of the second boat almost as much. He was aware, too, that for a second day the ship's larder had not been replenished. The vessel had provisions enough for this not to be of immediate concern, but you know the importance of well-fed men, especially on a ship lost in a strange place.

"'First, though, there were the sirens to be dealt with. An expedition to the spot was out of the question. The old sailor's report of the creatures had terrified the men. The captain suggested borrowing a trick from Homer and stopping their ears, but the crew would have none of it. Rather than risk rebellion, the captain ordered the ship's cannons loaded and trained on the sirens' location. Three volleys the Spaniards fired at the creatures. Their cannonballs felled two of the great trees, and stripped limbs from and struck holes in ten more. While the smoke still rolled on the water, the captain and four of his bravest men stuffed their ears with rags and boarded the remaining boat, which they rowed toward the sirens quickly. Upon reaching the spot, they found two of the creatures floating dead, the limbs of a third between them. A fourth swam in a slow circle, right beneath the water's surface, gravely wounded. The captain dispatched her with his sword, then had the men retrieve her body and those of her sisters. They towed the sirens' remains to the ship, where the captain instructed the crew to hang them from the mainmast.

"'Certain that an attack by Pan was forthcoming, flushed with his victory over the sirens, the captain prepared for battle. The armory was opened, the cannons were loaded, watches were posted. On the ship's forge, the smith crafted a hook to replace the captain's lost hand. All of this for a boy, eh? Yes, the Spaniards did not know Pan's true identity, but they had realized he was no normal child. His immunity to the sirens' music marked him as a supernatural being, himself. Many of the crew were sure he was a devil, and this Hell. The superstitions of sailors are legendary, and the captain, who worried about Pan more than his station would allow him to admit, did not want men's fears to undermine the ship's order. He pointed to grandfather croc's hide, to the bodies of the sirens, and told the crew that if this was Hell, then they would make the devils fear them. Brave words, and had Pan appeared at that moment, the sailors would have thrown themselves at him with all the ferocity they had reserved for the English.

"'During the days to come, the ship was the model of discipline. The men did not see Pan, but they had no doubt he was preparing his assault. The days became a week. The lookouts saw nothing in the great trees but brightly colored birds. One week became two. There was no hint of Pan. The crew grew restless. The captain wondered if the child had been struck by a cannonball and killed, but was reluctant to chance his remaining boat to investigate the speculation. With each passing day, the ship's provisions diminished, and this became as great a concern for the captain as Pan's skill with the sword. Hunger leads to desperation, desperation to mutiny, for sailors, at least. For those in command, desperation is brother to recklessness, and the arrival of one foretells the arrival of the other. As the second week of the ship's vigil tipped into the third, the captain called on his four best men and joined them in the boat. Together, they set out to look for Pan.

"'Their search took them to the place he had been seen last, the lair of the sirens. The Spaniards had blocked their ears, but there was no need: the spot was deserted. From that location, they rowed to every one Pan had showed them, from a rocky islet where grew a grove of lemon trees to a long sandbar whose grass fed a herd of goats. Nowhere was the god visible. They came within view of the rugged home of the Cimmerians, which Pan had cautioned them to avoid. Through his spyglass, the captain surveyed the island's huts, but could see neither the child nor the Cimmerians. A terrible suspicion seized him, which was borne out a moment later, when an explosion sounded from the ship's direction.

"'You can imagine, the men rowed with all the speed they could summon. When they reached the ship, they saw her canted to port, a column of thick smoke rising from the hole in her starboard side. A fierce fight was underway on the sloping deck between the sailors and a small army of men and women. They were bone white, these people, armored in the shells of the crab men they had slain, which proved little match for the Spaniards' steel. But their weapons, spears with fire-hardened tips, axes with sharpened rock heads, were no less deadly when they found their mark, and there were more, many, many more of the Cimmerians than there were of the crew. Dancing across the bloody boards, Pan stabbed this man in the leg, cut the hamstrings of another, jabbed a third in the back. The air was full of the grunts and cries of the sailors, the cracks of their swords on the shell-armor, and the battle song of the Cimmerians, which is a low, ghostly thing.

"'Once the boat was within reach of the deck, the captain leapt onto it, his blade at the ready. A swordsman of no small repute, he cut a path to the spot where Pan was engaged in a duel with the first mate, who had succeeded in scoring his opponent's legs and forearms with the tip of his sword. Just as the captain reached them, Pan jumped over the mate's swing and drove his blade into the man's chest. Enraged, the captain lunged at the god, but the blood of his lieutenant betrayed him, causing his foot to slip and him to lose his balance. A kick from Pan sent him tumbling down the deck, into the water.

"'Unlike the crew, the captain could swim. He was hindered, though, by his fine coat, whose fabric drank the water thirstily, dragging him deeper. Clenching his sword between his teeth, he used his hand to pull the garment from him. He was almost free of it when the right sleeve caught on his hook. Try as he might, the captain could not extract his arm from the coat; nor was he able to loosen the straps securing the hook. What air remained in his lungs was almost spent. There was no choice for him but to haul the coat with him, as if he were pulling a drowning man to safety.

"'By the time he climbed onto the ship, the battle was done. The crew were dead or dying. They had acquitted themselves well against their attackers, but the Cimmerians had the advantage of overwhelming numbers, and the assistance of a god. The captain found that deity's sword pointed at him, together with a dozen spears. However skilled he was with his own weapon, he was a realist who recognized defeat when it confronted him. He lowered his blade, reversed it, and offered it to Pan, telling him the ship was his.

"'If he was expecting his surrender to result in mercy, the captain was disappointed. Pan had sworn death to all the Spaniards, and a god will not break his oath. At his signal, the Cimmerians seized the captain's arms. A pair of them tore the coat from his hook, then used their stone knives to cut the bindings of the hook. They sliced away the captain's garments until he stood naked. They forced him to the deck, and held him there by the elbows and knees while an old woman pressed a sharpened shell to his thigh and began the laborious work of removing his skin.

"'She was skilled at her work, but the process took the rest of the afternoon. The captain struggled not to cry out, to endure his torture with dignity, but who can maintain his resolve when his skin is being peeled from the muscle? The captain screamed, and once he had done so, continued to, until his throat was as bloody as the strips of his flesh spread out to either side of him. Occasionally, the old woman would pause to exchange one shell for another, and the captain would survey the ruination fallen upon his vessel. The Cimmerians had taken the crew's weapons, and select items of their clothing, scarves, belts, and boots. Already, they had cut down the sirens' remains and were hanging Spanish corpses in their place. Grandfather croc's hide had been gathered from the bowsprit and folded into a mat, which Pan sat upon as he watched the Cimmerian woman part the captain's skin from him. He had donned the captain's fine coat, waterlogged as it was, and was holding the hook, turning it over in his hands as if it were a new, fascinating toy. Every so often, he would raise his right hand, his index finger curved in imitation of the metal question mark, and grin.

"'As the day was coming to an end, the old woman completed the last of her task, the careful work of separating the captain from his face. He had not died, which is astonishing, nor had he gone mad, which is no less amazing. Pan stood from his crocodile mat and approached him. In his right hand, he gripped the captain's hook. He knelt beside the man and uttered words the captain did not understand. He placed the point of the hook below the captain's breastbone and dug it into him. With no great speed, the god dragged the hook past the man's navel. Leaving it stuck there, Pan released the hook and plunged his hand into the captain's chest, up under the ribs to where the man's heart galloped. The god took hold of the slippery organ and wrenched it from its place. This must have killed the captain instantly, but if any spark of consciousness flickered behind his eyes, he would have seen Pan slide his heart from him, raise it to his mouth, and bite into it.'"

Mr. Haringa paused. The assortment of dark shapes within the crimson lights laded, brightening the room. The pocket watch dropped in volume, its tick-tock merely loud. When the teacher spoke, his voice no longer seemed to nestle in each student's ear. He said, "In his years at sea, Conrad had heard tales that were no less fantastical than this one. He had taken them with enough salt to flavor his meals for the remainder of his life. His inclination was to do the same with the narrative Heuvelt had unfolded, admire its construction though he might. The very location in which he Heuvelt delivered it, however, argued for its veracity with brute simplicity. All the same, Conrad found it difficult to accept that the boy who had seated himself at the front of the boat, where he had succeeded in prying open the pocket watch and was studying its hands, was the avatar of a god. He expressed his doubt to Heuvelt, who said, 'You know the story of Tantalus? The king who served his son as a meal for the gods? Why, eh? Some of the poets say he was inspired by piety, others by blasphemy. It does not matter. What does is that one of the gods, Demeter, ate the boy's shoulder before Zeus understood what was on the table in front of them. A god may not taste the flesh of man or woman. To do so confuses their natures. Zeus forced Demeter to vomit the portion she had eaten, and he hurled Tantalus into Tartarus, where Hades was happy to devise a suitable torment for his presumption. Demeter had been duped, but Pan sank his teeth into the captain's heart with full awareness of what he was doing. Nor did he stop after the organ was a bloody smear on his lips. He dined on the captain's liver and tongue, and used the hook to crack the skull to allow him to sample the brain. Sated, he fell into a deep slumber beside the remains of Diego de la Castille, captain in the navy of his majesty, Phillip II of Spain.

"'In the days after, Pan changed. The Cimmerians had departed the ship once the god was asleep, taking with them the captain's skin, whose pieces they would tan and stitch into a pouch to carry their infants. Alone, Pan roamed the ship, dressed still in the captain's scarlet coat. He loosened the hook from its collar, cut a strip of leather from a crew member's belt, and fashioned a necklace for himself. The captain's remains he propped against the mainmast and sat beside, engaging in long, one-sided conversations with the corpse. He was becoming split from himself, you see, this,' Heuvelt gestured at the child, 'separated from this,' he swept his hand to encompass their surroundings. 'The Cimmerians, who had faithfully followed the god into a battle that had winnowed their numbers by a third, grew to fear the sight of him rowing toward them in the ship's remaining boat, a strange tune half-hymn, half-sea shanty on his lips. He was as likely to charge them with his sword out, hacking at any whose misfortune it was to be within reach of its edge, as he was to sit down to a meal with their elders. The sirens, too, learned to flee his approach, after he lured one of them to the ship, caught her in a trap made from its sails, and dragged her onto the deck. There, he lashed her beside the captain's corpse and commanded her to sing for him. But the words that once had pleased the god now tormented him, and in a rage, he slew the siren. He loaded the captain's body into the stern of the boat, and roamed the islets of this place. He chased the herd of goats in and out of the water until they were exhausted and drowned. He hunted the flocks of bright birds roosting in the trees and decorated his locks with bloody clumps of their feathers. He piled stones on top of the rock opening in which he had tucked the head of the dismembered demigod, entombing him.

"'The transformation that overtook Pan's form as man affected his form as nature, as well. In days gone by, the routes here were few. A fierce storm might permit access, as might the proper sacrifices, offered in locations once sacred to the god. Now the place floated loose in space. Its trees would be visible off the coast of Sumatra, or in a valley in the Pyrenees. Rarely were those who ventured into the strange forest seen again, and the few who did return told of their pursuit by a devil in a red coat rowing a boat with a corpse for its crew.'

"'And you,' Conrad said, 'how did you come here?'

"'An accident,' Heuvelt said. 'The boiler had been giving me trouble, to the point of almost stranding me in the middle of the lake with a full load of passengers. Not very good for business. Compared to the trials I had faced on the open sea, it was modest, but a difficulty will grow to fit as much room as there is for it. I labored over the boiler until I was sure I had addressed the fault, and then took the boat out. I should have stayed in. There was a heavy fog on the water. But so obsessed had I become with the problem that I could not wait to test its solution. I flattered myself that my skill at the wheel was more than sufficient to keep me from harm.

"'Harm, I avoided, but I stumbled into this place, instead. You will appreciate my wonder and my confusion. I spied our young friend balanced on the ship's bowsprit, and when he challenged me, I knew enough of Greek and enough of Spanish to speak with him. Of course, I took him for an orphan (which from a certain point of view he was, abandoned by himself). Only later did I understand the peril I had been in. Our first exchange, halting as it was, gave me the sense that there was more to this boy than was apparent to my eye. When I left, I offered to take him with me, but he refused. For the gift of my conversation, though, Pan permitted me to depart unharmed.

"'Thereafter, I might have avoided the western end of the lake. Whether I judged my experience a waking dream or a visit to fairyland, I might have decided not to repeat it. As you can see, I abandoned prudence in favor of the swiftest return I could manage. I half-expected the way to be closed: I had made inquiries of several of my passengers the next day, and no one expressed any knowledge of strange rivers amongst the mountains. Yet when I searched for it that night, the passage was open. More, my young friend was eager to see me. Since then, I have visited whenever the opportunity has presented itself. I have learned my way around the tongue Pan and the Spaniards cobbled together. As I have done so, I have had his story, a piece at a time, in no order. The majority of these fragments, I have assembled into the tale you have heard; though there remain incidents whose relation to the whole I have yet to establish.

"'From the beginning, I had the conviction I must save this child, I must rescue him from this place. My own son died of a fever shortly after he learned to walk, while I was away at sea. I understood the influence this sad event exerted on my sentiments, but the awareness did nothing to diminish them. Each time I voyaged here, I brought candy, cakes, toys, whatever I guessed might tempt the boy away. After I understood what he was—as much as any man could—I continued my efforts to bring him with me. For if it is accounted a good deed to help a child out of misfortune, what would it mean to come to the assistance of a god?

"'Only the timepiece,' Heuvelt nodded at it, 'has continued to interest him. Every time I remove it from my pocket, it is as if he sees it anew. It fascinates him. Occasionally, I believe it frightens him. I have told him that, should he come with me, I will make a gift of it to him. The lure of the watch is strong, but not yet greater than the fear of venturing forth from his home. I think he will choose to accompany me into the world of men. It is why I have been able to travel the waters here so often. For the trespass he committed against his divinity, he must atone.'

"'What form would such a thing take?' Conrad said.

"'I do not know,' Heuvelt said. 'Perhaps he would live as a mortal, resolve the conflict in his being by walking the path we tread all the way down to the grave. Or perhaps he would require more than a single lifespan. How long is needed for a god to atone to himself? He might spend centuries on the effort.'

"There was a clatter from the front of the steamboat. Conrad glanced in that direction to see the child leap onto the railing and from there up to the roof. Another astonishing jump carried him from the boat to the tip of the ship's mainmast, which he caught one-handed and used to swing onto the mast. While he was running down the spar to the ship, Heuvelt brought the boat's speed up and turned the wheel in the direction of home. The child had left the watch on the deck; Conrad retrieved it and handed it to Heuvelt, who tucked it into his coat with a sigh. 'The next visit,' he said, 'or the one after that, perhaps.'

"Although Conrad remained at the Swiss spa another two weeks, and continued to take the ferry every day he was there, he and Heuvelt did not discuss their voyage to the wrecked galleon, their encounter with the figure

Heuvelt claimed was a god gone mad. He understood that the man had given him a gift, shared with him a secret mysterious and profound. But there was too much to say about all of it for him to know where or how to begin, and as Heuvelt did not broach the topic, Conrad chose to follow his example. Heuvelt did not invite him on a second expedition.

"Nor would Conrad speak or write of the trip until the last years of his life, when he spent fifteen pages of a notebook detailing it, more or less as I've related it to you. By then, he had been contacted by a number of critics, each of whom wanted to know about the sources of his fiction. He'd never made any secret of his life on the sea, but many of the letters he received sought to connect his biography to his writing in a way that stripped the art from it. He grumbled to his friends, but he answered the inquiries. He also recorded his experience in the Swiss mountains. Once he was finished, he turned to a fresh page and listed the titles and dates of a handful of narratives: 'The Great God Pan' (1890), 'The Story of a Panic' (1902), *The Little White Bird* (1902), *The Wind in the Willows* (1908), *Peter and Wendy* (1911). Under these, he wrote, 'A coincidence, or a sign Heuvelt at last succeeded in his quest, and delivered the god to his long exile?' Not long after writing these words, Conrad died.

"In the interest of scholarly integrity, I should add that the majority of Conrad scholars consider the notebook story a bizarre forgery. Even those few who accept it as Conrad's work dismiss it as a five-finger exercise. It's an understandable response. How could such a tale be anything other than pure invention?"

The pocket watch stopped. With a click, the crimson lights switched off, flooding the classroom with darkness. Something vast seemed to crowd the space with the students. Mr. Haringa's voice said, "Aidan, would you get the lights?"

After the dark (which took a fraction of a second too long to disperse), the fluorescent lights were harsh, prompting most of the students to turn their heads aside, or lift their hands against it. By the time their eyes had adjusted, Mr. Haringa was behind his desk, shuffling through the folders in which he kept his selection of relevant newspaper clippings. Without looking up, he said, "All right, people, you're free to go. Thank you for indulging me. Don't forget, next class we're starting Yeats, 'Sailing to Byzantium.' Anyone who feels particularly ambitious can take a look at 'Byzantium,' which is a different poem."

Still half in a daze, the students rose from their desks and headed for the door, some shaking their heads, some mumbling, "What was that?" A pair of students, the girls who competed for the highest grades in the class, paused in front of the teacher's desk. One cleared her throat; the other said, "Mr. Haringa?"

"Yes?" Mr. Haringa said.

"We were wondering: what do you think happened? To Pan? What did the Dutch guy do with him?"

Mr. Haringa straightened in his chair, crossing his arms over his scarlet waistcoat. "What do you think?"

"We don't know."

"You have no idea, whatsoever."

"Can you just tell us, please? We have to get to Pre-Calc."

"All right," Mr. Haringa said. "We know Heuvelt was using the watch to lure Pan out of his world and into ours. The question is, once you have him here, how do you keep him here? Or—that's not it, exactly. It's more a matter of, how do you accommodate him to this place, with all its strangeness? I'd say the answer lies in language, story, poetry, song. He knew some Spanish, so you might begin by reading him *Don Quixote*, a little bit at a time. As his fluency improved, you could introduce him to Lope de Vega, who wrote a long poem about the Spanish Armada. Yes, the same one the galleon had been part of. Maybe you would move on to Bécquer, his *Rimas y legendas*. Then—you get the idea. You teach him other languages, French, Italian, Dutch, English. You introduce him to Racine, Boccaccio, van den Vondel, Shakespeare. You bind him to our world with narrative, loop figures of speech around him, weight him with allusions. Does this answer your questions?"

"Kind of."

"Kind of?"

"Didn't you say Pan would have to atone, for eating the captain?"

"Ah." Mr. Haringa paused. "To be honest, I've wondered that, myself. I have no idea. I'm not sure how the god would figure out what he had to do, especially if he was cut off from himself, from that fullness of being he had known before his trespass. I can picture him telling and retelling the story of that event in an effort to discover whether the answer lay somewhere in its details. In this case, your guess is just about as good as mine."

"Um, okay. Thank you."

"Yeah, thanks, Mr. H. See you tomorrow."

After the class, Mr. Haringa had a free period. Once the hallway outside his room had grown quiet, he crossed to the door and turned the lock. Returning to his desk, he unbuttoned the scarlet waistcoat and shrugged it from his shoulders, draping it on the back of his chair. He opened the white dress shirt underneath down to his navel. A raised white scar ran up the center of his breastbone. His eyes focused on some distant, internal image, Mr. Haringa traced the ridge with the fingers of his right hand. Slowly, he dug his fingertips into the scar, grimacing as the toughened flesh resisted the tear of his nails. As his skin parted, he brought up his left hand to widen the opening. His sternum cracked and rustled. There was surprisingly little blood.

The hook was slippery in Mr. Haringa's grasp. Exhaling sharply, he slid it from his chest. He swayed, gripping the chair with his left hand to steady himself. Tears flooded his vision; he blinked them away, raising the hook to view. Stained and discolored with blood and age, the metal reflected Mr. Haringa's features imperfectly. The point of the implement had retained its sharpness. Mr. Haringa brought the hook to his mouth and pressed its tip into his lower lip. He remembered the bitter taste of the captain's heart, its chewiness.

"Si les dieux ne font rien d'inconvenant,
c'est alors qu'ils ne sont plus dieux du tout"
—Mallarmé

BREAKWATER

Only the main road to Breakwater had not been washed out, so Maureen had no choice but to take the most visible route into the town, around the Jersey state trooper parked in the middle of the road, his cruiser's lights flashing blue and red, miniature lighthouses in the storm's tumult. The cop stared open-mouthed at anyone heading toward the place; though he made no move to stop her. Her car, a gray Escort, was sufficiently nondescript to give the trooper little to remember. Even if it wasn't, the wipers pushing the driving rain back and forth across its windshield reduced her to an androgynous blur of lowered blue baseball cap and baggy white sweatshirt. To further diminish the cop's impression of her, she gave him the typical, compulsive glances of a citizen worried about an offense they weren't sure they were committing. As he didn't swing out to follow her, she assumed her act succeeded.

Either that, or Louise had paid him off to allow her entry. Which, come to think of it, was probably why he remained where he was.

Crossing the low bridge over the ocean inlet, she saw the height of the gray water, swollen with the week's unrelenting rain and storm-boosted tide well up over the docks lining each shore, halfway to the roofs of the intermittent boathouses. Leashed to their submerged posts, a scattering of orphaned sailboats, yachts, and speedboats struggled against the waves rising to their gunwales. On the other side of the bridge, she eased to a stop in front of the first of the town's two traffic lights. Although the gusting wind swung it almost horizontal, the light was functioning, its red lens flashing. Directly beyond the light, the road ahead was blocked by a half-dozen orange and white striped barrels, each with a round blinking yellow light on top of it. For a couple hundred feet, the street descended a gradual incline to the beach, where it dead-ended in a parking area. Since last Saturday, though, the Atlantic had worked its steady way up the slope, enveloping beach houses and businesses as it climbed, until now its foaming rollers were almost to the bases of the barrels.

Maureen flipped her turn signal and steered right, along Ocean View, the town's principal north-south street, which ran parallel to the ocean. Most of what she remembered about the ocean side of Breakwater, its crowded rows of oversized, pastel houses, its restaurants and shops, was gone, battered and swept away by the storm. Here and there, the upper floor of a house rose from the waves, the roof of a motel lifted a satellite dish to a signal it was no longer receiving. In places, the pavement dipped slightly, allowing the ocean to wash closer, and the sight of the frothing water reaching for the road tightened her fingers on the wheel. *Three hours*, she thought. *Two at the inside, four at the outside. Plenty of time.*

This was assuming, of course, the meteorologists were correct in their estimate of the number of hours remaining until the Atlantic rolled over this part of the town. From the speed with which it had coalesced, to its stalling over Breakwater, to the length of time it had raged with no appreciable diminishment, enough about this storm had been unprecedented, and to such a degree, as to render all predictions concerning it suspect. *Give me one hour*, Maureen thought. *Thirty minutes.*

A mile along Ocean View, Poseidon's Palace Motel stood on the left, two stories of sea-foam and pink cinderblock, a hold-over from days when Breakwater had attracted vacationers of more modest means. A foot of water rippled over the empty parking lot, washed the bottoms of the doors to the ground floor rooms, splashed the base of the sign whose neon letters, now dead, advertised neither vacancy nor full.

Not for the first time, Maureen wished she had acted on her impulse the moment Frank had said that sure, he used his EZ Pass on the drive here, why wouldn't he? and no, he hadn't shut off the GPS on his phone, why should he? On the spot, she had wanted to flee, to climb into her rental and take off while time remained before whoever Louise had hired to surveil her errant husband appeared, camera at the ready. Frank could join her if he wished, provided he left his cell in his car. Twenty-one years a private investigator, most of them spent gathering evidence on unfaithful spouses, and she had known what was going to happen. Hell, until Louise fired her, she had been the one with the telephoto lens, keeping a long-distance eye on the very handsome Frank as he roamed up and down the Hudson Valley from Wiltwyck to Manhattan, representing his ailing and reclusive (and significantly older) wife at gallery openings, philharmonic concerts, and benefit events for a range of charities. She had filled most of a thumb drive with the pictures she accumulated of Frank deep in conversation with this museum director, waltzing with that violinist at an after-party, laughing with the local TV anchor who was co-hosting the silent auction. None of those photos, though, went beyond the vaguely disquieting: Frank leaning a tad too close to a painter, or placing his hand on a cellist's elbow, or giving an enthusiastic hug to a socialite in a gauzy excuse for a dress. To the best of Maureen's not-inconsiderable ability to tell, Louise Westerford's husband enjoyed walking to within sight of the boundaries of their marriage but had not trespassed them.

No, for that he would require (oh irony!) two conversations, one short, one long, with the woman who had been his unseen companion for the better part of six months, the first in an upscale restaurant in White Plains the month after Louise told her her services would no longer be required, the second in the restaurant-bar of the Motel 6 off the Thruway in Wiltwyck. When Maureen had sat down in Louise's study with its assortment of occult paraphernalia—bookcases full of big, leather-bound volumes, stuffed ravens mounted on gnarled wire armatures, a crystal ball the size of a baby's head cradled by a stand decorated with grinning devils—a sudden surge of pity for this woman twelve years her senior, her terribly thin body wrapped in enough black scarves to make Stevie Nicks jealous, had stirred her to venture beyond her usual detailed summary of her findings and review of her expenses. It appeared to her, Maureen said, that while Mrs. Westerford's husband appreciated the company of attractive women, his admiration had not led to anything more. And if she didn't mind her saying, Maureen had noticed that Mrs. Westerford's husband appeared to be quite lonely. Those nights he wasn't committed to an event or social gathering, he tended to dine by himself at one of a half-dozen restaurants, spending his time reading on his tablet. Rather than paying her to watch him, Mrs. Westerford might consider the possibility of joining him for some of those dinners; she might find an hour or two of talking with him over a nice bottle of wine and a good meal would do as much to allay her concerns over her husband's fidelity as employing a private investigator to document his every move.

Throughout Maureen's speech, Louise Westerford had regarded her with her large, liquid blue eyes as if she were speaking a language Louise found both unintelligible and distasteful. When Maureen was done, Louise had summarily fired her and summoned a maid to escort her out the front door. It had been a long time—as in, going back to her first years as a PI—since Maureen had been dismissed so casually, and though she told herself it was not the reason she sought out Frank four weeks later at his favorite steak house, the lie was too blatant to maintain. Give her this much credit: it had taken a month of debating whether to approach the man before she sat down across the table from him and introduced herself. She had been blunt, to the point, meeting his inevitable disbelief in her tale by handing her phone to him and allowing him to flick through the selection of photos she'd uploaded to it. Mingled with his shock had been curiosity. Why was she telling him all of this? "Because I don't like being treated the way your wife treated me," Maureen said. "Plus, you don't seem as bad as she's afraid you are, and I thought you should know about this." What was he supposed to do now? he wanted to know. Maureen didn't have any answers for him. Soon thereafter, she left. He asked for a number he could reach her at, in case he wanted to discuss this some more, but she refused. "I'm not the one you need to talk to," she said.

Nonetheless, when he called the following week, she agreed to meet him at McCabe's, the restaurant-bar attached to the Motel 6. She wasn't especially surprised he'd located her. She'd provided him her name and profession; her contact information was one Google search away. She had no interest in speaking to Frank, but residual spite toward Louise prompted her to accept his request; though she countered his suggestion of Fulci's, whose waterfront popularity begged someone to notice them, with McCabe's, whose dim lighting and high-backed booths offered more in the way of privacy. He questioned the location, insisting he had nothing to hide. "Good for you," she said. "How do you suppose it's going to look for me if I'm seen out with a recent client's husband—a man, by the way, I've been investigating for possible adultery?" Her point taken, they had met at McCabe's.

Afterward, when they were lying on the bed whose blanket and sheets they had kicked off, Frank asked her if she had planned for this to happen. She denied it but was uncertain how honest her answer was. You invite someone who has learned troubling information about his spouse to meet you for a few drinks at a bar connected to a motel; you proceed to buy round after round of bourbon for him, tequila for you, exchanging life stories along the way; you inform him you're going to take a room for the night because you're too drunk to drive and you don't like to sleep in your car. How was that anything but a plan for seduction? She could imagine what the attorneys she worked with would make of any claims to the contrary. Her intentions were purer when she told Frank this was a one-time thing; although the vow held only until he appeared at her office door a couple of days later, as she was preparing to close up shop. They did it right there on her desk, with the door unlocked. Maureen wasn't a size queen (a good thing in Frank's case), but damn, did he know how to use what he had. No doubt, the illicit nature of what they were doing added to its thrill, as in the days to follow he continued to return to her office when she was about to leave, and they added the couch, both her office chairs, and the floor to the register of places on which they stirred one another to shuddering climax.

Yet if the sex was good, to the point of Maureen wishing she smoked, so she could light a cigarette after, the talks they had in the sodium light falling in orange stripes through the Venetian blinds were better. Maureen had experienced her share of good sex (though perhaps not at quite this level), but a partner with whom she could enjoy a decent conversation had proven more elusive. She told herself she was going to bring the affair to an end but settled for moving it from her office to her apartment, picking up Frank at a different location each time and driving him to her place via a new and circuitous route. Already, she was on the lookout for her replacement, the next PI Louise Westerford would have retained to trail her wandering husband. Maureen didn't like hotels, whose security systems were built around video cameras, as were those at the majority of motels; although there was a seedy place off 9W in Highland at which she and Frank passed a couple of dirty evenings. He thought her precautions charming, but within a few weeks was chafing under them, going so far as to ask if it would be that bad for Louise's agent to discover their affair. "Yes," Maureen said, sitting up in her bed. "Your wife is very rich. That makes her much more powerful than either of us. She could divorce you and leave you with nothing. Hell, with the lawyers she could afford, you'd wind up owing her alimony. She could call the politicians she's donated to and have them yank my license. Trust me, you do not want to fuck with the rich."

Frank accused her of exaggerating. Louise, he said, was far more interested in her mystical studies than she was in ruining either of their lives. Sure, a divorce would be unpleasant, but it wouldn't be the catastrophe Maureen was describing. His wife loathed public attention, which was why she sent him to represent her hither and yon. If they split, she would want the proceedings to be as low-key as possible. Although she knew he was underestimating the effect betrayal would have on a spouse, Maureen had not argued the point, as she had not argued a month later at Breakwater, when Frank admitted his failure to cover his tracks. In part, this was because of the promise implied by his words, a vision of a life together she found surprisingly compelling, even as she heard herself disabusing two decades' worth of adulterers of similar fantasies. Like them, she had become addicted to that most dangerous narcotic, hope, and her ability to recognize her disease did nothing to blunt its power. Yes, she wore large sunglasses and a sunhat, but as far as disguises went, the combination was lacking. At the end of their four-day excursion to the Jersey shore, when Frank expressed his intention to talk to his wife, Maureen didn't ask what he was going to discuss, nor did she attempt to dissuade him from his plan. Amazing, the effect a surplus of fine dining and athletic sex could have on her. She wasn't just addicted: she was overdosing.

Enough of her critical faculties remained, however, for her to be on edge when after four days, then five, then six, Frank had not communicated with her. Had he lost his nerve? Had his romantic sentiments been nothing more than the side-effect of the endorphins saturating his blood? *Patience*, she thought, trying to focus on her current caseload, to watch the news. Sandwiched between reports of the current scandals roiling Washington and Hollywood was a feature on a freak storm which had coalesced in the Atlantic and swung due west, toward central New Jersey. Maureen missed the explanation for why something that looked like a small hurricane on the satellite photos wasn't designated one and formally named, but she did notice the name of the location where the storm barreled ashore, the vacation town of Breakwater. As the days proceeded with no word from Frank, coverage of the storm elbowed its way to the lead of each broadcast. After lifting the ocean into a surge that had washed away much of Breakwater's shore, the storm had parked itself over the town. Instead of lessening, it gained in intensity, lashing Breakwater with driving rain and high waves, spinning off tornadoes like enormous tops, dragging the Atlantic higher and higher up the ocean-facing streets. What portion of the populace hadn't fled the storm's approach rectified their error and headed inland. Meteorologists struggled to explain the storm's behavior, employing increasingly elaborate models to account for it, predicting an imminent departure the system had yet to make. While she knew the location of the storm's landfall had nothing to do with her and Frank's excursion there, the coincidence was difficult to ignore. As his failure to send so much as a simple text reached the two-week mark, and her certainty that no such communication was on its way grew, Maureen began to take a grim satisfaction in the reports of the destruction of the place where she had been so stupid, so naïve. The storm came to seem an embodiment of the disappointment and hurt weighting her chest, its objective correlative, a term her brain retrieved from some college literature course or another.

Yet when her cell played its tinny version of the theme from *Magnum, PI* and she recognized the number of the Tracfone she had insisted Frank buy, she nearly dropped her phone in her haste to answer it. Her "Hello?" struggled to contain thirteen days' worth of anxiety and doubt. But damned if her heart didn't lift at the sound of Frank's, "Maureen."

Already, though, she heard the hoarseness in his voice. "What's wrong?"

Another voice replaced his. "I believe we all know the answer to that."

Maureen's mouth went dry. "Louise."

"Mrs. Westerford—at least for the moment."

There was no point in playing dumb. If Frank was there and she had the Tracfone, then Louise knew enough for any theatrics to be a waste of time. Maureen said, "What can I do for you?"

"Oh, I think you've done quite enough, already. From what my husband tells me, admirably so, much better than an old sack of bones like me." The fury in her words was terrifying.

"Mrs. Westerford—"

"Check your e-mail."

"I'm sorry?"

"I said, Check your e-mail."

Maureen was already at her computer. She opened her gmail account. The message had been sent while they were talking. Its subject line read, "Poseidon's Palace Room 211." Maureen clicked on the photo attached, and there was Frank, naked, roped to a chair, his flesh a patchwork of bruises, some purple and fresh, others green and yellow and old. Long cuts traversed his chest, biceps, and thighs, half of them scabbed-over, half weeping blood. The worst, though, was his face, which bore the marks of sustained beatings, the eyes swollen shut, the nose mashed and bloody, the lips torn, a handful of teeth missing from bloody sockets. Maureen stared at the image, her pulse pounding at the base of her throat with such intensity she feared she was about to throw up.

"Do you understand?" Louise Westerford said.

"You don't need to do this," Maureen said.

"You know nothing of what I do and do not need. Right now, my needs include seeing you at the location where this photograph was taken within the next twenty-four hours."

"All right. I'll come. Don't hurt Frank anymore. Please."

Louise hung up.

The screen of Maureen's computer flickered, and the image of Frank disappeared, to be replaced by the gmail login page, on which was the message "Error: Account Not Found." A second later, a pop sounded inside the computer's tower, and the screen went black. The machine sighed, and the power light blinked off. A strong odor of burnt plastic and metal issued from the stack. Maureen spent the next several minutes attempting to resuscitate it, but whatever malware Louise had employed had reduced the computer to an oversized paperweight. Maureen checked her phone, but it showed no evidence of her e-mail account, either. As more and more of her business had involved an online component, Maureen had armored her PC with successive firewalls, a squadron of the most efficient anti-malware available. For Louise to have slipped through all of it was more than a little intimidating. Maureen's phone buzzed; she checked it, only to discover it, too, had been rendered inert. Although the possibility existed that a specialist in electronic forensics might be able to detect Louise's fingerprints on the attack of her devices, such investigation required time she didn't have. Instead, Maureen retrieved a wallet from the bottom right drawer of her desk, checked its contents, and left her office.

Ten years past, Maureen had been hired by the wife of a local crime magnate to document his numerous infidelities. The case had been no more risky than most until, during a tirade fueled by box wine and cocaine, Mrs. LaPierre had boasted to her husband about knowing every last thing he had been up to, thanks to her private eye, which assertion Mr. LaPierre had taken to encompass his extra-legal as well as his extra-marital affairs. After gouging out the eyes of his head of security, the gangster had devoted the substantial resources of his criminal network to discover the identity of the person investigating him. The ensuing weeks had been the most perilous and tense of Maureen's career. Only by an exercise in bravado that had led to a sit-down with Étienne LaPierre in the palatial living room of his Catskill mansion had she survived them. The experience had prompted her to establish a series of protocols in case she ever should find herself again in a similar or worse situation. These, she put into action with a drive to the local bank, into whose ATM she inserted a debit card in the name of Irene Paretsky. The ATM would allow her to withdraw a maximum of five hundred dollars, which she did. Next was a stop at the Wiltwyck Trailways, where she used a Visa card signed Irene Paretsky to purchase a one-way ticket on the next bus to Montreal, leaving in two hours.

The same credit card paid for a Tracfone and a pair of hundred-minute phone cards at the Wal-Mart on the other side of town, along with a selection of toiletries, a small overnight bag in which to carry them, a pink and yellow sunhat, and a blue Yankees cap. She activated the phone, loaded the minutes, and punched in the number written on a slip in the wallet. It was for a small hotel on the outskirts of Montreal. While she was on the line with the front desk clerk, she asked for recommendations for car rental places, and once Ms. Paretsky's room was booked, called the second company the clerk had recommended. She reserved a sub-compact for two days from now, insisting she wanted a vehicle with good gas mileage.

Next to the bus station was a diner to the far side of whose parking lot she drove, parking and locking her car. She ordered a Monte Cristo with fries at the diner, which Irene Paretsky's Visa also took care of. Fifteen minutes before the bus was scheduled to head for the Thruway, Maureen exited the diner and joined the line waiting for it. Once she had identified the positions of the security cameras, she withdrew the sunhat from its plastic bag, glanced from side to side, and placed it on her head. After boarding the bus, she seated herself beside the college-age woman she had identified ahead of her on the line. Five minutes' conversation—and two hundred dollars, cash—was sufficient to persuade the woman, who was transferring at the station in Albany to a bus headed for Buffalo, to agree to wear the pink and yellow sunhat all the way to western New York. Maureen slipped off her jacket, folded and stuffed it into the bag that had contained the hat, pulled on the baseball cap, and as the driver was checking the tickets of a pair of last-minute passengers, left the vehicle, apologizing to the driver for having mistaken this for the bus to Springfield.

Hunched over, the bag containing her jacket clutched in her arms, Maureen scuttled across the parking lot, out of view of the cameras. She left her car where it was and walked four blocks south, to a cinderblock garage on a lot between a pair of two-family homes. A key on her keychain opened and allowed her to raise the door. Inside was a dirty white Ford Escort registered to Christie Sayers, which was also the name on the rental agreement for the garage. The keys to the car were in the glove compartment. Maureen started the Escort, backed it onto the street, and closed and locked the garage behind her.

She headed to a storage facility at the edge of the shopping plazas on the northeastern side of the city. A key duct-taped to the bottom of the driver's seat unlocked a storage locker the dimensions of a large walk-in closet. From plastic tubs stacked against the rear wall, she removed two sets of clothes, jeans, loose knit shirts, socks, and underwear. After changing into one outfit, she packed the other in a black duffel bag lying on top of a green suitcase. To it, she added the toiletries she'd picked up at Wal-Mart. The clothes she had been wearing, she pushed into a garbage bag she tied with a plastic tag and placed on top of the plastic tubs. From the footwear arranged to the right of the tubs, she selected a pair of Doc Martens, which she tugged on and laced up, and a pair of sneakers, which she added to the duffel bag. The locker didn't contain much in the way of men's wear, only a few pairs of sweatpants and T-shirts hanging from a short clothes rack. She selected pants and a shirt approximately Frank's size and folded and placed them in the bag. She returned the baseball cap to her head.

Last came the filing cabinet on the left, which she unlocked with a key concealed under a piece of duct tape beneath the plastic tubs. From the top drawer, she removed a flat metal box, which she set on a folding card table in the center of the locker. From the bottom drawer, she lifted a bundle wrapped in plastic and tape. The metal box contained five thousand dollars in five stacks of rubber-banded hundred-dollar bills, and, more importantly, a blue Argentine passport, driver's license, and a debit card for the Citi Belgrano in Buenos Aires. All were in the name of Mariana Highsmith. There was also a clasp knife, and a pair of books that had come from the Avila bookstore in Buenos Aires: a guidebook to the American northeast and a book of conversational English. She slid the Irene Paretsky debit and Visa cards from her wallet, dropped them in the box, and replaced them with Mariana Highsmith's license and bank card. She zipped the passport into a pocket on one side of the duffel bag, along with the money. The books went in with the clothes. Using the clasp knife, she cut the tape and plastic from the bundle.

Inside were a pair of .38 revolvers, a crumpled box of bullets, a pair of short plastic tubes, a plastic sandwich bag filled with cotton, another plastic sandwich bag filled with metal washers, and a roll of black duct tape. Careful inspection of the guns would have revealed their serial numbers filed down to the metal. Maureen loaded the cylinders, set the revolvers aside, and turned her attention to the tubes, cotton, and washers, from which she spent the next half hour fashioning two makeshift silencers she attached to the pistols using the tape. The silencers secure, she carried the guns and the tape out to the Escort, whose trunk she popped. Half a dozen empty plastic shopping bags littered the floor. She selected a bag for each pistol and wrapped the weapon in it. With the tape, she affixed one gun to the front right wheel well, the other to the rear left wheel well. Leaving the trunk open, she returned inside, where she zipped the duffel bag and exited the locker, whose door she lowered and locked. She deposited the bag in the trunk, then drove across town to the parking lot of the Holiday Inn near the Thruway exit.

She steered to the back of the building, easing the car into a space next to a beige minivan with Virginia plates. She shut off the engine, reclined her seat, lowered the baseball cap's bill over her eyes. Her nerves crackled with anger and anxiety; it was all she could do not to start the car and speed for the Thruway. Breakwater was a good three hours south, though, and that without the disruption of the storm battering it. There was no sense in compounding the fatigue of a long drive with the exhaustion of a sleepless night. Plus, she preferred to arrive in the town during the daylight. She could at least rest. Somewhat to her surprise, she dropped into a deep, dreamless sleep from which she was awakened by the minivan's family climbing into it for an early start. A stop at the Quick Check up the street allowed her to use the toilet, splash water on her face, and purchase a large coffee, sausage-egg-and-cheese sandwich, and a bag of trail mix. She paid cash, as she did for the tolls for the Thruway and, later, the Jersey Turnpike.

Which brought her to here, now, to the parking lot of the Porcelain Pig Family Restaurant (closed), across Ocean View from the motel where she and Frank had enjoyed their last happy time together. Rain sizzled against the Escort's windows, thundered on its roof. Wind gusted to a shriek, rocking the car. Between the rain and the distance, she couldn't tell if anyone in Room 211 had registered her arrival. Best to assume they had. She was guessing Louise Westerford had a minimum of three, as many as five, men with her. One to either side of the door, positioned to grab her as she entered the room. The others stationed nearby should it prove necessary to assist those two. Possibly a man hiding in the bathroom in case the situation seriously deteriorated. She pictured the room, the king-sized bed facing the room door, the bathroom down a short hall beyond it. Assuming he was still bound to the chair, Frank would be on the left.

She took a deep breath, released it slowly. With the Irene Paretsky identity, whose connection to her could be traced easily, she had set in motion one narrative, in which, frightened by Louise Westerford's threats, she had adopted another persona and fled the country. Assuming whatever hacker Louise was employing had discovered the alias and was tracking her through its purchases, the ruse should distract the older woman, cause her to divert resources in the direction of Montreal to deal with this fresh wrinkle. Because there was no doubt Louise intended the same or worse vengeance on her. Looking ahead, the same obvious link between Maureen and Irene would throw the police off her trail, at least temporarily.

She drew in another breath, let it out slowly. The Christie Sayers identity would be considerably more difficult to connect to her, and the time it would take the cops to do so, and then to search the video archives of the Thruway cameras for the Escort, and then to do the same for the Turnpike's video records, would extend her lead.

She inhaled deeply, exhaled slowly. In this day and age, you could hardly say something was untraceable, but the Mariana Highsmith identity was as close to it as a considerable sum of money could buy. If the police succeeded in doing so, it would be long after she had flown to Buenos Aires, emptied her account at the Citi Belgrano, and left in a rental car for the border with Uruguay. The only thing for which she had not planned was having someone else with her, especially a companion as grievously hurt as Frank. It was a complication, but not an insurmountable one. If she could get Frank to Newark, there was a small apartment on the western edge of the city rented to Ruth Abbot, where they could hole up for a few days while she sought medical care for him, and prepared for his departure from the country.

She took a deep breath, let it drain from her slowly. Thus far, Maureen had done her best to put the photo of his naked, wounded body from her thoughts. Now she allowed herself to remember it, to see the damage days of beatings had done to him. She pictured the wreck of his face. No doubt he had suffered internal damage, broken ribs, a bruised liver or kidney, a possible retinal detachment or blowout fracture. Cold, murderous rage rose in her. When she was ready to kill Louise Westerford, she zipped her raincoat and stepped out into the storm.

Rain lashed her. To her relief, the revolvers were where she had fastened them, which had been the idea, but as she crouched beside each wheel well, a surge of panic made her certain that pistol was gone, jostled loose by the combination of distance and weather. She stripped the guns of their covering, wadded the tape and bag into a ball, and tucked the ball into her raincoat's front pocket. Holding a revolver in either hand, she crossed the street. Water streamed from the baseball cap. Wind pushed her like an enormous animal, a dog or horse shoving her this way and that. Roaring filled the air overhead. She kept the pistols close to her legs, silencers pointing down.

On the other side of the street, she descended the short ramp to the motel's submerged parking lot. The water was cold, most of the way up her shins. She splashed across the pavement to a passage between the main office and the motel proper. A set of stairs climbed to the second floor. Her boots squelched as she ascended them. At the top of the stairs, she turned right, following the walkway that wrapped around the front of the building. Despite the rain pouring from the front of the cap, she could see the door to Room 211 open ahead. Louise's men weren't leaving anything to chance. They would be fast; she would have to be faster. Her sole advantage lay in the possibility Louise did not want her dead right away. She was at the doorway. She turned and entered it.

What happened next occurred with almost startling clarity. Maureen raised the gun in each hand to either side of her and squeezed the trigger. The pistols made a spitting sound, jerked slightly in her grip. The men flanking the doorway collapsed, one with a red hole in his throat, the other with a red hole in his cheek. Maureen swung the gun in front of her, to where Frank slumped forward in his chair, a man in a black turtleneck and jeans to his left, Louise—also in turtleneck and jeans—to his right, a bloody carving knife in her hand. Maureen shot the man in the chest and Louise in the chest. The man crumpled to the carpet. Louise stepped away from Frank. Maureen shot her again, also in the chest. Louise dropped the knife and sat. Pistols held out before her, Maureen advanced past Frank to the bathroom, through whose open door she saw a man in a black turtleneck and jeans rising from his seat on the edge of the bathtub, a .45 in his left hand. She shot him in the chest, the silencer on the right pistol puffing apart, sending washers pinging off the tiled floor and walls. The man tried to retreat, backed against the edge of the tub, fell into it, and did not rise. Guns leading the way, Maureen exited the bathroom.

She approached Frank, whose torso was covered in a sheet of blood from, she saw, the ear to ear cut Louise had made to his throat. Covering the room with the .38 in her right hand, she brought her left behind her and slid that pistol inside the waist of her jeans. With her free hand, she felt Frank's bloody neck for a pulse. There was none.

Maureen moved her hand to Frank's shoulder and lowered her head. The acrid smell of gunpowder mixed with the metallic odor of blood. Riding the adrenaline coursing her veins, grief rushed over her. Blood dripped and pattered from the chair to the carpet. Rain blew in the open door. A part of her mind was telling her she had to go, she'd been too late for Frank but at least she had ensured she wouldn't have to watch for Louise in her rearview mirror. Likely, after she murdered Maureen, Louise had planned on the storm destroying the motel, if not carrying the bodies of her husband and his mistress out to sea, then confusing the means of their deaths for anyone who cared to investigate. The same plan could work for Maureen, provided she wasn't here when the waves and wind brought the building down. She lifted her hand from Frank's shoulder to touch his hair.

And started back as his head jerked up. A horrible bubbling wheeze filled the air, the sound of someone attempting to breathe through a throat that had been slashed. Maureen dropped her gun, dug in the front pocket of her jeans for her clasp knife. Frank rocked weakly from side to side, struggling against his bloody bindings. She opened the knife, grabbed the topmost loop of rope, and sawed at it. The wheezing continued. She cut the next loop down, the two below that, and the remainder of the rope slackened, slithering to the carpet. Before Maureen could catch him, Frank pitched forward. She shoved the chair out of the way and knelt beside him, casting the knife aside so she could grab his shoulders and turn him over.

The wound to his neck gaped. (Was this why she couldn't find a pulse there?) His eyes bulged, his lips trembling with words he could not voice. "Shh," Maureen said. "It's all right." Which it most decidedly was not. Given the opening in his throat and the volume of blood he had lost, she could not understand how Frank could possibly be alive, nor could she imagine the story she was going to tell at whatever hospital she sped him to. As for how this was going to complicate her already complicated escape plans…

She heard movement behind her. In an instant, she had the .38 out from the waistband of her jeans and turned with it pointing at Louise Westerford, who was using the bed to pull herself to standing. Maureen considered shooting her again, hesitated. The front of Louise's black turtleneck was sodden with blood. When the older woman pressed her hand to it, her fingers and palm came away crimson. She stared at Maureen with her large blue eyes and said, with some measure of astonishment, "That hurt."

"It's called being shot," Maureen said, and squeezed the trigger. Having outlived its brief lifespan, the silencer did not muffle the BANG. Louise's head snapped back as a hole opened in the center of her forehead. There was surprisingly little blood. She closed her eyes, but remained standing. A moment passed, and then she said, "You are making it difficult for me not to kill you." She opened her eyes, and they were white, smooth marble orbs.

"What the fuck?" Maureen said, and aimed the gun at her again.

"Don't bother." Louise waved her bloody hand, and the pistol was wrenched from Maureen's grip and thrown across the room.

"What the fuck?" Maureen said.

"Oh, you have much bigger concerns," Louise said. "Why don't you check your beloved's heartbeat?"

Fearing him suddenly inert, Maureen glanced at Frank, who regarded the scene with the same wonder and horror as she. "He's fine. Well, except for where you tried to cut his fucking throat."

"I did not 'try' anything," Louise said. "I sliced his major blood vessels and windpipe. Go on. Tell me what his heart rate is."

Maureen touched Frank's neck, but still couldn't find anything. She caught his left arm, pressed her fingertips to his wrist. Nothing there, either, or from his other wrist. Finally, she leaned down and pressed her ear to his blood-soaked chest. It was silent. She lifted her head and looked at Frank, whose expression said that he, too, could not detect his heart's beating. She looked at Louise. "What is this?"

"Revenge," Louise said, "on my faithless husband and the woman with whom he betrayed me. Someone I hired," she added, her tone thick with contempt.

Wind gusted into the room, bringing with it a spray of rain that swept around Louise and splashed against the ceiling. How had Maureen ever thought this woman frail, weak? The very air surrounding her was different, darker. Maureen remembered the room in which she had met Louise to review her findings concerning Frank, the big leather books with their Latin titles, the crystal ball on its metal stand ornamented with devils, and said, "You're a witch?"

"Please," Louise said. "What I am is someone who has spent a lifetime mastering knowledge that was old when the ice sheets weighted the land. I have given more of myself than you can conceive to learning secrets that would crisp your nerves, char the bones inside you."

"Then why did you bother hiring me? Couldn't you have kept an eye on Frank, yourself?"

"My energies were required elsewhere," Louise said. "In general, I've found money as efficient a means of achieving my ends as the arts of the left hand. Your reputation was impeccable. I was concerned my rivals might attempt to strike at me through my husband. It seemed simpler to employ you to monitor him than to divert the strength necessary for me to do so, personally. Little did I know." She barked a laugh.

"Okay," Maureen said, "but once you did know, couldn't you have let him go gently? Did you have to hurt him like this?"

"Yes I did. Within my community, I have a certain standing to maintain. This does not include my husband committing adultery with a hireling. Beyond that, I loved him." Louise shook her gory head. "I loved him with everything I had. You cannot sully such a gift, you cannot spit on it and drag it through the mud and expect there to be no consequences."

"How self-righteous."

"I do not have to justify myself to you, of all people." White fire danced over her blank eyes. "I am the one who was wronged."

"So it's one down, one to go, is that it?"

"It's this entire miserable town to go."

"You're serious."

"I will not be satisfied until this place has been swept from the face of the Earth."

"The storm—"

"Yes."

"Jesus," Maureen said, not irreverently. "And Frank?"

"Will stay as he is. The waves will take him far from here, out to where the water is deep. There, he'll float while the water softens his flesh and the creatures of the sea consume him, all the while conscious of his slow devouring."

"I assume you're planning a similar fate for me."

"Oh yes," Louise said. "Unless—"

"Unless what?"

"I wonder what you would do to spare your beloved further suffering?"

"What do you mean?"

Louise flicked her right hand, and the carving knife she had been holding when Maureen entered the room lifted off the carpet and wobbled through the air to hang in front of Maureen, serrated blade down. She tensed, ready for the weapon to point at her and attack. "Go on," Louise said, "take it."

Still suspicious, Maureen reached out and caught the carving knife's pebbled hilt. When her fingers closed on it, whatever force had been suspending the blade released it. "All right," she said, "what now?"

"Cut your throat."

Maureen's stomach dropped. "What?"

"Press the edge of the knife to the left side of your neck and draw it across to the right. I doubt you'll be able to open the windpipe, but you should have no trouble with the major blood vessels."

"You aren't kidding."

"I am not."

Even through the blood streaking it, Maureen could see how sharp the blade's teeth were. She looked at Frank, who was watching her and Louise's exchange with an expression of terror. Her lips dry, Maureen said, "If I do?"

"Then Frank will be released."

"What happens to me?"

"This isn't about what happens to you; it's a test of your feelings for your beloved. Who knows, though? If you open your veins, I might decide this town has suffered enough."

"And if I don't accept your offer?"

Malice lit Louise's features. "Perhaps I'll let you live."

"You will? Why?"

"For this to be a true test of your commitment to Frank, your possible fate cannot be a factor. You might obey my request simply to spare yourself further suffering. Let's remove that from consideration."

"What about revenge? What about your standing in your community?"

"I trust the condition of this town has not escaped you. I know the condition of my husband has not." Louise smiled without humor. "Anyone who learns of either of these acts will be reminded that I am not to be trifled with. As for vengeance, if you understood anything of it, you would realize that the choice I am offering you is a far superior version of it than ripping the flesh from your bones."

Louise was right. If Maureen took the knife to her throat, Frank would have to watch her. Presumably, Louise would keep him alive until she had bled out, or was in the same half-life as he. That would be the sight he would take with him into death, the last of days of abuses. Maureen would have committed herself to who could say what? Nothing good, that much was certain. On the other hand, if she walked out the door, crossed the street, got into her car, and drove away, Frank would be abandoned by the woman for whom he had abandoned his wife, a betrayal he would take with him as the ocean carried him into its salty depths. Nor could Maureen expect to escape the consequences of such a decision, the guilt that would empty her as thoroughly as a coroner at an autopsy. She could practically see the empty Stoli bottles, the containers of sedatives spilled on her kitchen counter, Glock out on the coffee table, a round in the chamber.

"Well?" Louise said.

Surely, there was a third option, an avenue she had overlooked in the insanity of events. Was she close enough, fast enough for a lunge at Louise? Would—could it succeed? The leaking hole in Louise's forehead strongly suggested it could not. Was the attempt worth it anyway, as a last gesture of defiance? Where would that leave Frank, though? She glanced at him, at his savaged body. He was trying to tell her something, his swollen and bloody lips mouthing a silent syllable. *Go?* She wasn't sure.

"You can't prolong this forever," Louise said.

"This is part of the revenge, isn't it? The trying to decide."

"You're learning."

"You're a bitch."

"You're out of time. Make your choice."

On legs stiff from crouching beside Frank, Maureen stood. The carving knife was heavy in her hand. Her muscles tensed at what was to come next. Louise watched her with her blank, pitiless eyes.

ERRATA

Most of the errors in my books are my fault, either to begin with, or because I wasn't paying sufficiently close attention during the proofreading stage and missed something. The majority of readers are pretty forgiving of such slip-ups; although it seems there's always going to be someone to e-mail me explaining the difference between "insure" and "ensure" or between "principal" and "principle." (I can't decide if they're taking pleasure in correcting the English teacher, or if they're English teachers overly conscious of the scope of their powers and responsibilities.)

Without doubt the strangest example of this kind of e-mail appeared in my in-box about a month after the publication of my second novel, *The Fisherman*. Instead of identifying the usual sorts of errors, this writer (a Mr. Jyotisha of Seattle) took me to task for something new. The typography of page 85 of my novel was, he wrote, an utter and absolute disgrace, rendering the text all but indecipherable. Whoever had been responsible for laying out the page, he went on, appeared to have done so on top of another piece of printed material, an error he could not comprehend in this day and age of digital everything. Lest I think he was engaging in some form of bizarre jest, Mr. Jyotisha had attached a photo of the offending page of his book. Without considering whether it might be safe to do so, I clicked on the file. (In my defense, if this was a form of phishing or other e-scam, it was pretty specific.)

The image was pretty much what had been described, the words of my novel printed over other text. The resolution on the picture wasn't great, but it looked as if what lay beneath this section of my novel was a mix of words and images, the former elongated characters too narrow to be runes (though that was what they reminded me of), the latter sets of concentric rings scattered around the page. The effect of the under-text on the sentences floating over it was weird, difficult to describe. Where the long characters intersected my words, they seemed to pull them into bizarre, semi-abstract patterns that reminded me of pictographs; while the rings under my words seemed to bend them into one another, blending them into strange new lexemes.

I closed the file and reached for my copy of *The Fisherman*. I'll admit, when I turned to page 85, I was half-expecting to find the jumble I had been looking at repeated, an error of such magnitude I couldn't imagine how I could possibly have let it slip past me. (The perils of the same overactive imagination that had led to me writing the novel, I suppose.) In my book, however, the page was fine. The best thing for me to do, I decided, was to forward the e-mail to my publisher, Ross Lockhart, and see if he could work something out with Mr. Jyotisha, maybe send him another copy of the book. This I did, cc'ing Mr. Jyotisha in my e-mail to Ross.

As I didn't hear from either reader or publisher, I assumed the matter settled. At some point thereafter, I must have deleted Mr. Jyotisha's e-mail, because when I searched for it this past month, it was nowhere to be found. The reason I had gone looking for the message had to do with another book Ross had published, Orrin Grey's new collection, *Guignol & Other Sardonic Tales*, which I was reviewing for *Locus*. (From what I read of it, it's terrific.) When I arrived at page 94, I initially thought that the weird page layout was part of the story I was reading. For I'm not certain how long, I stared at the narrow characters branching among Orrin's words, making them parts of odd figures, the circular distortions warping his sentences into long curves of letters that almost cohered into new words, before I connected what was in front of me and the e-mail I had received a little more than two years before. When the lightbulb glowed over my head, I set the book down and turned to my computer. I was thinking I would compare what was on the page of my ARC with the photograph Mr. Jyotisha had sent me. But, as I've said, I could find no trace of the message.

While mildly annoying, this wasn't an especially big deal (nor much of a surprise: the number of e-mails whose deletion I've had cause to regret is embarrassingly [and frustratingly] large). Still, I thought I should drop Ross an e-mail, in case what had seemed a one-time printing glitch was in fact a sign of a more systemic and sustained problem. If nothing else, I figured he'd be amused by the coincidence of my encountering the same problem twice.

In the past, it's taken Ross a little bit of time to answer my e-mails, usually a few hours, once in a while as long as a day or two. On this occasion, his reply chimed in my inbox within five minutes. The subject line read, "Skype?" The message itself read "Give me ten minutes," which was followed by a number. I hadn't known Ross to engage in any form of video-conferencing, which is to say, I hadn't known him to engage in it with me, so I didn't see anything too unusual in his request. I propped my tablet on my writing desk (these days, my desktop's too old and unreliable for much beyond word-processing and basic internet surfing), opened Skype, and waited.

The video feed, when I accepted it, was poor. The picture kept freezing, then lurching into motion that was a half-second or so behind what Ross was saying. "John!" he said.

"Hey Ross," I said. "What's going on?"

"These books of mine," he said with a laugh. At least, I think that's what he said: a buzzing echo made him difficult to understand.

"Yeah," I said, "it's pretty weird. Do you have any idea what happened?"

Ross's eyes bulged, his face stilled. A long burst of feedback threatened to cohere into a sentence in a deep, rasping tongue. When the picture returned to motion, Ross was in the midst of speaking: "—from that church, or the one he found in the crypt beneath it."

"I'm sorry," I said, "I missed the first part of what you were saying."

Another blast of noise, this one sufficiently loud to make me wince and lean back from the tablet. Ross's face was caught in a rictus of either manic laughter or rage. Then he was talking, his features calm: "—because Norway doesn't have a formal extradition policy with the US, so he thought he'd be safe there." He shook his head. "You can file that one under irony.

"When I left to start Word Horde, I assumed I'd be okay, which seems pretty stupid, now. But at the time, I still didn't believe what he'd told me, not really. I was more concerned about money. I had the job at the bookstore to help pay the bills, but that might not be enough, depending on what happened. Anyway, there was one night, my last month working for the two of them, I stayed late to finish the cover design and layout for a book I was pretty sure wasn't going to be published. For a moment, I was positive there was someone staring at me through one of the windows. I looked up, and saw a face…"

"A face?" I said.

"I don't know," he said at last. "There was no way anyone could have been on the other side of the window, because we were four stories up. At least, that was what I thought. Now…"

"Wait," I said, "what did you see?"

"It could have been a mask," Ross said, "made out of some kind of paper, vellum or something. The surface was faded in spots, smeared with dirt. There was moss growing on one cheek, into one eye. The other eye was dull, cloudy. The face was wrinkled…" He glanced away, exhaled. "All of it was…wrong. The worst part—" A humming buzz replaced whatever he was about to say next. The video feed stuttered, Ross's face shuttling among half a dozen expressions. The sound went on for so long, I thought I was going to have to end the call. The connection righted itself in time for me to catch him saying, "—with a sacred book, any kind of textual mistake would have a real world effect. Think of this thing as a kind of errata made flesh or…whatever.

"Like I said, though, I didn't believe any of what I'd been told. I took the face at the window for a trick of the light, a consequence of too much time staring at Nick Gucker's cover art. If a little part of me wondered whether there might be some truth to Jason's story, I assumed I was safe. I mean, he was the one who'd removed the page from the book, not me.

"I'm still not sure how he…transferred the thing to me. I did have to fill out some paperwork when I left. I flipped through the packet, but I didn't read all of it. Who does? Maybe some page in there assigned the thing to me. How trite, right? I can't believe I would have fallen for something so hackneyed, so clichéd. I mean, it's a digital era: come up with something new. Whatever, it was a hell of a severance package.

"It took me a while to figure out what was happening. I had to see that vellum face another—" Although his mouth continued moving, a low buzz replaced the next several sentences.

"Ross," I said, "I'm having trouble—"

The audio cut back in, Ross going on as if he hadn't heard me (which made me wonder if the problems with the connection went both ways). "The idea was to disperse it," he said, "spread it among dozens, hundreds of books. The effects on the individual reader would be negligible. As long as they weren't exposed to more than one of the exits, they probably wouldn't notice anything."

Struggling as I was to assemble the fragments I had heard into a coherent narrative, Ross's words sent ice water down my spine. "Wait," I said. "These exits—what if someone saw two of them?"

"That could be a bit of a problem," Ross said with an apologetic smile. "Each successive exit has an exponential effect on the one before."

"I don't understand what that means," I said.

A tumult from the closet to my right made me jump out of my chair, heart leaping. The lower portion of the closet is crowded with stacks of books, overflow from my office's five bookcases. Three of those paper towers had fallen over, in the process dragging a pair of brown slacks and a white shirt down from the clothes rack above them, pushing open the closet door. Shirt and pants formed a flat, headless figure that looked as if it had lunged out of the closet toward me. A coincidence, but unnerving all the same.

When I glanced back at the tablet, the screen had gone black. Ross's voice said, "I'm really sorry," and cut out. I pressed the power button a couple of times, to no effect. (Later, the repair guy in town would tell me the device was hopelessly dead, its circuits melted. "What'd you do to this?" he asked; I had no good answer for him.)

Since then, despite numerous attempts, I haven't been able to contact Ross. He hasn't replied to my e-mails, my Facebook messages, or my direct messages on Twitter, this despite him maintaining a relatively active presence on social media, posting pictures of his dog, his day job at the bookstore, the books he's going to be publishing. I made an attempt to locate Mr. Jyotisha, which was no more successful. I couldn't bring myself to finish Orrin's collection, which is a shame, because what I had read, I enjoyed. But I couldn't bear to open the book again, even if what Ross had told me was patently ridiculous, impossible. There's a bookcase in the lobby of our local post office where you can donate and pick up used reading material. I contemplated recycling *Guignol* there, only to decide against doing so, my excessive imagination prompting me to place the book in one of my bookcases, between my copy of Laird Barron's *Occultation* and M.R. James's *Selected Stories*.

The same overactive faculty must be why I saw the face in the bathroom window two nights later, as I was rinsing my toothbrush. It was as Ross had described it: dun-colored, the left cheek and eye furred with moss, the entire surface mapped with wrinkles. He hadn't mentioned the tremendous rage, the sheer hatred the thing projected through the glass—my addition to the text, I suppose. The window was empty almost the moment I registered the face, but the resulting shock was enough to send me hurtling out of the bathroom and upstairs to bed without performing my usual nightly duties, rinsing whatever dishes remain in the sink and setting up the next morning's coffee. When my wife remarked on this the next morning, I didn't know what to tell her. I'd seen a scary face at the bathroom window?

A day or so after that, I received an e-mail from Arley at *Locus* headquarters, asking if I'd like to have a look at a couple of Word Horde's forthcoming titles. Something thumped in the hallway outside my office door. Heart in my throat, I stood to check it. Of course, the hall was empty. Although I had been eagerly looking forward to Carrie Laben's first novel, I wrote Arley that I would have to pass.

NATALYA, QUEEN OF THE HUNGRY DOGS

In Memoriam Lucius Shepard

I

When it came, Hunter's e-mail was brief, blunt. "Well," it read, "that's wife number three packed her bags and gone. Said she cared too much to watch this thing have its way with me. Pity. If she'd stuck it out a little longer, she'd have done quite well for herself. She may still. I haven't told the lawyers. Anyway. The doc says it's a matter of weeks, at most. Why don't you come up for a couple of days? Bring a bottle of something good. Maybe two. You know the way."

"What should I do?" Carl asked his wife after she had read the message over his shoulder.

"You mean you aren't going?" Melanie said.

"No, I am going."

"Then what…Ah. You don't know how long you'll be there."

"He shouldn't be on his own. Not now."

"Doesn't he have a daughter?"

"They haven't spoken for fifteen years. She stopped talking to Hunter when he married the second time. I suppose it's never too late, except it almost is."

"What about his brothers and sisters? Isn't he one of four?"

"They don't talk much. There's one brother he's on good terms with, but he lives in Austria."

"Well, it isn't as if he's alone."

"Nurses aren't the same as family."

"You aren't family."

"I'm close enough."

Melanie sighed. "You have coverage at the dojo?"

He nodded. "Indrani can do the 4:30 classes, and I'm pretty sure Tara and Jeff can teach the 5:30's. The only day I'm not certain about is Saturday. I'll have to call Carmen, see if she's available."

"You should take the Subaru. I'm pretty sure I read something about there being snow on the ground in Vermont already."

"Will do. And babe?"

"Yeah?"

"I love you."

"Of course you do."

II

Of the many stories Hunter Kang had shared with him over three decades of friendship, the one Carl Kimani returned to as he packed for the trip to South Burlington was that of Hunter's first death. "Not near death," Hunter had said. "Death. I was gone for at least five minutes before I was revived." They had been sitting at a booth in Pete's Corner Pub in Huguenot, drinking Heinekens, after a particularly grueling workout at their karate school. They had known one another six months.

"What happened?" Carl said.

"Riptide," Hunter said. "My dad decided to take the family to the Jersey shore. This was after my little sister died—I told you about Natalie, right?"

Carl nodded.

"That's right, I did. We had been in mourning for, it must have been a year by then. Dad packed us into the van, including Mom, who insisted she didn't want to go, and drove to Point Pleasant. Sprang for three rooms

144

at the Neptune motel, one for him and Mom, one for my older sisters, and one for me and my little brother. It was…" Hunter shook his head, smiling. "Man, it was fantastic. One of the best things my old man ever did. Maybe the best. We spent our days at the beach, with a break at lunchtime for subs at a deli a couple of blocks away. At dinner, we had pizza or hamburgers, and were allowed to watch TV in our rooms until 11:00, which was unheard of. You remember *Simon & Simon?*"

"Sure."

"That was the first time I ever saw that show. I loved it. Anyway, our second to last day at the beach, I swam into a riptide. The next thing I knew, I was being carried away from everybody, out to sea. I didn't know what to do. I tried swimming toward shore, but I wasn't strong enough to keep myself in place, let alone fight my way to the beach. I started to panic. It wasn't long before I was screaming for help, waving at the rest of my family. At first, they thought I was showing off. By the time they realized what was happening, I was going under.

"If you were forced to pick a way to die, drowning isn't the worst. Don't get me wrong, it's pretty bad at the start. You thrash and cry, struggling to keep the water out of your mouth and nose. In what seems like a matter of seconds, though, you're overcome by a feeling of tremendous peace, and you let the process that's started, continue. After I went under for the final time, I looked at the water around me, which was this luminous blue, and thought this was the color of death, and it was beautiful. Even at this age—we're talking eleven years old—I was aware that what I was experiencing was a kind of gift, not like what Natalie had been through, the year before.

"My sister Vicky was the one who reached me first, and not my other sister, Heather, which was strange, because Heather was on the swim team at her high school, and Vicky was captain of the chess club. Vicky also knew that the way out of a riptide is not to swim against it, but sideways to it, parallel to the shore, until you're free. This was what she did. As she was turning toward the beach, Heather joined her, and together, my sisters brought me in. When they delivered me to my dad, though, I was dead. No heartbeat, no breathing. If you could have hooked me up to an EEG, I'm sure it would have showed no brain activity.

"For what might have been the first time in his life, Dad froze. Here was a man who had immigrated to the US from Busan with a degree in graphic design and a bank account with just enough in it to let him live outside LA for three months. At the end of six weeks, he had a job with a small advertising company; within six years, he was chosen to head up their office in West New York. During that time, he met my mom, which meant dealing with her parents. Let me tell you, however progressive their voting record, when it came to whoever was dating their Lily, Grandpa and Grandma McMaster were not terribly thrilled with their daughter dating and then becoming engaged to an Asian. Apparently, Grandma said to her, 'Marriage is hard enough as it is. Why do you want to complicate it?' Nice, huh? But the two of them stuck to their guns, and when Dad moved east, he took his wife and young daughters with them. Together, they built a life for themselves in Jersey. The family expanded, two boys and another girl. At five, his youngest daughter was diagnosed with a rare form of bone cancer, which took two agonizing years to kill her. Throughout all of it, he had remained steadfast. Mom called him her rock, and I think the rest of us viewed him that way, too. Now here I was lying lifeless in his arms, a second child lost within the span of twelve months. It was too much.

"Fortunately for everyone, my mom hauled me away from him and dropped me onto the sand. She pumped my chest, turned me on my side to help the water pour out, rolled me on my back, pinched my nose, blew two breaths into my lungs, and started a set of chest compressions. My sisters, my brother, my father gathered around us, along with some other people who had witnessed Vicky and Heather dragging me out of the surf. One of the bystanders ran for a lifeguard (who, needless to say, were fucking useless). Dad started to speak to Mom, words to the effect of, 'Honey, he's gone,' but she stopped him with a look that killed the sentence in his mouth. She labored over me. She pressed down on my sternum one two three four five times, switched to my head to fill my lungs, went back to working on my heart. The seconds advanced, each one carrying me that much further from her, but my mother's pace did not slacken. She was a dentist—did I ever tell you that? Met my dad when he came in with an abscess. Romantic, eh? She was six years older than he was. Packed up her practice in San Marino and opened a new one in Jersey City, while managing a steadily-expanding family. When Natalie was given her diagnosis, Mom brought in a second and third dentist so she could spend the maximum time possible with her. She took my sister's death hard—not that the rest of us didn't, but with Mom, it seemed almost personal, as if death had targeted her child, in particular.

"Well. Mom put all of her effort—her concentration, he strength, her will—into her fight with the Grim Reaper. It was as if she was prying his grip from me one bony finger at a time. Right as the ambulance pulled up in the parking lot, I opened my eyes and sucked in a gigantic breath. Heather shrieked. Dad burst into tears. The EMTs insisted on taking me to the hospital, which my parents agreed to. Mom rode in the ambulance with me. Dad followed with everyone else in the van. On the way there, as the EMT was fussing over me, Mom leaned in close and whispered, 'You know what happened to you.'

"I nodded. The fact of my death felt too enormous to fit into words; it crowded the back of the ambulance with us.

"She glanced at the EMT, and when he looked away to check something, she said, 'Did you see anything?'

"I knew what she was asking. I nodded again. 'Natalie,' I said.

"Mom inhaled sharply. 'Really?'

"'Really,' I said. 'She was glowing—she was surrounded by yellow light. She was wearing the Hello Kitty T-shirt she liked, the purple one, and her favorite jeans. She held out her hand to me, said where she was was beautiful and peaceful. That's all I remember. The next thing I knew, I was sitting up on the beach.'

"'Oh, baby,' Mom said. She sat back, one hand over her mouth, her eyes full of tears. 'Oh.' If the EMT noticed, which I'm sure he did, then I'm also sure he thought she was overcome by what had almost happened to me. He was half-right. She didn't ask me anything else, not there, not during the day I spent in the hospital, not during the trip home. In fact, she never mentioned what I'd described to her again. But after that, I had the sense she wore her grief for my sister more lightly, as if it were no longer a heavy coat, but a light scarf."

Hunter raised his hand. "Before you ask, because how could you not, no, I did not see my little sister in a full-body halo. She did not speak to me. You want to know what I experienced while I was dead? Nothing. One moment, I was floating underwater, my vision closing off, and the next I was on the beach, coughing up the water still in my lungs. In between was a blank. It wasn't like being asleep. I had no sense of the passage of time, no sense of anything. I simply...wasn't.

"Of course, I couldn't tell my mom any of that. I knew what she wanted to hear—what she needed to hear. So, I told her. I lied, but I think the lie made the rest of her life easier. When she was dying, she was at peace with it. On her deathbed, she told my sisters Natalie was coming for her."

After a sip of his beer, Carl said, "Not to play devil's advocate…"

"What?"

"The kid who went to twelve years of Catholic school would argue you didn't see the next life because you weren't heading there. It wasn't your time."

"I was dead. That sounds like it was my time."

"Not if God didn't want it to be."

"Yeah, well, tell your inner Catholic child to come talk to me after he's been dead for five minutes. Then we can compare notes, talk about what God wants."

III

On a clear, cold Wednesday morning in early November, Carl took I-87 from the Beacon-Newburgh exit north to Route 7, on the other side of Albany, which he followed east out of New York into Vermont. Once he was over the border, he turned north again with 7, driving along the western edge of the state, toward South Burlington, a place Hunter had declared among the most civilized small cities he had spent time in, with the perfect proportion of bookstores and good restaurants, and within easy distance of Canada, his second favorite country. "Although," he had added recently, "the way things are going here, it's edging closer to the top spot." He had purchased a large house set on a hill a couple of miles southwest of the city, whose surround of evergreens did not diminish the view of Lake Champlain with the Adirondacks beyond from its windows. The fruit of Hunter's years as a photojournalist, as well as of a handful of prudent investments, the house was a source of mild envy for Carl, whose lodgings had not exceeded the modest Cape he and Melanie had purchased two decades prior, and which was, now that the girls were at college, plenty big enough for the two of them, especially with the garage converted into a study. But a big house, a spacious residence of the kind his friend had purchased to mark his semi-retirement from documenting the horrors of the world's worst war zones, had been Carl's fantasy since a childhood spent sharing fifteen hundred square feet of raised ranch with his parents, older brother, and younger sisters.

When he expressed his jealousy to Melanie, his wife reminded him that Hunter's abode had been paid for by bullets zipping past him, once pinging off the helmet he almost never wore, not to mention, by threats from local warlords and field commanders, a few of which had drawn perilously close to coming true. His Pulitzer, his books, his house had been earned risking his life to show the world sights it didn't want to see, but needed to. All of which was true, nor had success curdled Hunter's personality. He was essentially the same guy Carl had met when they started karate classes together in their early twenties, at the Double Dragon Dojo in Poughkeepsie. The principal difference in Hunter these days, as he himself liked to say, was that he could afford the top-shelf single malt he preferred. (In fact, he was part owner of a small distillery somewhere in Scotland; Carl couldn't remember its name.) Yet this did little to dilute the green which tinted Carl's eyes when he thought of his friend's house. As far as he was concerned, if you had to select a location in which to live out your last days, Hunter's was about as good as any.

Or so he thought. He wondered if Hunter shared his opinion, if he spent his time conscious of the understated beauty surrounding him, or if the prospect of his impending end, the one he already had had a taste of, chased all other concerns from his mind.

Without warning, Carl found himself remembering his first and only HIV test, taken at twenty-three, when he was not long out of a relationship which had given him a case of the crabs cured over one long night and trust issues which would require longer to treat. Over a pitcher of cheap beer, he had relayed the tale of his ex-girlfriend and her infidelities to a co-worker at the Office Max he was then assistant-managing. Instead of the chuckle and expression of commiseration he was expecting, though, Porter had stared at him with concern. "Dude," he said, "please tell me you were using protection."

"At first, sure," Carl said, "but then she was on the pill."

"Have you been tested?"

"For what?"

"What do you think? AIDS."

"Oh," Carl said, "I don't think I—"

Porter cut him off. "You were having unprotected sex with a girl who was cheating on you with someone who passed on crabs to her. Who knows what else he might have given her?"

"But..."

"You really want to chance it?"

He didn't, and so Carl had gone to the Department of Health to have his blood drawn; although, self-conscious about meeting someone he knew there, he drove twenty miles up the Hudson, to the office in Wiltwyck. After sitting on a molded plastic chair in the waiting room, Carl was directed to a closet-sized office, where he sat on another uncomfortable chair while a nurse dressed in a brown pantsuit and cream blouse asked him questions about his sexual and drug-use history before instructing him to roll up his sleeve. She filled a vial with his blood, taped a cotton ball over the spot on his arm, and gave him a slip of paper with his ID number on it and told him his results would be ready in two weeks.

Carl had passed most of that time not thinking about the test and its possible outcome. In unguarded moments, though, he would recall his older brother's best friend, Wayne Ahuja, who had suffered with and then died from AIDS-related complications over the course of a year and a half. Ever skinny, Wayne had become positively skeletal as his health worsened, his skin yellowing from the cancer consuming his liver. Toward the end, he had lost vision in his left eye, and for reasons of which Carl was unsure, had started walking with a cane. Throughout his decline, Wayne had retained an exasperated sense of humor, complaining that he was dying as a result of a fling with a paralegal, and not a debauched weekend with Freddy Mercury. While he refused to be despondent—at least, publicly—about a month before he entered hospice care, Wayne said to Carl, "You know, I'm really going to miss not seeing Paris."

They were sitting on the back porch of Wayne's mother's condo in Beacon. Manny, Carl's older brother, was helping Mrs. Ahuja in the kitchen. It was a warm spring day, but Wayne was wearing a cardigan and a blanket draped over his shoulders. Carl said, "Paris?"

"I'm treading perilously close to stereotype, I know," Wayne said. "I can't help it. I've always loved France. When my father was alive, he used to fly to France for business. He always brought me a souvenir, a little Eiffel Tower, French comics. The way he described Paris made it sound like the most amazing, wonderful city. In high school, I took French 1, 2, 3, and 4, all with Madame McCarthy, who was a flake. My junior year, there was a class trip to Paris, but we couldn't swing it, financially. My first real crush was on an exchange student from Besançon my senior year; he was beautiful and totally clueless, just thought I was very friendly. I'll say. In college, I majored in French. One of my teachers, Claude, was from outside Paris, and I used to ask her about the city in my terrible French constantly. I watched every French movie Blockbuster had on the shelves. I read *The Stranger*, first in English and then (slowly) in French. A lot of poets, too, Rimbaud and Verlaine, Baudelaire, Valéry. I liked Baudelaire the best; Rimbaud always seemed like he was trying too hard to play the bad boy.

"Anyway, my plan was, once I finished college, I would work for a couple of years, stay with Mom to save money, and then spend a summer in Paris. I intended to hit all the tourist spots, the Eiffel Tower, Notre Dame, the Louvre, Shakespeare & Co. I fantasized about finding a job while I was there, but hadn't figured out how to make that happen. I wasn't concerned. I assumed I had time. You know what they say happens when you assume?"

"You make an ass of you and me," Carl said.

"There you have it."

That was the last conversation Carl had with Wayne; the next he saw him, his brother's friend was lying in his coffin in a funeral home in Fishkill. The final expression on his face suggested disappointment, as if, after his lengthy suffering, whatever Wayne saw approaching was anticlimactic. Carl remembered the look, made uneasy by what it suggested.

As the days slid by and the date of his test result approached, Carl noticed a sensation at the limit of his perception, not unlike the feeling of pressure his ears registered during a change in altitude. No amount of swallowing or yawning affected this pressure; indeed, it strengthened each day. He noticed, too, the people and objects around him outlined ever-so-slightly in black, as if they were comic book illustrations and he aware of the inker's hand. He recognized the connection between the sensation and the black haloes and understood both as by-products of his escalating anxiety. Yet he could not shake the suspicion that this was more than an elaborate hallucination, that he was perceiving these things more than inventing them. Perhaps they had always been present, waiting for a situation of sufficient duress to disclose them.

By the time Carl was driving Route 9 to the Rhinecliff-Wiltwyck bridge, he had decided that what he had grown aware of was death, was the void, the non-existence atop which everyone and everything sat like soap bubbles quivering on the surface of dark water. At any moment, an individual bubble might burst, or dwindle to nothing, and the remaining bubbles would shift to close the gap, and it would be as if the particular bubble had never existed. Crossing the bridge high over the Hudson, he felt himself as hollow as any mix of soap and water blown into a sphere, his life a momentary structure fated to collapse.

Threaded through this apprehension, however, was another, of the sheer loveliness surrounding him. From the mid-afternoon sunlight bright on the corrugated surface of the Hudson below, to the chrome shine of the bumper in front of him, from the fine hairs on the knuckles of his right hand resting on the steering wheel, to the long blades of green grass nodding on the other side of the road as he drove off the bridge, beauty met his eyes wherever he turned them. A long line of passengers waiting to board a Trailways bus for Manhattan might have been figures in a painting by Brueghel. The buildings on either side of Broadway glowed with Technicolor vibrancy. A group of children running home from school could have stepped fresh from Renaissance marble. The impression swelled like a great piece of music rising to a crescendo, in its own way as pitiless as the sense of death with which it was entwined. Lightheaded, he parked up the street from the Department of Health. He was in the grip of an experience more profound than any he had undergone since the death of his father two years before, a moment in some ways adjunct to the earlier one. It continued as he once again entered the small office, where a different nurse, wearing a green dress and a necklace of large green beads, passed him a piece of paper on which he read the word NEGATIVE. Nor did it cease upon his return to his car, where he sat with the engine off and let relief spill through him. Perhaps the imminent dread of death lessened somewhat, but his recognition of the glory of the world did not. It held steady, even climbed a few rungs higher. By the next day, it would diminish considerably; while the morning following returned him to normal.

After that, the closest Carl drew to perceiving the raw, unfiltered beauty around him were the births of his daughters. Random moments in the intervening decades offered glimpses of loveliness, but nothing to compare with what he had known during his swing into death's orbit. He wondered if Wayne Ahuja had known the same beauty as he was dying, if perceiving the world's grace was compensation for losing it, if the disappointed expression on Wayne's face post-mortem was because whatever came next could not approach the beauty he was leaving.

On his left, the ground dropped to Lake Champlain, across whose shining breadth the Adirondacks stood in a line like the wall to some unimaginable kingdom, their jagged heights draped in snow.

IV

Despite previous assurances to do so, Hunter had not paved the long driveway to his house. It was a nod to privacy, a complement to the No Trespassing signs nailed to the trees at the end of the drive; albeit, one easily overcome by anyone willing to take the quarter-mile rutted dirt slowly enough to avoid scraping their vehicle's undercarriage. For most of its course, the driveway ran between dense rows of tall red pine. Amidst the trunks to the right, Carl glimpsed a figure in jeans and a red jacket, a woman walking beside a golden retriever, who ran and gamboled about her. That didn't take long, he thought; although the woman could as easily be Hunter's doctor, checking her patient's status, or his lawyer, here to review details of his will. She could have offered to take out the dog as a kindness. Or maybe she's the reason his third wife left him. Hunter had always been charming, to put it mildly. In fact, it was a particularly credible threat from one woman's angry boyfriend that had brought him to train at the Double Dragon. His flirtations and an extended affair had strained his first marriage far past what Carl had been certain was its breaking point; the end of the same affair had undone marriage number two. With Hunter's third trip to the altar, Carl had wondered if his friend might be ready to settle, but it would hardly be surprising to learn that, even in the face of a terminal diagnosis, Hunter remained restless.

And what business is that of yours? Melanie might have been sitting in the car with him. *That isn't why you're here, is it?*

"No," he said.

The trees thinned and fell away, revealing the short hill atop which Hunter's house sat. The architect had been after something in the spirit of Frank

153

Lloyd Wright, and had constructed a long wooden box with a flat roof and a western wall composed of two stories of windows, which Hunter said made the place a bitch to heat during the Vermont winters, but offered stunning views of the lake and the mountains. The driveway climbed through tall grass to a pair of garage doors set in the hillside below the southern end of the house. An olive, late model Range Rover was parked in front of one of the doors, an older blue Volvo before the other. Carl tagged the Range Rover as Hunter's, the Volvo as belonging to his dog-walking guest. He stopped far enough behind the vehicles to allow either's departure. He retrieved the plastic shopping bag with the bottles of Auchentoshan and Talisker in it, and stepped out of the car for the walk up the stone steps to the front door. The air was cold and damp, brimming with the promise of snow.

Hunter opened the door as Carl was leaning to press the bell. "Hey!" he said, "You made it!" He looked terrible. The weight he had accumulated with his semi-retirement was gone, devoured by his sickness. He was as thin as he had been when he and Carl had met, thinner. A belt cinched on its last hole secured his jeans to his hips, while his blue and white flannel shirt enveloped him like a small tent. A faded blue baseball cap shielded a face drawn to the bone from the sun. Carl embraced him, and his friend felt insubstantial, more fabric than flesh. *It's as if he's already gone.* They released one another, and Hunter gestured at the shopping bag. "Is that what I think it is?"

"Water of life," Carl said.

"Bit late for me," Hunter said, "although I swear, it's what's brought me this far. You know how long the docs gave me? Three months. 'Put your affairs in order,' they said. 'This is gonna be quick.' That was nine months ago, almost ten, at this point. Who could have guessed? But come in, come in," he said, retreating inside the house.

Carl followed, passing along the front hall to the living room, a vast open space across which were scattered couches, love seats, and easy chairs, all upholstered in the same black padding, each oriented more or less toward the large flat-screen TV hung on the wall to the left. A doorway in the same wall led down another hallway, past a number of closed doors on the right, a wall of windows on the left, which showed the tops of the red pines and, beyond them, a shining stretch of Lake Champlain, a cluster of the Adirondacks. They emerged into the kitchen, which was centered around a sizable island whose grey and white marble top glowed with the afternoon light. Hunter continued to another doorway, which admitted to a smaller room, its walls lined with tall bookcases stuffed with volumes shelved without apparent regard to size, subject, or author. Facing the windows and their view, a pair of easy chairs in the same black padding as the living room furniture flanked a small table, atop which rested a pair of glass tumblers and a jug of water. Seating himself on the far side of the table, Hunter nodded at the glasses and said, "There you go. I'll trust you to decide which bottle we finish first."

"You don't think it's a little early?" Carl said. "Don't you want to have lunch?"

"Early was a long time ago," Hunter said. "I'll have Annie order us a pizza when she gets back. You like mushrooms? Don't worry about it. We'll order two pies. You can get what you want."

"Fair enough," Carl said. He removed the bottles from the bag, set them beside the glasses. "As I recall, you favor the Auchentoshan."

"You recall correctly, sir."

He poured three fingers' worth into one tumbler, reached for the water. Hunter raised his left hand. "Don't bother."

"Do I have to give the speech about how the drop of water unlocks the Scotch's flavors?"

"At this point, I prefer my experiences undiluted."

"If you insist." Carl placed the bottle on the table and settled into his chair.

"Ahhh," Hunter said, smacking his lips after his first taste. "This is the stuff."

"It's even better with the water," Carl said.

"You don't let up, do you?"

"Nope."

"Dying's looking better and better."

Carl sipped from his glass. "What's the latest on that?"

Hunter shrugged. "We're in the bottom of the ninth, two outs, two strikes. Not much longer to go. Maybe a week or two. Maybe less."

"You seem in pretty decent shape, all things considered."

"You mean, for a guy who's already a skeleton?"

"Is that what's different about you? I thought it was your hair."

"You're not wrong about that." Hunter removed his baseball cap, revealing a head rough with stubble.

"Chemo?"

"Yeah." Hunter returned the cap to his head. "I stopped a month ago, once the docs told me there wasn't any point. Had you seen me while I was that stuff, you would've had no trouble believing the end was nigh. Since I discontinued it, I feel pretty good. You know, for a guy who's on his way out. It's strange: this is what got my mom. I'm five years older than she was, but in the end, heredity won." Hunter raised his drink, frowned. "Goddamnit, why is this empty?"

"Hang on," Carl said, and poured him another generous portion of Scotch.

"Good man," Hunter said.

"Still a no on the water?"

"Why do you insist on asking questions you know the answer to?"

"Hope springs eternal, or something." Carl's glass was almost finished. He refilled it with less than he'd served Hunter, added a splash of water. Outside, on the lake, a boat was heading south. Exactly what type of vessel it was, he couldn't say, only that it was neither sailboat or speedboat. A yacht? Maybe. It appeared to be making good time; long waves rolled away from it in a v.

"What about you?" Hunter said. "How's Melanie? How're the girls? Everything okay at the dojo?"

"Good, good, and yes," Carl said. "Melanie's not long back from a trip out west to a couple of shows. She did pretty well at one of them, may have found a new outlet for her jewelry. Deb has one more semester to go at Binghamton, then she's looking at NYU for her master's. Art History. Karen's at community college, leaning toward nursing. We're up to a hundred and fifty students at the studio, give or take."

"That is good."

"I can't complain." Carl tipped his glass at Hunter. "Any word from—it was Jill, right?"

"Gillian, yes," Hunter said. "And no, nothing. You never met her, did you?"

"Once," Carl said. "At the party you had for your book, the one about New Orleans after Katrina."

"*American Atlantis.*"

"That one. Melanie came with me. She met Jill, too. She didn't like her."

"Your wife is a very perceptive woman. Which is why I've never asked you what she says about me."

"It's not all bad. She thinks you have a good eye."

"Coming from Mel, that's high praise."

"I take it Francesca hasn't been in touch."

"Believe it or not, she has. Nothing like your old man's imminent demise to bring you to his doorstep. She was here last week for a few days. I wouldn't call it a good visit, but I didn't expect it to be. She had a chance to say what she wanted to. Where I could, I explained and apologized. Not everything that's happened to her has been my fault. We left things about as good as we could."

"I'm sorry, man."

"At least I saw her."

"How about the woman I saw on my way in? Walking a golden retriever? Is she—did you say her name was Annie?"

Hunter nodded. "Her name is Antoinette, Antoinette Mazarine; although she prefers to be called Madame Sosostris. It's…her professional name, I guess."

"Exactly which profession is she in?"

"She's a psychic, fortune teller, that kind of thing."

"Oh."

"What—did you think she was a dominatrix?"

"Well, no, not exactly, but with Madame as her title, my thoughts were tending in that direction."

"Trust me, man, this cancer's kicked my ass as much as any masochist could want. And then some. No, Annie's here to help me with some other stuff."

"Such as?"

"Drink up," Hunter said, emptying his tumbler and holding it out for more. Sunlight turned the lake into a sheet of bronze, made the mountaintops burn white.

V

At some point thereafter, Carl looked at the Auchentoshan and saw that the bottle was empty. Simultaneously, he realized that he was drunker than he had been in years, since his last visit with Hunter, when the two of them had stayed up after his book release party drinking their way down a bottle of high-quality rum, which Hunter took straight, and Carl mixed with various leftover sodas. The next morning, much to Melanie's mingled amusement and irritation, he had suffered a hangover so blinding he crawled into the back seat of the car and lay there while she drove them home. "Melanie isn't here," he mumbled, the statement filling him with crushing sadness.

"What?" Hunter said.

"Nothing." With great care, he leaned over and lifted the Talisker from the table. He attempted to remove the seal from the cap, which proved a far more laborious task than he thought it should be. Finally, he peeled the last bit of plastic from the bottle's neck and twisted the stopper free.

"At last," Hunter said. "I thought I was gonna die of thirst."

"You live next to a lake," Carl said, amazed at his ability to pour the contents of the bottle into his friend's outheld glass.

"So?"

"So, there's plenty of water there." He gestured at the windows, outside of which, the water was dark blue, the mountains heaps of shadow crowned by clouds lit red and orange.

"And?"

"You said you were thirsty."

"Did I?"

Carl nodded.

"It's okay," Hunter said, hoisting his tumbler, "I have this."

"Oh," Carl said, "right. Although, maybe we should have some water."

"Water? What for?"

"To drink."

"There's a whole lot of water," Hunter said, taking his turn to point at the windows, "out there."

"Yeah," Carl said, "but..."

"But what?"

"We're almost—we—we only have one bottle left." He nodded at the

Talisker, whose contents were already noticeably diminished.

"Don't worry," Hunter said, "we can get more. There's a liquor store in town."

"Sure," Carl said, "but neither of us can drive. Not like this, in this state, this state of drunkenness." He was finding it difficult to express himself; he wasn't sure the words he was using meant what he wanted them to.

"Not us," Hunter said, "her."

"Who?"

"Annie. Sosostris. Madame. When she goes for the pizza, she can pick up another bottle. Or two. Or three. Better make it three."

"Oh. That's okay, then."

"See? Problem solved."

"Wait."

"What?"

"Did we order the pizzas?"

"Of course we did. Remember? Mushroom for me, cheese for you."

"I never said I wanted cheese."

"Well, why didn't you? It's too late to change now."

"No—I mean, I don't think we called anyone."

"We didn't. Madame Annie did."

Had she? Carl couldn't recall anyone entering the study after the two of them, but neither could he bring the last couple of hours into focus. "Are you sure?"

"Sure I'm…" Hunter's voice trailed off. "Wait. Damnit. Didn't we?" He placed his glass on the gable. "Tell you what. One more, and if the pizza isn't here, we'll go order it. Mushroom for me, cheese for you."

"Hawaiian," Carl said.

"What?"

"Hawaiian," Carl said. "Or maybe you call it Canadian. I know I had it in Canada. At a knock down tournament in Toronto. Ham and pineapple."

"On a pizza?"

"It's delicious."

"Ugh."

"That's what I want. It's delicious."

"Whatever you say."

"Hawaiian is what I say."

"I thought it was Canadian."

"Either way."

There was more conversation after that, but Carl couldn't keep track of it. Some of it involved Hunter lecturing. He was a great one for holding forth when in his cups, was Carl's friend. "The French call them…What do they call them? *Les fantômes de*…something." Hunter's one last drink turned into another two, or three, and Carl tipped a couple more servings into his tumbler, and the Talisker was done, which seemed an unbelievable, a ridiculous amount for the two of them to have consumed in a couple of hours. Except the view out the windows had gone dark, and the room's track lighting was glowing—had Hunter switched it on? or did the study have some kind of light sensor? or maybe that woman, Annie, had looked in on them and turned on the lights. Did it matter? No, what mattered was that their pizzas hadn't appeared. Which meant that someone hadn't delivered them. Or ordered them. No pineapple and mushrooms for them. From the windows, a pair of middle-aged men regarded them from the comforts of their padded easy chairs. Jesus, when did we become so old? Still holding his glass, Hunter heaved himself from his chair with such force he staggered forward a half-dozen steps, almost losing his balance before recovering. Waving for Carl to follow him, he staggered from the room; although Carl wasn't certain of his friend's destination, the kitchen or some other spot deeper within the house. Either way, his eyelids had grown incredibly heavy, as had the rest of him. Full of Scotch, he supposed. Who knew alcohol weighed so much? He set his tumbler on the table, closed his eyes, and unconsciousness rose over him in a flood.

VI

He woke needing to pee, urgently. On legs not fully awake, he lurched from the chair, swaying with the effort not to tip over. The room spun like a carnival ride winding down. Still drunk, he thought, though not quite as much as he had been. The utterly disconnected feeling had subsided, replaced by the sense of being on a one to two second delay, requiring the slightest bit more time to respond to his surroundings. There was a bathroom somewhere nearby. At different moments throughout the afternoon and evening, he and Hunter had risen to seek it out. On the other side of the kitchen, on the way to the living room. Third door on the left.

Though the kitchen seemed to have expanded dramatically since he had crossed it last, he succeeded in navigating to the hallway where the toilet was. His bladder relieved, he exited the room and continued along the hall to the living room, whose assorted seating was dimly visible in the moonlight falling through the windows. Whether Hunter had shown him his room, he couldn't remember, nor was he sure enough of his recall of the house's layout, especially drunk and in the dark, to want to search for it. He would crash on one of the couches. Before he did, he would have to venture out to the car for his bag.

As he exited the front door, a pair of lights clicked on to either side of it. The temperature had plunged; his breath vented from his mouth in a cloud. Mist floated near the ground. The steps to the driveway sparkled with frost; he descended them with care. At the foot of the steps, another set of lights, these positioned over the garage doors, snapped to life. Down here, the mist rose higher, denser, catching the light and holding it, submerging the cars in a lake of pale radiance. It was colder here, too. Gooseflesh raised up and down his arms. Carl hurried to the Subaru and lifted his bag from back seat. He shut the door, and caught something out of the corner of his right eye.

Standing near the edge of the woods, a child regarded him. The mist reduced it to an Impressionist blur, but its size suggested eight or nine. It appeared underdressed for the cold in a red T-shirt and jean shorts. A sleepwalker? From where? Did Hunter allow campers on his property? Who would want to spend the night outside in this weather? Carl took a step forward, halted. There was something else out there. Closer to the tree line, a pair of shapes paced back and forth, weaving in and out of the pines. Lean, low to the ground, they could have been mountain lions, except their trunks were too long, their legs spread to either side in a way that suggested a spider's limbs more than a big cat's. Their heads, too, something was off about the heads, a disfigurement the mist would not allow him to see clearly. They were too long. Fear icier than the air sliced through his intoxication. Could these be dogs? They didn't seem to be menacing the child, at least, not yet. He dropped his bag and felt in the front pocket of his jeans for the knife tucked there (ironically, a gift from Hunter). He considered calling the house on his cell, but his friend was likely to be deeply unconscious; nor was Carl certain of Annie's location. Knife retrieved, its blade unfolded, he advanced toward the child, his eye on the twin creatures behind it.

The closer he drew to all three, however, the harder they were to see. The mist thickened until only the glow of the lights at his back indicated direction. Left hand up in a guard, right ready to stab, he moved in small steps, sliding the soles of his sneakers over the ground to minimize an attacker's ability to knock him off his feet. "Hello," he said. "My name is Carl. I don't know if you can see me, but I'm walking to you. I don't want you to be frightened, but there are a couple of animals out here with us. They're probably just dogs, but I don't know them, so I think it's a good idea to be careful. Can you tell me what your name is?"

In reply, the air erupted in high-pitched laughter, like the lunatic cries of a pack of hyenas. Carl started, his heart hammering at the base of his throat. He stopped where he was. The hysterical yelps subsided, replaced by a new sound, the scrape of skin over dirt. Something was treading a wide circle around him; he was reasonably certain it was not the child. The hairs on the back of his neck lifted. He turned with the noise, doing his best to keep the knife aimed at whatever was producing it. Of course, a voice in the back of his brain said, this would be a good way to distract you from an attack to the rear. "One thing at a time," he murmured. Should have held onto the bag, could have used it as a shield. "Too late, now."

Without warning, the lights over the garage went out. Momentarily blind, Carl tensed, listening for the paws he was certain were about to run at him. None did. As his eyes adjusted to the dark, he saw that the mist had thinned to a fine vapor, and that he was at the edge of the woods. Of the featureless child, the strange predators, there was no sign. He stared into the trees, but if anyone was standing amidst their dim ranks, he could see neither them nor any animals.

For a second time, manic laughter filled the air. Glancing over his shoulder as he went, Carl retreated to his car, bending at the knees to retrieve his bag. Finally, the garage lights popped on. He was half-expecting to find the child standing at his elbow, one of the big predators ready to pounce, but there was no one there.

VII

Certain he would not be falling asleep any time soon, if ever, Carl dumped his bag next to the biggest couch in the living room before heading to the kitchen. Although his nerves were humming with adrenaline, he could feel the drag of the alcohol his system had not processed. He found a glass in one of the cupboards and poured and drank four and a half cups of water. Given how much Scotch he had imbibed, there was no way he was escaping a hangover, but he figured he would do what he could to minimize it. Depositing the glass in the sink, he returned to the living room, where he settled onto the couch. He had no idea what time it was, only that it was late, far later than he was accustomed to being awake these days. Old, he thought, you're so old.

The next he knew, he was climbing out of sleep, prompted once more by the urge to urinate. No time seemed to have passed, but a look out the windows showed the sky washed with faint light, herald to the dawn. He found the bathroom more easily this time, and forgoing modesty, left the door open while he peed. The chamber music echoed through the hall. While he was washing his hands, he heard mixed with the water's hiss another sound, what might have been the squeak of sneakers on the floor outside the bathroom. He shut off the tap and waited, listening.

Nothing. He dried his hands and walked to the kitchen. Another couple of glasses of water, then back to the living room, where the couch was waiting to receive him.

VIII

Breakfast smells (coffee, sausages, toast) and sounds (the stuttering burp of the coffee maker, the sizzle of oil in the pan, the ticking of the toaster) roused him to late morning sunlight. Head complaining at the effort, Carl sat up. It wasn't as if he hadn't seen this coming. At least he'd remembered to hydrate; otherwise, the hangover would have been mortal.

Hunter was waiting in the kitchen, standing at the stove cooking sausages in one pan and scrambled eggs in another. A gray tracksuit floated around him. Aside from a pair of sunglasses, he showed scant evidence of any effects of the previous day's excess. "Hey, Sleeping Beauty," he said, "how're you feeling?"

"About two steps from death," Carl said. "How is it you're even moving around?"

"Please," Hunter said. "You think that's the most I've ever had to drink? I tell you about the time I was in Chechnya, following a squad of Russian *spetsnaz*? Those guys spend all night working their way through a case of vodka, then are on the move at dawn, fighting by breakfast. If you want to run with them, you have to be able to keep up with them."

"I'm amazed your liver survived."

"Yeah, well, I did lay off alcohol for about a month after I came back from that assignment. What do you want to eat? Eggs? Sausage? Both?"

"For the moment, this'll do," Carl said, lifting the mug of coffee he'd poured. "I don't suppose you have any oatmeal."

"Yeah, there's a box of the instant stuff in the cabinet to my left. Apple and cinnamon, I think."

"That'll be fine, thanks."

They sat on high stools at the kitchen island, Carl with his coffee, Hunter with a plate of sausage and eggs. Through the windows, Carl watched a hawk skim the tops of the evergreens. "Actually," Hunter said through a mouthful of food, "that was among the drunkest I've been."

"No 'among' for me."

"Yeah?"

"I've never been what you'd call a heavyweight, but I've put away my fair share of booze. Not like that, though."

A smile broke over Hunter's face. "Good. I like the idea of our final visit being marked by a memorable event. You'll always be able to say, 'The last time I saw Hunter, we drank more Scotch than I ever had before or since.'"

"Couldn't we have gone out for a nice dinner, instead? Or a game of miniature golf, maybe?"

"Nah. Think of it as being like Vikings on the eve of a big battle, working themselves up for it."

"We're fighting a battle today?"

"What would you say if I said yes?"

"I'd say I wish I stayed home, sent you a nice card, instead: 'So long, nice knowing you.'"

"A card? Really?"

"A nice card. You'd love it. They'd show it off at your funeral."

"After I was killed in the battle you bailed on."

"It would be some card," Carl said. "Speaking of which, are you planning a memorial service?"

"Yeah," Hunter nodded. "Immediately after I go, there'll be a small gathering in Burlington, at one of the galleries. Then, in the spring, there'll be a bigger event down in Brooklyn, a retrospective of my work with remarks by a few of my friends and colleagues. If you're available…"

Carl's throat tightened. "Sure."

"Good. Thank you. I'm just about done writing your speech. I figured we could rehearse it later."

"What? You don't trust me to tell the truth?"

"That's exactly what I'm afraid of."

"So: what's the plan for today?"

"Finish your coffee," Hunter said. "You should probably have your oatmeal, too."

IX

After breakfast, Hunter led Carl to the guest room, which was on the other side of the study, up a flight of stairs and along a short hallway. "I'll see you for lunch," Hunter said. "I have some dying stuff to attend to."

"Right," Carl said.

The room was on the east side of the house, what Carl thought of as its back side. Instead of a wall composed of glass, a pair of regular-sized windows gave a view across an overgrown field behind the house to the tree line. Low hills rolled in the distance. Resisting the temptation of the queen-sized bed, Carl showered in the attached bathroom, dressed, and called home.

"How hungover are you?" Melanie asked.

"It could be worse," Carl said.

"That bad."

"Yeah."

"Did you leave any Scotch for today?"

"Technically, it was today when we finished the second bottle. I think it was, anyway."

"Wonderful. Well, I'm sure Hunter has more liquor, just in case there's anything left of your liver. How is he?"

"Honestly, he's in better shape than I was expecting. Don't get me wrong:

he's skin and bones, with an emphasis on the bones. But I imagined he'd be confined to bed, too spent to say much; instead, he's up making scrambled eggs and sausages this morning. As far as I can tell, he's as sharp as he ever was."

"He's led a pretty active life. He must have a lot to draw on."

"I think you're right."

"Has he said anything about his ex? Jill, was it?"

"Gillian, yeah. Not really—only that he hasn't heard from her. There's another woman staying here, Annie something. I saw her yesterday on the way in, walking the dog. I haven't met her, yet."

"Really."

"Apparently, she's a psychic. Hunter says she's here to help him. I don't know with what."

"I'll avoid the obvious remarks," Melanie said.

"I thought the same thing, but I'm not sure it's the case."

"Either way, Hunter's a big boy. Anything else going on?"

Carl hesitated, weighing a description of his early morning driveway encounter with the child and the weird animals. Already, though, the event seemed distant, dreamlike, if not a product of the Scotch, then colored by it. He settled for, "Not much. I ran into a couple of coyotes when I went out to the car for my bag." The instant the words left his mouth, he realized how false they sounded. Even through liquor-clouded lenses, the things he'd seen had not moved like coyotes. He remembered their strange, spread-eagled crawl, their elongated skulls. No, not coyotes, and not cougars, and not anything with which he was familiar.

"Holy crap," Melanie said. "What did they do?"

"Oh, they prowled back and forth in front of the woods for a minute or two, and ran away."

"Be careful. It's more wild up there."

"Yeah," Carl said, but he had an obscure feeling it was too late for caution.

X

There wasn't space for him to practice his morning (now afternoon) kata in the guest room, so once he and Melanie had said their good-byes, Carl made his way downstairs. He was considering finding a spot outside, but during the time he had spent in the guest room, clouds had thickened the sky, obscuring the Adirondacks and releasing torrents of snow. In the kitchen, he stopped to watch the crowns of the red pine swaying this way and that, as if engaged in a vast conversation about the snow accumulating on their branches. Behind him, a voice said, "It's supposed to last all day."

He turned, and saw a woman standing on the opposite side of the kitchen island. Late twenties, he guessed, dressed in a white cable knit sweater and jeans, her chestnut hair pulled back in a ponytail. On the marble in front of her, a number of oversized cards had been arranged in a circle—Tarot cards. The woman was holding the rest of her deck in her left hand. "Sorry," she said, "I didn't mean to startle you. I'm Annie."

"No need to apologize," Carl said. "I'm Carl. Hunter maybe said I was coming?"

"He did. I saw you on the driveway yesterday."

"You were walking a dog."

"Rufus, yes."

"Where is he? I haven't seen him at all since I've been here."

"Hunter's rehoming him with some friends. I took him over there yesterday afternoon."

"That's…oddly responsible of him."

"You aren't the first person to say that to me." Annie picked up the card at the top of the circle and returned it to the deck.

"Am I interrupting you? Because if I am, I can get out of your way."

"It's all right," Annie said. "I was done, anyway."

"I take it from the cards you're Madame Sosostris."

"Guilty as charged."

"What were you doing the reading for? Or can I ask you that?"

"I was—you might say I was checking on Hunter."

"And?"

"Your friend is very sick."

Carl nodded. "Yeah. A week or two, he said."

Annie lifted the last card from the island. Without looking at Carl, she said, "It's a little less. Days, really. If he passed this afternoon, I wouldn't be surprised. You shouldn't be, either." She placed the deck on the island.

"That's…" The words were a roundhouse kick to his unprotected head. "I mean, I knew he didn't have long. It's why I'm here. But I assumed we'd have a little time together. He's—he seems fine."

"Hunter possesses more willpower than any man I've ever encountered. I'm fairly certain that's what's keeping him going at this point."

"He's always been stubborn."

"Yes, I can believe it."

"We met in karate class," Carl said, crossing to the island. He slid out a stool and seated himself on it. "I don't know if he's mentioned this. There were some things he was good at right from the start. Free sparring, in particular: he was fast, and he was ferocious. He would hit you four times before you knew what was happening. The forms, though, the kata, were a challenge. He had a hard time remembering the sequences of moves, and then performing them at the proper pace. For some students, this would not have been a big deal. They would do whatever kata they were responsible for well enough to earn their next promotion, and that was that. Not Hunter. He wanted his forms to be perfect. Every time he made a mistake, it was back to the beginning, running through the form until he had it right, no matter how long that took. I used to practice with him after class was over. We would stay an extra hour, longer. While we were training, his focus was absolute. Those sessions made me a better martial artist. Without them, I doubt I'd have ended up with my own studio."

"He told me a version of that story," Annie said. "In it, he wants to go home, but you insist he keeps working until he does the form properly."

"Well, there may have been a little of that," Carl said. "What about you? How did you meet Hunter?"

"On a message board. He had some questions he was looking to have answered, and he reached out to me. We corresponded for about a month, then he invited me up here."

"Oh."

"I'm not sleeping with him, if that's what you're wondering."

"No," Carl said, glancing away. "I mean, it's none of my business if you are."

"You're right," Annie said, "it isn't. But I don't want anything distracting you from what we have to do."

"Which is?"

"Help him as he leaves this life."

"That's why I'm here."

"I'm not talking about another marathon drinking session."

"Thank God," Carl said, and smiled. "It's been years since Hunter and I discussed these things, but time was, he didn't have much use for notions of the afterlife. I'm guessing that's changed."

"Yes and no," Hunter said, entering the kitchen. He had changed from his gray track suit to a white long-sleeved T-shirt and jeans. His faded blue baseball cap perched on his head.

"Hey," Carl said.

"You're ready?" Annie said.

"Getting there," Hunter said. "First, my friend and I need to discuss a few things."

"We do?"

"Why don't you make yourself some lunch? There's plenty of stuff in the fridge." Hunter pulled a stool toward him and climbed onto it, adding, "I'm not hungry."

"All right," Carl said. "How about you, Annie? You want anything?"

"Thanks, I'm fasting."

While he was retrieving bread, cold cuts, and mustard from the refrigerator, Carl heard Hunter say, "Well?" and Annie reply, "It's as good a time as any. You see what's happening outside." Hunter said, "I take it you checked the cards." Annie said, "I did. Let's put it this way: it's a good thing your friend is here." Hunter grunted.

His smoked turkey and swiss assembled, a glass of milk poured, Carl resumed his place at the island. "So," he said to Hunter. "What is it you want to talk about?"

"It's my sister," Hunter said.

"Which one, Vicky or Heather?"

"Neither," Hunter said. "Natalie. The dead one."

XI

"Come again?" Carl said.

"I lied to you," Hunter said. "All those years ago, when I told you about me dying."

"Your first death."

"Yeah. Don't get me wrong, the drowning part was true. My heart stopped.

I was gone. My mother had to resuscitate me. The lie was me saying there was nothing after I died."

"Okay."

"I'm just gonna describe what happened," Hunter said. He swallowed, licked his lips. "Start with me underwater. My vision closing off, contracting to a single point. It was like the reverse of the stories about moving through a bright tunnel. I seemed to be traveling backwards along a dark passage, away from the light. Or, could be the light was moving, leaving me behind. It was a little frightening, but mostly, I was sad watching it go. I'm pretty sure the sensation of floating was the last thing I felt.

"And then I was on my hands and knees, gasping. I was no longer in the water. I was back on land. Not the beach, though. My fingers and knees were pressing into thick, grey mud. I was still wearing my swim trunks. I looked up, and saw the mud rising to a line of scrub grass. Overhead, dense grey clouds blocked off the sky. I stood, and glanced behind me. An enormous brown river, so wide its other shore was a distant line, flowed from left to right. Patches of mist hung above its surface, which swirled and eddied with competing currents. Despite that, I had the oddest impression I was watching a gigantic snake, something fit to wrestle Godzilla, sliding to a destination I didn't want to know. I turned and headed for the grass. The mud made it slow going; I kept tripping and almost tripping. I wasn't upset or scared—well, maybe some, at the prospect of a monster snake. What I mean is, I wasn't especially freaked out at slipping under the waves and opening my eyes next to a river. Could be, I was stunned, overwhelmed, but I mostly remember being curious about this place, which didn't resemble the afterlife I'd learned about in Catholic school. I knew enough Greek mythology to think of the River Styx, except there was no sign of Charon the ferryman, and the rest of the shore was empty.

"As I approached the grass, I saw stands of trees, birches. In their midst was a structure—when you were a kid, did you make forts out of old cardboard boxes? You know, big ones, like the kind an appliance comes in?"

"Sure," Carl said.

"What was in front of me was the biggest box fort I had ever seen. It was the kind of thing my siblings and I would have fantasized about building. There were boxes of all sizes, some large enough to hold a refrigerator. A low wall of cereal boxes separated a cluster of the biggest boxes from individual boxes scattered around its perimeter. Some of the boxes had pictures on them, the kind of crude figures small children draw, done in mud. Seeing the fort filled me with happiness. This was the kind of afterlife I wanted. Plus, I assumed the fort meant there were other kids here. I didn't know who, but if they built something like this, I was sure we would get along. I hurried forward.

"As I passed one of the boxes outside the low wall, I saw the word JAIL written on it. From inside, someone whimpered. I stopped beside it. The box was washer- or dryer-sized. I circled it to see if there was an opening in one of its sides, a door to the jail. None. I leaned in close to it and said, 'Hello?'

"Right away, a pair of voices burst out crying, 'We're sorry! We'll be good! Please let us out!' One of them started sobbing, the other went on pleading to be released. They both sounded young, four or five.

"'Hold on,' I said, 'I'll get you out of here.'

"Upset as the kids were, I thought they'd be happy to be released. But the one who was crying cried harder, and the other one shouted, 'No!'

"'Why not?' I said. 'You guys don't sound like you're having much fun.' I ran my hands over the top of the box, searching for a loose corner to pull on, but the flaps were sealed tight.

"'No,' the kid said again. 'If she finds out, we'll be in trouble.'

"I said, 'Aren't you already in trouble?'

"'Please,' the kid said. 'We have to stay here.'

"'How come?' I said. 'What did you do? Who put you in here?'

"'The Queen,' the kid said. 'We made her mad, so we had to go to jail.'

"'Who's the Queen?'

"The other kid's sobs had diminished; my question revved them up. 'She's awful,' the first kid said. 'You should probably run away before she sees you.'

"The second kid stopped crying long enough to wail, 'I don't wanna be a dog!'

"I didn't know who this Queen was, but if she was ruling over a box fort, I guessed I could handle her. I said, 'This isn't fair. You guys shouldn't be in here.' Which only provoked more protests and sobs. I crouched, sliding my hands along the base of the box in search of a hole or tear an opening I could work to enlarge. Nothing. When I stood, I saw my sister, Natalie, standing on my left, between the jail and shoebox wall.

"She looked the same as she did in the photographs hanging around the house. In the year since we'd buried her, I had stared at those pictures a lot, afraid that, if I didn't, I would forget her. Her hair had grown in to what it was before the chemo took it, down well past her shoulders. She was wearing a cardboard crown, a red T-shirt, and jean shorts. She was barefoot. She cocked her head and said, 'Hunter? What are you doing here?'

"'Nat!' I said. Strange as it sounds, I think this was the moment I realized I was dead; I mean, when it really hit me. I ran over and threw my arms around her, the way I never had while she was alive.

"She stiffened. 'This is my place,' she said.

"I released her. I said, 'You're the one who put those kids in that box?'

"She nodded. 'I'm the Queen,' she said.

"'They're little kids,' I said. 'One of them's crying.'

"Natalie walked to the box and bent over to it. She said, 'I'm the Queen. Isn't that right?'

"'Yes!' the kids shouted. 'Yes, you're the Queen! Yes!' The first kid added, 'Please let us out, Your Majesty. Please. We'll be good. We'll do everything you say.'

"'Come on, Nat,' I said. 'Listen to them. They're really scared.'

"'They're fine,' she said. Leaning on the box with her left hand, she trailed the fingers of her right over the cardboard. She said, 'They're going to be my dogs. Aren't you? You're going to be my dogs. Aren't you? Aren't you?' She turned the question into a song: 'Aren't you, aren't you, aren't you?'

"In response, both kids cried. I mean, they cut loose, with the kind of full-throated abandon kids can tap into. I said, 'Nat, come on.'

"'Shhh,' she said, holding her index finger to her lips.

"The crying continued, until it wasn't crying anymore, it was laughing, the screaming, hysterical laughter of someone who's been overwhelmed by the joke. It sounded too big for the box. The kids started to pound on the walls, shaking it.

"'Nat!' I said. 'Please! Will you let them out?'

"'Here,' she said. She straightened, put her hands on top of the box, and pulled the flaps apart. The pounding ceased, but the laughing continued. With a mocking bow that was pure Nat, my sister stepped away. 'Happy?'

"I ran to the jail, ready to lift one or both of the kids out. The cardboard prison was empty. The laughter seemed to surround me. For a moment, I thought my sister had played an elaborate joke on me, allowing the kids to exit the box while I was distracted by her theatrics. I circled it, but aside from the laughing, there was no sign of them. 'What's going on?' I said. 'Where are they?'

"Natalie didn't answer. She gave me this look—her face went blank, except for her eyes, which burned like blowtorches. She said, 'Shut up,' and the laughter died away. 'You don't belong here,' she said to me. 'This is my place. I'm the Queen here.'

"I said, 'Nat—'

"'Stop calling me that!' she screamed. 'That was my old name. Now I have a new one. I'm Natalya, Queen of the Hungry Dogs.'

"I started to laugh, but her expression stopped me. I decided to shift to big-brother mode, because even in the afterlife, I still had that over her, right? I returned her stare with a frown of my own and said, 'Listen—'

"Apparently, my sister hadn't gotten the memo about me still outranking her. She said, 'No, *you* listen. You don't belong here. I don't want you here. This is my place. I made it. You need to leave.'

"'I can't leave,' I said. 'I drowned. I can't go back.'

"'I don't care,' she said. 'Leave.'

"'Nat,' I said.

"'Queen Natalya.'

"I had forgotten how stubborn—how ornery my little sister could be. I was annoyed, and under that, scared at the prospect of spending the rest of eternity with someone so unreasonably hostile to me. I mean, I was her brother, for God's sake. Shouldn't we be sticking together?

"From the way Natalie was acting, the answer to my question was no. I felt my irritation bubbling into anger. 'Well, Queen Natalya,' I said, 'what if I don't want to leave?'

"'Then I'll make you,' she said.

"'You and what army?' I said, a favorite taunt from our childhood.

"'This one.' She raised her right hand to her mouth, put her index and ring fingers between her lips, and blew. Her whistle was sharp and clear. Immediately, the laughing returned, but louder, as if it was coming from dozens of throats. I saw movement in a stand of trees to my left, and watched as a pack of animals raised themselves from where they'd been lying on their bellies and sides. I glanced at the other groups of birches, and the same thing was happening in each of them, these animals standing."

"Animals?" Carl said.

"Man, I don't know," Hunter said. "They were on all fours, which made me think they were the Hungry Dogs Nat had referred to. But they didn't look much like dogs. They were hairless, and tailless, and their heads— there was something wrong with their heads. They were misshapen, no two in the same way. Some were long and knife-like, others squashed flat. This one's jaw was too big for its mouth, that one's ears flared like fans. You might have thought they were a child's drawings, brought to life. Or death, I guess. They were the source of the laughter, each one a voice in the mad chorus. They started in our direction, and they didn't move like any dogs I'd ever known. They crept along the ground, the way you would if you were sneaking up on someone. Of course I could see them, but I had the sense this didn't matter. They wanted me to watch them coming closer. I was suddenly conscious of myself in my bathing suit, with no means of defense but my hands and feet, which seemed woefully inadequate for the job. The laughter seemed to draw a line under that fact, to emphasize how defense-less, how vulnerable, I was. I didn't know if I could die a second time, but I guessed I could be hurt. I turned to Natalie and said, 'All right, I'm sorry. Maybe there's someplace else I can go.'

"'Too late,' she said, with all the smugness of a gambler holding a winning suit.

"'Nat,' I said.

"'Queen Natalya,' she said, 'sovereign of the Hungry Dogs. Who are go-ing to tear you to shreds.'

"I bolted. There was no point in running any direction but the river, so that was what I did. At my back, I heard Natalie whistle, and the thunder of the dogs' feet as they leapt into pursuit. My hope was to reach the river, splash in and let its current carry me to safety. Or at least, away from my sister and her animals.

"In the time I'd spent talking to Natalie, however, the distance between her box fort and the muddy shore had expanded to the length of a couple of soccer fields—not so far apart as to place the shore beyond reach, but enough to give the dogs a decent chance of bringing me down. I'd always been a fast runner, faster than anyone else in my grade at school, or two grades ahead of me, for the matter. A glance over my shoulder at the assembled dogs chasing me spurred my feet to move even quicker across the grass. But the dogs were running on four feet, which had to give them the advantage. By the time I was halfway to the river, the leader was right on my heels, its laughter dropped to a low chuckle. I veered right, left, faked right, trying to do what I could to increase the distance between us. The dog's teeth snapped at, missed me. My heart was pounding so hard it felt like it was about to burst out of my chest; my lungs were filled with fire. Funny, a small part of me picked up on this and thought, *Wait a minute. You're dead. How can you be getting tired?*

"It didn't matter. I had reached the shore. At the edge of the grass, I threw myself forward in what I intended to be a long jump, but was more my arms pinwheeling, my legs flailing, as if I could swim through the air. I landed off balance, in a half-skid, and my feet went out from under me, dumping me on my back, hard. Before I could do anything, the dog was on me. Its snout tapered to a jagged blade. It raised up on its hind legs, and drove the blade into me, right here." Hunter's hand pressed the middle of his shirt.

"Holy shit, did that hurt. I had never experienced that kind of pain before; in comparison, drowning had been almost pleasant. It stunned me, as if I'd been plunged into freezing water, this full-body shock. The dog jerked its head loose from my mid-section. Blood splashed my face. I wanted to raise my hands, protect myself from its next strike, but the most I could force my arms to do was tremble madly. The dog prepared to skewer me again. This time, its target was my throat. I shut my eyes.

"And nothing happened. No stabbing pain pierced my neck. I opened my eyes to darkness—no dog, no shore, no river—and then the world rushed at me. I was still on my back, but my mother was above me, her knotted hands pressing my sternum, my older sisters and younger brother leaning in to watch Mom's efforts, my father standing just beyond them, as if afraid he'd jinx Mom if he was too close, too hopeful. After that, it was pretty hectic: the paramedics, the ambulance ride to the hospital, the exams to check my status. I didn't forget what happened to me while I was dead, but I…put it to the side, you could say. There was no doubt in my mind as to its reality. I still hurt where the dog had impaled me. But since this reality didn't align with anything I'd been taught to believe about the life to come,

I needed time to process it. I can't remember: did I ever tell you about my mom asking me if I'd seen Natalie?"

"You did," Carl said. "You told her she was happy, surrounded by glowing light."

"Yeah," Hunter said, "because how could I say her daughter was ruler of her own little hell?"

"Is that what you think it was?"

"Not exactly," Hunter said, "but not too far off."

"So, wait," Carl said. "What about the whole 'I died and there was nothing' bit? Not to put too fine a point on it, but for as long as I've known you, you've been pretty insistent about that."

"Like I said, I lied. Or, not exactly. By the time you heard the story of my first death, I pretty much believed what I was saying. Or I believed I believed it. I don't know. In my late teens, I went through a phase where I became obsessed with near-death experiences. You know, rising out of your body, moving along a tunnel of light, being greeted by all your loved ones. I read every account I could lay my hands on, searching for a narrative that matched up with what I'd been through. I couldn't find one. I moved on to scientific studies of near-death phenomena, and learned that there were biochemical explanations for all of it. The tunnel of light was caused by the firing of certain neurons as your eyes shut down. The vision of your loved ones was a last-minute effort by your brain to fool itself about what it was undergoing, a final delusion. It made a sense I couldn't argue with. I had always been a creative kid; my brain had just come up with a more elaborate fantasy. Yes, it had felt real at the time, but a lot of things had seemed real to me when I was a kid. I used to be very religious; I'm sure I must have told you."

Carl shook his head. "You didn't."

"Oh yeah. Altar boy, morning and evening prayers, Bible study, the works. My parents had this series of books, *The Catholic Encyclopedia*, big, oversized volumes with gold covers, and I would slide one out from the bookcase and sit leafing through it. I didn't just believe in Catholicism intellectually, I felt it viscerally. Jesus, Mary, the saints were these living presences I swore I could sense, as was the Devil. By the time I was a teenager, though, my faith had started to waver, mainly because I discovered girls, or maybe I should say, they discovered me. Either way, I knew all of the

Church's prohibitions against anything other than the most chaste kissing, but when Marcie Roy unhooked her bra, all of that went out the window. I was smart enough to be able to rationalize what we were doing, but I also recognized my mental gymnastics for what they were, a type of bad faith, believing my own bullshit, and this revelation was the first crack in the wall. Considering how devout I had been, my belief crumbled remarkably fast, undermined by good old sex.

"The point is, if I had been wrong about religion, which had been at the center of my life, then the chances seemed petty good I had been mistaken about my post-death encounter with Natalie. If there was a difference between the two, it was that what I'd been through with my sister and her dogs retained the vividness of actual experience. I told myself it was due to the extremity of the situation which had produced it. Let's face it, you're probably thinking something along those lines right now, aren't you?"

"You were young," Carl said, "and it was a horrendous event. It wouldn't be a surprise if your mind tried to protect you from it. Although…"

"What?"

"If it were purely a matter of distracting you from your end, you would think the fantasy would have been more pleasant, less threatening. You go into the light, you meet your sister, and that's all, folks. This is way outside my area of expertise, though, so there could very well be another explanation I'm not aware of."

"Like residual guilt over the death of my sister."

"I suppose. If what we're talking about is some kind of defense mechanism, I'm not sure that works."

"You're right," Hunter said, "it doesn't. I want to say it took me a long time to reach the same conclusion, but I knew, on some level, I knew all along. I couldn't admit it, was all."

"What changed? The cancer?"

"Before that," Hunter said. "About six years ago, I saw Natalie again. I was back in Afghanistan, Kabul, to shoot a piece on the rise of heroin addiction there. I was working with a journalist from the *Guardian*, Janet Singh, and she had been told about a spot under one of the local bridges where the addicts gathered. We took a taxi to the place, and sure enough, there were all these men sheltering under a structure that might have gone back to the Soviets. This was in the middle of winter, January, and it was freezing. Janet found someone to talk to, a young guy who had the worn-out look long-term users get. He had a frankness I associate with certain kind of addict; it's like their drug use has reduced everything in their lives to the essentials, which is maybe not so strange.

"Anyway, we asked the guy the usual questions. How did you start using? How did it affect your relationship with your family? Is the drug hard to come by? Are you afraid of the police? My Pashtun isn't very good, but it didn't need to be. The guy gave the same answers you get from addicts the world over. Until it came to his dealings with the cops, when he said something that caught my attention. There are good cops and bad cops, he said, but the men are more worried about the little girl. The little girl? Janet said.

"Yeah, the guy said. For about the last week, a girl had been showing up among them. It wasn't unusual for there to be kids under the bridge, but this girl dressed like a westerner, in a red T-shirt and shorts. Taking her for the child of an aid worker or a journalist, one of the older men tried to shoo her away. In return, she did something to him.

"Did something? Janet said. What? What did she do?

"The guy became embarrassed, looked at his shoes. She put her finger to his forehead, he said, and the old man fell down in a fit. His eyes rolled back in his head; foam came out of his mouth. At the end of it, he was dead. Since then, everyone avoided her.

"Janet took the story for a variety of collective hallucination, which is the rational interpretation. I hadn't thought about what happened after I drowned for I can't tell you how long—not consciously, anyway—but right away, I was back beside the box fort. It was as if I'd been punched in the solar plexus. All the air rushed out of me. I bent over, hands on my knees. Janet noticed, asked if I was okay. I shook my head. Hard as it was to speak, I asked the guy if the girl was wearing anything on her hair. I didn't know the word for crown, so I swirled one hand around my head. His eyes grew large, and he nodded, said she had on a *taaj* like a child would make. Who is she? he wanted to know.

"I couldn't think how to answer him. Janet wanted to know what was going on. I started to say nothing, but it was obvious that wasn't true. Did I mention I'd been in the country for a week? I didn't, did I? You could guess, though. I looked up at the guy, and standing ten feet behind him, there she was: Queen Natalya, ruler of the Hungry Dogs, my dead sister. She hadn't changed much since I'd seen her last, four decades earlier. She glared at me with hatred pure and freezing as an Arctic gale. I panicked, told Janet we had to leave, apologized to the guy we were interviewing, dug in my pocket for some cash to press into his hand. I was terrified Janet was going to notice the girl in the red T-shirt and jean shorts, wearing the cardboard crown, which of course she did while I was attempting to hustle her from under the bridge. The addict had already turned and seen Natalie, and he leapt back the way he might have if he'd seen a cobra raised to strike. Who is she? he asked. You know that little girl? Janet said. I told the guy to steer clear of her. I didn't know the word for ghost, so I settled for calling her bad. Janet said, How is this child bad? She was trying to step around me, to get to Natalie, who was radiating malice, who was radioactive with it. Please, I was saying, we need to go. We can't stay here. But Janet was having none of it. We have to find out what this girl is doing here, she said. No, we don't, I said. While we were arguing, Natalie turned and ran the other way, out from beneath the bridge. Everyone gave her plenty of room. Janet pushed me aside and set out after her."

"What did you do?" Carl said.

"I walked to where the cab was waiting, got in, and returned to the hotel, where I sat at the bar consuming more alcohol than I had in years. This wasn't convivial excess; this was shot after shot of overpriced vodka to numb the memory of what I'd seen. Eventually, Janet showed up. She'd chased Natalie into a maze of alleys where she'd lost her. She was tired, and pissed, and wanted answers I was too drunk to give her. Let's face it, though: had I been sober, I doubt I would have told her the truth, either. I was deeply afraid, in a way I'd never been. Scratch that. The fear—the absolute dread hollowing me was what I'd experienced as a kid, when I worried about Hell. The joys of religion. Once you know about something like that, you start to wonder if you might wind up there. It leaves you with the sensation of being horribly exposed, as if your skin is made out of glass and everything you are is on display. It did for me, anyway. Part of an over-developed superego, I thought when I left the Church. Sitting at the bar, I felt all the old fear, vulnerable in a way I hadn't standing across a tent from a Sunni chief pointing his .44 magnum at me. I finally told my friend I'd freaked out because the girl we'd seen looked exactly like my long-dead sister, which had triggered all kinds of emotions I wasn't prepared for. If you're going to lie, keep it as close to the truth as you can, right? Janet wasn't satisfied. We'd been in enough high stress situations for her to know I didn't lose my shit, not like that. But she let the matter drop, for which I was grateful. It was the last time we worked together, though. Two days later, I left Kabul on the first flight I could snag. I spent the intervening time firmly ensconced at the bar.

"So that was weird," Hunter said, "but maybe it was an isolated incident, right?" He shook his head. "Nope. On and off since then, Natalie has appeared to me. While I was shooting wild fires in the hills above LA, she was visible between a pair of tall trees wrapped in flame. In eastern Ukraine, she was in the middle of a group of rebels creeping through high grass. I saw her on the roof of a burned-out car on a side street in Aleppo. Always, she wore the same, hate-filled expression.

"My most recent encounter came the week following my cancer diagnosis. I decided I wanted to drive down to the Jersey shore, revisit the site of my first death. Morbid, perhaps, but there you have it. Do you know, in the years since, I hadn't been back to that beach once? Not so surprising, I guess.

"With traffic, it was a ten-hour drive. I went alone, didn't want to bring Jill with me. I suppose that was a sign the marriage was on its way out. I left at breakfast, arrived in the early evening. The town had taken a beating during Sandy: there were still gaps where beach houses had stood. I had an idea I would find a motel room, spend a couple of days on the shore. I stopped at a deli, bought an Italian combo hero and a Coke. Being there might have been all kinds of traumatic, but parking on a side street, walking toward the beach, I was kind of exhilarated. The sky was hung with low puffy clouds the sun was filling with red and gold light on its way to the horizon. I strolled onto the beach, which was mostly empty, sat down halfway to the ocean, and ate my dinner while the waves rolled in. If there was one place I was certain of encountering Natalie, this was it, ground zero for our first meeting. Or, not first, but you know what I mean. Our first posthumous run-in. I wouldn't go so far as to say I wasn't concerned about it, but I was less worried than you would have anticipated. Maybe what I needed to do, I thought, was to confront my sister here, where everything had started. Call it a version of taking the fight to the enemy.

"All my bravado went straight out the window when I saw her running toward me. She burst from the waves, already moving full-tilt, her arms out low to either side, her fingers curved into claws. Her mouth was open in a scream that made me nearly piss myself. Where the ocean foamed behind her—I don't know how to describe this—it was full of the Hungry Dogs, I couldn't say how many of them, rising from the water and falling back into it, as if they were trying and failing to gain form. Natalie's bare feet pounded the sand. Her clothes were dry, as was the cardboard crown. I'm not sure I can convey how frightening it was. It—she had lost none of the intensity, the single-mindedness kids have, and that we spend our adult lives attempting to recover. She didn't hate: she was hate. She was no bigger than she'd ever been, but her screaming surrounded her, made her part of something enormous and terrifying. I swore I could hear the dogs laughing in the waves.

"I didn't waste any time. I left my sandwich wrapper and bottle where they were and fled for the car, which sounds easier than it was. My feet kept threatening to slip from underneath me and dump me on my ass. At my back, Natalie's scream expanded. Legs burning, I reached the pavement. Natalie's scream was deafening; it vibrated right through the center of me. I glanced over my shoulder, saw her a dozen steps away. Whether I was going to reach the car before she reached me was looking like a close thing. Thank God for keyless entry; I jammed my hand in my pocket, found the remote, and pressed the unlock button. My shirt jumped as Natalie swiped at it, missed. As we drew even with the car, I sped up, running past the driver's side door and then dodging left, around the trunk, to the passenger's side. It was the kind of trick I used to play on her when we were growing up, and it worked now, as it had worked then. I flung open the passenger's door, threw myself into the car, and hauled the door shut, locking it.

"Natalie was furious. She circled the car three times, and I swear, her scream was as loud inside the car as it had been outside. My heart was pounding, my head swimming. How ironic would it be for me to die from a heart attack here and now? I forced myself to move. If Natalie gained entry to the car, I had no plan. I sidled into the driver's seat, started the engine. My sister came to a halt directly in front of me and stood there, screaming. I'll admit, I considered shifting into drive and stepping on the gas."

"Why didn't you?" Carl said.

"Because whatever she had become, she still looked like my little sister. I reversed away from her, and burned rubber out of there. Natalie didn't pursue me, but her screams rang in my ears the entire way home."

XII

"I assume this is when Hunter called you," Carl said to Annie.

"Eventually," Hunter said. "For the first twenty-four hours after I pulled into the driveway, I was certain Natalie was on her way, that I'd look out the window to see her springing up the front steps. I didn't, but I didn't sleep all that much, either. I started chemo a couple of days later. My oncologist had recommended aggressive treatment as my only hope. As I believe I may have said, it kicked my ass. I was terribly afraid Natalie would appear while I was sitting on one of the hospital's comfy chairs, IV'd to the stuff that was nuking my body in hopes of frying the cancer first. I was tense, irritable. Jill was gone from the house a lot, which I can't say I blame her for.

"Finally, I decided I had to start talking to people about Natalie. I don't mean psychologists. I already had a decent idea of the interpretation they would offer me. My original experience was a fantasy constructed ad-hoc by my mind to fool itself into believing it wasn't facing extinction. Its ambiguous nature owed itself to unresolved guilt over my sister's death. My recent visions of her were the result of decades of poorly treated PTSD brought about by the accumulated stress of the places I'd covered. What had happened was a full-blown psychotic incident, precipitated by my recent diagnosis and its poor prognosis. That sound on target?"

"I'm not a shrink, but yeah, I guess so."

"The people I was interested in were the ones who would take my story at face value. I started with the local Catholic priest. Faith of our fathers and all that. He was followed by Episcopalian, Lutheran, Greek Orthodox, Methodist, Presbyterian, Baptist, and Unitarian clergy, after which, I moved to conservative and reformed Judaism, then Zen Buddhism and Tibetan Buddhism. I didn't have much luck with any of them. Assuming they didn't think I was playing some kind of weird joke on them, most of the men and women I spoke to opted for the psychological view. The Episcopalian and Unitarian were more flexible; each of them suggested I might have encountered a Hell that was adapted to me, specifically. The Tibetan Buddhist raised the possibility that what I took for my sister was a kind of wrathful god, a figure who appears to you once you're dead to frighten you toward the right path. There was no doubt Natalie had scared me, but none of our meetings had driven me to enlightenment. And I couldn't understand why my younger self would have merited a trip to Hell, and why my little sister would have been waiting for me there. No, none of it was especially helpful at explaining the story I told. I went online, hung out on all sorts of out-of-the-way message boards. This was how I found Annie." Hunter nodded at her. "There was this woman on one of them. She was being—I guess you would call it harassed by what she thought was her brother, until she found out he was out of the country, on a month-long trip to New Zealand. This…figure was making all kinds of weird shit happen to her. Annie wrote a long response to the woman's post which made me think she might be the person for me to talk to. I messaged her, sketched out the parameters of my situation, and asked if she had any insight into it. She replied straight away, said she'd do some research and let me know in a day or two. Which she did.

"And to cut to the chase, here we are."

"Here we are," Carl said. He stood from the kitchen island, carried his dish and glass to the sink. "If one of you could tell me exactly where here is, that would be helpful. Specifically, what is it you're planning, and why do you want me to be part of it? I mean, I assume that's the point of all this, to persuade me to assist in your—are you going to perform an exorcism? some kind of casting out of the evil spirit?"

"No," Hunter said. "All I need is for you to walk with me for a little while."

"This is one of those it's-more-complicated-than-it-sounds deals, isn't it?"

"No," Hunter said. "Or yes. Somewhat. Annie, feel free to jump in."

"Hunter's telling you the truth," Annie said. While Hunter had been telling his stories, she had quietly removed six Tarot cards from the deck, and placed them at what appeared to be the points of a hexagon. "He has to cross dangerous terrain. Having a friend with him, especially one he's known for so long, will help."

"Dangerous?"

"She means Natalie's turf."

"The box-fort place?"

"Her kingdom, yeah. With the Hungry Dogs."

"I don't think I understand."

"Hunter's become entangled with his sister's domain," Annie said, "to an extent that will make it difficult for him not to be caught in it. I've worked out a map to guide him through it. However, once he sets foot there, Natalie is going to do what she can to keep him with her."

"You want me to fight your sister for you?" Carl said.

"I'll deal with Natalie," Hunter said. "It's the dogs I'm worried about."

"I'm protecting you from them? I'm still not sure what they are."

"They're souls," Annie said. "Of children, as far as I can tell. Drawn into Natalie's sphere and warped by her."

"Jesus," Carl said. "What are we talking about? I thought she was a ghost."

"Imagine," Annie said, "that when you die, you have to cross from the land of the living," she placed her index finger on the card at the top of the hexagon and slid the digit to the card at the bottom, "to the land of the dead. Let's not worry about that place. What concerns us," she moved her finger to the center of the space, "is what lies between."

"Isn't that supposed to be a tunnel of light?"

"Or the river Styx, or a Valkyrie leaning to grab you from her winged horse, or—you understand. It's reactive. You're likely to encounter whatever you expect to. The majority of those who enter it succeed in reaching the other side. A few turn back, try to return to this life, which generally doesn't go well."

"Ghosts."

Annie nodded. "Among other things. A few souls become lost in this middle ground. They see somewhere they want to remain, so they do. Call it Limbo, albeit, of a highly personalized kind. There, the dead change, go feral."

"Hunter's sister is a feral ghost?"

"Yes, and from everything he's described, she's a powerful one. She's learned how to employ the landscape's reflective quality to alter other souls."

"But she's a kid—was a kid."

"You have children?"

"Two, daughters."

"Then you have direct knowledge of a child's creativity and will power. What do you suppose would happen if you placed a particularly bright and strong-willed child in a place where those qualities would have an immediate effect on her surroundings?"

"Okay," Carl said, "you have a point. But what are the other kids doing there to begin with? I'm guessing there's some kind of connection among family members, which would explain why Hunter was drawn to the place. Those kids, though, the ones Natalie's transformed, what brought them to her? Shouldn't they have been traveling their own paths?"

"Most do. As I said, it's possible to lose your way, and once that happens, to wander into someplace like Natalie's domain. There, you're liable to her influence."

"To what end? Why would she do all this, change other kids into monsters, chase after Hunter?"

"Boredom," Annie said. She began to collect the Tarot cards in front of her. "Eternity is long. She wants Hunter because he escaped from her, because he escaped back to life. Think of a frustrated child. I would guess she's been searching for a way to extend her pursuit of him ever since that afternoon. How she accomplished it, I'm not sure. Single-minded persistence, obviously, but combined with some quality of the places Hunter went which allowed her to push through into them. Possibly the connection to trauma, to pain, suffering. Those kinds of extreme states weaken the barrier between our world and Limbo."

"If she's this strong, why not grab him, drag him off to her kingdom?"

"I don't know," Annie said. "To do something like that requires tremendous power and knowledge. Natalie has the one, but may not have the other. Or she may know he's dying, and have decided it's easier to wait."

"So you kick off," Carl said to Hunter, "and Natalie's waiting to turn you over to her dogs for a rawhide bone. I understand you have Annie's map through Limbo, but I don't see how you ever get to use it."

"Because we're cheating," Hunter said. He doffed his baseball cap and set it on the kitchen island, grabbed the bottom of his T-shirt and pulled it over his head. In the wintry light, his chest and arms were pale, the skin tight against the bone, painful to look at. His flesh was covered in designs executed in pale red ink, what might have been a child's approximation of letters, except the longer Carl studied them, the more they grew to resemble not so much letters as animals, fantastic creatures whose outlines stirred the hairs on his arms. He said, "What...?"

"Camouflage," Hunter said. "It won't hide me from Natalie, but it should make it harder for the dogs to track me." He folded the T-shirt, placed it beside the baseball cap.

"Should," Carl said.

"Hey, none of this is the kind of thing there are manuals for. We're doing the best we can."

"What about me? Where's my camouflage?"

"You don't need any." Hunter unbuttoned and unzipped his jeans, and lowered them. Underneath, he was naked, his emaciated skin a canvas for more of the strange characters.

"Dude," Carl said.

"Our theory," Annie said, "is that Natalie and the dogs will be focused on Hunter. The sigils will throw the dogs off Hunter, while your presence will confuse them further."

"A living guy in Limbo is not something they've seen," Hunter said. He folded his jeans, set them on top of the T-shirt.

"Are you saying they can't hurt me?"

"No," Annie said.

"You're the living weapon, remember?"

"Seriously? I run a small dojo in small city in the Hudson Valley. Most of my students are under ten. Half my classes I spend in fun activities so the kids won't get bored."

"Don't sell yourself short."

"You want to know the last time I was in a fight? Not a sparring match, but an actual fight? I was thirteen, and the other kid cleaned my clock. And this was a human being, not some kind of monster."

"All right," Hunter said, "how about, you're all I've got?"

"That's hardly a ringing endorsement. What happened to your *spetsnaz* buddies?"

"Dead," Hunter said, "except for the one who's in Syria."

"Son of a bitch," Carl said. "How am I even supposed to accompany you?"

"At the moment," Annie said, "the next world is very close. When you're talking about this kind of geography, the places move in relation to you. Just over the border, Natalie and her dogs are waiting. She's so concentrated on Hunter, she won't notice if I slide our place and hers into conjunction."

"You can do that?"

"Under normal circumstances, no. You need knowledge and power, remember? I have plenty of the former, but nowhere near enough of the latter. Natalie has power to spare, however, and I've worked out how to siphon off a sufficient amount to put my knowledge to use."

"Annie's gonna drop us behind enemy lines," Hunter said, "so to speak. We'll have a head start on our pursuers; plus, we'll be that much closer to our destination."

"Your destination," Carl said. "I still have to return from this excursion. Which I'm going to do how?"

"Once Hunter has reached the other side of Natalie's domain, I should know. I'll release the spell holding the worlds together, and you should be carried back here."

"There's a hell of a lot of maybe to this plan."

"Yeah," Hunter said, "there is."

Carl sighed. "It amazes me that I'm having this conversation."

"You've always been pretty gullible."

"Very nice," Carl said. "Okay. When is all of this supposed to happen? Do you know how much longer you have?"

"Until about two hours ago," Hunter said.

Snow filled the kitchen, swirling around the three of them.

XIII

"What do you mean?" Carl said. "You're…?" Unsaid, the word lay leaden on his tongue. Heavy, wet snowflakes pattered his face. The temperature was plunging.

"Don't worry about it," Hunter said. He crossed to Carl, grabbed his left shoulder with a hand that felt as solid as it ever had. Snow stuck to his bare skin; his breath misted the air. A mix of emotions, grief, incredulity, anger, surged in Carl's chest, making him sway as if still drunk. His eyes moistened, dissolving the snow clinging to his lashes.

"We're on the clock," Annie said. She had fanned the Tarot deck on the marble in front of her and was using both hands to push certain cards out of it. Snowflakes eddied about her, condensing into clouds which rushed away from her.

Hunter relaxed his grip on Carl. "Madame Sosostris," he said, "thank you. I couldn't have done this alone."

Without looking up from the cards, Annie said, "You're right."

"Come on," Hunter said, moving toward the hallway to the living room.

"One moment," Carl said. He wiped his eyes. A magnetic strip on the wall to the left of the sink held a series of rubber-handled knives hung points down in ascending order of size. He selected the second-largest, just shy of the butcher knife at the end, and tugged it loose.

From the doorway, Hunter said, "Ready?"

"No," Carl said, testing the knife's weight, its balance.

"Excellent."

In the hall, the snow thickened, the flakes becoming smaller and denser, almost ice-pellets. They rattled against the windows, clattered on the wall, stung Carl's face and hands. Raising his left hand to shield his eyes, his right ready with the knife, he said to Hunter's back, "This already sucks."

"Yeah, well, try doing it naked."

"About that: couldn't you have found a way to do this clothed?"

"Sorry. I didn't realize you'd be so intimidated."

"Intimidating is not the word I'd use for your scrawny ass."

Carl glanced at the windows, but the storm outside had reduced the view to driving snow. At his feet, mist carpeted the floor, rising to his knees as he moved forward. "I feel like we should be having some kind of heartfelt conversation," he said. Icy snow clung to his hair, his ears, the back of his neck.

"What is it you want to talk about?"

"I don't know. Did it hurt? Dying?"

"I took some pills," Hunter said. "I went to sleep. At the end, I panicked a little, thought, 'Oh my God, what am I doing? What if all of this is bullshit, and I'm killing myself because of it?' But it was already too late; the only thing I could do was trust the plan Annie and I had come up with."

"How about now?"

"How do I feel? Weird. Half of me is elated. It's like, it worked! Here I am! The other half of me is scared shitless. I've deliberately made myself vulnerable to my sister and the Hungry Dogs. Those things, man..."

"I know."

"What do you mean?" Hunter slowed, cast a glance over his shoulder.

"I saw them," Carl said. "Last night. Or technically, I guess it was this morning. When I went out to the car for my bag. There were a couple of animals at the edge of the woods. I couldn't see them very well. Even with the garage lights, it was pretty foggy. I thought they might be coyotes, except they didn't move like any coyote I've ever seen."

"Sounds like them."

"I think I saw your sister, too. There was a kid dressed in a red T-shirt and shorts."

"She probably wanted to check you out."

"That's reassuring."

At the end of the hall, a framed eight-by-ten photograph hung. Hunter paused to study it, giving Carl time to join him. One of his better-known efforts, Hunter had taken it in the aftermath of Katrina's inundation of New Orleans. It showed a man and woman waist deep in water, straining to hold onto a rowboat crowded by four frightened children, a pair of dogs, and an assortment of worldly goods, including a cooler, a microwave, and a television weighing down one corner of the boat. Water foamed around the hull, the man appeared to be on the verge of losing his grip, the woman's face was contorted with effort, two children were crying, one of the dogs was attempting to scramble over the side. The photo was one of those iconic images of the disaster, part of the visual library news directors and documentary filmmakers went to for their pieces on the storm. Now, every last one of the figures in it had been replaced by Natalie, including the dogs. She looked on with concern at her struggling attempt to fight the current threatening to carry her away. Tongue lolling, she leaned against herself, who wrapped her arms around her tightly, eyes closed.

"Well," Carl said.

"Yeah," Hunter said.

As they emerged into the living room, the snow lost its ferocity. Carl lowered his hand. The space was full of trees, red pine mixing with birch, rooted in the hardwood floor. Couches and chairs scattered among them. The mist reached above his and Hunter's heads. He said, "I love what you've done with the place."

"I wasn't sure," Hunter said.

"No, it totally works," Carl said. "Gives a real, 'You're going to suffer a horrifying death here' vibe."

"Exactly what I was aiming for."

They advanced quickly, Hunter aiming for a group of three pines beside a recliner. About four feet up, the trunk of the middle tree had been scored with a series of short, shallow cuts, forming a symbol somewhere between a diamond and an eye. Hunter gestured at the mark. "All right. That's one of the runes Toni's using to stitch everything together. We can use them to guide us. More importantly, you can follow them out of here."

"I thought I was supposed to be whooshed to safety."

"That's the plan, but I figure we should have a backup."

"Can't argue with that."

In the middle distance, a larger pine was faintly visible. Skirting an end table, Hunter set off toward it. The snow had returned to large, damp flakes, which dropped around them in slow, lazy motions. To the left, a shape appeared: a brown box, big enough to hold a washing machine. On the side facing them was written HUNTER in childish letters. "Jesus," Carl said. Hunter did not comment.

The same blend of diamond and eye stared at them from the second tree's bark. Hunter brushed it with his fingertips. "Okay," he said. "The next part is tricky. We have to walk in a more or less straight line until we come to a tree that's forked at the base. It shouldn't be too far, but distances can be tricky, here. The important thing is to maintain our direction."

Carl nodded. He switched the knife to his left hand, flexed the fingers of his right. "After you."

Two steps from the tree, the mist congealed, rendering Hunter dim, insubstantial. In the dim light, the red figures written on his skin appeared clearer, as if the mist were a lens bringing them into sharper focus. Carl had the momentary impression the symbols were carrying Hunter, a mix of strange creatures and unfamiliar characters taking him through the mist. "You with me?" he said. The mist muffled his voice, making him sound farther away.

"Yes, sadly."

First on the left, and then the right, Carl heard the click of claws on hardwood. They were being paced, by several animals, from the sound of it. Glances to either side showed only mist. He returned the knife to his right hand. "Hey," he said.

"I know," Hunter said. "Nothing to do but keep going."

Now the claws were behind them, as well. The skin between Carl's shoulders tingled. He said, "I thought you were supposed to be camouflaged."

"Who says it's me they're tracking?"

"Great."

Another box, this one tall and narrow, loomed directly in front of them. "Shit," Hunter said. HUNTER'S FRIEND was scrawled on it. Carl's mouth went dry. He approached the box, reached out his hand to touch the words. The mud in which they were written was still damp. He wiped his fingers on his jeans. He felt his distance from Melanie, the girls, from everything he knew, a gap vast and profound. The claws herding them slowed but did not stop. Cold filled him, his interior weather mirroring the exterior conditions. "Oh," he said, "I am fucked."

"Not yet you're not," Hunter said. He stepped closer to Carl, caught his elbow. "Come on." Carl nodded, allowed Hunter to tug him around the obstacle.

On the other side of the box, the dogs struck. To the right, claws scrabbled on the floor. Raising his left hand to guard, dropping his right to stab, Carl pivoted at the sound. As he did, another set of claws raced at him from the rear. He half-turned in that direction, and the first dog smashed into his left knee. The pain was instant, overwhelming, taking him from his feet. Although he landed on his elbows, adding injury to injury, he held onto the knife. With the shock broadcasting from his leg, it was the most he could do. His assailant continued into the mist, as did the decoy, passing close enough for him to feel the drum of its paws through the wood. In this position, he was horribly defenseless, his back open to the teeth of the next attacker, but he could not move, could not draw sufficient breath to voice the curses streaming through his head: *Fucking fuck oh motherfucker fuck me you fucker fuck.*

Laughter burst around him, a shrieking choir whose volume suggested it issued from a hundred throats. Had it not been for the hurt lighting his nerves, they would have glowed with fear. As it was, he registered the approximate number voicing their delirium and added one more curse to his mental litany: *Shit.*

Hunter crouched beside him. "What happened?"

"My knee," Carl said, nodding at it.

He felt Hunter's hands on his leg. "No sign of a bite or cut."

"No. Hit it with their head."

"Right," Hunter said. He caught Carl under the armpits, started to lift. "Let's go. You don't want to stay here."

Of course he was right. With Hunter's help, Carl pushed himself to standing. His knee protested, but took his weight.

"You need to lean on me?" Hunter said.

"I think I can manage."

Accompanied by the laughter, and under it, the snicker of claws on wood, the two of them resumed their trek. The snow had tapered to scattered flakes, which circled them like moths. Cold numbed Carl's fingers, ears, face, made his nose run. He passed the knife back and forth between his hands, tucking whichever hand was free under the opposite armpit to warm it. At least the movement helped the pain radiating from his knee, allowing him to breathe more freely. But as the hurt ebbed, a tide of dread pushed in to take its place. A solid shot from one of those things and he was left helpless. How was he supposed to handle the laughing mass accompanying them?

A red pine materialized in the mist, split at the foot into a pair of thick trunks whose lower branches were barkless, dead. On the trunk to their left, Carl recognized the diamond/eye symbol. The right fork was inscribed with the figure, too, but this one was surrounded by a tall rectangle, above and below which were cut short horizontal lines. Hunter stood beside the left trunk and pointed into the mist at about a forty-five-degree angle from where they were standing. "This way," he said, and set off in the new direction.

At first, Carl thought it was his imagination, or an acoustic trick played by the moisture around them, but as they left the latest signpost behind, so did the laughter diminish in intensity. He wouldn't have sworn to it, but it seemed to be moving away from them. For a brief time, individual yips and screams continued to sound perilously close, and then the only noise was his and Hunter's feet on the floor. He said, "Is this the part where I say it's too quiet?"

"Another one of Annie's tricks," Hunter said. "Won't last forever, but it'll allow us to put some room between us and the dogs."

The mist was thinning, trees coalescing to either side. Hunter veered slightly to the right, to a young pine whose slender length bore the familiar mark. At the tree, he turned ninety degrees to the left and continued walking. "You know," Carl said, "I'm not sure I'm going to be able to remember this route."

"Relax," Hunter said. "You won't have to, remember?"

"And if something goes wrong? What happened to the contingency plan?"

"Nothing's going to go wrong," Hunter said. "We made it this far, didn't we? Jesus, when did you become such a worrywart?"

"Two kids and one business ago."

"It's fine. Everything's fine. Why do you have to be like this?"

"Because I'm the one looking at a future as the chew-toy of the damned."

On their left, a collection of geometric silhouettes, smaller rectangles and larger squares, appeared through the mist. Another couple of steps, and the shapes resolved into a series of shoeboxes stood on end, forming a half-circle before a pair of square boxes. Beyond this arrangement, further boxes were visible, clusters of low boxes interspersed in front of a line of bigger boxes, which were joined in what might have been a tunnel whose ends continued into the mist. Behind the tunnel, assorted boxes stacked three, four, and even five high formed precarious towers. Here and there, a birch rose in the midst of the constructions. Clearly, this was the box fort of Hunter's story, but it had grown from fort to metropolis, its full dimensions obscured by the mist. There appeared to be writing on some of the boxes, but between the distance and the mist, Carl could not read any of it. He said, "Wow."

"Natalie was never one for half-measures."

"I can't help thinking how cool this looks. Is that crazy?"

"You have to respect her dedication."

They proceeded within sight of the cardboard city for ten minutes, more, past long, narrow boxes balanced to form a succession of archways, past a massive collection of coffee-mug-sized boxes meticulously layered into a ziggurat whose flat top stood as high as Carl's head, past tiny jewelry boxes arranged upon the floor in great spirals and stars. Mixed with his admiration and dread, Carl was aware of a new emotion, pity, for a child whiling away the endless days of her afterlife in yet another game. "Do you suppose," he said, "your sister has anyone else with her? Not the dogs, I mean another person."

Hunter shrugged. "My previous trip, she was the only one I saw. It's hard for me to imagine her tolerating another kid for very long. If an adult wandered into this place, I expect she'd consider them a threat to her authority."

"She must be lonely, though."

"Yeah, well, she's kept herself busy, hasn't she?" Anxiety strained Hunter's words.

"Is it much further?"

As if in answer, Carl saw a trio of red pines ahead. The trees on the right and in the center bore Madame Sosotris's symbol. Hunter strode between them. Carl followed. "We're most of the way there," Hunter said.

"That's good. Right?"

Instead of replying, Hunter stopped. Carl was on the verge of asking him what was wrong, when he saw the girl standing directly in front of them, a large animal behind her.

Natalie Kang might have been any nine- or ten-year-old entering an early growth spurt, all long skinny arms and legs. Her thick black hair reached past her waist and was in need of a brush. She was barefoot, wearing denim shorts and a red long-sleeved T-shirt. A cardboard crown circled her hair. Looking at her there in front of them, Carl was reminded of his daughters at that age, brimming with energy, possessed of surprising depths of melancholy and reflection, as well as titanic mirth. She was much smaller than he remembered, which was a ridiculous observation, because she was a child, but Hunter's stories of her had caused her to grow in Carl's memory to a raging monster, twelve feet tall.

When she shifted her large brown eyes from her brother to Carl, however, any reassurance her appearance might have caused withered. The gaze she directed at him was of pure, distilled malice, of hatred concentrated into its coldest form. He thought of Deb and Karen unhappy, of the rages they could fly into, the expressions of raw anger that would lower their brows, straighten their mouths. What was scalding him now like a jet of liquid nitrogen was the same emotion focused over decades, refined to a degree far in excess of what was humanly possible, tolerable. Briefly, he had wondered if Hunter might have misjudged his sister, misinterpreted her actions; now, he saw, his friend had not. Her eyes swung to Hunter, and it was as if Carl's skin warmed.

"You're naked," Natalie said. Her eyes narrowed, as if she was attempting to decipher the characters on Hunter's skin. Something was off about her voice; it had a worn quality, as if it had been too long at the same pitch. Carl found it simultaneously frightening and sad.

"Yeah," Hunter said. "Hi, Nat."

"Don't call me that," she said. She raised her chin. "I am Natalya, Queen of the Hungry Dogs, and you are trespassing in my kingdom. Who is this?"

She pointed at Carl.

"He's a friend. He agreed to come with me on my way through here."

"Why does he have a knife?"

"To protect himself. There are some pretty scary things in these parts."

"You mean my dogs."

"Yes, I do."

"You're right," Natalie said, "he should be afraid of them." She glanced behind her, and the creature at her back crept into view.

At the sight of it, Carl's stomach dropped, and despite himself, he said, "Jesus Christ."

The size of a big dog, a Great Dane or an Irish wolfhound, it slunk close to the floor, slender limbs out to either side like an enormous insect. Its hide was the damp white of flesh left days under a band-aid. Its head was awful, a pair of jaws distended by a cage of fangs the length of Carl's hand. Eyeless, it tasted the air with a fluttering white tongue whose edges were ragged from its teeth. A low chuckle rolled from its throat. The Hungry Dog positioned itself in front of Natalie, sitting as best the awkward arrangement of its limbs would allow and turning its monstrous head in search of the palm she laid on it. She said, "This is Sam."

"Hi, Sam," Hunter said.

"Don't talk to him," Natalie said, her words laced with contempt. "He's mine."

"Okay," Hunter said, hands held out in apology, "I'm sorry."

"They're all mine," Natalie said. "Now you are, too."

"Can we talk about that?"

"No."

Left hand low, palm forward, right hand holding the knife close to his body, Carl slid next to Hunter, who said, "Are you sure? I'm going to the summer country; maybe you could come with me."

"Why would I want to do that?"

"To see Mom and Dad."

"Them? They let me die."

"I don't think that's—"

"Shut up," Natalie said. "When I got sick, I asked them if I was going to die. 'Oh, no,' they said, 'we would never let that happen.' I did everything they told me to. I took their stupid medicine, which made me feel terrible.

All my hair fell out. And it didn't work. I died anyway. Before I did, Mom and Dad promised me I was going to heaven. 'You'll be lifted up by angels,' they said, 'and brought straight to Jesus. You'll see Grandpa Hugh again.' But there weren't any angels. I didn't see Jesus, or Grandpa Hugh. I wound up here. I saw a box fort and stopped at it. I didn't know where I was. I thought I was in Hell. I didn't know why; I didn't know what I had done. For a long time, I was so scared. Then I got tired of being afraid and got mad." Natalie lifted her hand from the dog (Sam) and he lurched to his feet. She said, "I knew when Mom and Dad died. I was ready for them. I was going to show them this place. I was going to ask them why they'd lied to me. I was going to make them apologize. Only, I missed them. Both of them. I went to find them, and I couldn't. It was like they didn't want to see me. Don't you think they would have? Don't you think they would have come looking for me?"

"I'm sure they did," Hunter said. "After I returned from here—after I was resuscitated—you were the first thing Mom asked me about. 'Did you see Natalie?' she said while we were in the ambulance."

"She did?"

"Yes, really."

"What did you tell her?" Eagerness blended with Natalie's anger, softened the stern cast of her features.

"I said I'd seen you."

"Did you tell her about my kingdom?"

"No, I did not."

"Why not?"

"To be honest, I was pretty freaked out by it. I thought Mom would be, too."

Natalie's face hardened. "So even if she had wanted to find me after she died, she couldn't have, because you didn't tell her the right place to look."

"Whoa," Hunter said. "Hang on a minute."

Carl didn't pick up on the exact cue Natalie employed, but he caught the dog rocking back, gathering himself to leap, and pushed in front of Hunter as the creature sprang. For an instant, the Hungry Dog hung in the air, his abundance of fangs spread wide. Ice water flooded Carl's chest. Sam drew nearer in fits and starts, as if in a series of slides caught in a stuttering projector. Somewhere inside Carl's head, a voice was saying, *Move*

move move move move. When the dog was an arm's length away, he did. Aiming for Sam's throat, he snapped the knife straight out, exhaling sharply as he twisted his right hip into the strike. The dog came in lower than he anticipated, however, and the knife drove into Sam's open mouth, piercing his tongue and lower jaw. Fangs tore Carl's hand as the dog jerked his head left in an attempt to avoid the weapon that had already wounded him. His momentum carried him into Carl, who released the knife and stumbled backwards, thudding against Hunter and knocking the two of them to the floor. Sam landed next to them, thumping on his side, and immediately started wailing, a frantic cry halfway to a laugh. On his ass, Carl scooted clear of the thrashing dog, colliding with Hunter and forcing him back, too.

"Dude," Hunter said when they were a safe distance, "your hand."

Carl raised it. It was bright red with blood streaming from the furrows Sam's fangs had dug in it. "Jesus." His head swam. He was aware of pain, incredible pain, astonishing pain, the moment his ravaged hand came into view, but he was more concerned that neither his thumb nor his middle finger seemed capable of movement. Nausea fought with panic in his throat.

"Holy shit," Hunter said.

At first, Carl thought his friend was commenting on his hand, until he saw what was happening to Sam. All over him, the dog's pale flesh was quivering, losing its solidity, becoming gelid, sliding partway from his limbs and torso onto the floor, then regaining its integrity and retracting up his frame. In some places, what reformed was not the shape of the Hungry Dog, but of a child, a seven- or eight-year-old, Carl would have guessed. An arm, a leg, a hand, a foot, a shock of curly red hair, a green eye wide with agony and fright, all blended with the dog's monstrous features, while he continued his laughing wail, pawing at but unable to dislodge the blade buried in his lower jaw.

"Hush," Natalie said, and Sam's cry diminished to a whimper. Mingled with his whining were sounds that might have been words; Carl thought he could pick out, "Hurts." Natalie crouched in front of the dog, her left hand on his head, her right reaching amidst his fangs to grab the handle of the knife. She murmured something to Sam, too low for Carl to hear, and tore the knife from his mouth with a downward stroke that spilt his lower jaw to the throat. Carl and Hunter shouted. The halves of his jaw flapping, pinkish blood venting from his open neck, Sam reared on his mismatched hind legs and fell over. His eye rolled frantically, then fixed. He sighed, shuddered, and was still. His body began to slide apart.

"What the fuck, Nat?" Hunter said.

"You broke him," Natalie said. She dropped the knife, stood, wiped her hand on her shorts. "He'll go back to his doghouse until I can fix him."

Hunter raised himself to his feet. He held out his right hand to Carl, who took it in his left and used it to help him up from the floor. The pain from his injuries was excruciating. "How're you doing?" Hunter said.

"Have I mentioned how much this sucks?" Trying to keep the hand elevated, Carl pressed his right arm across his chest.

"You might have."

"I don't think I'm gonna be much good for anything else," Carl said. Natalie had kicked the knife away.

"That's okay. It isn't too far from here. I'm pretty sure I can make it on my own."

"You are going nowhere," Natalie said.

"Are you sure?" Carl said. "Do you know which direction you're supposed to be heading? Because I have no idea."

"I said, You are going nowhere." Natalie advanced toward them.

"Yeah, I think so," Hunter said. "Hang tight; it shouldn't be too long."

"That's assuming you succeed."

"Ever the voice of encouragement."

"I SAID, YOU ARE GOING NOWHERE." Natalie was standing beside them. This close, hatred poured from her in freezing waves. "You are mine," she continued, addressing Hunter, "and so is your friend. I rule here. What I want to happen, happens. I want both of you to suffer, so you will. There's a box waiting for you, big brother. I've been preparing it for a very long time. Maybe I'll sic what comes out of it on your friend. Maybe I'll let the dogs have him, for what he did to their brother."

"Nat—"

"Queen Natalya."

"Yeah." Hunter shook his head, and leapt at his sister, catching her in a tackle that brought them crashing to the floor. Almost too fast to see, Natalie twisted, planting her feet against Hunter's chest and kicking with enough force to shove him away from her, mist rolling about him. She sprang up, ready for Carl, but he was hurrying to Hunter, who grimaced, his left arm wrapping his ribs. "Well, that worked," Carl said, extending his left hand.

Behind him, Natalie's voice thundered, "GIVE IT BACK!"

In his other hand, Hunter held his sister's crown. Waving away Carl's help, he staggered to his feet.

"GIVE IT BACK!" Trembling with fury, Natalie glared at the two of them. Loosed from the cardboard circle, strands of her hair lifted as if in a breeze. "GIVE ME MY CROWN, HUNTER!"

Hunter shook his head. "No can do, Nat."

In response, Natalie screamed, an ear-splitting shriek which lasted longer than Carl would have thought humanly possible. Somewhere deep in the mist, a distant pack of laughs answered. "Now you'll see," she said. "I won't bother putting you in your box. I'll let the dogs get you. You're going to be so sorry, Hunter. They're going to hurt you so bad."

"Thank you," Hunter said to Carl, "for coming with me. I don't know if I could have made it this far without you. I'm sorry about your hand."

"That makes two of us."

"I love you, man."

"I love you, too. I hope you make it."

"That makes two of us." Crown in hand, Hunter turned left and ran.

"HEY!" Natalie shouted after him. "HEY! COME BACK HERE, HUNTER! HUNTER!"

Already, the mist was closing around him, rendering him ghostly, dulling the slap of his feet on the floor. For an instant, the strange red symbols written on him appeared to float in the air, then they faded from sight, as well.

Natalie didn't waste any more time. Without another glance at Carl, she sprinted after her brother, her long black hair streaming behind her like a banner.

XIV

Laughter roared around Carl, raged, together with another sound, the rumble of many feet, of hundreds of feet, running at him. The floor shuddered with their approach. How many Hungry Dogs were there? Carl's hand throbbed. If one of them left the chase, he was in trouble; two, and he was finished. Hang tight, Hunter had said. Easy for him to say. The laughter swelled. The floor jumped under him. Hang tight.

As fast as his legs would carry him, Carl ran, aiming ninety degrees from the direction in which Hunter and Natalie had vanished. Laughter pursued him, enveloped him. The floor bounced like a trampoline, throwing him into a stumble that almost sent him sprawling. To his right, a stand of birches waved like reeds in a wind. He considered sheltering in them, rejected the idea. An arm's length in front of him, a dog loped from right to left, its head an assortment of blades. Closer still, another crossed behind him. This direction, the mist was heavier, which he supposed was equal parts to his advantage and disadvantage.

Snow rushed against him. He slowed, shielded his face with his left hand. "HUNTER!" Natalie's voice boomed on his left, made him flinch. He quickened his pace. The Hungry Dogs' laughter ebbed, swelled, ebbed. The shaking of the floor subsided. Ahead, someone panted with exertion. "Hunter?" Carl said. Faintly, he heard Natalie shouting, but could not decipher her words. Snow stuck to his skin, clung to his hair. At least it numbed his injuries.

His feet were starting to drag. There was something to the right, a squat form about which snow swirled. Its outline was too regular for a tree. Carl jogged over to it. Made of grey brick, it stood waist high, a foot and a half on each side. Set in its flat top was a shallow bowl of dull metal. Snow silted the bowl, spackled the column's sides. Carl walked around it, but could see no markings on it, no hint of its purpose. One of Natalie's creations? He couldn't be absolutely sure, but didn't believe so. He squatted to study it more closely, using his left hand to balance himself. As he did, he realized his fingertips were touching not wood, but soil. Pulse leaping, he brushed his hand over the ground, confirming his discovery:

He had left Natalie's domain, and Madame Sosostris's path through it. He was lost.

XV

For a long time, Carl stood beside the brick pillar, as snow drifted against it and the blood flowing from his wounds began to freeze. He could attempt to find his way back to Natalie's kingdom, but there seemed little point in doing so. If Hunter had succeeded in escaping her, then Madame Sosostris would have performed whatever action was necessary to unlink Limbo from the world of the living, and Carl would be entering a hostile environment from which there was no escape. He did not imagine Annie would or could keep the worlds locked indefinitely—she had mentioned the tremendous power required to do so, hadn't she?—so if Hunter did not reach his goal, if Natalie caught him or if he ran off course, there would come a moment when she would have to effect the separation, anyway. Which would yield the same result for him returning to Natalie's domain, except he and Hunter would be suffering together. He could continue into this new precinct of Limbo. The brick column was evidence at least one other person inhabited or had inhabited the area. But what if that individual was as hostile as Natalie, another feral ghost? What if they were worse, at the head of their own army of monsters? Although it was possible he could be found should he remain here, the risk struck him as less than that incurred by wandering further into this territory.

The snow continued.

XVI

At some point, he crouched against the brick pillar, thinking it would offer him a modicum of shelter from the elements. He supposed it did; although it sharply curtailed his view of his surroundings. He was too cold to let that sway him. How long had it been since Hunter and he had set out on their journey? A couple of hours? Was that possible? It felt as if he'd followed Hunter along the hallway out of the kitchen days ago. Attempting to conserve body heat, he huddled tight. Could he die, here? Given that he could be hurt, it seemed likely. What would it mean, to die in the afterlife? Would he notice? Or was there some deeper level of existence waiting under this one?

His family would not know what had happened to him. Presumably, Annie would call 911 to report Hunter's lifeless body. One look at the empty pill bottle beside it would tell the cops how he had exited his life, while a conversation with Hunter's doctor would explain why. No doubt, the investigating officers would have plenty of questions for Annie, but Carl didn't think she'd have any trouble answering them. He was less certain how she'd respond when they asked about the owner of the other car parked in the driveway. Her best option would be to hew as close to events as she could, to admit she didn't know. In short order, what started as a call about the death of a famous photojournalist, apparently at his own hand, would have developed into a missing person case involving his long-term friend, the owner of a Shotokan karate studio in Beacon.

What would the cops assume had happened to him? More importantly, what would Melanie think? She would have leapt in the car the instant the call to her ended. An accident would seem the most reasonable explanation. In this version of events, he went for a walk in the woods surrounding his friend's house and suffered some kind of mishap, tripped, fell, knocked himself unconscious, then froze to death in the storm. A heart attack would work as well, despite a clean bill of health at his last checkup. The lack of any trace of his body on Hunter's grounds would lead to the search being expanded to neighboring properties, possibly down to Lake Champlain, whose cold waters would offer a compelling explanation for the absence of his remains. The cops might posit he had slipped and fallen into the lake. How long would it be until the search was called off, suspended? What would the official verdict be? Missing, presumed dead? Yet the coincidence of him vanishing at the same time his friend ended his life would lend his disappearance an aspect of mystery which would birth conspiracy theories as quickly as the internet could midwife them. The prospect was almost enough to bend his mouth into a smile, except that the same openendedness would haunt Melanie and the girls.

From Carl, from Dad, names which over a lifetime had become synonyms for stolid, calm (if unexciting), dependable (if forgetful), the man who had been one quarter of the family would assume a new identity, or rather, lack of identity. He would become a cipher, a blank onto which Melanie, Deb, and Karen would write whatever anxieties and doubts they'd had about their relationships with him. Melanie would fear he had left her for a new life with another woman, one of the younger black belts whose fawning she teased him about. Deb and Karen would worry they'd been abandoned by a father who had only ever feigned interest in them and their lives. With time, perhaps the girls would accept that he had died in an accident which had hidden his body, but he doubted Melanie would. She would know something was not right about his vanishing; the low-level marital telepathy they had developed over their decades together would tell her the situation was off. Would she seek out Madame Sosostris, demand more of an answer than the woman had provided the police? And suppose Annie acquiesced to her request, told her everything? What then? Assuming Melanie didn't take Annie as either lying or insane, what could she do? What options could Annie offer her? Without the power she had drawn from Natalie, she could not access this place. The best Melanie could expect was to know her husband was forever lost to her. Grief for her, for what she had not learned she already had lost, shot through him like a steel pin fixing an insect to a board.

Nearby, footsteps crunched in his direction. Wondering if Hunter had failed in his efforts and had managed to track him here, he raised his head. But no, he did not recognize the young man advancing toward him. For one thing, he was clothed, wearing a peach dress shirt, charcoal slacks, and black loafers. For another, everything about him, the colors of his clothes, the tone of his skin, even the shine of his eyes, glowed with a rich light, as if the midday sun were shining full on him. The man's expression, however, indicated he knew Carl. Squinting at the snow pelting his face, the man approached Carl until he was standing over him. In a pleasant voice, he said, "Your ride's here, kiddo. Time to go."

XVII

"Who are you?" Carl said through chattering teeth.

"The gift horse you're looking in the mouth."

"I'm sorry," he said, bracing himself against the pillar as he struggled to stand, his legs complaining as they unbent. "It's just—"

"Your friend's sister, yes."

"You know about her?"

"Some."

"Can you tell me if Hunter got away from her?"

The young man shook his handsome head. "I can't. What I can offer you is a way out of here."

"Is this a trick?"

"This is not a trick."

"Then why are you doing this?" Sudden suspicion widened his eyes. "Are you an angel? A god? God?"

The young man burst into hearty laughter. "That's terrific," he said.

"What a difference a change of clothes makes, I swear." Noting the blend of consternation and embarrassment on Carl's face, he added, "I'm sorry. I shouldn't have expected you to know me. The last time you saw me, I was in considerably worse shape. Actually, the last time you saw me, I was lying in the coffin in the Miskowski Funeral Home in Fishkill."

Here, Carl realized, was Wayne Ahuja, his older brother's friend, dead these many years, one of the multitude consumed by AIDS and its attendant infections. The delay in his recognition was understandable. Even before his sickness, Wayne had been skinny, the type of kid, it was joked, who had to stand in the same place twice to cast a shadow, who had to run around in the shower to get wet. In contrast, the man in front of him had the robust dimensions of an Olympic swimmer. He wore vitality with the same ease as his immaculately tailored shirt. Nor did the difference end there. When Carl had known him, Wayne had been reserved, guarded, a consequence of being out at a time and in a place whose attitudes were struggling to advance. This Wayne was suffused with self-confidence. It was as if he was seeing Wayne not as he would have been had he lived, but as the best possible self he could have been. Wonder and bewilderment competed to find their way into speech; what emerged from Carl's mouth was a compromise: "Why?"

"Are you saying you want to stay here?"

"No," Carl said, "no, no, of course not. It's—I don't understand. I thought I was trapped in this place."

"I supposed it does seem a little deus-ex-machina-y, doesn't it? Just when all hope seems lost, the handsome ghost from your past swoops in to rescue you. Well, more like, trudges across a snowy waste, but you get the picture. It's because of that," Wayne said, pointing at Carl's torn right hand. "Blood was spilled. Whenever that happens in this neck of the woods, it creates all kinds of opportunities."

"Like what?"

"Don't ask. Be glad your friend's sister didn't know about it, or she wouldn't have spent two seconds on him." Wayne turned to the pillar, on top of which a couple of inches of snow had accumulated. With the flat of his hand, he swept it clear, then scooped out the snow remaining in the metal bowl. He waved to Carl. "Give me your hand. No, the injured one."

Carl removed his hand from its position against his shoulder and held it out. Wayne took it in his warm grasp and guided it over the bowl. Rotating the wrist this way and that, he inspected Carl's mostly frozen wounds. "I'm sorry about this," he said, and squeezed Carl's hand tightly.

Pain burned his fingers and palm. He yelped, went to jerk away, but Wayne's grip did not lessen. From numb, Carl's hand was aflame, flesh and bones luminescent. Fresh blood streamed from the grooves in his skin and pattered onto the bowl, striking it with a tinny music. "That should do," Wayne said, and released him.

"Fuck!" Carl said, cradling his re-injured hand.

"Again, I apologize." Wayne peered at the bowl, watching Carl's blood slide down its sides into a crimson bubble. The blood quivered, elongated, shooting up the bowl's curve in a straight line. Wayne pointed in the direction it indicated, about twenty degrees to their left. "This way," he said.

Snow whirled around them. "There's a hell of a lot more walking in the afterlife than I expected," Carl said.

Wayne chuckled. "It isn't far."

"Can I ask you something?"

"You want to know what it's like."

"Heaven, yeah. Hunter called it the summer country."

"What makes you think that's where I come from?"

"You didn't?" Carl glanced at him.

"No, I'm teasing you," Wayne said. "If your friend reaches it, he'll be happy."

"I would hope so, after all this."

They proceeded in silence for a minute or two, until Carl said, "That's it?"

"That's it."

In front of them, a low wall made of flat black stones layered thigh high barred the way. "Here we are," Wayne said. "Do you think you can get over this on your own, or do you need a hand?"

The stones were a single layer deep. Carl stepped across with a minimum of effort.

"And there's my answer," Wayne said. "All right. Continue straight on and you should see your destination in about five minutes."

"Thank you," Carl said. "I wish I could come up with something better to say."

"You're welcome."

"I still don't understand why you were the one who came for me. Not that I'm complaining; I just wondered."

"Do you remember the last conversation we had?"

"Yes. You told me about wanting to go to Paris."

"That was a bad day. A horrible day. I was in a lot of pain, and I was starting to understand I didn't have much longer. All the stuff about France had been such a central part of who I was, how I saw myself, and it was going to be lost, to go down to the grave with me. I was depressed and I was afraid. You allowed me to talk about something I loved one more time—for the final time, as it turned out. It was comforting, at a time when comfort was in short supply. For my remaining days, I appreciated that.

"Plus, you did a good thing for your friend. I admire that. I could help you, so I did. You get a Get-Out-Jail-Free card. Why not, right?"

"No argument here," Carl said. "One last thing?"

"Yes?"

"If you happen to see my friend—Hunter—tell him I'm glad he made it."

"Should I see him, I will."

"Thanks."

"Go home," Wayne said.

Carl did.

XVIII

More like ten minutes after he departed Wayne, Carl noticed the mist thinning, disclosing the trunks of trees around him. The snow had not let up; indeed, it had gained in intensity, accompanied by a wind that sliced through him to the bone. Carl advanced to one of the trees, saw that it was a red pine, and his heart lifted in his chest. Moving from evergreen to evergreen, he continued forward. The wind whipped away the last of the mist. He was walking through the woods lining the driveway to Hunter's house; through the blowing snow and the trees, he could see his Subaru, and beyond it, the steps climbing the slope to the house's front door.

A tremendous wave of emotion rose in Carl, sent tears flooding his cheeks. The snow, the trees, the car, glowed in his sight, suffused with beauty. The wave broke, became joy and relief and a fierce love for the world and everyone in it. The snowflakes were a miracle, the trees astonishing, the car a work of art. He could not contain himself: he broke into a run toward the house, where his old friend's body lay on the bed in the master bedroom, an unreadable expression on its cooling face.

EPILOGUE

The surgery to repair Carl's hand took place at the UVM Medical Center. He had blamed his injuries on an attack by a stray dog he encountered when he went outside to practice his kata. The explanation was simple enough to repeat to the police convincingly; although it necessitated a series of rabies shots he couldn't refuse and maintain the illusion. The doctor who treated him at the ER strongly recommended operating as soon as possible, which opinion the surgeon on call endorsed. Already on her way up, Melanie met him at the hospital, where a slot had opened early the following morning. "Holy crap," she said when she saw the bandages wrapping his hand. "A dog did this?"

Although he hated lying to her, Carl said, "Yeah. It was the craziest thing." Which was perhaps not as much a lie as he had thought.

After the surgery, while he was in the recovery area, surrounded by tall green curtains through which various nurses came to check his vitals, Hunter appeared to him. Melanie had ducked out to run to the cafeteria for a cup of coffee and a snack. Carl was lying with his eyes shut, riding in and out of consciousness. He heard the curtain rings jingle, felt someone sit on the end of the bed. He assumed it was Melanie, but when he opened his eyes, saw Hunter. Still unclothed, his skin still a canvas for the red figures, Hunter was wearing Melanie's cardboard crown, perched unsteadily atop his larger head. On the floor beside him, a Hungry Dog sat awkwardly, its head an elongated wedge.

Carl was aware that he should be terrified, but whatever drugs were coursing through his system dulled the emotion to a mild concern. He said, "You're still naked."

"Yeah," Hunter said.

"I take it this means the plan failed."

"No," Hunter said, "it didn't."

"Then why are you here?"

"I couldn't do it." Hunter looked down. "I made it. We made it; Natalie chased me all the way there. We must've made some sight, me running bare-assed down the middle of this cobbled street, her hot on my heels, screaming her head off. She finally brought me down, started punching and kicking me. I wouldn't let go of this, though." He pointed to the crown.

"Wait," Carl said. "Heaven has cobbled streets?"

"This part does. You know what it reminded me of? Have you ever been to St. Andrew's, in Scotland?"

"Heaven is like Scotland?"

"I'm sure the Scots would agree with that. It's not important. Anyway, there we are, me on the cobblestones, Natalie beating the shit out of me, and the next thing, there are people in the street. I want to say they were there all along, it just took us a minute to see them. I don't know what the hell that means, either. Their clothes were these incredible colors…. I can't say exactly how, but they separate the two of us, form a circle around Natalie. She's furious; she's shouting at the crowd, running up to and pushing them, punching a couple. They don't react. Or, they don't react the way you would expect. They talk to her, reassure her, tell her it's okay, everything's all right. As they do, they're doing this thing with their hands," Hunter mimed moving his back and forth, as if he were playing tug of war and drawing the rope to him. "I'm thinking I should run, escape my sister while I have the opportunity, but I can't stop watching. I swear, I can almost see these people drawing something out of Natalie, like long, silvery webs. Eventually, she goes from running around inside the circle, to standing still, to sitting, then she lies down and falls asleep right there in the middle of the street. Some members of the group leave, others keep on with the hand stuff.

"I was so relieved; I can't tell you. A woman approached me, said we should see about getting me settled. 'What about my sister?' I said. 'Oh, her too,' she said. Just like that. As if Nat hadn't been this raging monster.

"And it hits me, what about the Hungry Dogs? I'm thinking about Sam, about what we saw happen to him. I'm thinking about I don't know how many of these creatures, these kids, there without their queen. I'm thinking about what I've witnessed with Natalie. If there's a way to, I don't know, get her back from whatever she had transformed into, then shouldn't there be a way to reclaim them, too? But who's gonna do that? I can't bring Natalie out there, and I can't ask any of these people I don't know. I can't say it isn't my problem, because…well, I can't. How could I enjoy this place knowing this pack of kids was wandering around the box fort, wondering what happened? I asked the woman I was talking to if she could help my sister, could connect her with our parents. She said she would, so I put the crown on my head and set off the way we'd come.

"It wasn't hard to find the path back to Natalie's kingdom. Once I arrived, most of the dogs avoided me. I could see they recognized the crown, but had no idea what it meant for me to be wearing it. A few approached me, but this guy," Hunter nodded at the dog at his feet, "was the only one to stay. So far. I can't say why, but I think his name is Rudy."

"Hi, Rudy," Carl said.

The dog stared at him blankly.

"Although I could be wrong," Hunter said.

"How are you planning to retrieve them," Carl said, "who they were?"

"I have no idea," Hunter said. "If Natalie could transform them into these things, then I figure there's a way to return them to who they used to be. I just have to find it."

"Sounds like it could take some time."

"It's not as if I'm doing anything else." The bed creaked as Hunter stood. So did the Hungry Dog (Rudy?). "Okay, I just wanted to drop by, check on you. I don't foresee myself having a lot of adult conversations in the immediate future." He moved toward the green curtain.

"Be careful," Carl said.

"I'm already dead."

"And for God's sake, get some pants, your majesty."

"Kiss my ass, peasant."

The curtain rings sang, the dog's claws clicked on the floor, and Carl was alone. When Melanie returned, she saw her husband wiping his eyes with the back of his unbandaged hand, but she did not ask him about it, not then.

> "And if he were wrong, well, what would be the harm in that?
> Better to be wrong forever than to live without hope."
> —Lucius Shepard, "Limbo"

OSCAR RETURNS FROM THE DEAD, PROPHESIZING

To distract my son after his first breakup, I told him a story. It was the only thing I could think to do.

—Do you remember Oscar? I said. We were in the car, heading north on the Thruway. We were going to Albany International Airport, to meet my wife's return flight from Seattle.

—You mean Dylan's lizard? Jordan said. He was staring out the window at the fields rushing by.

—Leopard gecko, I said. You know he died, right?

Jordan sighed. In the fire, he said.

—No, before that. When we were watching him.

—What? Jordan said. No, he didn't.

—Yes, he did.

—That's bull—that isn't true, Jordan said.

—It is, I said. You were gone, at a sleepover. At Owen's, I think. The weather had turned incredibly hot. I had the idea that Oscar would appreciate a little time in the sun. His tank wasn't heavy, so I moved the heat lamp off it and carried it out to the porch. I set the tank down next to the doorway, away from the direct sunlight. Then I went back inside, and forgot about Oscar.

—How long did you leave him there?

—Too long. I wasn't the one who noticed he was gone. After Mom got home and had dinner, she said, Where's Oscar? And I said, Oh no. Actually, that isn't what I said, but you understand. I raced onto the porch. The sun was down, but the wood still burned my feet. I hefted the tank and ran into the kitchen. Almost dropped the tank on the kitchen table. Not that Oscar would have minded.

—He was dead, wasn't he?

—Yeah. During the afternoon, the sun had moved, and the tank had turned into a little oven. Oscar had…shriveled, dried out.

—Mom must've been upset.

—To put it mildly. Which was fair enough. Although it was an accident, I had cost Dylan his pet.

—What did you do?

—Mom called around to the local pet stores until she found another leopard gecko. The next morning, I drove up to Wiltwyck and purchased Oscar 2.0. Cost me forty dollars.

—How about the first Oscar?

—We removed him from his tank, wrapped him in a couple of dish towels, put him in an empty chocolate box, and buried him in the backyard.

—Where?

—Under the pine tree next to the fire pit. It was the only place the soil was deep enough, and which was sufficiently out of the way for you not to notice. I had a couple of pieces of slate left over from when you and I had dug the pond at the side of the house. I laid them on top of the box before I filled in the hole, to keep any animals from digging Oscar up. The whole thing was done—new lizard bought and housed, old lizard interred—by the time you returned from Owen's.

—I can't believe I never noticed.

—You had lost interest in Oscar by then. At first, you were fascinated by him. Do you remember watching him chase the crickets we fed him for dinner?

—Yeah.

—We were supposed to be able to handle him, but the first time you stuck your hand in the tank, he snapped at you, and that was that. Which worked out for us, in the long run. It meant you didn't notice when we swapped him for his replacement.

—Did Dylan know?

—He didn't, but that's a little complicated.

—How so?

—The pet we returned to him was the first Oscar.

—What do you mean?

—Four or five days after Operation: Fresh Gecko, I heard a noise from Oscar 2.0's tank. This was around noon; I was sitting in my office, catching up on email. I walked into the kitchen. I heard the sound again. It took me a minute to figure out it was gravel, spraying against the tank's sides. I crossed to it, and was just in time to watch the original Oscar swallowing the last of the other gecko's tail.

—Where was Oscar 2.0?

—I couldn't find him. I knew leopard geckos could drop their tails in stressful situations, which is what I assumed was the case, here. But there was no trace of the other Oscar. There wasn't any place in the tank he could have hidden that completely, so I concluded he had been eaten, too.

—Wait.

—What is it?

—You're making this up.

—I am not.

—You're a horror writer. This is what you do for a living.

—I am not making this up.

—Dylan's lizard died, came back to life, and ate the lizard you bought to take his place.

—Granted, when you put it that way, it sounds like something I might have written. Although, a leopard gecko?

—You always say you're open to new ideas.

—True, but an undead pet?

—Invent from what you know: isn't that another one of your sayings?

—You really are your mother's son. You have an answer for everything.

—I take that as a compliment.

—Do you want to hear the rest of the story or not?

Jordan shrugged. If you feel like telling it.

I was sufficiently irritated to want to spend the remainder of the drive in silence. Jordan's effort to discredit it, however, was evidence that the story was fulfilling its purpose of shifting his attention from the breakup. I sighed

JOHN LANGAN

and said, I hate to leave a story unfinished, especially when it's true.

—Or true-ish.

—Very funny. All right. I was pretty freaked out. I could not understand what had taken place. Because I wasn't prepared to believe that Oscar had returned from death to consume his successor. It was—there are moments of strangeness, instances when some feature of your surroundings doesn't make sense, and it puts a strain on everything else. You hear a voice in another room in a house you know is empty. You get out of bed in the middle of the night to have a pee, and there's a shape moving on top of the dresser. You're out walking the dogs, and you see a figure in the woods, watching you. Most of the time, these moments resolve. The voice you heard was a clock radio whose alarm turned on the radio. The shape in the bedroom is your reflection in the dresser mirror. The figure in the woods is the trunk of a tree in whose bark your brain picked out a face. You realize what's actually happening—what was always happening—and the strain you felt relaxes.

—Sometimes, though, it doesn't resolve. This was how I felt after your grandfather died. The world had been wrenched into a new configuration, and the sensation of it was terrible. Granted, it was on a much smaller scale, but seeing Oscar in the tank, I experienced something like this. There was a case of Gatorade sitting unopened on the kitchen table. I grabbed it and lifted it on top of the tank, then backed away, in case it wasn't enough to contain Oscar.

—What did you think he was going to do? Jordan said.

—I had no idea. Just the fact that he was there was bad enough. Not to mention, the whole cannibalism thing. He looked awful. His skin was shrunken right to the bone. There was no sign whatsoever that he'd eaten the other gecko's tail, let alone the rest of him. His claws were yellow, most of the ones on his forelegs cracked and broken. His eyes had a white film over them.

—How did I not notice a zombie gecko?

—You were a lot shorter, then. You had to stand on one of the kitchen chairs if you wanted a good look into the tank. Which, as I've said, you no longer did. And Oscar didn't make me think of a zombie so much as he did a mummy. He had that white, pebbled skin, and it had shrunken and bunched around his skeleton in a way that reminded me of a mummy's wrappings.

—Not to mention, you had buried him in his own tomb, in a kind of sarcophagus.

—Right. I'm sure you can guess what I did next.

—You called Mom.

—I called Mom. She was in her office.

—What did she say?

—Pretty much the same thing you did.

—She thought you were pranking her?

—In a particularly tasteless way. It took me what felt like forever to convince her I was serious. Of course, she didn't believe Oscar had come back from the dead, or that he had eaten Oscar 2.0. As she saw it, Oscar must not have been dead when we put him into the ground. He had clawed his way out of the grave and made his way to his home, where he had discovered the other gecko and chased him away. In the process, Oscar 2.0 had dropped his tail, which the original Oscar, in need of sustenance after his interment, had gobbled up. It was all very reasonable—or, not as unreasonable as my version of events—though it meant there was a second leopard gecko hiding somewhere in the house, and we should find him before you came home from school and were confronted with the evidence of our deception. And in a house with three dogs and three cats, a solitary lizard's chances of survival were not good.

—So while I was certain I would find no trace of him, I spent the next hour and a half conducting an exhaustive search for Oscar 2.0. I went through cabinets; I opened drawers; I looked under tables and chairs. I shifted the refrigerator; I pulled out the stove; I removed the cushions on the couch. I went through the laundry hamper. I sifted the recycling tubs. I lifted the garbage bag out of the garbage can. The entire time, I could feel the original Oscar behind me. I had the craziest impression he was…not watching me, but aware of me, of the search I was conducting. It was as if he'd returned from the grave accompanied by a presence he hadn't possessed before.

—Well. I turned up no trace of the second Oscar. I tidied the house as best I could and was left with forty-five minutes till I had to meet you at the bus stop. I decided I had better check the spot where we had buried Oscar.

—What did you find?

—The grave was open. Obviously. The earth at the spot had mounded, pushed up by the pieces of slate I'd laid over the chocolate box. They had been shoved away from the coffin with considerable force. There was a hole at one end of the mound, through which Oscar had escaped his tomb. I dug with my hands until I could see the edges of the pieces of slate. They were hot. Not warmed-by-the-sun: these things might have come out of a baking oven two seconds before. I couldn't touch them. There was a gap between them, through which Oscar's coffin was visible. The heat from the slate had caused it to blacken and shrivel. Nevertheless, I saw the hole Oscar had clawed through its top. The box was beginning to smolder. I pushed earth over it, filling the grave, tamping down the mound. Once I was finished, there was barely enough time for me to run into the house, wash my hands, and run down to the bus stop.

—Why didn't you leave it open?

—I didn't want you poking around in it. Unfortunately, this meant that, when Mom came home, she had to take my word about what I'd found.

—Did she?

—Let's just say that your mother is possessed of a healthy skepticism. She could credit Oscar tunneling to the surface—she had to: he was sitting in his tank in the kitchen—but she was less convinced about the shifted pieces of rock that were also burning hot. It sounded to her as if a larger animal had scented Oscar and attempted to get to him. Maybe Oscar had been moving in the box and a racoon or a bear heard him. The animal dug until it reached the pieces of slate, which it levered up, allowing Oscar to escape.

—That sounds reasonable.

—Of course it does. I had witnessed Oscar's grave, which in no way looked as if it had been excavated by a hungry predator, and I half-believed her explanation. She couldn't account for the temperature of the slate, said it was probably from the sun. Which, as we had learned in the recent past, could be plenty hot.

—What did she say when she saw Oscar?

—Oh, she agreed he looked pretty horrible. We would, too, if we had been buried alive, with no food and water, for almost a week. A lizard's metabolism was much faster than a human being's, especially if he was tearing through the box, tunneling to the surface. It was a wonder there was anything left of him.

—Makes sense.

—Except it doesn't. The math didn't compute, so to speak. As I saw it, if his metabolism was that amped up, then Oscar should have run out of gas long before he dug his way to freedom. Not to mention, there was the problem of how and why he had found his way from his grave to his tank. Wouldn't it have made more sense for him to flee into the woods? Instead, you have to imagine he scrambles across the lawn, around the porch to the stairs, climbs the stairs, leaps through the doggy door into the mudroom, traverses the mudroom, leaps through the doggy door into the kitchen, races across the kitchen, and scales the cabinet to his tank. There, to confront and devour the interloper. It's like a twisted version of one of those Disney movies about the loyal dog who follows his family cross-country, only with undeath and cannibalism. Even if I could accept that we had mistakenly buried Oscar alive, the rest of the situation defied sense.

—Okay.

—I'm just saying.

—I know. What happened next?

—Nothing, really. Mom and I had a brief, somewhat contentious debate over what to do with Oscar. I thought we should remove him from the tank and destroy him. Dylan's family weren't going to move into their new home until the end of the summer. That left us plenty of time to find another leopard gecko. Mom wasn't having any of it. As far as she was concerned, Oscar's miraculous return, after we had almost killed him twice, obligated us to ensure his safety until we could reunite him with Dylan. She won the argument, though I succeeded in persuading her that we needed to replace the pack of Gatorade I'd set on top of the tank with a heavy board.

—Did Oscar try to escape?

—Nope. In fact, he didn't do much of anything. Just squatted in the middle of the tank and stared out at the kitchen. Half the time, I was sure he had died. Again. That I could tell, he didn't eat, either. I continued to tip a few crickets in with him every couple of days, and they evoked no response. They hopped all over the place—they hopped onto Oscar, and he remained motionless.

—Maybe he was hunting them when you weren't watching him.

—It's possible he might have eaten one or two, but from what I could see, the overall population stayed the same. Finally, I stopped adding crickets to the tank. It had reached the point that, if I was up late writing, I could hear them chirping.

—Oscar number one ate the other lizard's tail.

—He ate the other lizard.

—Either way, maybe that gave him the nourishment he needed.

—For a week or two, I could believe. But this lasted two months. I had left off feeding Oscar and turned my attention to the insects, making sure they had food and water. And then they all died at once.

—All of them?

—Every last one. I was working on a story that was well past its deadline, and I realized that the house was quiet. I had the impression that the crickets had been singing not that long before, but I couldn't say when they had stopped. It was strange enough to cause me to walk into the kitchen and flip on the light. The crickets were motionless. Some were on their sides, some on their backs, some upright. I want to say I wasn't sure what was going on, but that isn't true, not exactly. Right away, I knew they were dead. I could feel it, as if their lives were water that had rushed down a drain, and the pipes were still gurgling. Oscar sat in their midst, his lower jaw hanging open. There was a sound coming out of him, so soft and low I almost missed it. I had to lean in close to the tank—much closer than I liked—to make out what it was.

—What was it?

—A word. A single word was broadcasting from his mouth, in a creaking, raspy voice that might have belonged to an old, old man—an ancient man.

—Seriously?

—Yes.

Jordan sighed, but said, What word?

—Life.

—That's...odd.

—You're telling me. I went to the butcher block, withdrew the butcher knife. I was halfway to the tank when I hesitated. Already, Oscar had come back from being baked. Who could say if a knife would work any better? I needed fire, to incinerate the lizard and scatter his ashes. I couldn't figure out how to accomplish this without making so much noise I'd wake Mom and you. That was not a conversation I wanted to have. Honey, what are you doing? I'm setting the gecko on fire because he talked to me.

Jordan snorted.

—And besides, Oscar's mouth had closed, and the voice had stopped. I slotted the knife back into the block. That night, I slept on the living room couch. I told myself I was guarding Mom and you from Oscar. I don't know what I thought he was going to do. I don't know what I thought I was going to do to stop him. But I felt better positioned there. Surprisingly, I fell asleep. When I checked the tank the next morning, the crickets were gone.

—Oscar ate them?

—Presumably. You still wouldn't know it to look at him. He was as shriveled as ever—desiccated, is the word I want. I didn't know what to do. Things that seem obvious to you at night become less certain during the day, and vice-versa. I tried to do research. I went to Oscar's grave and carefully opened it. I was hoping to unearth some clue to the cause of his return. I wore heavy gloves, in case the pieces of slate remained hot. Which would have been weird—at this point, Oscar had been back in his tank for a solid couple of months. It was almost time for us to hand him over to Dylan. But the whole situation was so bizarre, I wouldn't have been surprised if the rock had retained its heat. It hadn't, though. It had crumbled to pieces, to sand, as had the box and towel beneath it. I dug down another foot and a half, in case whatever was responsible for re-animating lay deeper. I didn't find anything.

—Next, I tried the internet. Most of the hits for mummified animals led to sites concerned with ancient Egyptian burial practices. They were informative, but not helpful. There was one pharaoh whose tomb's contents included a mummified crocodile, which seemed as if it might be relevant, but it wasn't. In the end, I knew no more than I had at the beginning.

—What did you do?

—Nothing, really. For the remainder of Oscar's stay with us, I slept on the couch. I told Mom I was having trouble sleeping, which was not as much a lie as it was an incomplete truth. I listened for that old man's voice, but I didn't hear it—although there were a couple of times I woke up certain it had just been speaking.

—In the end, we returned Oscar to Dylan. We loaded him in his tank into the car, and drove him to the Lucases' new house.

—I remember that, Jordan said. Kind of. Dylan showed me his room. There was a secret passage to the stairway.

—It was an old house. It had lots of peculiarities like that.

—Wait: what did Dylan do when he saw Oscar?

—He didn't say much of anything. Nor did his parents, for that matter. For the week leading up to it, I had rehearsed my responses to Dylan and his folks reacting to Oscar—to what Oscar had become. I was prepared, I thought, for tears, for shouting, for angry recriminations. But they barely paid attention to him. They were too caught up in unpacking. I swear, I had to stop myself from pointing to the tank and asking them if they noticed anything different about their pet.

—No one said anything?

—John, Dylan's little brother, wrinkled his nose at Oscar, but that was it. And that could have been an expression of distaste at a lizard. I left the house like someone backing away from a bomb. The minute the Lucases paused and took a good look at Oscar, I was sure they would be on the phone. They never did, though, and then when the house burned down a few months later, Oscar was the sole casualty.

—Was that after Dylan's parents got divorced?

—During, but it didn't help matters.

—Huh, Jordan said. You know, it's been a while since I've seen Dylan. Maybe after we pick up Mom—when we're home—I'll call him and ask if he wants to come over. If that's okay.

—Sure. I don't think we're doing anything tomorrow.

—Cool. Do you mind if I put on some music?

—Go ahead.

Jordan tapped the screen of his smart phone a couple of times, and soon was singing along with Bon Scott about the dirty deeds they would do dirt cheap. I had expected him to comment on the end of the story, ask me if I was certain Oscar had met his end along with the Lucases' house, maybe press me again on inventing the entire thing. He might later. My own teenage years lay long enough in the past for me to have lost touch with the peculiar schedule of their mental processes. Should he question the veracity of the narrative, I was prepared to answer honestly and say that everything I had told him was true. Should he question the story's close, I was prepared to lie and say that it had concluded with me setting Oscar's tank on the Lucases' kitchen table.

Because there had been more. Not much, but enough to make its omission a dishonesty. It began with a phone call three months after I returned

OSCAR RETURNS FROM THE DEAD, PROPHESIZING

Oscar. Van Lucas, Dylan's dad, was on the other end. Despite the time that had passed, I flinched when I heard him, trying to remember the lies I had prepared for his discovery of Oscar's state. I needn't have worried. Since we had deposited Oscar with them, we hadn't heard anything from the Lucases, which was unusual, as we saw them for dinner every few weeks. I speculated their silence had something to do with the lizard; my wife chalked it up to the move. I decided her explanation was more likely. As Van started talking, I learned that there was a third reason for their silence. Their marriage had collapsed, and they were getting a divorce.

I was shocked. Van and Polly Lucas had been together longer than Denise and I, and theirs had seemed to me one of those unions of opposites that proves the cliché. Of course, there's a great deal in every marriage that remains hidden to those outside it. Polly's mother, I knew, had died suddenly as the Lucases were closing on the new house, which was more than they could afford, except its previous owners had defaulted on their mortgage, and the bank had put the place up at a price that was a steal. My experience with buying and moving into our house had taught me how stressful the process could be, and this was on its own, with no concomitant tragedies. Van refused to say any more over the phone, so I met him at the Starbucks in Huguenot. There, he told me the reason for his and Polly's split. While up late one night, Polly had heard her mother speaking to her. Her message was simple: you and your husband don't love one another. It's time for you to leave this loveless marriage and find a better life for yourself. Crazy, but Polly believed the voice that had spoken to her immediately and without reservation. You didn't have to be much of a psychologist to know that she was using this supposed incident as a way to lever herself out of a relationship she had grown tired of. Van wanted her to see a doctor to ensure she wasn't suffering from some affliction physical or mental, a brain tumor or psychosis, but Polly found a lawyer who said there was no requirement for her to do so, and from there, their split had been accomplished with frightening speed. She had moved out, found a new place in Joppenburgh. Really, the only major thing that hadn't been settled between them was the house.

—I swear, Van said, some nights, I stand in the kitchen, hoping that I'll hear someone telling me what to do, my father or grandfather, you know? But it's just me and the gecko, me and old Oscar.

I must have blanched, but Van didn't notice. I said, Is that where you keep him?

—The lizard? Yeah. Dylan didn't want him in his room, any more, so we left him in the kitchen.

—And that was where Polly said she heard her mother?

—Yeah. Pity we can't question Oscar about Polly's voice, get him to tell us what really happened, right?

—Yeah.

Two weeks after that, I was breaking into the Lucases' former home. Technically, I wasn't breaking in, since the back door was unlocked. There was no one there. Polly was at her new place with Dylan and John. Van had gone up to Lake George for the weekend to visit his mother and stepfather. The house looked much as it had my previous visit, full of boxes of clothes, books, and toys. In the kitchen, Oscar's tank was on the counter near the stove. According to Van, he and Polly couldn't agree about custody of the gecko, either. Oscar was in his familiar position, surveying the room. He did not register my presence.

Although it was late, past one in the morning, I had parked several streets over and crept through a number of backyards and a stand of trees to reach the house. The night was quiet, but I didn't want to take any chances of being seen, which was why I was wearing a black turtleneck, black slacks, and black shoes. Prior to entering the house, I had pulled on a pair of rubber dish gloves I brought with me in a small rucksack. I was still carrying the rucksack with my left hand. When I saw Oscar, I opened the top of the bag and withdrew the butcher knife I'd stowed in it. The knife was old, from the junk box in my basement. I'd sharpened the blade and wiped the whole thing down for fingerprints. I moved to Oscar's tank. I had returned the tank with the heavy board I'd kept over its wire top at our house, but the wooden lid had been removed. This made it easier for me to lift the screen. I was ready for Oscar to attempt an escape, but he stayed put, didn't acknowledge the exit I'd provided him. If it was possible, he looked worse than he had the last time I'd seen him. His skin had contracted around his bones to the point he appeared more skeleton than flesh. Had I been told he'd been found in some minor pharaoh's tomb, I would have believed it.

I thought I was prepared for Oscar's jaw to drop open, for that ancient voice I'd heard to claw its way out of his throat. I was wrong. What emerged from the gecko was neither the old man's voice I had heard the night of the great cricket massacre, nor the old woman's voice that had encouraged Polly to end her marriage. This was another old man speaking, one whose low tones could have belonged to my father, dead the past decade. It was mixed with a hissing noise, like sand pouring over stone. I froze as it said my name, then continued speaking.

What my father uttered in slow, halting syllables was horrible. The kitchen tilted, as if I had been punched in the head. On trembling legs, I stepped forward and stabbed the knife down into the tank. It struck Oscar at an angle, cleaving his head and right foreleg from the rest of his body, and stuck in the glass under him. His mouth snapped shut, and the voice ceased. I had intended to remove the butcher knife once it served its purpose, but the prospect of touching something that had touched this thing made my stomach churn. From the rucksack, I slid a small can of lighter fluid and a box of matches. The pungent odor of the liquid stung my nostrils as I soaked Oscar's remains. I replaced the lighter fluid in the rucksack and reached for the matches.

After all this time, I still wasn't sure exactly what went wrong. I hadn't used that much lighter fluid, yet when I dropped the lit match into the tank, the air inside ignited in a swirl of blue that leapt straight to the ceiling. I looked for a fire extinguisher, but already, the ceiling had caught, flames racing across it. The glass of Oscar's tank cracked, then burst outward, spraying flaming shards around the kitchen. Ten, twelve struck boxes, setting them alight. In no time whatsoever, the situation was out of control, the ceiling rippling with fire, the boxes flaring like torches. Soon, the flames would find the gas line snaking into the stove, and the house would be lost. I had left my cell in the car, and could see no sign of a house phone. I chose the only option left to me, and fled out the back door. Panicked as I was, I had enough sense to retrace my route through the woods and backyards. I was almost to my car when a distant WHUMP announced the propane tank's detonation. As I drove home, I heard the first sirens.

Needless to say, the destruction of their house and about fifty percent of their material possessions did not help the Lucases' divorce. Apparently, it was obvious to the investigators that the fire had been deliberately set, but Van's alibi of being with his mother was rock solid, nor was there evidence of any suspicious activity in his phone or internet histories. For a short time, a good deal of interest focused on Polly, a consequence of some intemperate threats she had made to Van within earshot of their respective lawyers and their aides, but that didn't lead anywhere, either. I spent a month in near constant dread of the knock on the door that would herald my discovery, but the door remained silent; though it was another year until I felt I could truly relax. But the guilt I felt at having destroyed my friend's home, however accidentally, continued to surge in me at unexpected moments, sometimes with such force I had my phone in hand and was halfway to entering Van's number before I gained control of myself. Of course, there was no way he would believe my explanation, and he was well on his way to a new life, so I felt justified in continuing to conceal my responsibility for the blaze. The gas explosion had been severe enough that the evidence of my dispatch of Oscar had been obliterated; Van would likely take my attempt to explain events as nothing more than a sign of mental illness.

But if the lizard was gone, and my part in his demise a secret, the words that had been delivered to me through him had lodged in my memory. I had done my best to forget them and, failing that, to ignore them. Every time Denise flew to another conference, though, I heard the voice I did not want to accept had been my father's saying, The landing gear will fail. The plane will split, catch fire. Your wife will survive, but the two of you will wish she hadn't. Your son will suffer the most. It will be the end of your family.

There had been no way to convey the prediction to Denise, not without revealing my role in the destruction of the Lucases' house. She wouldn't have believed it, any more than she could accept that a dead gecko had returned to life (or, had I told her, that it had channeled the voices of the dead). So every time she flew, I was there to see her off and to greet her, in hopes that my presence would act in some way as a good luck charm. I didn't like to bring Jordan, but he had asked, and with the bad breakup, I hadn't wanted to say no.

There wasn't much further to go. Traffic was heavy; we were going to be late. Call Mom, I said to Jordan, tell her were almost there.

After a moment, he said, She isn't answering.

In the rearview mirror, I saw the flashing lights, racing toward us.

ALICE'S REBELLION

1

Freshly cut, the block of wood sat in the center of the scaffold, a white box. It was a peculiarity of the Prime Minister to insist on a new block for each of the condemned. Given the number and pace of the executions, there wasn't time to finish the chunks of wood, whose surfaces were rough, covered in splinters, a final indignity. As long as the headsman's blade was sharp, his eye true, it wasn't one Alice would have to endure for long.

He stood to the left of the executioner, the PM, another of his idiosyncrasies. Surely, there was more important business for him to be attending to than this spectacle. Yet so much of his rule was built on exactly such public displays that Alice supposed this was exactly where he was supposed to be. A light breeze tousled his colorless hair, caught his long red tie and made a banner of it. His babyish features wore their usual distracted look, as if he were trying and failing to remember a favorite clever story. Behind him and the headsman, a forest of poles held the heads of those whose feet had preceded Alice's up the stairs to the scaffold. The Mock Turtle's mouth hung open next to the glazed eyes of the Unicorn, whose tongue protruded from between his cracked teeth black and swollen. The thickness of his strong neck had proved a challenge for the executioner, who had required ten strokes of his weighted sword to sever it completely, and then halted the proceedings to inspect and sharpen his implement. The wind rocked the heads right to left, making them appear restless, impatient for what was to come.

As Alice stepped onto the scaffold, the PM's attention returned from its internal distance, his eyes focusing on her with such intensity they practically bulged in the sockets. He shuffled his feet, gestured at the wood block sheepishly, as if embarrassed by the event the two of them were part of. Alice walked to the block. In front of it, there was a piece of rolled up carpet for her to kneel on, the fabric sodden with blood. Of course, Alice thought. The PM grimaced. With her right foot, Alice slid the carpet to the side. Fear pressed her chest, made each breath an effort. In the far distance, over the ruined red brick walls hemming in the execution grounds, the sea was a gray line. She stared at it as the PM's cough drew her back to the matter at hand. Or at head.

The surface of the scaffold was smooth against her knees. She leaned forward until her throat touched the rough top of the block. The odor of pine flooded her nostrils, and underneath it, the mingled pungency of bleach and blood. Out of the corner of her right eye, she watched the headsman pass his over-sized sword to the PM, who took it with none of his usual bumbling, but rather a butcher's practiced hold. I suppose I should be flattered, Alice thought. He adjusted his grip on it, then swept the blade over his head, tugging the edge of his shirt out of his trousers in the process. Without looking directly at him, Alice said, "I liked you better when you were Tweedle Dee." She saw the executioner flinch.

The sword crashed down, a first time and a second.

2

Though unpleasant, the Caterpillar's attentions were a price Alice told herself she was willing to pay for shelter beneath his great mushroom. Safety from the Red Queen's Numerals was worth the sensation of his fleshy legs crawling over her skin. Honestly, she wasn't clear as to all or even most of what went on when the Caterpillar began to heave his bloated mass in her direction. The vents along his baggy sides released enormous clouds of the violet gas that collected and hung in the air over the mushroom, her head would start to spin (or perhaps it was everything else spinning and her head remaining still), and Alice would lose hold of herself in the resulting maelstrom. Sometimes she would think she had caught hold of her self, only to find she was looking out of six eyes instead of two, her sides rippling with a motion not unlike exhaling, and she would release that self and try for another. Rarely was she successful before the effects of the violet gas had subsided. In the meantime, she might recline in a rowboat drifting on a lazy river under a hot summer sun, her companions a pair of young girls in blue and white dresses, or she might rush burbling through tulgey woods, her wings tucked in close to avoid the branches, her waistcoat tightly buttoned. Afterward, she would lie on her back staring up at the mushroom's underside, the striations like the ribs of a whale, while the Caterpillar struggled to his hookah on top of the mushroom to begin inhaling the dense smoke the engine of his body would refine to purple vapor.

It was during one of those other selves that Alice first encountered the idea of (or for?) mathematical logic. She was a tall man seated at a wooden desk, the pen in her hand scratching row after row of symbols onto the paper before her. For the time she was in the self, her brain was packed full with theorems, each one linked to another, sometimes more, the whole a sort of web whose strands tugged the world into order. Once more herself, Alice could not remember most of the equations she had written, but the idea of things being arranged into systems of cause and effect, with boundaries and limits, remained fixed and burning in her mind. The Caterpillar was no more interested in discussing it with her than he was anything else, but Bill the Lizard proved surprisingly amenable to conversation. Once he was finished brushing out the Caterpillar's vents and inspecting his hookah, he accepted a cup of milky Oolong from Alice and sat with her for the time it took him to drink it.

"I think what I mean," Alice said, "is that the world should not revolve around us, so to speak."

"Ooh, I don't know about that," said Bill, his tail flicking nervously. "If things wasn't to revolve around us, then wouldn't we revolve around them? I'm afraid I should find it awfully dizzying."

"Not exactly," Alice said. "It's more a case of, both we and things would orbit something else, a third thing, a set of...rules."

Bill looked as dubious as a lizard could.

"Or," Alice said, "there wouldn't be any spinning. Things would stay where they were, as they were. When the Red Queen had someone's head chopped off, their blood wouldn't turn into a fresh pack of cards."

"What would it turn into?"

"Nothing. It would remain blood."

"Hmm," Bill said. "That has rather a fatalistical sound."

Alice said, "I suppose it does."

3

"If this plan of yours succeeds," the Dodo said, "I should be extinct."

"It's not my plan, exactly," Alice said. "A great many people have already agreed to it."

"All the same," the Dodo said.

"Well, yes," Alice said.

4

Light clung to the windows of the Jabberwocky's eyes for a long time after its chorus of hearts had ceased to beat.

5

"You know what they say about omelets," Alice said.

"I'm certain I do not," said Humpty Dumpty.

6

"You mean to turn nonsense on its head," the Mad Hatter said.

"I mean to turn nonsense on itself," Alice said, "and to continue to do so until it becomes nonsensical to itself."

"How odd," said the Hatter. "How would such a thing happen?"

"I'm not exactly sure about all of it," Alice said. "But I think that, if you were to fold nonsense onto nonsense, then onto nonsense again, and so on, you would begin to notice places where the nonsense started to…fall into line with itself. Which would mean it was becoming more sense and less non-sense. If you were to continue folding, the sense would replace the nonsense, until all you were left with was sense.

"Or mostly sense," she added.

"What a fascinating idea," the Hatter said. "However would you accomplish it?"

"It would require frightfully complex equations," Alice said. "And blood: an enormous quantity of blood."

7

The Red Queen shouted, "OFF—"

"Shh," Alice said, placing her index finger against the monarch's fleshy lips. "You don't get to say that anymore."

8

For an instant, Alice felt everything about her become heavy, as heavy as it was possible to imagine, as if she were being pulled down, down underground, down past all the clocks, and the teacups, and the coffee spoons, down past the crust, the upper mantle, the lower mantle, the outer core, all the way to where the inner core spun burning in the darkness, 11,000 degrees Fahrenheit, a measurement in a system she understood, as she understood the hemoglobin in her blood to have a chemical formula of $C2952\ H4664\ O832\ N812\ S8\ Fe4$, and $F=ma$ to be an expression of Newton's Second Law, and 1558 to be the year Mary I (aka Bloody Mary, surely a Red Queen if ever there was one) died, and numbers and names, essays and equations, sciences and stories, all the nails necessary to tack down existence, secure it. In that instant, as everything was crystallizing but not all the way solid, Alice cast away the Caterpillar and his mushroom sanctuary, the Numerals and their insistent flatness, the Red Queen's scarlet expression, cast away all of it, let words take it, sentences wrap it and bind it between leather covers. She threw away the sun-drenched afternoon, the placid river, the girls in the rowboat, left it to anecdote and rumor.

The world set. She was twenty-four years old, pursuing graduate studies at the London School of Economics. She was renting a nice (if tiny) flat in Wimbledon, and she was seeing a nice veterinarian who had his practice in Croydon.

9

Six good years: not great years, not perfect years, but lit by a quiet glory, a radiance arising from the splash and tumble of water from the faucet as she washed her hands, the sizzle and pop of an egg frying in the pan, the warm weight of the duvet on cold winter nights. There was no shortage of badness: the veterinarian turned out to be married, the chef she took up with after him generally horrible, and she broke her wrist when she tripped running for her train. Even at their worst, though—when she was standing in the doorway to her flat, arms crossed, as Yasmine, Nathan's wife, screamed at her from the hallway, while he hid locked in the bathroom—events unfolded within an underlying framework of order and predictability. Alice finished her degree, found a decent position with the Royal Bank of Scotland, took her holidays in Dubai. She considered moving into a larger flat.

Ironically, BBC 1 gave her the first warning things were unraveling. During one of their roundtable discussions, a pithy older woman described the new prime minister as Tweedle Dee to the American president's Tweedle Dum. Although Alice had the TV on mostly for background noise while she did her yoga, the comparison caught her attention. A number of political cartoonists picked up on the allusion and for the next several days, the print and online editions of a host of newspapers published cartoons illustrating it. Right away, Alice was struck by the almost preternatural accuracy of the journalist's words, and each drawing to appear reinforced her growing conviction that the Tweedles had not only found their way to this new existence essentially intact, but were prospering within it. She did her best to ignore the icy dread rising within her, to put faith in her coworkers' assurances that everything the PM was promising would be splendid. "He'll take things back to the way they used to be," more than one person said to her.

"Yes," Alice said, "that's what worries me."

10

How the Prime Minister (whom she could not stop thinking of as Tweedle Dee, now that she had started) succeeded in picking apart the stitches with which Alice had sewn together this new world, she did not know. Of course, she had been aware not everyone was in favor of her plan to remake their existence, but the Tweedles had not seemed terribly bothered one way or another. And it wasn't as if the PM undid everything. Instead, he and his trans-Atlantic counterpart confused matters sufficiently to throw the world into turmoil. Soon decks of cards were roaming the streets of London and several other large cities, assaulting anyone they thought looked foreign, while flamingos and hedgehogs invaded football and cricket pitches. It was no longer safe to eat oysters, and a knight in battered white armor was reported roaming tube stations, waving his longsword threateningly. It was ever harder to follow the news, which proliferated in the time it took to switch from one channel to the next. A batch of bad tea cakes caused the necks of any who ate them to lengthen a foot and a half. Feral bagpipes were sighted on the Scottish border.

When the mirror war erupted, Alice sighed and submitted to the inevitable. The Dormouse and the Greens were ecstatic, gathering behind her; the Unicorn joined them. Although Alice smiled to see the Unicorn once more, her outlook was grim. There were creatures fighting for the Prime Minister she had not previously encountered, heaps of scrap metal, rusted hulks whose ranks advanced in rigid lock-step. Their thick feet crushed the Dormouse, trampled women and men. For all his ferocity, the Unicorn was hard pressed to defeat their armored mass, while their crude blades splashed his ruby blood across the floors of the living rooms, churches, and department stores where they battled. What members of Alice's forces survived the Heaps were attacked by drones whose propellers separated hands, arms, and sometimes heads from bodies with brutal efficiency. Once Alice had been steeped in blood, had waded through rivers of it, washed her long hair in it, worn its rich stink as a perfume. Now the copper reek through which she moved kept her every meal burning at the back of her throat. She was still capable of single-minded ruthlessness, but so was the Prime Minister, so was everyone else in this existence.

She had a single conversation with him, a week before what was to be the final battle of her failed war. They met at a coffee stand in Waterloo Station. Alice recognized the nervous proprietor as a former Numeral, a Six of Hearts, she thought. Security was heavy. The PM did not bother sitting at the wobbly table on which had been set a pair of china mugs, sugar bowl, and milk jug. Alice slid out her chair, sat, and prepared her coffee light and sweet. Behind her, she could feel the Unicorn tense as she brought the mug to her lips. She wasn't concerned. Poison was far too sophisticated for the PM. The coffee was better than she would have expected from this sort of establishment. She looked at the proprietor (who had been a Six, yes) and nodded approvingly. He ducked as if she'd thrown something at him.

"I do hope you're going to surrender," the Prime Minister said.

Alice paused. "I was planning to say the same thing to you."

"Whatever can you mean? You're losing. Every time your forces have met mine, we've crushed you, we've slaughtered you. Your supporters are deserting you in droves. If you lay down your weapons now, ask forgiveness, I could pardon you. Perhaps. Anyway, at least no more of you would have to die."

"I mean," Alice said, "that you've done fundamental damage to this existence. You've loosened what was sealed with blood. I don't know if it can be repaired. Even if there's no fixing it, we should be able to prevent it from becoming worse. Yes, we. This is why I'm here, to ask you to lay down your arms and join me in finding a way to keep things from coming apart any more than they have."

"But I don't want to," the PM said. "I like what's happened. My friends like what's happened. My followers like what's happened. Why on earth should I want to change it?"

"Because it's not sustainable," Alice said. "Because what you've started is going to harm everyone."

"Oh, I don't know about that."

"I do."

"Look," the PM said, "will you surrender or not?"

"I will not," Alice said.

"The penalty for insurrection is death," the PM said, "I hope you understand."

Alice finished her coffee, stood. "The way things have been going," she said, "I'm not sure death is what it used to be."

11

The final battle began on the streets outside and spilled into the aisles of Harrod's. Mannequins that had not picked sides held up plaster hands in protest at this invasion of what was supposed to be neutral ground and were cut down by the weapons of both sides. Display cases were smashed, racks of clothing doused in blood. The fight was over depressingly fast. Through sheer force of numbers, the Heaps overwhelmed Alice's troops, killing those they could not capture. Although she knew he wouldn't be, Alice was hoping the Prime Minister would be there to witness his side triumphant. She entertained a fantasy of fighting her way to him and splitting him down the middle with her blade, Tweedle Dead. But he was nowhere to be seen, unless he was concealed in a back room, watching the battle through the store's security cameras. Failing in her plan for the PM, Alice was hoping for death under the swords of her foes. This did not happen, either. In the end, she was borne to the bloody floor by the combined efforts of a quartet of the largest Heaps.

The inevitable show trial was mercifully brief.

12

The first blow of the heavy sword missed her neck and instead struck the top of Alice's back. Pain blinding white detonated across her shoulders, robbing her of breath. She was able to recover her thoughts sufficiently to think, Naturally, he'd bollocks this, too, before the Prime Minister's second attempt cut clean through her neck.

Alice's blood sprayed across and down the sides of the wooden block into which the executioner's blade had lodged. So pleased with himself was the PM (who was still bristling from that Tweedle Dee snipe) that he released the sword and reached for Alice's hair. Her head weighed more than he expected. He lifted it until he was face to face with it. The eyes had rolled under the lids; the mouth hung open. Already, the head looked more like a prop from a movie and less a part of a living person. The PM licked his lips and said, "I've been reading about what happens to you after you're beheaded—to your consciousness. Apparently, there's some evidence it may hang about for a minute or two. Well. In case you're still there, I wanted to let you know, I've decided I'm going to keep your head. I intend to have it mounted on the wall of my personal chambers, together with those of your principal co-conspirators. At the next Guy Fawkes, we'll find a way to work your likenesses into the festivities."

The head did not answer. Had the PM looked down, at the base of the block along whose sides Alice's blood continued to drip, he might have noticed the pools into which it gathered quivering. Had he inspected them more closely, he would have been astonished to see tiny playing cards lifting themselves out of the red liquid and fleeing for the edge of the scaffold, in the direction of the sea.

SNAKEBIT,

Or Why I (Continue to) Love Horror

1

Here's the thing: I've been answering questions about the beginnings of my relationship to the horror field for a little bit of time, now, some in written interviews, some on convention panels, some on podcasts. I've referred to the experience of reading Stephen King's *Christine* during the fall of 1983, in my freshman year of high school. I've described the way the novel catalyzed me, discussed the way in which its portrait of adolescent existence felt true, even though I recognized many of its details as exaggerated. From there, I've moved forward in time, to credit the importance of reading (and rereading) Peter Straub's *Ghost Story* and *Shadowland*, not to mention, T.E.D. Klein's *Dark Gods*, Clive Barker's short fiction, and the *Year's Best Horror Stories* series Karl Edward Wagner edited for DAW books. I've also gone backwards from that high school moment, to writing and reading a horror story to my sixth grade English class, to writing and illustrating a King Kong vs. Godzilla story in my first grade English notebook. I have referred to watching an adaptation of *Frankenstein* I've never been able to identify with my father at an age I'm unsure of.

I've discussed the two heart attacks that almost killed my dad in the fall of 1982, and the two months in the ICU at what my family did not realize was the actual end of his life a decade and change later. I've considered the effect of being raised Roman Catholic by devout parents on my youthful imagination. I've revisited the oldest memories I have, which are of surgery for a tiny piece of metal that had infiltrated the cornea of my right eye when I was two and half.

Given such an accumulation of anecdotes, my becoming interested in horror narratives is perhaps not that surprising. Indeed, you might call it overdetermined. But starting a relationship is not the same as continuing one, is it? To ask why I love horror is, as I see it, to ask what it is about the field that has allowed and even encouraged me to sustain a creative engagement with it in a professional sense for the last twenty-four years (as I'm writing this). It's the equivalent of asking how you've remained in love after many years with your partner. Answering this question requires a different type of explanation. Rather than another trip through my interior archives, we need to go a little further along, to the workshop that adjoins the archives. As a shorthand to explain the way my creativity functions, I've recently employed the following example: "Give me a story about a college professor having a mid-life crisis, and I'm not that interested. Add a Lamia to the mix, however, and I'm on board."

Let's take a look at this shorthand in action.

2

To begin with, here's a character. We'll call him Tom, Tom Alero, using a name that's been rattling around inside my brain for at least the last decade, when he was supposed to be the protagonist of a story called, "Five Million Tentacles, Five Million Bullets." This Tom—as perhaps that other, earlier Tom—is an assistant professor of English at a college in New York state, about an hour and a half north of New York City along the Hudson River. As a nod to the novels of the terrific Carol Goodman, I've used the name Penrose College in previous stories; I believe this is where Tom teaches. (Penrose is also a leitmotif in James Joyce's *Ulysses*.) He's a small (5'8"), trim (140 lbs.) man who maintains his health with an early morning run around the college's extensive network of footpaths, which he follows with a shower at the campus health center. He likes to say he hates running but loves having run, hates the way his legs burn and his chest heaves as his sneakers pound the ribbon of pavement that takes him around the school's mix of late Victorian and Modernist buildings, but loves the feeling that settles in him not long after he's left the health center and is walking toward his office in Irving Hall, a sensation of having been cleansed, all the detritus of the previous day left in the carefully mowed grass lining the paths, washed down the shower drain. Tom is in his early forties—forty-three, to be precise—an age which bothers him more than he knows it should. Yes, his thick black hair has receded, but only enough for someone staring obsessively at his hairline in the mirror to notice. And there isn't enough gray in it for anyone to notice (except for the obsessive mirror-starer). The dark circles under his brown eyes are no worse than they've ever been, and the trio of lines cut into his forehead don't mark him as almost-fifty, just older.

On the mental checklist he doesn't like to admit keeping, but to which he has been returning with increasing frequency the past couple of years, Tom can mark as completed most of the items there. Ph.D.: check, and from Columbia at that. (Tenured) position at a more than respectable school: check. Publication of books (two) by prestigious academic presses and articles (seven) in peer-reviewed journals: check and check. (One of the books, a meticulous study of the English Romantic poet John Keats's long poem, "Lamia," was a finalist for a minor award.) The list goes on, but you get the point: career-wise, Tom is doing about as well as the younger self who chose to pursue a doctorate, as opposed to opting for a career as a high school teacher, could have hoped. Every year, he attends the MLA convention in whatever city is hosting it, and the panels in which he participates are among the best-attended at the sprawling event. He is on the editorial board of two scholarly journals. His photograph and professional biography feature prominently on the Penrose website. It's always possible to wish for more from one's career, an endowed chair at a larger institution, a Brown or Stanford, but such aspirations are not the source of Tom's unease.

Well, perhaps it's his personal life, right? Or his lack thereof? He's one of those people whose overachievements in one part of their life have come at the expense of deficits in the rest of it. Maybe he lives in an underfurnished apartment whose sparse, almost monkish decor speaks to an underdeveloped aspect of his existence. But no: at five eleven this particular afternoon, let's follow him as he leaves campus in his green Subaru Outback—vehicle of choice, he likes to joke, for liberal professors condemned to contend with the region's unpredictable, sometimes ferocious winters. He drives twenty minutes south and a little east from Penrose to a development of split-level houses through whose looping streets he steers until he arrives at one set atop a small, steep rise. He turns into its short driveway beside his wife's car (another Outback, brown, which he is surprised to see already there) and shifts into Park.

Possibly, he remains in the driver's seat after he has switched off the engine, his eyes seemingly staring at the garage door in front of him, closed although if it were open, there would be no room for the car, as the space is occupied with all manner of boxes and clutter, most of it connected to the two children who throw open the front door to the house with a crash and race down the concrete steps to the driveway, Bess, the younger, holding onto the metal railing with her left hand as she descends each step, while Barney, the older, ignores such precautions and jumps two and three steps at a time, almost overbalancing himself when he attempts four, only to catch himself at the last moment, his round seven-year-old's face lighting with pleasure at his success. Tom was on his way out of the car as Barney braved four steps, his heart already in his throat in anticipation of scraped and bleeding skin, possible broken bones, streaming tears and sobbing. Barney's triumph renders his father's surge of panic unnecessary, though the emotion fails to subside right away, threatening to erupt from Tom in a torrent of reproach directed at his grinning son. "What have I told you about jumping on the steps?" he can hear himself saying, his voice taut and nasal from exasperation. No matter that Barney will apologize immediately, is on his way to doing so before Tom has said anything, as the sight of his father's expression has reminded him of the no-jumping-on-the-front-steps rule.

Shame clouds Tom's fear like ink dropped in boiling water. Lightheaded from the tumult of emotion, he forces a smile at Barney and says, "Hey, buddy," in a tone he hopes betrays nothing other than happiness at seeing him. Barney responds with a, "Hey, Dad," of his own, a myriad of feelings flitting across his face like startled sparrows: the tail end of fear at having realized his mistake; suspicion at the mildness of his dad's greeting; relief at thinking Tom didn't notice his rule breaking. Tom exchanges a high-five with his son then steps past him to catch Bess in a hug that lifts her off the bottom step and into the air, shrieking laughter. Five, she responds to Tom's exaggerated embraces with an unfettered delight from which her older brother has withdrawn since entering second grade. Oh, Barney still appreciates a good hug, but lately he has favored more restrained displays of affection. Of course he does, Delilah, Tom's wife says. He's growing up, maturing, which Tom concedes their oldest is; it's just that the process seems to be happening in fits and starts, which Tom wishes he found less confusing and occasionally exasperating than he does.

His marriage has been teetering on the edge of a similar period of flux for some time, and the instant we hear this, we probably assume we have arrived at the source of Tom's discontent. The more things change, and all that. Compounding the cliché, Delilah Spenser is in the kitchen when Tom carries Bess through the front door and up the short flight of carpeted stairs to the house's upper level, Barney pulling the door closed behind them with a mighty grunt. "Hi, hon," she calls from the countertop where she is using a butcher knife to cube a large tomato. The strong, pleasant odor of garlic sautéing in the pan on the stove meets Tom as he reaches the top of the stairs, where he deposits Bess to the left so she can run into the living room where the Disney channel is playing on the 55-inch flatscreen fixed to the wall. He enters the kitchen to obey the command on his wife's green apron to kiss the cook. She is about the same height as Tom (5'7"), unless she wears the shoes and boots with the chunky heels she prefers but he secretly finds ugly, in which case, she stands anywhere from one to three inches taller, a difference highlighted by her hair, whose off-blond curls bestow another couple of inches to her, especially if she wears it up. This afternoon, she is in the comfortable orange sneakers that barely increase her height, together with jeans and a gray St. Stephen's College T-shirt. Located twenty-five miles farther up the Hudson than Penrose, St. Stephen's is a much smaller, if no less famous, institution where Delilah, whose Ph.D., also from Columbia (where she and Tom met), is in Art History, is assistant chair of the Fine Art department. While her administrative duties earn her a release from one of the courses she would otherwise be required to teach, her attention to those responsibilities generally consumes at least as much time as would preparation for a class.

Tom is more than surprised to find her home before him, preparing dinner: he is this side of shocked. Typically, he is first in the front door, relieving Melanie, the younger of their next-door neighbors' two daughters, who supplements her part-time job at the McDonald's drive-thru window with the cash Tom and Delilah give her for meeting the kids off the school bus and watching them for the hour and half to two hours before a parent pulls into the driveway. Dinner tends to be Tom's responsibility, and it's one in which he takes a certain private pride. While he can't put together a lasagna or meatloaf as adeptly as his wife, he's entirely capable of heating chicken nuggets and fries and serving them to the kids with a side of grape tomatoes and baby carrots, plus cups of diluted fruit juice to wash it down with, even as he boils tortellini for him and Delilah topped with a local red sauce he bought at the farmers market in Poughkeepsie on Sunday.

"Well, this is a pleasant surprise," he says, mostly meaning it, trying his best to dismiss the irritation this unexpected change in his routine arouses. Yes, Delilah says, she received some very good news this morning, so she decided to take the afternoon off and make a bang-up dinner in celebration. There's champagne chilling in the freezer, alongside an assortment of Ben and Jerry's finest ice creams. When Barney, who has been hanging around the kitchen doorway, his eyes on the TV screen, his ears listening to his parents, hears his mother utter the magic names Ben and Jerry, he turns his head to his parents and puts on his surprised face, eyes wide, eyebrows raised, mouth open. *They're having Ben and Jerry's?* he says, speaking the words with the fervor of a fanatic for his favorite sacrament. They are, Delilah says, and they have *four different flavors*, her tone mirroring her son's. Barney calls to his sister to share the news and in no time at all the kids are hopping up and down, chanting, "Ben-and-JERRY'S! Ben-and-JERRY'S! Ben-and-JERRY'S!" Delilah exits the kitchen to join the refrain for a few rounds; though she skips the jumping. Tom smiles as he watches his family express their collective delight. After Delilah's voice falls off, he raises his hands, palms-out, and hushes the kids, laughing as he does to show he's still part of the celebration, and adding that he needs to ask Mommy about her very good news, which is more for his wife's hearing. Throughout the kids' childhoods, Delilah has accused him of being too uptight with them, too rigid and impatient, charges he has both admitted to and resented. If he fails to contextualize his call for quiet, he fears, he will spark a conflict with Delilah that will torch the rest of the night. His strategy appears to succeed: Delilah echoes his request to turn the volume down.

Once Barney and Bess have lost interest in their chant, distracted by whatever cartoon is playing on the TV, Tom follows Delilah into the kitchen and says, "Is it the island?" To which she replies with a delighted, "Yes!" throwing her arms around his neck and giving him a kiss through which he can feel her smile. "Congratulations," he says while their lips are still joined, which makes Delilah laugh and extend the kiss. Tom feels his face flush, not unpleasantly. Finally, she steps back from the embrace, fanning herself with her hands and letting out a, "Whew! Honestly, sir," she adds, "there are young children in the house!"

"I know," Tom says with his most rakish grin. "Where do you think they came from?"

"Oh, you," she says. She returns to the stove, turning the gas back up under the pan. As she continues dinner preparations, and Tom sets the dining room table, Delilah elaborates on her good news. For the last year and a half, she has been in negotiations on behalf of St. Stephen's with the owner of a small island just off the eastern shore of the Hudson, at the southernmost tip of the college's property. It's as much a peninsula as a proper island, since the twenty yards between it and the mainland is a tidal marsh. (Yes, there are tides this far up the river.) Magdaline Island is a narrow oval of approximately five acres. A spine of bedrock runs north to south through its center, with a mix of hemlock, birch, and maple on either side of it. At the southern end of the island, there's a grassy meadow where most of the houses (and once, a castle) have been built and let fall into disrepair. A smaller cottage, still in use, sits amidst the rocks at the north end. For such a small piece of land, the island has an extensive and eccentric history. The Lenape who inhabited this stretch of the river called the island Snake Island, due to the number and variety of the reptiles reported to inhabit it. It was purchased from the Lenape by that scion of old New Amsterdam, Peter Stuyvesant. From his calloused hands, it passed via marriage and purchase into the hands of other of the region's famous families, the Van Rensselaers and the Van Tassels, as well as several lesser known though equally wealthy individuals. In the mid-nineteenth century, Beryl Magdaline, whose inheritance upon the deaths of her parents and older brothers in the crash of the steamboat *Swallow* included the island, a mansion on the mainland, and an astonishing sum of money, made of the island a kind of open-air display for a collection of statues she gathered

243

from all over the world on the two-year trip she took following her entire family's fiery demise. Many, Beryl was supposed to have found during her travels, in Mexico and Honduras, Greece, Turkey, what was then called Persia, and India. Prior to his death, Beryl's father, Constable, had ordered the construction of a number of partial structures on the island, arches, columns, and walls, to give the impression of ruins, as was the fashion of the time. Beryl modified her father's instructions, transforming the faux wreckage into displays for her imminent purchases. From the manor on the mainland, she relocated to the cottage she instructed be built on the island's north end. There, she entertained visitors, whom she took great delight in guiding around the island, leading them to her statues. The same visitors reported the artworks they saw were of women, albeit women of an unusual, even monstrous type. All had some connection to snakes. In a few, the woman depicted was accompanied by snakes, surrounded by snakes, draped in snakes. In others, the figure itself appeared part-serpent, either in its hair or its arms or in place of its legs. The extended reference to the island's original name seemed clear, which her visitors assumed was Beryl's point. After settling on the island, she took to walking it at night, in various states of undress. The behavior drew a good deal of condemnation in the editorial columns of the local newspapers (though the reproaches were couched in oblique language) and a good deal of interest from the local men who took their rowboats and canoes out for night-time paddles around the island, especially when the full moon made every tree, arch, and scantily clad woman glow with pearly light. Despite visits from the clergy of the local houses of worship, all of whom found Beryl gracious, charming, and fully clothed, if somewhat cold, the island's sole inhabitant continued her nocturnal excursions for the remainder of the nineteenth and the first decades of the twentieth centuries. As late as 1913, those who spied her moving in and out of the nighttime trees said she appeared no older than she had ever been. At some point thereafter, she withdrew from view, literally and figuratively. By 1920, she was reported to have been dead for an indeterminate amount of time, possibly a victim of the flu pandemic that followed the Great War. The supposed cause of death raised more questions than it answered, as there was no record of her exposure to the disease. Nonetheless, the management of her estate was assumed by a law firm based in Manhattan. For over a century, these lawyers, and the ones after them, ensured the upkeep of the island, its statues, and its cottage.

Visitors to the island have been rare. Strange rumors have attached to it, most of them involving a specter haunting the place. It is a woman, of course, though reports of her describe her as having the slitted pupils of a snake. Over the years, local high school seniors, by and large boys, and freshmen at St. Stephen's, also largely boys, have attempted to demonstrate their courage by stealing onto the island after sunset. The majority of these have ventured no farther than the rocky shore when they have been over-whelmed by a sensation of utter dread, the way you might imagine feeling were you to find yourself faced with a tiger, its muzzle gory. The emotion has chased them off the island, over the water, and pursued them home. The next day, with the sun brightly shining, they have explained away their reaction, attributed it to overactive imaginations, but you would be hard-pressed to convince any to make a return trip. As for the small number of trespassers who have fought their fear and pressed ahead into the trees on shaking legs, none will say anything about whatever passed during the subsequent hours they were on the island. Their faces tighten at the slightest reference to the place, their mute memories exerting a terrible gravity on their flesh. Every decade or so, one of the local papers will run a feature on the island, its history, and its legendry in the local interest section. Several years ago, when the scholar Dennis Mitre hosted his PBS series surveying the history and significance of monsters, he included a segment on the figure he called "the Hudson River's *Belle Dame sans Merçi*." While he was filmed standing on a boat on the river side of the island, pointing out its features and discussing its history and rumor, he did so with the midday sun flashing on the water, and he did not attempt to set foot on the rocky shore.

Delilah knows the tale of Beryl Magdaline—because this is who the ghostly woman must be—and has become quite adept at relating it to friends and family over dinner. It is part of the island's history; though not the part in which she is interested and on which she has been focused since she was pregnant with Bess. Given her position as an art historian, it is perhaps no surprise that her attention has been directed to the assortment of sculptures Beryl bought and displayed on the island. During Beryl's life-time, a handful of visitors were allowed to photograph the art works. For a long time, the only way to view these pictures was in black and white, in the pages of a slender, expensive volume printed in collaboration with the

Metropolitan Museum of Art. (Line drawings of individual pieces made their way into several of the better-known textbooks.) At the turn of the millennium, the photographs were digitized and placed online and since have become widely available. There are also color pictures of the sculptures taken during the nineteen-sixties, but these were shot at a distance, through dense summer foliage, and do not reveal quite as much of their subjects as a viewer would hope. They, too, are online, which is how Delilah first encountered them, when she was working on her doctorate. The color photos led to the black and white ones, and the line drawings, and as much information as she could locate concerning Beryl Magdaline. In the opinion of her dissertation director, there was not enough available about the woman who transformed a small river island into her private open-air museum to justify a dissertation. Yes, Professor Otoni had agreed, there was probably a decent amount concerning Beryl and her island waiting to be discovered, not least of it the island, itself, whose exact topography remained surprisingly vague. The process of accessing and compiling said information was likely to consume years, and Delilah's advisor was of the firm opinion that a dissertation was a hoop to be jumped through with all due haste. Once she was secure in a decent job, then would be the time to commit herself to unearthing the story of those lonely statues. Delilah followed her mentor's advice, wrote her dissertation on Peggy Guggenheim, revised and published it to gain tenure at St. Stephen's, and when she received the provost's letter informing her of the P and T committee's recommendation, set to work on the project she had put on hold almost a decade prior.

Her research since then has been exhaustive. She has visited the archives of every newspaper, library, and historical society between Albany and Manhattan. Always the more socially adept half of the marriage, she has formed friendships with a score of librarians, historians, and enthusiasts of local history, not a few of whom have taken her up on her offer to contact her whenever and have sent her important bits of information. Through a process of slow, polite email correspondence, she has won over the law offices of Angstrom, Howard, and Roth, under whose auspices the island is administered. This has led to her receiving permission to visit Magdaline Island in the company of one of the newer lawyers and the island's caretaker, of whose existence Delilah was unaware but who apparently has been living in the cottage on the north end since before COVID. Delilah and the lawyer hit it off, and although the caretaker, a striking young woman with high cheekbones who wore her black hair up, was reserved to the point of cool, she listened to Delilah describe her interest in Beryl Magdaline and admiration for what she created on the island. The trip went well enough for Delilah to be allowed a second, during which she was able to examine (but not photograph) one of the sculptures up close, a figure of a woman standing turned away from the viewer, her head to the left, allowing her to look back over her shoulder, the hint of a sly smile on her lips. Her robe was at her hips, leaving bare the perfect expanse of her back. A snake wound around her, draping her shoulders, the tip of its tail curled at her right bicep, circling her waist, the neck arcing down and out from her left hip, the heavy head tilted to direct the round eye at the viewer. Under the close supervision of the lawyer—whose name was Ciaran Barth—and caretaker—whose name she had not yet learned—Delilah inspected the piece, which been stationed at the western side of the island, at the edge of a stand of hemlocks, as if asking the viewer if they were following her into the once-sacred trees.

Broadly speaking, the style in which the statue had been carved was classical Roman; indeed, it reminded Delilah of the Venus Callipyge, though the mood of this sculpture was decidedly less playful than the first century BCE portrait of the goddess of love lifting her skirt to show off her idealized buttocks. In answer to her questions, Ciaran Barth admitted he had no idea of the age of the piece; while the caretaker gave it as two thousand nine hundred years. From the standpoint of the development of artistic technique, such a number was pretty much out of the question; not to mention, the statue's pristine condition argued against it. As any number of armless, legless, and headless examples demonstrated, the passage of time was not kind to sculptures, especially those parts of them protruding from the central mass. Delilah responded to this effect, but in a manner and tone designed not to offend the caretaker. This type of exchange would continue on her third visit to the island, when she would be led on a hike up the island's crest to examine a serpent's head carved from a block of gray granite in the dramatic style of the Aztecs at the height of their power. The bolder-sized piece was set on a flat ledge and positioned south, as if keeping watch on the river with its stony gaze. During her fourth visit, which took her to the meadow at the island's southern end, where she stepped carefully through the tumbled walls of a small castle constructed (hastily and poorly) in the eighteen-forties in imitation of a medieval English fortress to a niche carved out of a boulder, in which was a relief portrait of the Hindu goddess, Manasa, seated on a lotus under a canopy of seven cobras with their hoods open, another cobra hugged to her torso by her left arm. Delilah's knowledge of Indian sculpture is limited, but she recognized the style's general age as somewhere in the vicinity of a thousand years; though as before, the presence of the unbroken cobra heads appeared to belie such an estimation, an observation she put forth with what was becoming her customary tact. Her continuing ability to voice her opinions without alienating the still-nameless caretaker built the foundation for a relationship (if not quite a friendship) whose long-term benefit has been the woman endorsing the plan Delilah has proposed for the future of Magdaline Island. (On behalf of the law firm, Ciaran Barth agreed to Delilah's project after their first tour of the property; during the phone call in which he informed her of this, however, he added that the caretaker's approval would make what was already certain even more so, a semi-cryptic remark suggesting Angstrom, Howard, and Roth's support might evaporate should the caretaker oppose Delilah's idea.) With the caretaker's blessing, the news of which came this morning, what Delilah regards as the major work of this segment of her academic life can proceed. It will be a multi-part, multi-year undertaking. There will be a book, naturally, a biography of Beryl Magdaline centered on her creation of the sculptural display on the island. This will be accompanied by a documentary film, in which Delilah has solicited interest from no less a director than Sarah Fiore. As part of book and film, intensive (but careful and respectful) analyses of the assorted statues (there are some thirty-two placed around the island, most quite small) will be performed with an eye toward establishing their respective provenances. Coming out of this study will be an interactive, online archive of the island, to be administered by the Fine Arts department of St. Stephen's in close consultation with the law firm and the caretaker. Finally, a pair of senior art majors from St. Stephen's will be selected for a monthlong internship on the island each spring.

It's possible that, as a result of these investigations, some or all of the island's statues will be revealed as fakes, clever forgeries. It is possible the research will show that Beryl was duped; it's also possible evidence will come to light of her having commissioned the sculptures, herself. None of these outcomes bothers Delilah. Indeed, if the statues should turn out to be the stony brainchildren of Beryl's ultimate design for the island, Delilah will find the fact no less fascinating and worthy of discussion than if she collected a small museum's worth of distinctive sculptures in almost supernaturally pristine condition. This is the kind of large-scale endeavor that makes an academic career. For Delilah to be on the cusp of it is indeed worthy of celebration.

The rest of the evening is a success. Encouraged by the prospect of the four tubs of ice cream waiting in the freezer, Barney and Bess make short work of their dinners. In an extension of the celebratory spirit, Delilah and Tom allow the kids to carry their bowls of (small) scoops of *all four flavors* through to the living room, where they spoon the steadily melting mix of dessert into their mouths while watching the animated *Mulan*. By the end of the movie, the wave of sugar the kids have surfed through the film is crashing, washing them onto the shore of unconsciousness. Together, Delilah and Tom help them change into their respective pajamas, use the toilet and brush their teeth, and climb into bed. At Bess's request, Delilah joins her under the covers, where Tom knows his wife will remain until the early hours of the morning.

Although Tom was hoping the night might conclude with sex, Delilah spends enough nights in with Bess, always a nervous sleeper, for his disappointment to be mild. He is more unsettled by what he foresees as the amount of time Delilah's new undertaking will require of her. As he moves through the house, clearing the dining room table, washing the dishes, picking up the kids' toys, switching off the lights, he anticipates long afternoons and evenings, weekends without Delilah. This shouldn't bother him the way it does, he knows. When he was turning his dissertation into a proper book, then during the two years he spent writing the follow-up, Delilah allowed him enormous swathes of time to work. It is no less fair for him to return the favor. What troubles him has to do with the light her imminent success casts on his accomplishments, which appear considerably more modest in its radiant glow. What are two books, however well-received by those in his field, compared to the type of groundbreaking work Delilah is about to begin? Given the sheer number of hours Tom has put into his scholarship, you would assume him to be confident in his achievements. It certainly seemed as if he was when we first met him on the Penrose campus. Now, as he enters his and Delilah's bedroom to change into his pajamas, he is as insecure as any teenage boy beset by anxiety and acne. Sufficiently self-aware to understand his wife's success subtracts nothing from his, he nonetheless struggles against a feeling of darkness crowding the edges of his vision, a non-literal experience that almost crosses into the real. He has been subject to this emotion more days of the week than not, which Delilah has suggested is a manifestation of depression and recommended an appointment with their family doctor to discuss, but which Tom suspects is a malady of a less biochemical nature, a manifestation of the condition his Neapolitan grandfather called *noia*. Asked to define the word, Tom's grandfather waved his hand in a gesture that took in all their surroundings, accompanied by a noncommittal grunt. His father was no help in explaining it; though his mother said it was like *ennui*, or *angst*, another pair of words whose meanings Tom lacked but which he could look up in the family dictionary. All three words circled the same territory, a perception of the world's essential emptiness, of a kind of senselessness underlying everything.

3

We've left Tom in the position of many of the protagonists of the best-known novels and stories of the last hundred and seventy-five years, give or take: at a moment of personal crisis, in which discontent with the particulars of his life coincide with a sense of existential emptiness in a kind of chicken-and-egg dance. A list of similar characters would require pages, and I imagine there would be debates about whether (say) Flaubert's Emma Bovary or Dostoyevsky's Underground Man belong in the same column, but the discontented protagonist—particularly in its white, male, middle-class iteration—is a recognizable enough figure to have become an archetype, if not a stereotype. The many instances of the type suggest potential avenues for Tom's story to take.

The first involves adultery, that great passion of the western novel. He might begin a (secret) affair with a woman or man, at work or in the neighborhood, possibly via that great enabler, social media. The romance may have been simmering for a while, or it may be a spur of the moment thing. He may become involved with a student in one of his classes, or Melanie the babysitter. (Granted, these last would be problematic in ways beyond the breaking of his marriage vows, to put it mildly.)

The second route Tom's story could take involves a different kind of deviation from the norm. He could undergo an awakening religious or political, abandon his tenured position in favor of an occupation he finds compelling, leave his family to embark on a pilgrimage personal or traditional. In the end, he may succeed in his quest for an authentic life, but in one of those ironies that tend to wait at the end of this path, his return to the desperate Catholicism of his grandfather is as likely to drive a wedge between him and Delilah as if he travels a more dissolute route, if the bottle of single malt whose contents he employs occasionally to reduce the volume of his *noia* migrates from the liquor cabinet in the dining room to the drawer of the desk in his office at Penrose, and from there to a thermos in the black knapsack he carries with him around campus. It's as if any action taken in response to discontent with one's marriage is doomed to end in disaster. ("What about *Ulysses*?" I imagine some wag calling from the back row. Its many innovations of style and form notwithstanding, I'm not sure Joyce's novel succeeds in making a case for the saving grace of adultery.)

Both possibilities we've considered fall within the remit of what tends to be called realism; though I prefer Salman Rushdie's use of "mimetic naturalism" to describe this kind of fiction. Whichever term we use, there's an underlying assumption that this approach to narrative has the advantage of representing its readers' experience in its most typical and therefore recognizable form. So many instances of mimetic naturalism aim at a form of epiphany (here we are back to Joyce). Either the protagonist achieves a moment of sudden insight, or the protagonist doesn't but the reader does. In its formal construction, the epiphanic story reminds me of the Shakespearean sonnet, in which the twelve lines spent expressing a complaint or dilemma must be answered by the final two. Effectively executed, it rings in the reader's mind like a cathedral bell; the risk is that the conclusion of the piece will not be adequate to what preceded it.

There's nothing inherently wrong with either mimetic naturalism or the epiphanic plot; indeed, many of the novels I alluded to at the beginning of this section make fine use of both. Let's be honest, though: if we look to justify our realist narrative through an appeal to what is usual, then we have to admit that Tom's dissatisfaction could lead him down avenues (perhaps) less probable but no less possible. He might become implicated in/involved

251

in illegal activity. He might stumble upon a political conspiracy. He might encounter a hidden community, a group of UFO enthusiasts constructing the strange, apparently unworkable device they are sure they have been given instructions to during their abductions. He might run afoul of someone monstrous, a serial killer. Each of these options takes Tom's story into the precincts of other kinds of fiction: the crime, thriller, science fiction/fantasy, or horror genres, respectively. Brought into contact with the conventions of these fields, what we might describe as their formal qualities, Tom's story, which already has certain formal qualities of its own, opens in new and interesting ways. You might compare it to what happens when a fly fisherman slides on a pair of polarized glasses, and the bed of the stream in which they're standing appears in amber-tinted clarity, the clusters of rocks, the waving weeds, the trout hanging in the current. If such is the result of bringing Tom into the suburbs of a given field, then it seems reasonable to argue that a trip to the town center holds the promise of still further revelations.

There's the opportunity for a kind of amplification or energization to occur at the symbolic level, the thematic level, which allows the narrative to resonate in the remote deeps of the reader's mind, to achieve a kind of emotional verity.

I realize all of this sounds a bit abstract, a bit technical, but I've been publishing horror fiction for a couple of decades, now, and reading it for twice that number, and when you spend so much time with something, you think about what it does and how it does that. For me, this has been a way to continue to develop as a writer. There's nothing wrong with the appeal to taste, i.e. "I like what I like," but this explanation limits further discussion.

If you'll permit me to remain among the gears and levers for a moment longer: the type of fiction I find most productive to bring into contact with the stuff of everyday life (however we corral that) is found under the circus big top that is horror. While there are many ways into a story for me, I'm especially fond of being given a prompt, which may take the form of an invitation to an anthology with a specific theme or may result from a request to write about a particular monster or topic. Placing an apparently random creature into an otherwise mundane situation allows for a kind of narrative synchronicity to take place, for the yoking of two disparate elements to produce something unexpected. (Am I borrowing Eliot's description of metaphysical poetry? You bet.)

In a sense, this has already happened here, in my expansion on the example of the unhappy English professor meeting a Lamia. (The Lamia, as I recall, was requested of me quite some years ago by Justin Steele.) In terms of Tom's book and Delilah's multiform project, the Lamia has infiltrated the story, become part of its texture. If I want, I can include additional information about Keats's poem, possibly by means of a conversation Tom has with a (very attractive) student with whom he's conducting an independent study on images of the supernatural feminine in nineteenth century English literature. (In addition to "Lamia," the plan of study features another Keats poem, "*La Belle Dame sans Merçi*," Bannerman's "The Mermaid," Dacre's "The Skeleton Priest," Coleridge's "Christabel," Gaskell's "The Poor Clare," Rosetti's "The Hour and the Ghost," Tennyson's "Lady of Shalott," and Le Fanu's *Carmilla*.) Or the poem's details could feature in a discussion between Tom and Delilah, possibly as pillow talk after she slips into their bed in the wee small hours of the night, naked and amorous. Before the actual Lamia has made her appearance, Keats's poem and the various sculptures on the island are able to bounce off one another, not to mention, off Tom's story, creating a kind of echo chamber.

4

At this point, we're waiting for the meeting between Tom Alero and the Lamia, who it seems must be Magdaline Island's caretaker and probably—no, definitely Beryl Magdaline. In the matter of Beryl, several questions present themselves: what happened to her to transform her from human to monstrous? Are the statues displayed on the island connected to this? Was the island the site of her transformation? It would be possible to answer these questions in a way that picks up the monster's association with witchcraft, which would add a dimension to Beryl's history of self-empowerment. This would resonate with Delilah's success, too; though it risks associating such accomplishments with the monstrous, which is an implication I prefer to avoid. The ages and origins of the island's sculptures suggest a more ancient route for Beryl's change, an encounter, perhaps, with an old power of the Earth, a darker version of the meeting between Keats's Lamia and Hermes. I suppose you might ask what such questions and their (potential) answers contribute to the story, beyond indulging what the writer M. John Harrison described as "the great clomping foot of nerdism." At an ontological level, they help to give the Lamia more substance, to establish her as part of the fabric of the imagined world. In so doing, they expand the reader's sense of things, pointing to depths of time and space and being. To paraphrase Keats, they tease us out of thought, as does the idea of eternity.

Did Beryl seek out this figure? Was she, too, riven by a sense of the fundamental meaninglessness of her existence, possibly stemming from the death of her entire family, or possibly originating long before the disaster which only confirmed it? Did this lead her to use her new fortune to embark on a trip whose ultimate destination was a cave in the Apennines, in whose rocky depths services sacred to the snake goddess Angitia were once—and perhaps still—performed? Did she walk into darkness that enclosed her almost immediately, and did she hear the rasp of scales sliding over stone? Did her mouth go dry, her heart pound as a sibilant voice flicked in her ear?

Yes, I believe she was. And yes, I believe she did.

5

How does Tom encounter Beryl Magdaline? Does the meeting take place at a single—and singular—event, or do they have a series of meetings, at parties, Art Department functions, dinners for those involved in the Magdaline Island project, which Tom attends as a faculty spouse, "Mr. Delilah Spenser," he jokes to his wife? As one of these dinners, it may be, he's seated next to the striking young(er) woman with whom he's previously exchanged pleasantries but now engages in a conversation that develops over the entire lengthy meal, from drinks to appetizer to salad to main course to dessert and coffee. (This dinner takes place at the Beekman Arms, an upscale restaurant whose location in the center of the town of Rhinebeck dates back to the eighteenth century, when it served as a stopping point for those traveling up and down the Hudson. The sprawl of rooms, with their low ceilings, exposed beams, and brick fireplaces lend the establishment a cozy, intimate feel.) This may be the moment when Tom discusses Keats's "Lamia," if for no other reason than the idea of him talking over the poem with this story's Lamia is too much to resist. Does Beryl prompt him? Maybe.

For much the same reason, I think this is when Beryl reveals at least some of the details of her long-ago trip to the Apennines. Perhaps she expresses surprise at the Keats poem's content, which, she says, is remarkably similar to the diary entries Beryl Magdaline wrote about an experience she underwent during a tour of northern Italy. Suppressing his tendency to be pedantic and declare the entries in question must have been composed in imitation of Keats (which in fact they were not: the younger Beryl preferred Byron, Tennyson, and Elizabeth Barrett Browning), Tom instead asks the woman he, like his wife, still identifies as the caretaker to tell him about Beryl Magdaline's record of her time in Italy.

To either side of and across the table from them, the rest of the diners murmur to one another, call to friends and colleagues, shriek with sudden laughter. Cutlery clinks on porcelain; the odors of bread fresh from the oven, vegetables roasted with garlic and honey, beef seared on the outside and pink on the inside, float through the room. The red wine in Tom's glass, which threatened to ascend into sharpness, levels into a fullness that spreads over the tongue. The caretaker—remember, Tom has no idea of her true identity, and although we may have our suspicions, they have yet to be confirmed—narrates Beryl's mountain journey in an allusive, impressionistic manner, referring to local traditions in that region of the mountains regarding the older divinities who were driven deep into the caves and up amid the peaks by the coming of the newer gods, Jupiter and Juno, as they in turn would be exiled by the advent of the Christian God and His angels and saints. She describes Beryl's search for something, some knowledge, some answer that led her into the heart of the Apennines, to a cave to which her guide agreed to take her but refused to enter. You already know about the voice like a serpent's forked tongue tickling her ear. Tom asks what the voice said. The caretaker says the sound conjured an image in Beryl's mind, one of such vividness she was half-sure she could see it next to her. She pictured a woman, naked, her breasts full, her hips firm, draped in snakes—snakes ribbon thin circling her head and neck, snakes wide as a belt looping her shoulders and arms, snakes thick as a man's arm winding up her legs, living garlands of green, black, and gold—the pink gums of her open mouth filled with a snake's needle-like fangs. Tom feels his cheeks flush with adolescent embarrassment (and perhaps a hint of excitement) at the description, a silly response, except there is something about the way the caretaker looks directly into his eyes as she describes the vision's generous breasts, the curve of her belly down to her thighs, which evokes in him a vision of the woman—of the caretaker as the woman. Sweat prickling the back of his neck as if the thermostat has just been raised ten degrees, he reaches for his wine with an unsteady hand and asks what happened next.

It's too unbelievable, the caretaker says. He'll have to read it for himself. She has the diary in her cottage on the island. Perhaps he'll come visit her there—the next time his wife comes over. Tom takes advantage of the glass at his lips to delay his response. When he has swallowed the wine, he says that sounds wonderful. He's certain Delilah will love to read the diary.

By now, we're near the end of dinner. It's allowed me to do a number of things, most important among them, to bring Tom and Beryl together for an extended conversation during which she has provided him a plausible reason for visiting her on the island. Of course, Delilah has noticed her husband's interaction with the attractive caretaker, and she quizzes him about it on the long car ride home, beginning with gentle mockery about the interest he showed the young(er) woman that is much nearer the truth than she realizes. Tom, who's feeling the effects of his three generous glasses of wine with an acuity he has not experienced since he was a college freshman, can find no better explanation than the truth. He and the caretaker spoke about "Lamia," then she told him about something in Beryl Magdaline's record of her Italian trip. As he relates what he remembers of the account—most of it, actually—Delilah falls quiet in the particular way she does when she is listening intently to what is being said. After he has finished, Delilah waits a moment, then says, "You're serious?"

"Hand to God," he says.

"Holy shit," Delilah says, the expression equal parts wonder and delight at what this has the potential to add to her project.

Although Tom is relieved at his wife's response, he is aware of a vague sense of uneasiness at not having told her about the caretaker's (deliberate, he is pretty sure) effect on him, as if in so (not) doing he is committing one of the sins of omission his childhood self worried about. Keeping his tone light, he says, "You're okay with this strange woman inviting me to her cottage to look at her historical documents?"

"Whatever it takes," Delilah says with equal lightness. "If you have to do her on top of the giant Aztec serpent head for us to get a look at Beryl's diary, that's a sacrifice you'll have to make. Besides," she says, voice more serious, "I'll be there, too."

"Which could be what she wants," Tom says, the jest forced.

"Nah," Delilah says. "You know how much time I've been spending with her, and I have to tell you, your girl there is about as reserved as they come. Cold as—"

"A fish?" Tom says.

"I was going to say a snake," Delilah says. "Seriously: you know I trust you. And even if I wasn't a hundred and ten percent sure about you, I have zero worries about her. If something came up and I couldn't be there, I would not worry in the least."

Delilah's expression of faith in him, buttressed as it is by her appraisal of the caretaker, causes a shift in Tom's interior weather, like a strong wind pushing fog from a landscape. The obscure guilt that's clung to him throughout the car ride dissipates, its place taken by gratitude. It isn't enough to banish his underlying sense of *noia*, but the feeling retreats. Later, after they have received Melanie the babysitter's summary of her evening with the kids and paid her, Delilah will lead Tom downstairs, to the guestroom whose door they lock when they want to have uninhibited, vigorous sex. During their exertions, Tom feels his erection begin to sag, a consequence of the alcohol, or the hour, or (terrifyingly) his age. Delilah does not appear to notice. Tom casts around for something, some memory or fantasy to firm his member. He recalls the caretaker staring at him as she described the naked woman of Beryl Magdaline's vision and is instantly hard, almost painfully so. He imagines fulfilling his wife's facetious instruction to have sex with the caretaker on the great Aztec sculpture and is overtaken by the orgasm the image produces. Afterward, as sleep rises around him, he feels a pang of fresh guilt at his mental substitution, but the emotion is muted, its grasp weak, and the tide of unconsciousness floats it away from him.

6

By this point, Keats's "Lamia," which remains my touchstone for envisioning the monster, has been brought fully into the story and set up to bounce Beryl Magdaline's tale off. Keats's version of the monster reverses the figure Beryl's story describes, representing the Lamia as a fantastically colored snake with a woman's mouth and teeth, which is what enables her to plead with Hermes to change into human, not to mention, to betray the nymph the god is pursuing in exchange for his assistance. Her mouth symbolizes the human concealed within the beast. Beryl's Lamia suggests the monster waiting within the human. There's a very real, very tangible threat in those fangs, which is different from the abstract peril in which Keats's Lamia places the young man who is the object of her desire. And desire, yes—desire in its most carnal iteration is now front and center. Until this point, you could say that desire has been expressed in a number of ways: in Tom's longing for a way out of his *noia*, in Delilah's ambitions for Magdaline Island; in what we may have inferred about Beryl Magdaline's original transformation on the island. While each of these remains present, they are sublimated into the warmth that colors Tom's cheeks at unexpected moments, when memories of the fantasy that facilitated his lovemaking to his wife steal into his thoughts. Wrapped—coiled around his physical desire is another and in some ways more insidious type. The number and variety of people who might arouse our lust is no doubt a respectable, if not considerable amount. Although this form of temptation is the one most partners worry about, because it is obvious, immediate, highlighting our insecurities about our appearance, it's not nearly as dangerous as the attraction to someone's personality, the blend of wit, intelligence, imagination, and empathy that makes us what we are. During their dinner conversation, Tom found himself talking with the woman seated next to him in a way he hasn't for years. Yes, he and Delilah speak constantly, but the subjects they address are entirely different: the kids' health, their experiences in second grade and kindergarten, their teachers, their friends, their friends' parents, routine maintenance on their cars, unexpected repairs on their cars, routine maintenance on the house, unexpected repairs on the house, monthly bills—you understand. When their respective careers come up, they do so within the context of departmental politics and gossip, the latest instance of administrative idiocy (of which there is an ever-renewing supply). Tom understands the shift as an inevitable consequence of the course his life has followed, and he's been able to find a reasonable replacement for the conversations he and Delilah used to share in discussions with his better classes, but there are moments he is overcome by nostalgia so acute it's like a punch in his solar plexus for nights on the fire escape of his closet of an apartment in West New York, drinking cheap red wine under what stars could shine through the light pollution and talking about everything, words another way to learn each other's secret places. The couple of hours he passed with the caretaker have brought him closer to the feeling of those graduate school conversations than anything since.

So the stakes for Tom are not only physical, in ways he does not fully comprehend, but moral, in a sense he recognizes and appreciates more fully. Whatever erotic fantasies he may have entertained up to this point, none has approached as close to reality as he thinks this one may be, and the proximity fills him with equal parts dread and excitement. Were his response solely one or the other, it would simplify his character. Either he would flee the opportunity presenting itself or he would embrace it. Keeping him balanced on the horns of this dilemma, however, helps to create an additional layer of suspense for the story. We know he'll be walking across the wooden foot bridge arching between the mainland and the island; the caretaker's invitation, compounded by Delilah's reaction to it, pretty much assures it. Because his wife expressed her trust in him making the visit without her, that is also what will happen, due to some type of plot mechanism. (I'm tempted to say a snake bite, but that seems a little too much, doesn't it? Even in a world in which the supernatural is present, you can overdo things. Instead, let's attribute her absence to a twisted ankle. Nothing life-threatening, but sufficient to prevent her returning to the island. Although Tom offers to delay the trip, she insists, says she'll pay Melanie to stay longer and help her with Barney and Bess. It's really important he gets a look at that diary, she says.)

If we feel the need for symbolism, we can pause Tom midway across the footbridge, have him gaze at the long low shape of Magdaline Island, covered in trees still holding their leaves, the faux ruins visible through their trunks bright in the late afternoon sun. Perhaps he looks back to his car, parked in the small gravel lot at the foot of a gently sloping hill covered in grass untended and tall. Returning his attention to the island, he sees the Hudson shining beyond it like a river of fire. What is he expecting? Does he know?

7

Writing about constructing the climaxes to narratives in her excellent book, *Storyteller*, Kate Wilhelm posited that for every story, there is an obvious ending. She advised avoiding this and whatever its opposite would be. Instead, she wrote, find something else, a third option. We know that Tom is on his way to a confrontation with a Lamia. In this scenario, the obvious ending would be for the monster to kill him. Perhaps he sees her as he steps onto the island, waiting in the midst of a stand of hemlocks, near a statue. (Which one? I believe it's the sculpture of the woman faced away from the viewer, her back bare, her shoulders draped with a snake, her head turned just enough to allow her to look behind her.) Despite a slight chill in the air, Beryl is wearing a magenta dress through whose gauzy fabric Tom can distinguish the snakes tattooed on her in deep blues and dark reds, luminous green and gold. They wrap her legs, coil around her hips, wind over her stomach, slide up between her breasts, and extend along her arms. A bronze armband in the form of a snake circles her right bicep. The front of her dress shifts, and Tom registers with shock the sizable snake (a boa?) hanging from her neck under the dress, its scales the same mix of purple and red as her tattoos. As Tom enters the trees, Beryl pivots away from him. With a shrug, she sends the dress slithering down to her hips. He sees the loop of snake sliding on her skin. Beryl inclines her head to the left, just enough to permit her to peer over her bare shoulder at Tom, a sardonic smile lifting the corner of her mouth. Yes, she's copying the statue's pose, but in her imitation, Tom apprehends something, his brain makes a connection he cannot articulate, but which floods him with dread. Beryl shifts her hips, and the dress completes its earthward transit. As she executes another turn, bringing her full nakedness into view, what Tom a second ago would have sworn was a large snake unlike any he had seen in zoo or nature documentary is revealed as another tattoo; although it still seems as if the decoration is moving, as if all the snakes incised on Beryl's skin are in motion. Her lips, which have not lost their smile, part and the teeth drop from her mouth like so many pearlescent stones. There is little blood; rather, a viscous, amber-tinted liquid spills down her chin. Sliding up from her exposed gums, Tom sees the curved fangs of a snake.

After this, it's all over for Tom. There may be a few motions to go through—he might try to flee, race toward the bridge, or decide that's too far and rush deeper into the island; he might decide to swim for it and run to the rocky beach, splash into the Hudson. Whichever way he goes, though, Beryl and her deadly bite will find him, and his story will conclude in searing pain and panicked regret. Its final image could be Tom's lifeless body floating on the river's shimmering surface. Depending on how harshly you've judged Tom's shortcomings, you may derive a certain grim satisfaction from his agonizing fate. It's not the worst ending for a story, but it seems to me the equivalent of a burger from a fast-food chain: satisfying in the moment, but nothing especially memorable.

Pretty much the same thing is true should we flip the action of the climax, have Tom emerge victorious from his contest with Beryl. This version of events could remain the same as the previous one, up to and including the instant of Tom's flight. This time, however, he will succeed in reaching the meadow at the island's south end, where he would trip over one of the many bricks scattered in the long grass. This obstacle puts him within reach of Beryl's long stride, but it also provides him with a weapon, which he smashes against the side of Beryl's head as she moves to bite him. It's doubtful a single blow could kill such a figure, but the half-dozen that follow succeed in bringing Beryl's long, strange existence to an end. Even with her skull crushed, her body will thrash on the ground for a long time, with such violence it appears the snakes ornamenting it are taking part in her death throes. This version might end at the river, too, with Tom washing his hands in its shining water.

Granted, there are times fast-food is perfectly adequate to your hunger. But while you may remember such a meal for the people with whom you shared it, rarely will you recall *that* particular burger and fries for their own sake. That resonance is what I'm after, both as a reader and writer. It's what leads me past the obvious ending, past its reverse—each of which has its virtues—in search of something else, a third option.

It occurs to me, nothing could happen. Tom could cross to the island and find it empty of everything except its statues. He could wander it for a time, locate the cabin at the north end and discover its door unlocked, its interior bare. I won't lie: there's a part of me that takes a certain perverse pleasure in the idea of such an ending. Talk about upending the reader's expectations, right? You can be sure this would stick with them. Except: this feels like a bit of a cheat, doesn't it?

Not only does it not seem fair to the reader, it doesn't seem fair to the story, does it? It doesn't seem justified by what's led up to this point; nor is the effect of its dissonance interesting or provocative enough to argue for it.

What about this? We leave the beginning of the climactic scene unchanged, with Tom crossing to the island unaccompanied. Halfway over the footbridge, he still pauses. He feels as if he's wearing one of those lead vests the technician puts on you in the dentist's office before they x-ray your mouth. A not-insignificant part of him would like to walk back to his car and drive home, tell Delilah the caretaker never showed. The two of them can figure out a time to meet later. It's as if he's caught in the gears of an enormous machine, moving him relentlessly forward. Such a comparison, he knows, minimizes his agency, mitigates his responsibility for what may be about to happen. He straightens and continues to the island.

There, he sees Beryl waiting for him in the midst of the hemlocks, beside the same sculpture of the woman with her back to the viewer. At the sight of her in her filmy dress, Tom's heart leaps into a hard gallop. His vision swims. He is aware of himself teetering at an interior precipice, a limit whose crossing will be profound and unforgivable. He registers the snake sliding under the folds of Beryl's dress, his shock at the sight of it overwhelmed and absorbed by his astonishment when she turns and allows the dress to slide first to her hips, then to the ground. In between these motions, he recognizes the link between the figure represented by the statue and Beryl, and as Beryl steps out of the puddle of her dress, all strength drains from his legs and he drops to his knees. Emotion he cannot name, but which somehow feels like grief, envelops him. Great sobs tear themselves from his chest; tears flood his eyes. Amidst the sobs, a keening sound rises from him. Vision a watery blur, he does not witness Beryl's teeth drop from her mouth, the fangs rising in their place. He hears the soles of her feet scraping over the ground and understands that she is walking toward him, but the fact means little. The *noia* which for him has been primarily an intellectual phenomenon, if not pretension, howls along his nerves. Beryl's hands press lightly on his shoulders as she lowers herself to a crouch in front of him. He smells wet earth and cinnamon as her head moves next to his, her hands sliding under his jacket, pushing it down his arms, then moving to his shirt, whose top button is already open, and whose next button her fingers undo. Despite everything, the certainty that his life is a house collapsed on its rotten foundation, Tom feels a small thrill at the whisper of Beryl's breath on his neck, the tug of her elegant fingers on his shirt. He lifts his hands in protest, brushes the smooth skin of Beryl's forearms. Swallowing a sob, he forces out a, "N-no."

Beryl bites him.

The pain is astounding. For an instant, everything goes blank, the world stuttering out and back into existence. Though he is aware of doing so only at the periphery of his perception, at the edge of the blazing white pain spreading from his neck down to his chest and up to his skull, Tom pushes away from Beryl, scrambling backwards through the grass like a kid doing a crabwalk. Before he's traveled very far, his arms and legs stop supporting him, dropping him onto his back. His limbs tremble, convulsing, the nerves webs of fire. He feels the blood wet on his neck, slaps a palm against the skin and when he pulls it away sees his skin shining scarlet mixed with another, honey-colored fluid. His hand spasms, splashing the combined liquid across his face. He blinks, barely avoiding a heavy drop in his left eye. He does not want to look directly at Beryl, who is a dark presence at the lower limit of his vision, because the prospect of seeing her—what she is, must be to have done whatever this is to him, envenomed him, is one he cannot bear. His shock and rage at her teeth (fangs) breaking his skin, his surprise at the injury and anger at the betrayal (and possibly, his regret at how this will appear to Delilah) have dissipated as the bite has its effect on him. He has no choice, Beryl is approaching him, and while the muscles of his irises are spasming as much as the rest of his body, taking the trees looming over him from pillars of fire to faint charcoal sketches and back again, Tom sees Beryl's mouth smeared with (his) blood and the other stuff, the amber liquid turning his nerves into fuses sizzling toward a simultaneous detonation. Now he registers the fangs that have replaced her other teeth, her human teeth, and incredibly notices the longer pair where the canines would be. He recalls poring over the pages of a book on reptiles with Barney, reading to his son about the way these teeth fold up against the roof of the mouth until the snake needs them, when they swing into position.

Tom does not know what Beryl is. Despite their discussion of the Keats poem, he fails to complete the connection between that figure and the one staring down at his suffering. Silly to say he can't believe in her when she's standing right there, but the reality of her, the difficulty such a being's existence causes to his thoughts, seems to exacerbate the pain crisping his nerves, to add injury to injury in a way that seems terribly unfair. He has no doubt he is dying; he cannot conceive this level of pain having any other result. It is an awful death. And it has been delivered to him by a creature whose existence should inspire a kind of ecstatic wonder. Even in so fantastic a death as this, it seems, the *noia* that has dimmed his life continues to cast its shadow. If the pain were not so extreme, were not burning away everything around him, everything of him, he might feel disappointed.

8

I know, I know: at this point, you're muttering to yourself, "I thought this ending was supposed to be different from the others. How is this not just the first option (with maybe slightly more introspection on Tom's part)?"

9

This is how: eventually, after a long, indeterminate time, Tom comes back to himself, which he experiences as a gradual return to his surroundings, a movement from gray formlessness to color and shape. He is still on his back in the grass. It is early evening, the sun drained from the sky to a white glow at the horizon, diffusing up into the steadily darker blue. A cool breeze blows from the river. Tom is aware of the wound to his neck, throbbing and burning yet. The rest of his body seems all right; though his muscles ache in the deep way they do after he joins some of his younger colleagues for the occasional game of pick-up basketball after classes. His clothes are saturated, heavy with his sweat and probably piss, both liquids cooled. Head pounding with the effort, he raises himself to sitting. The hurt on his neck screams its displeasure. The hemlocks are hung with shadows. Across from him, the statue is a white blur.

It moves, splits in two, and Tom understands he is watching Beryl stepping away from it. His heart jolts, and it is as if the motion carries him to his feet. Heat vents from his neck. He staggers. He is hot, unbelievably so. Fresh sweat envelops him. His clothes cling to him. He struggles out of his jacket, grabs the front of his shirt and tears it open, buttons flying free. With much the same motion he used to remove his jacket, he shucks his shirt. The remainder of his clothes—T-shirt, shoes, socks, khakis, boxer—join those flung on the ground.

Freed of his clothing, he is still intolerably hot. Heat fountains from the wound in his neck. As if he could stem its flow, he presses his hand against the punctures and feels the skin loose, papery. Before he can stop himself, he pinches it and tugs. The flesh tears free in a long strip which winds halfway round his neck then veers down his chest, coming free just above his left nipple. Horrified, he lifts the length of skin to inspect it. Translucent, it is streaked with blood dried dark and traces of the other, honey-colored substance. He opens his fingers and watches the ribbon of skin flutter to the ground. The newly exposed portions of his neck and chest are cooler, blessedly so. Tom's fingers trace the uncovered path, which is soft, dry. From its edges, his (old) skin curls away. The remainder of his burning flesh seems to sag, as if untethering from him. The sensation is maddening. Tom works the fingertips of his right hand under the skin lifting from the right side of his chest and peels. A large, almost clear piece of skin comes away with a crackling sound like wax paper, taking the terrible heat with it. Tom frees a patch of crisp hot skin from the left side of his chest. He pulls skin up and over his shoulders, down his arms, off his hands, the emptying flesh turning inside-out as it tugs from his fingers. Coolness wraps his chest, his arms. He reaches behind him, grasping at his back. Pieces of dried skin litter the grass around him, a jigsaw assortment of his form. He peels dead flesh from his hips, his legs, his feet. He is panting. With both hands, he works the skin from his face. When he removes it, he turns the crinkling mask over and considers the open mouth, the vacated eyes, and lets it join the rest of his old flesh on the ground, where it stares up at the stars appearing in their familiar configurations. His vision clouds. He blinks, the eyelids rasping over the corneas. He lifts his right hand first to his right eye, then his left, pinching the dried covering off each.

To his exposed eyes, the hemlocks stand in gray ranks, the grooves in their trunks trenches filled with darkness. Across the grove, the statue blazes white. Overhead, the stars flare uncomfortably near, his discarded skin shining in their austere light. Coolness eddies around him, encircles his legs and arms, shifts over his hips and chest, embraces his head. Somewhere deep within him, in the densely packed space beneath his heart, an answering sensation flows forth in an icy wave. Whatever remains of the *noia*, whatever charred fragments and flecks of his hereditary affliction have survived the conflagration that has harrowed him, is swept away in a freezing tide. Tom wonders where the caretaker is, imagines she has returned to her cabin, or departed the island, perhaps taking his car, and realizes she is right in front of him, a tower of shadow his eyes have not registered, his brain not accepted. Beryl looms over him, an impossibly tall form composed of writhing night, a titan who might stretch up one of her arms and burn her fingers on a star. An awful expectancy streams from her face. Tom feels its weight force him back to his knees. A strip of abandoned skin crackles beneath one kneecap. He reaches down, slides the scrap from under his leg, and starts to gather the scattered pieces of his discarded skin, sorting them by size before piling them largest to smallest. The bits of skin rustle against one another. The exception to the arrangement is his former face, which he sets on top of the heaped skin. Still kneeling, he slides his hands under the evacuated skin and lifts it to the power regarding him. He keeps his head bowed as he waits for her to judge his offering.

10

That's where we leave Tom, I believe. Of course there are plenty of questions still unanswered, chief among them, What happens next? It hardly seems as if it can be anything good, does it? Even if this aspect of Beryl—perhaps it's simply Tom's enhanced perception of her, perhaps something else—is satisfied by Tom's gesture—propitiated may be the word I want—this experience, what has happened to him on a small island in the Hudson, must have a profound, a life-altering effect on him. How could it not? Should Tom return to the mainland, drive home, and never see Beryl again, his life will still be unalterably changed, in ways it would take another story, at least, to explore. And who can believe this will be his final encounter with her?

Why do I love horror? Why has my relationship with it persisted over decades; why do I anticipate it continuing for whatever time I have left me? This is why: Tom Alero's encounter with a figure from literature and legend on a few acres of rock and dirt lapped by a great river under the night's vast canopy; the juxtaposition of the local and sublime; the suggestion of other stories before and after this one. If I have succeeded in what I set out to do, then some portion of Tom's narrative—up to and including the whole thing—will have slithered into the folds of your brain and at an unexpected moment in the future, you will feel its coils slide over one another, somewhere in the depths behind your eyes. In that instant, perhaps you will think of walking through a darkened house when everyone else is asleep, or of sitting at a restaurant table beside someone to whom you are too much attracted, or of stopping on a footbridge in the early evening. Or you may imagine walking into a cave whose darkness is absolute and hearing something in there with you. Or of peeling a length of brittle skin from your throat. Or of genuflecting in the presence of something ancient and immense.

Or it could be, you'll shudder and continue with whatever it was you were doing. I can live with that.

I flatter myself that you and I are at the table in the nice restaurant, the one from Tom and Beryl's story, with its warren of cozy dining rooms, the relics of its history displayed on its walls, the tables set with fine china and silverware. Around us, the air is laden with the conversation and laughter of our fellow diners, but I am talking to you, directly to you, telling you a story that is only for you. The food is delicious, surprising yet satisfying. *And then*, I say. *Because. And then. Because.*

In reality, I know we are not in a pleasant, upmarket restaurant, finishing our main courses and anticipating dessert. Where we are, the sculptures of old gods stare at us from their places amidst the surrounding trees. The moon is a yellow scythe hung against a backdrop of pitiless stars. Somewhere nearby, water washes onto a rocky shore in an ongoing, irregular tide. Cool but not cold, the air smells of fresh green things, crushed parsley and mint, under them a fouler smell, that of decay, of flesh on its way to dissolution. In this secret, holy place, I kneel in front of you naked, head bowed, lifting in my bloody hands the ragged things I have cut out of myself and arranged for you. My lips are trembling, but I whisper, *And then. Because. Because. And then.*

CLAPPING TEETH
AND DRIVING BEATS:

CONCERNING ZOMBIES IN THE SPRINGTIME,

AND THE ZOMBIE PROM

S pring is the worst time for zombies.

I know what you're thinking: "What is he talking about? You see zombies at Halloween." And it's true that the fall does bring an uptick in zombie activity, as the cooler temperatures make them more active after the summer heat, which tends to render them sluggish, slow-moving. But it's in the spring that you have to be most careful. That's when they're coming out of their long winter's nap. As the mercury plunges and the snow piles up, the living dead become…dormant, I guess you might say. If they can find a place to shelter, a cave or an outbuilding no one's using, they'll conceal themselves there. They've been known to bury themselves in loose soil, leaves, even. A few always get caught out in the open, usually somewhere in the woods near or up on Overlook, where they freeze in place. You may have run across them while you're looking for your Christmas tree. Corpsicles, the locals call them. Weird to look at, but harmless, inactive. That's the best time to deal with them.

Once the days start to grow longer, though, and the snow retreats, and soil starts to thaw: that's when the zombies who survived the winter begin to stir. They awaken—if that's what you want to call it—and they rouse from wherever they've been hungry. They open their mouths wide, move their jaws from side to side, take a practice bite out of the air. I don't know if you've ever heard a zombie's teeth clap together, but if you have, then you know it's a sound you don't forget. It's the noise of a hunger that cannot be satisfied, that drives the living dead to lurch from their hiding places in search of food, of…flesh. (Conventional wisdom says they prefer brains, but I've never heard of zombies turning up what's left of their noses at any part of their victims.) When I think of zombies, it's the teeth I imagine, the mouths distended in what appear to be grins, but are actually them preparing to take the biggest bites they can. No matter what condition they're in, no matter what style of clothing they're wearing, no matter if they're among the rare few capable of carrying on a conversation, each and every last one of them is aching to fasten their teeth on something warm and alive.

The other thing about zombies in the spring—it has to do with music. As the weather improves, people open the windows of their houses, their cars, turn up whatever's on DST or Spotify or on disc or record. It's one of the signs the season is changing, isn't it? But music…it *draws* zombies like almost nothing else, almost as much as the promise of food. Especially if it has a good beat, a solid bassline, maybe a guitar or two, the walking dead will seek it out no matter how faint, how distant it is. No one's sure why this is. There's a theory that it connects to our earliest memories, the memories we have before we know we're having them, of our mothers' heartbeats keeping steady time for us in the womb. That kind of primal experience, the theory goes, is so deeply rooted in our brains that it can survive the traumas of death and reanimation. It makes as much sense as anything, I guess. Whatever the reason, put on music—play music live, and the zombies will be there. There are stories about local musicians who have taken advantage of this, who have disguised themselves as zombies, set up their instruments, cranked up the volume, and let it rip, all with the goal of attracting the living dead. The Zombie Prom, it's called. It's something to imagine, zombies swaying and shuffling to Blue Oyster Cult, Oingo Boingo, and of course Michael Jackson. Some of the performers, the rumors say, escaped to tell the tale. Others were not so fortunate. It makes for a good story, but I don't know: who would want to be part of something like that?

So now that you're up to speed on zombies in the spring, you'll know what to be on the lookout for. If you hear music playing—worse, if you come to a place where musicians are setting up, tuning their instruments, be on your guard, because it won't be long before the living dead will be joining you, and if you aren't careful, *you* could wind up joining them.

STORY NOTES

I sometimes think that the story notes I include with each collection are becoming a weird, oblique kind of autobiography—a sort of fragmentary, discursive record of the (frequently winding and even crooked) routes my development as a writer has gone down. There are times my brain feels as if it's become crowded, congested—a possible side effect of my most recent bout of COVID, and of the last several years in general—and it's nice to have these records to look back on. This time around, I'm struck by how many of these stories have their origins going back years, even decades. I've said often enough that this is how I operate as a writer, accumulating characters, ideas, place, and details over time until something catalyzes a certain arrangement of them into a story. The contents of this collection bear that out.

As ever, if you find some use to these notes, that's great. If not, I hope to see you next book.

"Madame Painte: For Sale": The brilliant Australian horror writer, Kaaron Warren, all of whose work is required reading, posted a picture of a garden gnome on social media. There was something off about the way the figure had been painted, which made its smiling face somehow sinister. It was as if the slapdash decoration had revealed the benign expression to be a form of camouflage. In the comments section of Kaaron's post, I said I was going to write a story about the gnome. The opportunity to do so arose when I was invited to contribute a story to Doug Murano's anthology, *Behold! Oddities, Curiosities and Undefinable Wonders*. I had been thinking about Detective Roberto Calasso of the Albany, NY, police department. He's been an exception in my work: unlike many of my contemporaries, I tend not to revisit characters from story to story. A background figure in a couple of earlier stories ("City of the Dog" and "Children of the Fang"), he had been the protagonist of his own narrative, "The Communion of Saints." The end of that story had left the detective in an uncertain place. Following the events of which he had been a part, it seemed to me unlikely he would or really even could continue in his role with the police. I thought he might become a private investigator, but the possibility struck me as a little too clichéd. I suppose I might have left him where he was, but Doug's anthology prompt suggested a new role for him: proprietor of an antique and secondhand shop, on whose shelves and in whose aisles—outside whose front door— might be found certain...unusual objects, ones with histories eccentric and menacing. Because there was no doubt the figure I had christened Madame Painte was in possession of just such a background. Given that the original inspiration had been provided by Kaaron's photograph, Australia seemed the appropriate setting for the meat of the story. At the same time, I was leery of fetishizing the location, making this another story of a monstrous being from an exotic place. Instead, it struck me as more interesting (and more consonant with historical practice) to have Madame Painte shipped from her European home to someplace far away, a distant location where whatever malign power is attached to her might be dumped and forgotten. (Her appearance in upstate New York a version of the Freudian return of the repressed? Sure.) I liked the idea of having Calasso take a step back, not all the way to secondary character but to narrator. Having been the subject of so much narration before, it interested me to have him assume the position of narrator. When I started the story, the ending, which strikes me as particularly nasty, was not in my thoughts at all. It was only as Madame Painte's story drew to a close that it occurred to me the person listening to it might have a very dark reason for considering the figure's purchase. Did they return after the story's last line? I can't say, but it would mean Madame Painte would be out in the world once more. I'm not sure where that would lead. Perhaps we'll see. Will Calasso appear in another story? I wouldn't bet against it. (As a bidder at an estate sale, his eye on another object Kaaron posted a picture of? Hmmm.)

"Lost in the Dark": Beginning with *The Blair Witch Project*, found-footage horror film has blown up during roughly the same time I've been publishing my fiction. (Were I to be pedantic, I would contend that the horror genre writ large has made use of faux-documentary elements and effects for much longer, starting with Poe and his love of the hoax, then moving to M.R. James's stories with their old documents and their even older histories, and on to H.P. Lovecraft, who presents a story such as "The Call of Cthulhu" as an assemblage and collation of different found documents. But I pontificate.) Some of my favorite horror films sit under the broad umbrella of this approach, from the original *Blair Witch* to *Session 9* to the [REC] films to *Lake Mungo*. At some point, the question occurred to me, what if a director made a film that was in fact a weird documentary but was mistaken for a found-footage horror movie? The answer to the question started to coalesce when Ellen Datlow and Lisa Morton invited me to contribute to an anthology focused on legends old and new surrounding Halloween. The area I live in is full of caves, some naturally occurring, many made by mining during the nineteenth century. (Cement was a big local business.) Before we were married, I kicked around the idea of setting a story in the caves with Fiona; I thought the miners might have awakened a dragon, or something like a dragon. (The influence of the Lord of the Rings on this idea seems unmistakable to me now, but at the time, I was thinking of Beowulf.) (Writing this I realize that this idea would hang around and form the spine of something called *The Tunnel*, a sequel-of-sorts to *The Fisherman*.) When our son was very small, Fiona and I used to walk with him along the rail trail that lay about a five-minute walk from our tiny yellow house. Sometimes we would head south, between the steep rock walls through which the trains had passed up until the later decades of the last century; others we would head north, past a set of caves in front of which stood a set of tall concrete silos. It seemed as if this must have been part of a cement mining operation, but a pool of water of indeterminate depth lay in front of the caves, and I did not have much desire to chance it. Later, when David was older, we walked around the Snyder Estate in Rosendale, where some of the cement used in the construction of the Brooklyn Bridge was produced. We ventured into a couple of the caves on the property, but we were without flashlights, so we didn't go any farther than the daylight would allow. All the same, the empty bottles and old skin magazines we saw scattered on the dusty floors indicated that these spaces had been used by local kids to host (and hide) parties. (There was, as I recall, a machine in one of them, yellow, about the size of a washer, maybe a little bigger. It might have been the kind of thing you would use for paving a driveway, but I'm not sure.) All of these experiences and more were in my mind when I began working on the story. Anyone who's read my previous work knows, I'm a big fan of invented histories, secret histories, and this story is no exception. Some of my filmmaking friends like Phil Gelatt and J.T. Petty may be surprised to discover they were involved in projects of which they have no memory (not to mention, of which there is no trace); the same is true of figures such as Larry Fessenden and Takashi Shimizu. On the fictional side of things, Stephen Graham Jones graciously let me borrow Sean Mickels from one of his short stories. The figure of Bad Agatha and her ominous history came to me pretty much all at once. In imagining the film franchise built on her, I liked the idea that each entry's approach to Bad Agatha would in some way be affected by—you might say refracted through—whatever the current trend in horror movies was. (Which aspect of the story relates it to the following story in this collection, "My Father, Dr. Frankenstein.") I enjoyed the challenge of imitating the model of the IMDB movie summary. Most of all, I took great pleasure in constructing the parallel narratives of the feature film and the original documentary out of which it was sculpted. The contrast between one story full of steadily escalating incident, and the other full of increasingly large, empty spaces, delighted me. In the years since the story was first published, I've read descriptions of it as a vampire story, which wasn't at the forefront of my mind when I was writing it, but I can see how the early references to classic vampire movies might lead a reader in this direction. Neil McRobert of the Talking Scared podcast (to which you should listen if you like smart, witty conversation about horror books) is of the opinion that this story is in some way connected to the cosmos of *The Fisherman*.

Which I hadn't thought of before he mentioned it. Now, though...

"My Father, Dr. Frankenstein": The original idea for this story, a father modifying his son in an attempt to suit him for a series of catastrophes, occurred to me a long time ago, in the late 2000s, I think. From the start, I wasn't interested in repeating the plot of Mary Shelley's novel: I was more intrigued by the idea of documenting the ongoing series of transformations the father works upon his son as he becomes aware of each new (global) threat to him. I imagined the story might end with the son confined to an underground lake somewhere deep in the Rockies, reduced to a giant, single-celled organism, floating in darkness, insensate but safe from the possible catastrophes of a gamma ray burst or asteroid strike. I suppose you could interpret the idea as projecting and amplifying my anxieties about my own role as father, especially in a world grown ever more violent, ever more perilous. When Darren Speegle emailed asking if I would contribute to an anthology he was putting together on the theme of human evolution, I thought this idea might be a good fit for it. When I published my first horror story, "On Skua Island," in the *Magazine of Fantasy and Science Fiction*, there was another debut in the issue: Charles Coleman Finlay's terrific "Footnotes," which as the title suggests presented its narrative as a series of footnotes to a missing text. I loved this conceit, and as I set to work on my story for Darren, I realized this was the time to employ it. Already, I had accumulated pages and pages of notes on the catastrophes over which we have obsessed in the decades following the Second World War, as well as still more notes on how the human form might be modified to facilitate its survival in such situations, as well as some relevant references to religion, literature, and film. The footnote format struck me as a particularly elegant way to handle and present this abundance of information while still leaving room for the reader's interpretation. Typing these notes, it occurs to me that this story has much more in common with "Lost in the Dark" than I realized, as both run through different types of prose in order to relay their narratives. Working on the story, I became aware in a way I never had before of the extent to which my life, and those of everyone living alongside me, has been overshadowed by the prospect of apocalypse, of annihilation reinvented on a regular basis. Yes, it's possible to trace the deep origins of such concerns to the New Testament and specifically the Book of Revelation, but I wonder to what extent the most recent iterations of the concern are tied up in Modernity-writ-large?

As I've continued to progress as a writer, I've grown increasingly fond of stories that leave room at their end for questions, for me as well as for the reader. In this case, I think about those possible humans, the Yeti, the Cockroach people, the Alligator folk. How far did the planning for their creation go? Amidst the snowy mountains of Alaska, is there a small band of what the few who catch a glimpse of them assume must be polar bears, albeit unlike any they have seen before? Do the Russian military bases across the Bering Strait experience occasional raids by terrifying creatures? Is there a derelict building in Natick or maybe Boston which is rumored to be inhabited by a group of furtive, deformed children? Do local kids dare one another to push open the rotting door to its basement and step inside? Do some of those kids not return? In the canals that separate the backyards of the houses in Pensacola, are there glimpses of men and women lifting their heads from the water to survey the surrounding terrain, then ducking back under not to reappear? Is there something subtly wrong with their skin, a certain coarseness, roughness, even?

Oh brave new world, indeed.

"A Song Only Partially Heard": This story was written for an anthology whose title was *The Beauty of Death: Death by Water*, which seemed a pretty straightforward prompt. I thought of something of such beauty that if you died while looking at it, you would feel as if you were being killed by that beauty. Obviously, this death had to be connected to water. I've spent the last several years teaching the Odyssey to high school sophomores, so it was perhaps not a surprise that I would think of the sirens. These merged in my imagination with the mermaid, another figure I'd wanted to write about but been unable to find a story for. A great deal about the appearance of this mermaid came from the Beta fish my younger son and wife have owned. The setting of the story was suggested by a small shipyard along the banks of the Rondout River, just on the Kingston border, which I've driven past I couldn't tell you how many times. The workforce is as far as I can tell Latino. I have no idea whether these men are immigrants; though I assume some of them must be. On a regular basis, they work on tugboats, many of which are much larger than I appreciated. They repair and build barges, as well, and there have been other ships docked there, most memorably, a former hospital ship David discussed writing a story about with me. There are ways in which this story is cousin to "To See, To Be Seen," which you can find in my fourth collection, *Children of the Fang*, and which focuses on another set of immigrant workers dealing with unearthly things. (For that matter, there's the central narrative of *The Fisherman*, too.) The sharp-eyed reader will notice a reference to Robert Chambers's Carcosa in the flag of the tanker dumping its waste water in the Hudson (at times a real enough problem in this stretch of the river), and thus a possible origin point for the mermaid. (I wouldn't swear to it, though.) I also think the story draws inspiration from a fishing spot to which I used to take David in his spin-casting days. Located maybe a quarter-mile up the Rondout from the shipyard, next to a narrow turn-off, this water along this stretch of the river could be especially clear if you sat beside it in the later afternoon. All kinds of underwater scenery became visible. I thought the river was maybe three or four feet deep; my son said it was more like seven or eight. Some horror and weird stories are about confrontations with the extraordinary; some are about near-misses. This one is definitely among the latter.

"A Song Only Partially Heard" begins a sequence of stories in which water features prominently, from rivers to shorelines to oceans real and invented. (Possibly, it was already underway with "Lost in the Dark" and its subterranean lake.) I'm unsure why my imagination kept turning in this direction, what it signifies about this period in my writing and my life. My relationship with large bodies of water is marked by both love and fear. The Penobscot River in Maine, the River Clyde in Scotland, the Atlantic shore at Acadia National Park in Maine, the Hudson River from Albany down to Manhattan, the Jersey shore, the Atlantic shore at Cape Cod, Boston Harbor, and Gloucester, and more are spots I remember with great fondness. At the same time, I find video of water surging up the streets of coastal towns and cities during storms deeply unnerving. I sometimes think it would be nice to live beside water, but every time I see footage of waves climbing the sides of houses and businesses, I think maybe the ridge on which my house sits is just fine.

"The Deep Sea Swell": In the winter of 2002, about six months after we married, Fiona and I flew to Scotland, where we took a trip from her home in Kirkcaldy first to her old university stomping grounds of Aberdeen and from there up to the Shetland Islands, where her first college roommate lived with her family. The Shetlands are as far north as you can go and still be in Scotland; though as I learned during our trip, many of the residents prefer to emphasize their connection to the Vikings who once held the islands. For a dizzying few days, we were driven all over the main island of Shetland, where we visited various relatives and friends of our hosts, and had brief excursions to the adjacent islands of Yell and Unst. There were few trees, and the ocean was always visible. I ate mutton and Bannocks, drank prodigious amounts of beer, and attended a Ceilidh. The sun rose late and set early. I heard ghost stories and watched a replica of a Viking longship set ablaze and pushed into the main harbor. I saw the house called the House of Windows, which would give me the title of my first novel. The sail up to the islands was pleasant enough; the voyage back to Aberdeen in the mist of a winter storm was tumultuous and terrifying. (And the anecdote about the staff member looking for his twenty-pound bribe is one hundred percent true.) When Ellen Datlow invited me to contribute to an anthology of sea-related horror stories, most of my material was already waiting for me. The monster must have been inspired both by the great Mike Mignola's drawings of old diving suits and by a graphic novel Paul Tremblay and I talked about writing together, which concerned a haunted costume. Doggerland was an actual place; as I was writing and doing research for the story, it emerged as a way to tie together the various elements I was including. Late in my work, I remembered the Tennyson quotation, which seemed to resonate with the story in ways unexpected and satisfying.

There's at least one more story about Shetland waiting for me to write it. Honestly, there's probably more than that.

"Haak": Once again, my friend Jack Haringa was the impetus for the writing of a story. In this case, it was prompted by an extended period of bad health for him that led me and several other of Jack's friends to assemble a collection of stories and poems under the exhortation, *Jack Haringa Must Live!* Together with Laird Barron, Michael Cisco, Nick Kaufmann, Sarah Langan, and Paul Tremblay, we put our energy into a single edition intended to buoy Jack's spirits, which we presented to him at that year's Boskone. My favorite contribution may have been Paul's short, Reanimator-esque piece in which Jack was a snarky head kept alive in a tray and served by a headless, furious Cisco. My contribution was inspired by a project Laird and I had kicked around a few years before, a darker take on Peter Pan. We had considered titles such as Peter Hook or Peter Hoek. I think it was Laird who was of the opinion that Peter Pan, left to his own devices, would have become a sociopath, and I didn't necessarily disagree with him. Laird and I never moved ahead with the story, but I thought I might use it now. I had visited a couple of Jack's high school English classes at Worcester Academy to talk about Joseph Conrad's life and work with them. (I had written the introduction to a Barnes and Noble edition of Conrad's collected stories and Jack's students were reading *Heart of Darkness*.) For that talk, I had studied both the novella and the details of Conrad's life on which it drew, and these seemed as if they not only could but should in some way feature in the story. At the same time, I had been struck for several years by the appearance of the figure of Pan in a number of the literary works written in the years surrounding the turn of the twentieth century. All of this coalesced in a classroom lecture whose surface resemblance to my earlier story, "Technicolor," was I hoped eclipsed by its substantially different plot. In the process of writing what became a much longer story than I initially anticipated, I found the sisters of the mermaid from "A Song Only Partially Heard;" I also found crab people who clambered out of an old issue of the first Conan the Barbarian comic book. There was Greek mythology, of course, and also the Spanish Armada, which I did not anticipate. (Their flight around the north of the British Isles after their defeat was a fact I had not learned in my high school history class; I owe it to my mother's older brother, my Uncle Bobby.) There was an Alpine lake with a passage through to a secret ocean.

Our plan worked, and Jack was cheered. His health since then has at times still been a struggle, but I'm glad he's with us.

"Breakwater": I'm a big fan of noir fiction and film. There's a considerable overlap, I would argue, between the world of noir and that of horror. From William Hjortsberg's *Falling Angel* to DC comics' John Constantine to Clive Barker's "The Last Illusion," not to mention the film adaptations of all three, certain narratives have explored the shadowy territory where noir and horror intersect. Since Ellen Datlow's 2011 *Supernatural Noir*, to which I contributed a story, there have been an increasing number of anthologies mapping the region. "Breakwater" arose in response to an invitation to another of them, *Ashes and Entropy*. The idea for it is the very oldest in this collection, reaching back to the mid-to-late-nineteen-nineties. In its earlier incarnation, the destructive storm which could only be dispersed by the willing self-sacrifice of the protagonist was created by a young man whose disappointment at finding himself at the losing point of a romantic triangle led to him killing the woman with whom he had been involved and then himself, using the deaths to fuel the spell that sustained the storm. The image of the storm engulfing a beach town I found powerful and unsettling, but even at the time the premise struck me as cringeworthy. Flip the genders, though, and the situation became more interesting, particularly when grafted onto what must be one of the archetypal noir plots: that of the person hired by a wealthy individual to protect or surveille the employer's (much younger, attractive) partner, who subsequently becomes involved with the partner, resulting in all sorts of (frequently fatal) complications. Honestly, I was less focused on that dimension of the story than I was on what I guess I would call the process element of it. So many noir stories focus almost obsessively on the details of whatever crime lies at their center: how many ways, for example, have stories, novels, and films come up with to rob a bank? In the case of my story, I wanted to figure out a reasonable way a person who wanted to disappear in this era of digital footprints and constant cameras could do so. I wouldn't say the answer I arrived at was perfect, but I was reasonably pleased with it. The Jersey shore was a location I visited a couple of times in my mid-twenties, and I thought the slightly faded glory of its motels and restaurants made a good setting for the story's climax; not to mention, the towns I remembered were places that might be consumed by an ocean whipped to fury by an angry sorceress. (Was I influenced by the photos and video I had seen of the aftermath of Superstorm Sandy? I must have been.) The literary critic in me wants to point out that any shore is a liminal space, a location where two things border one another, which is both a nice trope for the margin where noir and horror abut.

In thinking about the story's ending, I decided I wanted to leave things ambiguous. Yes, the last image we have is of Maureen lifting the knife as Louise looks on, which some readers have taken to mean Maureen cuts her own throat, but it seems equally possible to me that she will either throw the knife at Louise or leap at her and stab her with it. Of course this won't kill Louise, but Frank's sacrificial blood still on the weapon will give it a potency Louise has not counted on. I can imagine a sequel of sorts to this story in which Maureen and the undead Frank are on the run from Louise, in whom the entire fury of the storm has been confined by the blade protruding from her chest...

"Errata": I've known Ross Lockhart for a while. We first met when I was visiting San Francisco in the early 2000s with Fiona and David. He had just been hired by Night Shade Books, back before they imploded in such spectacular fashion. Ross worked with me on my first novel, *House of Windows*;

after Night Shade collapsed, he left to found his own publishing company, Word Horde, where he took a chance on my second novel, *The Fisherman*, and my fourth, fifth, and now sixth collections. (He also reissued my first collection when it went out of print.) Ross has been ideal to work with: responsive, calm, and obliging. When his wife emailed to ask if I would write a short story for him for his birthday, I immediately agreed. A story about publication/printing seemed the obvious choice. I had in mind Michael Cisco's brilliant story, "Machines of Concrete Light and Dark," as I started writing. In Cisco's story, he describes certain entities as having their existence spread across a range of spaces and times. I wondered if this arrangement might be a way to disperse a malevolent supernatural agent, over an assortment of texts—which might also mean that exposure to more than one of said texts might allow the threat to reconstitute itself. I guess you could read the story as an updated version of an M.R. James tale like "The Mezzotint." It occurs to me, too, that this piece features another being with a ruined face.

Oh, and you should read Orrin Grey. His stories are terrific, and he's one of my favorite writers on horror film.

"Natalya, Queen of the Hungry Dogs": The title for this story owes itself to an online exchange among myself, the terrific Nadia Bulkin, and a few others, which resulted in Nadia being crowned queen of the hungry ghosts. When I asked her if I could borrow the title, she agreed. By this time, Ellen Datlow had already invited me to contribute to an anthology of ghost stories which was to be, she said, a big book, a doorstopper. Write me something long, she told me. Almost right away, I thought of Ellen's previous ghost story anthology, 2003's *The Dark*. Published when I was first starting out as a writer, the book featured stories by Jack Cady, Glen Hirshberg, and Lucius Shepard. It was the publishing event of the year, Lucius's contribution its standout. "Limbo" was a sprawling novella which began as a James M. Cain-esque tale of carnal passion and violence before transforming into a vision of a maze-like afterlife. He would revise it for his 2007 collection, *Dagger Key*, but the essentials were already in place. I decided I would write a response to "Limbo," and I would do so in memoriam of Lucius, who had died in 2014 after a short illness.

I've written elsewhere about Lucius Shepard both in general and in response to specific books. Although I had been aware of his writing for decades, it wasn't until the early 2000s that I started to read him in earnest, and when I did, I was floored, to the extent that when I had a chance to meet him in late 2003, I was as nervous as I've ever been. ("Buy him a drink," Fiona said, right as always.) In those days, Lucius was part of an online group of writers including Jeffrey Ford, Elizabeth Hand, and Paul Witcover. Perhaps presumptuously, I thought of them as the older siblings, so to speak, of my group of writers (myself, Laird Barron, Michael Cisco, Stephen Graham Jones, Sarah Langan, Paul Tremblay), which was to say, established in ways we were not, but not as distant from us as such parental figures as Stephen King, Peter Straub, and Clive Barker. I admired Jeff, Liz, and Paul for all sorts of reasons, but I felt closest to Lucius in large part because of his prose style, which was lush, elegant, passionate, and discursive, capable of giving you a character's life in a single long paragraph. In his work, tropes drawn from the very heart of genre fiction were rendered with a baroque sensibility not dissimilar to that of Conrad, Ford, and García Márquez. He was a brilliant writer of shorter things, stories, novellas, and short novels; though his novel, *A Handbook of American Prayer* (2004), is not to be missed. I never felt Lucius received his due as a writer, either within the field of genre fiction, or the adjacent mainstream. The story I began working on for Ellen would be my way of acknowledging the debt I felt to Lucius's work. Its opening lines were inspired by the beginning of *Harrison Stark*, a 1978 novel by Russell Banks, one of Lucius's compatriots. (I had read a great deal of Banks's fiction in my early twenties, and *Continental Drift* [1985], *Affliction* [1989], and *The Sweet Hereafter* [1991] remain as good a run of American novels as I have encountered. The first line of *Affliction* is as far as I am concerned perfect.) Lucius's example and Ellen's instruction encouraged me to be expansive in my storytelling, to include incidents drawn from my life (such as the HIV test and acquaintance with a young man who was one of the approximately half-million American casualties of the AIDS epidemic), as well as characters from other of my stories (Madame Sosostris, who first appeared in my short novel, *Sefira*), and locations I had employed previously (specifically, the Jersey shore). In addition to the shore, there was other water imagery, from Lake Champlain, seen at a distance through the windows of Hunter's very nice house, to a quick glimpse of post-Katrina New Orleans, to the great river bordering the muddy beach of the next world. I incorporated elements of Lucius's character in both of my protagonists, Hunter's globe-trotting and checkered romantic history being the most obvious examples. As the story progressed, it came to echo "Limbo" in ways of which I would not be fully aware until working on these notes. The labyrinthine, ramshackle afterlife, the malevolent, vengeful female antagonist, the cryptic woman offering help, the open, uncertain ending, all draw inspiration from Lucius's original. This was still another story whose ending I struggled with. My initial plan was to conclude with Carl's return to the house, leaving Hunter's fate unknown. But the thought of the monstrous children left abandoned bothered me to an extent I was not prepared for, with the result that I had to write an epilogue to show them not forgotten.

Hope, it seems, is necessary even in the afterlife.

"Oscar Returns from the Dead, Prophesizing": The writer Daniel Braum, with whom I share a love of the 1982 film *Conan the Barbarian*, was putting together an anthology of mummy stories. While my first published story, "On Skua Island," employed a variation on the traditional mummy, I had not returned to the monster since (unlike, say, the vampire, who has appeared to drain his victims in a number of my stories). I took Dan's prompt as a challenge to find another approach to the monster. This coincided with what I came to think of as a Season of Divorce among the parents of David's third grade classmates. Out of the blue, it seemed, couple after couple were splitting up, some proclaiming it loudly on social media, others doing so more quietly. It may be impossible to know what lies at the heart of a marriage, but the couples who were parting had appeared to have solid relationships. It was disconcerting. There was one case in particular in which one partner claimed to have received via a medium a message from a departed parent instructing them to seek the divorce they so obviously wanted. This joined with a story I had heard about a pet-sitting disaster much the same as the one described in the story, a hapless reptile overheated to death and then replaced by an identical one. (No house accidentally burned down, though.) What, I wondered, if the shriveled creature returned from its clandestine burial spot to consume its would-be replacement? And what if its mummified form was animated by some kind of supernatural force? And what if that force spoke through the undead creature to utter dire secrets and predictions? Not long before writing this story, I had discovered a series of holes drilled through the concrete floor of our house's basement. They did not appear new; in all likelihood, they had been there since the house's construction in the 1950s. I wasn't sure what their purpose was, but I imagined something or someone had been buried or confined under the basement floor. I considered including this information in the story, allowing the reader to make more sense of its action, but decided to leave it out, preferring the increased weirdness of a reanimated lizard delivering awful prophecy. The ending of the story, which chills me, only occurred as I was close to finishing it. I knew the narrator would have heard something awful from the lizard, but I didn't know it would be this awful.

As for the space under the basement floor: I'm pretty sure there's something there.

"Alice's Rebellion": The long-term inspiration for this story came from an anthology Ellen Datlow edited of new stories inspired by Lewis Carroll's Alice books. I wasn't invited to contribute, which was fine, but I wondered what I would have written if asked to submit. I read the Alice books in my midteens, when their sheer weirdness disturbed me in a way I'm not sure it would have when I was younger (although I think it probably would have), and I taught "Jabberwocky" to so many poetry and English literature classes I can recite most of it. Aside from a rather conventional idea of someone having to fight the Jabberwocky (another dragon story) I didn't have any definite ideas until several years later, when the twin disasters of Brexit in the United Kingdom and the (first) election of Donald Trump to the Presidency of the United States began the unraveling of the world that was probably never as stable as I wanted to believe it had been in the first place. There's no need to quote Yeats's "Second Coming" at length to describe the feel of that time; his line about the worst being "full of passionate intensity" puts the dart in the bullseye, I think. Seemingly out of nowhere, I had my idea for an Alice story. It was to be a tale of order bought from chaos through blood and violence and then betrayed back into chaos by greed and stupidity. Until the very end, the narrative flew from the tip of my pen. The last lines of the story, however, took me a while to write. Given the darkness of my mood, my first impulse was to leave the situation in hopelessness and defeat, perhaps with some remark about the Prime Minister striding off the stage, looking forward to the meeting with his American counterpart. Despite the heaviness in my chest, I didn't want to end on quite so bleak a note, so I thought about the very blood that had helped birth this sabotaged reality escaping, heading for the sea and maybe the chance of something better.

"Snakebit, Or Why I (Continue to) Love Horror": Given the self-reflective nature of this story, additional commentary on it may seem redundant, if not self-indulgent, gilding the lily, as it were. Accordingly, I'll keep things to a minimum, except to note, this piece began as an essay for a collection of essays to which I was kindly invited to contribute by Becky Spratford. The theme, as the title states, was *Why I Love Horror*. The essay was supposed to be about four thousand words long, but as usually happens, grew in the writing. As I wrote in the piece, itself, for me, the question wasn't so much how I had fallen in love with the horror field, but how I had stayed in love with it. I very much liked the idea of walking the reader through the writing of a horror story to show what the genre offered, how my relationship to it had continued. During one of our weekly phone conversations, Paul Tremblay told me his supremely talented daughter, Emma, had contributed illustrations to his essay. I asked my daughter, Kayla, if she would consider creating a single image. She agreed, we discussed the details and possibilities over a couple of car rides to the school where we both work, and the picture she drew became part of the writing of the (ever-longer) piece. At some point, Paul said to me, "It's gonna be late and three times the length." The essay-cum-story wound up about thirteen thousand words, so he was right, there, and had I turned it in, it would have been incredibly late. But when I was about nine thousand words through it with a substantial amount still to go, I realized doing so would have been an unfair imposition on Becky, who would have had either to accommodate this monster of a thing or to reject it and find another writer to fill my space. So I quickly wrote an essay that met the length requirements and sent that to her, only severely late. Yet I still wanted to complete the first piece, this hybrid essay-story. I was at the time writing another overlong and overdue story whose prose I was trying to keep deliberately plain (its working title "The Fleshy Side of the Bone"), and I enjoyed the opportunity what I would come to call "Snakebit" gave me to luxuriate in language. This was another narrative centered on a poem (like "Shadow and Thirst" from my previous collection, *Corpsemouth*) which allowed me to play around with a number of other literary references. (Thus the Apennines, a mountain range in northwest Italy which figures in some of the early classics of Gothic literature and of which Henry James famously wrote, "What are the Apennines to us?"

Contextually, James's question makes sense, but I couldn't resist the chance to say, in effect, "This is what the Apennines are to us, Henry."). At about the point I realized I had to write a shorter replacement essay for Becky, it occurred to me the story-cum-essay might be the original piece in my next collection, and this pleased me on several levels. Here was another story expanding the secret history of this region I call mine. Here was another story in which water, which I had realized by now threaded through most of the stories in the book, features significantly. Despite the significance of the Hudson River to this area, I haven't written very much about it, an oversight I was happy to address. Here too was a chance to mention Dennis Mitre, who figures prominently in the novel on which I'm currently at work, *The Cleaving Stone*. Looking over the story after it was done, I saw that Tom Alero is a bit more callow than I intended but decided this was in keeping with the kind of narratives I mentioned in the beginning of the piece, those mid-twentieth-century novels of men in crisis.

I'll admit, I do wonder what's next for Tom following his transformation. Yet another reason to love horror, the opportunity it gives me to ask myself, "What's next?"

"**Clapping Teeth and Driving Beats**": To wrap things up, a digestif. A few years ago, the Rock Academy of Woodstock, at which David was a student, was scheduled to be part of a community zombie walk. Jason Bowman, the school's director, asked me if I could find an appropriate excerpt from a story or novel to read to kick off the event. Although I searched my library, I could not. So I wrote my own. Jason was pleased and grateful—and then the walk was canceled due to weather and could not be rescheduled. My account of the spring zombie thaw remained on my computer, until it occurred to me it might serve to conclude my sixth collection. Which, here it is.

Be careful out there, people.

ACKNOWLEDGMENTS

To be honest, when I published my prior collection, *Corpsemouth and Other Autobiographies*, in 2023, I thought it would be the last book of stories I'd be releasing for a while. But enough people asked me when the *next* collection was coming out for me to think that sooner might be a better idea than later. Then I looked at the stories I planned to include, noticed the connections among them, and decided to go ahead. Thanks to everyone who offered their words of encouragement; as much as anything, this book is here because of you.

There are some other thank-yous I have to make. There's a reason I dedicate everything I do to my wife, Fiona. Twenty-three and a half years in as I write this, our marriage continues to develop and grow in ways I never could have anticipated, and remains a source of deep and abiding joy to me. Thanks, Love.

I've benefitted, too, from the love and support of my younger son, David, with whom I've had long and wide-ranging discussions about writing and music as we've roamed the Catskills in search of fly-fishing spots. As a result, my musical education is now 67% more complete. (Who am I kidding? It's more like 23%. But I'm trying.)

And who knew I had a daughter? Kayla Heikkinen has been the biggest and one of the best surprises of the last several years. I love you, kid, and I'm so glad you're in my life now. Thanks for your encouragement, talks in the car and in school, and for your terrific artwork.

John Langan

In looking over the story notes for this book, I notice how often I mention fellow writers. I'm happy to have the friendships of Laird Barron, Stephen Graham Jones, and Paul Tremblay. Nadia Bulkin, Michael Cisco, Brett Cox, Gemma Files, Sarah Langan, and Kaaron Warren are pretty cool, too. Special thanks to Victor LaValle for writing such a generous introduction.

I count myself lucky in my agent, Ginger Clark, and her assistants, Nicole Eisenbraum and Maria Ministreri. And in my editors: Daniel Braum, Ellen Datlow and Lisa Morton, Jodi Renee Lester, Alessandro Manzetti, Mark Morris, Doug Murano, Darren Speegle, and the Wilsons. This marks the fifth time Ross Lockhart has published me, and I continue to be grateful for his support and for producing such lovely books. (Scott Jones deserves credit for his contribution to the process.) Once again, Matthew Jaffe hit the ball out of the park with his cover illustration.

Finally, a sincere thanks to you, my reader, for picking up this collection. I'm grateful for the gift of your time and attention. You make books like this possible, and I thank you for it.

PUBLICATION HISTORY

"Madame Painte: For Sale" originally appeared in *Behold! Oddities, Curiosities and Undefinable Wonders*, edited by Doug Murano (Crystal Lake 2017).

"Lost in the Dark" originally appeared in *Haunted Nights*, edited by Ellen Datlow and Lisa Morton (Blumhouse/Anchor 2017).

"My Father, Dr. Frankenstein" originally appeared in *Adam's Ladder: An Anthology of Dark Science Fiction*, edited by Michael Bailey and Darren Speegle (Written Backwards 2017).

"A Song Only Partially Heard" originally appeared in *The Beauty of Death II: Death by Water*, edited by Jodi Renee Lester and Alessandro Manzetti (Independent Legions 2017).

"The Deep Sea Swell" originally appeared in *The Devil and the Deep: Horror Stories of the Sea*, edited by Ellen Datlow (Night Shade 2018).

"Haak" originally appeared in *New Fears 2*, edited by Mark Morris (Titan 2018).

"Breakwater" originally appeared in *Ashes and Entropy*, edited by Dreamx Wilson (Nightscape Press 2018).

"Errata" originally appeared on johnpaullangan.wordpress.com (December 14, 2018).

"Natalya, Queen of the Hungry Dogs" originally appeared in *Echoes*, edited by Ellen Datlow (Saga 2019).

"Oscar Returns from the Dead, Prophesizing" originally appeared in *Spirits Unwrapped*, edited by Daniel Braum (Lethe 2019).

"Alice's Rebellion" originally appeared in *After Sundown*, edited by Mark Morris (Flame Tree 2020).

"Snakebit, Or Why I (Continue to) Love Horror" is original to this collection.

"Clapping Teeth and Driving Beats" is original to this collection.

ABOUT THE AUTHOR

John Langan is the author of two novels and six collections of stories. For his work, he has received the Bram Stoker and the This Is Horror awards. He is one of the founders of the Shirley Jackson awards and continues to serve on its Board of Advisors. He lives in New York's Mid-Hudson Valley with his wife, younger son, and the late night calls of owls.